*W*hat the critics are saying...

Five Stars "Nuworld: The Saga Begins by Lorie O'Clare is like a rare blended whiskey; alone the elements science fiction and romance are delicious... woven together by Ms. O'Clare, they create something more that truly works!" ~ *eCataRomance*

Five Coffee Cups "This story, with its twists and turns, is an excellent framework for a bigger saga. The characters are clearly drawn and the story is rich with possibilities." ~ *Coffee Time Reviews*

Five Angels "I cried and hurt along with these people and was sorry to see the story end." ~ *Fallen Angels*

"Ms. O'Clare leads the reader down a scintillating path of excitement, adventure and some wonderful sex scenes between the hero and heroine. Rich in dialogue, descriptive prose and wonderful secondary characters, this story has the potential to be the start of a very good series about Nuworld and its characters." ~*Love Romances*

"NUWORLD: THE SAGA BEGINS quickly sucks the reader into the story and doesn't let go until the surprising ending." ~ *Romance Review Today*

Lorie O'Clare

NUWORLD
The Saga Begins

Cerridwen Press

A Cerridwen Press Publication

www.cerridwenpress.com

Nuworld: The Saga Begins

ISBN #1419953168
ALL RIGHTS RESERVED.
Nuworld: The Saga Begins Copyright© 2005 Lorie O'Clare
Edited by Briana St. James
Cover art by Syneca

Electronic book Publication May 2005
Trade Paperback Publication January 2006

Cerridwen Press is an imprint of Ellora's Cave Publishing, Inc.®

Also by Lorie O'Clare

℘

Nuworld 2: Tara The Great
Nuworld 3: All for One
Nuworld 4: Do or Die

If you are interested in a spicier read,(and are over 18) check out her erotic romances at Ellora's Cave Publishing (www.ellorascave.com).

Cariboo Lunewulf 1: Taming Heather
Cariboo Lunewulf 2: Pursuit
Cariboo Lunewulf 3: Challenged
Fallen Gods: Tainted Purity
Fallen Gods: Jaded Prey
Fallen Gods: Lotus Blooming
Lunewulf 1: Pack Law
Lunewulf 2: In Her Blood
Lunewulf 3: In Her Dreams
Lunewulf 4: In Her Nature
Lunewulf 5: In Her Soul
Lunewulf 6: Full Moon Rising
Lunewulf 7: Blue Moon
Sex Slaves 1: Sex Traders
Sex Slaves 2: Waiting For Yesterday
Sex Slaves 3: Waiting For Dawn
Torrid Love: The First Time
Torrid Love: Caught!

About the Author

෨

All my life, I've wondered at how people fall into the routines of life. The paths we travel seemed to be well-trodden by society. We go to school, fall in love, find a line of work (and hope and pray it is one we like), have children and do our best to mold them into good people who will travel the same path. This is the path so commonly referred to as the "real world".

The characters in my books are destined to stray down a different path other than the one society suggests. Each story leads the reader into a world altered slightly from the one they know. For me, this is what good fiction is about, an opportunity to escape from the daily grind and wander down someone else's path.

Lorie welcomes mail from readers. You can write to her c/o Ellora's Cave Publishing at 1056 Home Avenue, Akron, OH 44310-3502.

Nuworld: The Saga Begins

ຂ

Chapter One

❧

When would she ever learn?

Patha *had* warned her about taking the Gothman for granted, and Tara cursed her foolishness. She scoped out how the flat plains had now disappeared, replaced by more dominant hills, and she knew without a doubt that she was surrounded. She couldn't see them, but they were there, keeping their distance. The Gothman—the other warrior race—hid themselves well...but *her* skills were better. *Much* better.

While she had a moment to breathe, Tara reflected on the information she'd gleaned recently. The plains, known as the Freelands, were completely behind her now. *And good riddance.* Although the land there was healthy, the wildlife plentiful, and the seasons on a continual cycle, the people were boring.

Having been bred from a warrior race, she found it hard to relate to the Freelanders, even though they were polite to Runners. Tara knew from the stories told by her people, that Freelanders were more inclined to welcome her people than other races. But that didn't mean she felt comfortable around them. She still had a hard time imagining a race working the land and making no effort to develop a militia. Their weapons were primitive and used mainly to hunt.

"Oh yes, I can just picture it, invaders creeping across the land and they draw a rake and quiver out a slight *Halt*," she said aloud. She couldn't contain the chortle catching in her throat. What a way to protect a race! She nodded her head in agreement with her initial assessment. The agrarian society of the Freelanders was definitely a little too dull for her liking.

Ever since she'd grown out of adolescence and arrived at the *Age of Searching*, Tara had begun to crave knowledge of the world, just like all her fellow Runners. The tales told by clan elders about other races were no longer enough; she wanted to see these people and their lands for herself. Tara knew of no other way of doing it than by striking out on her own.

Tara sighed. She had always moved with the clan, traveling from one territory to another, learning the skills of the warrior and racing on her motorcycle with the other children. She'd also helped to raise the younger Runners, and cooked and cleaned along with the other girls and boys. While these activities had always contented her, they did no longer.

Of all the stories told around the fire, Patha's stories of the Gothman intrigued her the most. Runners and Gothman had a hatred for each other that transcended the winters. She had asked the elders time and again why this was so, but no answer ever satisfied her. For many winters she'd thought about the causes. The only reason she could see for Runners and Gothman despising one another was that each race thought the other inferior.

Tara meant to find out for herself which race was correct.

Now that she'd made her decision, Tara realized she had the perfect opportunity to see what kind of warriors the Gothman actually were. Of course entering Gothman wasn't what most Runners would view as an opportunity. *More like a suicide journey.* She shivered as icy fingernails traced patterns along her spine. The growing hills spread around her. Rugged countryside was a sure indication she had entered Gothman territory. She checked for her laser, running her fingers over the smooth metal as the weapon rested, secure, on her belt. Not for the first time, Tara hoped her plan would prove productive and not be her demise.

She wove in and out of the protruding rocks half-buried in the ground and navigated her motorcycle with expertise, keeping most of her attention on the surrounding area. All of a sudden, her leisurely jaunt became much more than a drive through a new country—it became a lesson in survival.

An explosion vibrated the air, causing her to nearly crash her motorcycle into a tree.

"Ahhh!" The daughter and heir of the leader of the Blood Circle Clan couldn't believe she'd just screamed.

She'd heard stories about the weapon that exploded when shot, leaving a foul smell in the air, but she'd always thought them ridiculous. But now…now she realized it was true. It was *actually* true. Tara's heart pounded in her chest.

"Stay focused, warrior," she whispered under her breath. "Don't let yourself be distracted."

This was no time to think about her past. They'd seen her and then actually fired one of those bang sticks she'd always thought were mythical. By the grace of her schooling as a warrior, she'd managed to evade the legendary weapon. But for how much longer?

Another shot flew through the air, and a large branch crashed to the ground.

She screamed again and leaned closer to the body of her cycle.

Where were the Gothman? Behind the rocks? Somewhere in the approaching forest? How far could they shoot?

"Primitive or not, these Gothman weapons can do damage," she muttered quietly. Tara licked her dry lips. She'd looked forward to meeting the Gothman, but she hadn't expected to encounter them this soon, or under such savage conditions.

Quickly, she propelled her motorcycle into the cool, sweet-smelling forest, and dismounted once the woods surrounded her. She parked the cycle between two embedded boulders and pulled her personally encoded landlink off the handlebars, slipping it in her pocket. She left her bike, hoping it would be safe for the time being. Tara knew the Gothman would find great pride in retrieving a Runner's bike. No other race in the world had achieved the perfection her machine represented.

As she searched for a place to hide, some of the Gothman lore she'd heard occupied her thoughts. Gothman only taught their men to fight. Gothman women weren't educated.

"What a waste!" she snorted. "Imagine! Half of a race needing protection!" This made no sense to her. Runners viewed men and women as equal. All were taught the same skills.

More bang sticks ripped through the air. Tara broke into a run.

"You men want to play with this woman? Then come get me!" She moved easily through the scattered trees, adrenaline flowing from the thrill of being the hunted.

Her Runner breeding was apparent when she managed to live through the second round of fire. She turned quickly to see two more Gothman approaching on foot, moving stealthily from protruding rocks to a large tree. She could smell the explosives and could feel her heart racing as she watched part of the tree next to her disappear after one of their bullets attacked it. She returned fire with her laser weapon, the silent weapon giving no clue of her location, and two Gothman lay dead on the forest floor.

Tara ran through the pines as fast as her small agile body would allow. Within minutes she'd eliminated another three Gothman. Patha was right; these people loved to fight but hadn't mastered the art of being true warriors.

She slowed to a trot and listened to the breeze as it carried the scent of the pines through the air. Trees stood far enough apart to allow wide sunbeams to graze the ground. Grass and patches of moss glowed an emerald green, offering a bright contrast against the patches of crisp, clear sky. It was a deep blue and she knew the sun would set soon. With twilight, the long shadows would make it more difficult to spot a sole traveler, especially one clothed in the color of night. Still, she had to be cautious.

Tara studied every bush, tree, and rock. Hearing a sound she stopped, wondering if more Gothman waited to waylay her. No. It was nothing more than a forest creature. The Gothman had so successfully controlled these lands for hundreds of winters she found it hard to believe there weren't more lying in wait for her. Where was their skill?

She continued walking at a slow pace, getting her bearings by studying the sun shining through the trees. The silence grew eerie in its stillness, and Tara knew something was very wrong.

The Gothman weren't gone. She could smell them, sense them watching her. But why just watch? Why didn't they try and kill her? Instinct told her to run. Run like hell. Get away as quickly as she could. But those same senses also urged her to go on. After all, the Gothman had seen her plenty of times in the last few minutes, yet they kept their distance. She'd even taken out a handful of their men, yet they didn't retaliate.

Why?

The smell of the pine invaded her thoughts, telling her she was now deep in Gothman territory. Her chances of walking into another ambush were significantly higher.

Taking her training into account, she used the natural shield of the rocks to her advantage and switched her laser to scan for life-signs. The Gothman controlled large amounts of land. They certainly couldn't do so if it weren't adequately guarded.

Something caught her attention.

Wood burning.

She searched the pines in front of her for its source.

A small wooden house with a stone foundation appeared through the trees.

Yes! I found it! Tara gloried in how well she'd listened to Patha's stories.

Had he known she would use his tales to explore the different nations? Of course. He must have. All good Runners used the accounts of their peers to learn about places they'd not yet explored. They could move through anyone's land with that knowledge.

The old Runners would retell the information they had heard from others. If there were several old Runners around an evening fire, they would always try to outdo each other with their tales. A good listener could always discern fact from fiction in their stories.

Tara was young, just a few more than twenty winters, but even she knew Patha had elaborated on many of his stories. She'd heard some of them numerous times, and noted the changes as he told them around the fire to any new Runner visiting their clan.

Before her stood the house Patha described over and over again. It had to be.

Tara approached it cautiously, making sure to stay hidden by the trees until she was sure of its occupants.

Light flowery, faded curtains covered glass windows. They were closed however, prohibiting Tara from seeing into the house. Voices trailed through the night air, and the front door of the house opened.

She moved nimbly through the natural camouflage until she could see inside the house.

"It will go well for you to notify us immediately if you notice anyone, it will." The loud grumbling voice broke the night air.

While the thick Gothman accent had been described to Tara before, it still sounded strange hearing it for the first time.

"Of course, I'll call immediately if there be any disturbances, to be sure. I daresay you're too kind to protect an old lady, you are."

Tara could see two large men appear out of the shadows as they moved toward motorcycles. A petite woman stood on the porch of the house and wrapped a knit shawl tightly around her shoulders.

"Tell his Lordship that I'll be sure to have a warm pie to his house in time for lunch, I will. I look forward to seeing his mama. Is she well?"

The two men grunted in answer and took off down a gravel road, raising dust into the night air.

Tara studied the woman who stood on the porch and watched the Gothman warriors until the sound of their motorcycles was barely audible.

The woman continued to stand there, looking up into the sky, apparently surveying the first of the stars as twilight faded to darkness.

She tightened her grip on the shawl and finally turned toward the trees. "You can come out now, you can. I'm a simple woman and I'm no threat to you, that's for certain. I know the Runners, and you didn't come to my house by accident, so come out and allow me to be hospitable, yes."

Tara didn't move.

Patha had talked about the Gothman woman, Reena, many times. This lady definitely fit the description. She was a small woman, her features petite but in nice proportion. Dark gray hair wrapped around her head in a wide bun. Her skin wasn't wrinkled although laugh lines could be seen next to her eyes. The lone light hanging from the porch ceiling accented the woman's features with graceful shadows.

Tara needed to be cautious, though. She could defend herself if this woman did try to call the Gothman back, but she couldn't tell if there were more in the house. Even with a thorough scan of the area, the Gothman could have any number of places to hide their motorcycles.

The old woman must have read her mind. "Now, I know you're there, Runner. I can smell your leather, I can. I know you're armed, and I daresay I don't have a gun. I don't feel like going back into my house, wondering who be outside watching me, no. That much is certain. So, come out now!" The old lady's voice had become authoritative.

She had thought her Runner attire would aid in hiding her, but the old lady's comments made her rethink that decision. She needed to blend in. But apparently with her dress, anyone in Nuworld could recognize her instantly. Tara glanced down at her clothing. Her black leather boots laced to her knees and thin black gloves fit like a second skin, adding to the practicality of clothes required for the lifestyle of a Runner. The thick leather protected her skin in battle. The black Runner material, known throughout Nuworld as being virtually bulletproof, was woven with a thread made from crushed glass.

Tara shrugged. Ridding herself of her Runner clothing would be helpful. Maybe the old lady could prove useful.

She moved out from behind the rock and walked up to the porch. She didn't watch the woman, but instead focused beyond her through the open door, looking for movement. She needed to reassure herself that she wasn't walking into a trap. She ascended the porch stairs as silent as a cat and faced the old woman.

"Well now, you are a Runner, you are. The black leather does hide you well in the shadows, doesn't it? Come on in. I promise I'm quite alone, I am. So tell me your stories. How do you know of me?" The old woman spoke without taking a single breath even as she turned and walked back in to her home.

Tara followed her.

Reena stepped to the side, allowing Tara to view the interior before she shut the door behind them and moved to a kitchen that was merely a wall along the side of a small living room. She put a tall thin pot onto the stove and lit a match to start the fire underneath it. A pie was produced out of an off-white icebox and the old woman pulled a plate out of the freestanding cupboard. Reena placed a large slice of the pie on it.

"It's apple. I reckon I'll make another one in the morning for the Lord's family, I will. It helps to show my loyalty, you know. Lord Darius knows I've entertained Runners before, but I like to keep peace in the family, so to speak." She placed her hand over the pot, then reached for a rag hanging on the icebox and removed the container from the stove. "Do you like your coffee hot?"

"That'll be fine. Thank you." Tara couldn't believe it. The woman had coffee. That was a coveted treat. The plants making the rare drink didn't grow in their nation and could only be obtained through the right connections. How did a Gothman woman have such connections?

Reena picked up a wooden knitting needle and gathered together a project she'd obviously been working on for some time. It appeared to be a sweater, and Tara wondered at the patience required to take on such a task.

Crow's feet appeared next to the old lady's eyes as she smiled, then used one of the knitting needles to point to a lumpy couch with a multicolored quilt thrown over the back of it. "Sit. I'll be curious to see how you plan on eating that pie with your Runner headscarf wrapped around your face, and I'll be mighty offended if you refuse my food, I will. My pies are known throughout Gothman and if you traveled through the trees with the usual Gothman hospitality to greet you, I daresay you should be hungry, yes."

Tara unwrapped the black scarf from her face as she stroked her finger across the red circle that surrounded the embroidered red drop of blood—the symbol of the Blood Circle Clan, to which she proudly belonged—and she sighed. The symbol meant so much to her, she only hoped she was worthy of all that it entailed. Very carefully she set the scarf on the couch next to her.

She placed the mug of coffee on the wooden table in front of the couch and eagerly tasted the sweet dessert. It was as good as promised and she quickly took bite after bite.

"I'm thinking if the Gothman guards knew they were chasing such a beautiful wench as you, they'd have fought a bit harder to capture you, they would."

The woman's laugh tempted the corners of Tara's mouth.

If a person could be judged by their home, then Reena was a warm, caring person with patience and a solid foundation in her culture. The small cabin offered several different aromas that Tara easily distinguished.

The wooden walls and floors offered the spicy scent of the forest. The pungent smell of brewed coffee mixed with the sweet bouquet of baked apples. Other aromas floated through the air as well, not as easily defined — the pungent tang of spices and herbs used either for cooking or medicinal purposes, and a sterile smell, possibly soap used for laundry or bathing lingered in the air.

Tara also noticed a variety of handcrafted items in addition to the faded patchwork quilt on the sofa: a knitted afghan hung over the back of a rocker that waved back and forth as Reena gently rocked, and several embroidered wall hangings framed the walls. These items shared a bit of the woman sitting across from her, smiling peacefully and glancing at her occasionally with gentle blue eyes.

* * * * *

Reena tried hard not to stare at the beautiful young woman. Her light brown hair fell gracefully past her shoulders and was as supple and shiny as silk. Her complexion was fair although she had a red tint much as a person would from the sun. Reena realized it probably came from riding without a headscarf. Her skin was smooth, at least what Reena could see of it, with no scars or marks of battle on the young face. A novelty among Runners. The girl's sapphire eyes took in everything around her, conveying intelligence and a bit too much wisdom for her age.

"My goodness, you're barely a woman, and so beautiful. The men of these parts won't take kindly to knowing a looker like you avoided them so skillfully, I'm thinking. Their women don't learn the skills you've learned, they don't."

"So I've heard."

"Well now, what's your name and whose stories bring you here?"

"I'm Tara of the Blood Circle Clan."

"Ah, Patha's stories sent you here, they have." Reena nodded and started to rock a bit faster in her chair.

She's finally come to me.

So overjoyed was Reena to have the young woman sitting in her home, her heart forgot to beat for a second. "I'm Reena and you may call me that. Now, are you Patha's daughter?"

"I gained that honor at the age of four, but not by birth." Tara chewed as she spoke. "I'm at the *Age of Searching* and have heard the stories about you. Those stories also told me that Gothman don't like women."

Reena noticed her laugh interrupted Tara as the youngster stopped to look up from her pie with inquisitive eyes. It was hard not to get up and move closer to this young Runner.

"Gothman like ladies just fine," she said, still laughing. "They like them in the kitchen and in the bedroom. An unclaimed woman such as you will be plenty liked in this world, I fear."

The woman stopped laughing. "So, Tara of the Blood Circle Clan and daughter of the leader of all Runners, I would think you've come here with your head full of stories of Gothman, you have. I know a Runner doesn't enter a land aimlessly without a plan, so let's hear it."

"I—"

"You must be an excellent warrior, I would think," Reena continued on, "to get past the guards. But if you display your abilities you'll be detected instantly, to be sure. Gothman women don't fight, that is true. You're young and unclaimed, yes. I daresay your destiny here is to be raped continually until you're claimed, it will."

"I'm no stranger to being attacked, and I don't fear Gothman men." Tara gestured with her fork. "I came here to see if you had clothing that will help me mingle among the Gothman and learn their ways."

"I'm sure your skills are outstanding, but ten men against one woman aren't good odds…even if that woman is a Runner, no."

"I thought—" Tara began.

Reena didn't hear her. "I might be able to find some clothes that will fit you, yes. You're small, like me you are." Reena chuckled again.

"Would you be willing—" Tara's rush of words were cut off once more.

"I daresay in my youth I had much of your beauty. But the more you change to fit in, the more trouble you'll bring on yourself, that much is true."

"So you'll help me?" Tara's expression brightened.

Reena could see her warning had been ignored, but she answered just the same. "Yes." Reena tried to hide the excitement in her voice. Patha had sent Tara to her; she just knew it. There was no way she could let this young woman out of her home without getting to know her first. "I've known a Runner or two in my day, I have. You want to know the Gothman, and if I don't help you I'm sure you'll resort to a backup plan, you will. You'll stay the night here, though. I'm sure Lord Darius' guards will be keeping an eye on the woods for a Runner through the rest of the night, they will."

* * * * *

Tara watched the old lady get up from her rocking chair and open a door leading to a bedroom. Tara didn't move, but the woman continued to talk to her. From what Patha had taught her of Gothman society, Tara wondered why the woman didn't have a man around.

"I'm sure I've an extra nightgown for you, I do. We need to get you out of those clothes immediately, yes. I've many visitors and to be certain we'll have to come up with a story to explain your presence, we will. The women around here use me for a midwife and the Gothman like to reproduce. I stay quite busy, that much is sure." Reena laughed again as she retreated down a hall and into a dark room, her voice trailing off as she moved.

"Let's see." She returned a minute later holding up a long paisley nightgown with white ruffles around the collar. "This is quite becoming, and I do think it might fit, it will. I'm thinking I'll have to wash some clothes for you to wear during the day. Not to worry, I'll provide you with a modest wardrobe, yes. Go change into this. We'll figure out the rest in the morning. Tomorrow is a new day, you know. Now move along, get going."

Tara took the feminine nightgown to the bathroom and slowly disrobed. She felt ritualistic as she shed the black leather pants and jacket of her Runner heritage. She told herself, as she discarded her sleeveless black undershirt, that along with her clothes she also needed to shed the actions of the Runner. From this point forward she would be a Gothman woman, outwardly void of any rights, passive and submissive. Somehow she would do her best to be subservient and domestic. *Oh boy! Talk about choosing a foreign lifestyle!*

Her thoughts drifted back to her first encounter with the Gothman in the forest.

She hadn't planned on making such close contact with the brutal race so soon. Now they knew she was here. It still didn't make sense to her that she'd managed to get through the soldiers unscathed. Considering the close range when they used the bang sticks, she should be wounded or captured, if not killed.

Tara couldn't help but wonder if leaving her unharmed hadn't been the plan all along. When she heard the knock on Reena's front door, those thoughts quickly flew out of her head.

Chapter Two

ᔬ

Tara opened the bathroom door quickly. *More Gothman soldiers?* She hoped not. She began moving into the hallway when she stopped in her tracks. What happened to her vow of submissiveness? Her goal of blending in? Here she was, ready to protect the old lady who had been so hospitable toward her by barging in to the living room. And giving herself away in the process.

Passive, she warned herself, *be passive*. Slowly and quietly she left the bathroom and tiptoed to the end of the hallway.

"Joli, my dear, you're not here for a social call at this hour…am I right?" There was sincere concern in Reena's tone.

From her post at the end of the hallway, Tara caught a glimpse of a very pregnant young woman standing in the middle of the living room, her gaze focused on the ground.

Tara heard the thud of boots moving with slow determination, making floorboards creak. She pressed her body flat against the wall. She couldn't see as well, but she definitely felt more protected.

Just then somebody else entered the small house. The pitter-patter of small feet sounded everywhere. A young boy, with strawberry-colored curls that bounced ridiculously around his face, came into view for a split second.

Tara didn't move. Luckily the boy didn't look her way but paid attention to another person in the room.

"She's got the pain, Reena. And I daresay it isn't her time yet." A booming male voice echoed off living room walls.

Tara edged to the end of the hallway, but knew if she peeked around the corner, she would chance being seen. Instinct had her reaching for her laser. She felt naked without her Runner attire for added protection. In the flowing nightgown she was vulnerable, exposed. Although the evening air felt cool against her skin, small beads of perspiration formed in the center of her cleavage.

"I know it isn't her time yet," Reena snapped at the man, showing no fear of the burly man who stood almost twice her size. "Togin, you're wound tight, you are. This is woman's work...be gone with you. I'll call for you when I need you."

"I know you can help, Reena. She isn't taking it easy like you said, that's for certain."

A shadow spread across the carpet, and floorboards moved beneath a heavy burden. From the sounds, Tara guessed the man was moving toward the door.

"I'll be at the tavern in town when you need me. Some of Lord Darius' guards are hovering down that way, I hear. Figured I'd see what's about in the town."

"Then I shall call for you there, should I need you." Reena's tone gave no indication that guards in town bothered her in the slightest.

The door closed soundly. Tara heard a loud sigh escape the young Gothman woman and the chattering questions of the small boy and another youngster. A girl. The tension in the room had disappeared with the hollow thud of the door.

"Likely you can't be taking it easy when he has you waiting on him hand and foot. I'm sure he's not much help with the young ones either. My now, look how the three of you are growing, you are." Reena's words suddenly had laughter in them.

Tara crept to the end of the hallway and spotted a teenage girl hovering over the pregnant woman.

Reena ran her fingers through the girl's pale red hair. "Most likely, you'll be getting claimed before you're much older, as pretty as you're getting to be. That much is certain."

The young girl giggled and blushed.

"Reena, the pains are steady. I fear I've thrown myself into labor."

The woman called Joli looked down the hallway and noticed Tara. "Oh my goodness, you're already with someone, you are. Togin should have noticed before he left."

"Nonsense, this is my niece, Tara. My brother sent her to me just today. One of the Barg brothers wants to claim her, and my brother will have no doings with the likes of them. He sent her to me to see if I could get her claimed here in town, he did." Reena gestured for Tara to come to her. "Help me get Joli into my bed, will you? I'll get my herbs to brewing…they should stop that child from coming before his time."

Tara and Reena walked Joli into a large bedroom, which was no small feat, given that Joli was close to full term and quite heavy. Tara literally carried her to the bed, taking as much weight onto her shoulders as she could. She realized the old lady could not possibly handle the burden herself. Tara welcomed the distraction of making sure Joli felt comfortable, or as comfortable as possible.

Having a fair bit of birthing knowledge through the winters with the women in the clan, Tara knew Joli had dropped; the babe already rested between the woman's hipbones. Although Tara had never had a baby, she knew that cramping was common when the baby was positioned so low in the womb. She could also tell by the slender figure hinted at under the woman's swollen breasts that the woman would be thin after the baby came.

Tara remembered helping a clan member thrown into labor. Only a child at the time, Tara could still recall the memory of pounding Wild Yam root into powder to help soothe the pain.

"Joli dear, I save this bedroom for all my special ladies who visit me," Reena cooed as she pulled an old, but clean, blanket to the end of the bed.

Tara half placed, half dropped Joli onto the sheet. The woman struggled in her arms, making it hard to place her gently.

"Grab some more blankets from that shelf in the closet." Reena pointed to a closed door and Tara turned. "I'll put the kettle on to boil." The older woman scurried from the room.

"If we can get you to lie on your left side, it should stop some of the stomach discomfort, yes," Tara said quietly, trying to match the dialect of the Gothman. She helped the woman but didn't think she looked too comfortable when Tara finally left to find the old lady.

Reena was digging through a drawer in one of the cupboards when Tara entered the living room. She saw the three children standing awkwardly in the middle of the room, their large brown eyes showing fear and worry for their mama.

"Ah, not to worry, little ones." Tara knelt in front of the three children and reached her arms out to hug them. "We'll take care of her now, we will."

"I'm thinking you'll have to give up the back room tonight, my dear," Reena said to Tara. "Let's give the children some of my pie, and then we can put them down in the bed back there. We have a long night ahead of us, I fear."

After a quick check of her herbs on the stove, Reena set out plates on the counter and began slicing pie. "Seems more nights than not, my house will fill with family members, it will. I get accustomed to having the bodies around. I daresay there's plenty of blankets."

Tara sat the three children around Reena's kitchen table and fed them each a slice of the pie she'd so recently enjoyed. The children eagerly took in the sweetness and had it gone in no time. Tara grabbed a cloth and started applying it to the fingers of the youngest before he could damage Reena's house. The boy, who couldn't be school-age Tara decided as she looked at his soft baby skin, immediately fought his restraints.

"My mama always sends me out to the water buckets," the boy complained.

Tara kept a firm grip on the sticky hand until all remnants of pie were gone. "It's dark outside."

"Being scared of the dark is for women." The child stood in defiance and forgot to run when Tara released him.

She ruffled his curls, bringing him back to reality, and then smiled at the older daughter who was clearing dishes.

"Reena?" Joli called out, then groaned.

The old lady patted Tara's shoulder as she passed on her way to Joli.

Joli's grunts grew louder, and the children stared at the closed door.

"Let's check out the sleeping arrangement, shall we?" Tara herded the children toward the hallway.

"I want to say goodnight to my Mama, I do." It was the first time the middle child, a skinny girl with a shapeless dress hanging on her bony figure, had spoken.

"As soon as your mama's cramping has eased, I'm sure she'll come gather the lot of you." Tara smiled at the child, who didn't smile back.

She nestled the three under thick quilts covering the bed. A small lamp on a tall narrow dresser provided the only light for the room and sent long shadows up the wall. Tara sat with them and hummed quietly. She realized after a few minutes that she hummed a Runner lullaby. The children stared glassy-eyed at the ceiling and didn't comment so she continued until she noticed eyelids bobbing.

"Does it hurt terribly to have a babe?" the oldest asked, continuing to stare at the ceiling.

"I've never had a baby, so I don't know," Tara whispered the half-truth, watching as the youngest curled into his sister and plugged his thumb into his mouth.

"When our neighbor had her last baby, she screamed through the whole thing, she did. Couldn't talk more than a whisper for almost a cycle after that. Her claim says he is gonna keep her with child just to keep her quiet." The brief tale was said without inflection, and Tara couldn't guess from the young girl's expression how she felt about such an atrocity. Tara wanted to tell her the brute should be castrated.

"I should be with Mama," the oldest whispered, after pausing long enough to glance at her now sleeping siblings.

"I'm thinking your Mama would appreciate you keeping an eye on your brother and sister for her. They will be scared if they wake in a strange bed, they will be." Tara hoped she didn't exaggerate the Gothman brogue, but the young girl seemed relaxed speaking with her.

Tara remained with the children until she felt sure they were asleep then went into the kitchen.

"You've a way with the young ones," Reena said as she stirred something over the stove. She reached beside her and picked up a bottle containing a green powder, then set about sprinkling it into her concoction.

"I've had a fair bit of experience in that area." Tara thought of all the children who were often left in her charge when the clan traveled. More times than not, she had longed to share in the adventures of the adults, instead of playing nursemaid. But she couldn't deny she had learned from the experience of babysitting.

"I daresay your knowing that will come in quite handy in these parts. As my niece, you're now *officially* my apprentice. Come here and sift the root from the brew."

Tara accepted the strainer ladle. She slowly stirred through the dark tea, lifting the bark and placing it on the plate next to the unused portion.

Reena observed Tara until she seemed satisfied with her work, then left for the bedroom.

It was a long night. Tara stared at the almost empty pot on the stove, thinking there was no way Joli could possibly consume more of its liquid. She knew if she helped Joli to the bathroom one more time, her muscles would be too sore to defend herself against Gothman soldiers if the need arose.

Suddenly, beneath the sound of branches brushing the roof, Tara was certain she heard someone moving outside the small wooden cottage. No one else in the house seemed to hear the boots crunching out front. Tara guessed the branches were loud enough to conceal the sound from them. Still, she knew what she heard, once even aware that someone had stepped onto the porch. The squeaking of wooden floorboards had given away their position.

The curtains were drawn, and she had no light from outside to aid in seeing into the darkness. And that put her at a disadvantage she didn't like. She knew whoever was outside could see through the thin curtains and into the cottage. With the two lamps in the living room and the overhead light burning in the kitchen, she felt on display to anyone who cared to look.

No one ever came to the door, though. Tara ached to go outside and investigate but knew Gothman women wouldn't carry out such an act.

A short time later, Reena plopped down on the couch in the living room. "Well, the pains have stopped, and I am not afraid to say I don't know as I could have helped her without you." She smiled at Tara. "You were a smart one to stay out of sight when Togin was here, you were."

Tara glanced again at the curtains that hid the window. She didn't hear anything else, and Reena showed no indication she'd detected sounds outside. For the time being, she would stay quiet and alert.

Hot tea seemed in order, as the two of them enjoyed the first calm moment since Tara's arrival. Tara joined Reena on the couch and offered her a mug steaming with the hot brew. She blew on her own tea, but didn't comment.

Reena continued her quiet musings. "I couldn't speak on this when his claim was still awake. She'd be loyal to him, she would. He's a member of the Lord's army, and I'm a thinking he could have slipped his wife some powder to bring the baby just so he could get another look in here."

Tara nodded her head and leaned back against the couch, rearranging the pillows around her.

* * * * *

Joy coursed through Reena at the realization that Tara had made herself at home. She took her time with her tea, enjoying the warmth it offered and Tara's presence nearby. Finally, she rose and moved into the kitchen, dumping the remnants of the pot in the sink.

She glanced up at those pale sapphire eyes that took in everything being said without comment. For a moment, Reena wondered if she'd looked that wise when she was Tara's age. She shook her head, doubting it.

"We'll do the dishes in the morning. I'll call Togin and let him know he can fetch his family come morning."

* * * * *

Tara had heard stories of Gothman communication devices and was curious to see one. She knew their use was limited—only one person could be heard at a time. Tara thought they must not be very reliable since she also knew the person speaking couldn't always be heard accurately. She considered suggesting that Reena call Togin now, so she could watch the device operate. But Tara didn't wish to pry by asking where Reena kept her device.

As she struggled to remember what the devices were called, exhaustion began consuming her. Tara decided the matter could be dwelled on later.

She heard Reena say, "I'm afraid, child, you'll be sleeping on the couch tonight."

"It sounds more comfortable than the places I've slept for the past cycle."

Reena smiled as she lowered the lights so the room was almost dark. "I'm glad to have you here, Tara. We will have more time for each other tomorrow. Good night now."

Tara watched the older lady disappear down the hallway before stretching out on the couch.

"Goodnight, Reena of Gothman. Nice to have met you."

Morning came sooner than Tara would have wished. Surprisingly, the homemade quilt, which she had pulled over her sometime during the night, provided a very nice sleep. Tara inhaled the many smells from the cottage the quilt had absorbed, and felt a strange sensation of peace consume her. The irony of it all brought a smile to her face while she stood and folded the blanket. She was in enemy land, being hunted. Peace was the last sensation she should be experiencing.

Tara entered the bathroom to shower and found a plain peach-colored dress hanging on a hook. The streaming hot water felt good after her long journey and late night. The soap Tara used didn't smell like Reena, and she wondered if the lady had put it in the bath just for her.

She would have savored the hot water longer, but knew adventures awaited her on this new day. She was ready to experience all of them.

The dress fit surprisingly well. The thin material was light on Tara's skin. After a lifetime of wearing thick Runner material, she felt almost naked. She adjusted a matching belt, which accented her narrow waist and displayed her figure nicely. A pair of plain tan cloth shoes finished the picture. Looking in the mirror, Tara stared at her Gothman appearance.

"Tara-girl? Do ya know what you're getting yourself into?" She stared at her reflection once more and nodded. Then she turned and left the bathroom.

Tara entered the living room in time to say goodbye to the children.

Togin stopped in mid conversation with Reena to stare at the girl entering the room.

"This would be my niece, Tara." Reena walked over and wrapped her cool fingers around her *niece's* arm. "She was a great help last night in saving your unborn child."

"Mighty fine-looking lass you are." Togin tipped his hat and then turning to his claim, pulled her out the door.

"You're welcome," Tara muttered sarcastically as he walked across the porch.

Tara washed the dishes and made the beds. As she straightened the rooms, she reflected on how much she enjoyed the mundane tasks.

Reena seemed surprised when she came out of the bathroom and saw the condition of her house. "Goodness me, child. You're mighty full of hidden talents for a Runner, you are. And just look at you, would you? You're more stunning than any lass I've seen in this town, to be certain. It will be his Lordship himself taking a notice in you, I'd be sure."

"His Lordship?" Tara frowned as she studied the pattern of the quilt folded over the couch.

"Oh yes, my dear. The Bryton house has ruled Gothman since the winters of my grandmama. They've always been quite powerful, and each generation has added land to our nation. Lord Jovis Bryton ruled for over forty winters. He passed on last spring and his son, Darius, is now lord."

Tara followed Reena to the small bedroom Joli had occupied and listened as the woman continued.

"Lord Jovis' eldest son, Juro, was to rule, he was, but shortly after his papa's death he drowned in the river to the east. Darius was next in line, and so now he rules." Reena pulled the sheet from the bed, and paused, lowering her voice to a whisper as she met Tara's gaze. "It was murder, were the rumors, although just rumors, mind you. Not one would stand up to Darius and challenge him, I know that much. He's a ruthless warrior, he is, although he has much to learn."

Tara didn't try to hide her smile. If last night's attempt to capture her was any indication of the man's abilities, then he definitely had a lot to learn.

"This is quiet talk, child hear me, not to be muttered outside this home, even as gossip. Lord Darius will not hear a word spoken about his dead brother. He's powerful, and many stand behind him."

Reena hurried out of the room without another word.

Tara followed with her arms full of the used sheets and blankets, dropping them in the basket that Reena indicated.

The lady then moved to the kitchen and stepped in front of the oven. "Oh to think, an old lady's memory must always be checked, shouldn't it?" She chuckled to herself. "I put the apple pie for the Lord's family in the oven while you were showering. I'll be struck down, to be certain, if it's cooked a moment beyond perfection."

She pulled the pie out of the oven. It filled the room with a wonderfully enticing smell. Reena set the pie to cool on the kitchen table.

Tara felt a twinge of hunger in her stomach as the scent of the sweet apples filled her nose.

"Some fat added to those bones will make you look more Gothman, I'm thinking." Reena chuckled as she pulled a plate of sweet rolls from the overlarge breadbox on the counter.

Tara and Reena enjoyed honey rolls for breakfast, washed down with fresh cool milk. Then Reena washed the sheets used the night before. Tara marveled at the antiquated machine that vibrated to an off-rhythm beat as it spun the sheets around and around. Most things in Reena's household consisted of basic domestic items; the type of things she anticipated finding within a Gothman community. But then there were mysteries like the coffee, and no man around in a functioning household. The main thing Tara had learned was that Gothman women relied on their men to provide for them, yet Reena didn't appear to have one in her life.

Tara went outside and began chopping firewood. Extra fuel would be needed to help keep the house warm as the nights grew cooler. She stacked the logs in a pile alongside the house and then sat on the front porch to nurse some scrapes. "It'll take some time to get accustomed to this light material you have me wearing," Tara admitted as Reena applied a salve to one of her scratches.

"It'll be easier for you, it will, if you accept the women's chores and leave the men's chores to the men. But I have a feeling you will do what you want, I do." Reena smiled at the young shapely woman. "You might as well make me aware of the other talents you possess before we go to town. Do you sew? Have you done any quilting? The Gothman do not take well to strangers, but they welcome family with open arms, they do. Announcing you as my niece will help you in town, to be sure."

"Well, I've—"

"You can obviously keep a house and you're good with the children, but the women socialize over their chores. We'll go to town and stop at the market to pick up a few necessaries. The women folk'll be there doing the same after they've taken their sons to school. It's a social time for us, it is, and the gossip's usually good and plenty. You do like gossip, don't ya?"

"I'm not much—" Tara gave up trying to talk as it appeared needless. Reena would continue without her input.

"On Saturday mornings we meet for a quilting session. If you can partake, I'll announce your presence for this Saturday. It will send quite the talk through the town, it will." The old lady smiled. "I enjoy good gossip, I do. And you, my dear, will put a mark on Gothman that won't soon be forgotten. I can feel it in my bones." Reena paused and looked at Tara. "So, what is it you can do?"

"Well," Tara said, then waited for the interruption. When none came, she continued. "If you're talking about the blanket thrown over the back of your couch, I've never seen one like it before. I'm a quick learner, though."

"Hmm, it won't do to have a novice quilter. Not at your advanced age. The gossip'll fly on that one faster than the news of your being here. You'll offer to watch the young ones while the rest of us quilt. I dare say that'll work. I'll try to teach you on the side, ah, that will do, yes it will."

Tara wrapped the pie in a cloth and placed it in a wooden basket. Reena scurried from room to room preparing for their trip to town. The old woman chatted the entire time, showing obvious excitement about introducing Tara to the women of the town. Slowly the couch filled with items to take into town—the pie for his Lordship, stacks of quilting patterns, some clothes left behind by a previous caller that Reena had washed and needed to return. And last of all, a sweater made from a rough yarn Tara didn't recognize, which Reena had thrown her way to wear if needed. Tara found herself leaning against the counter in an effort to stay out of the way.

She took this opportunity to place her small laser, easily concealed due to its size, in her dress pocket. She wasn't going to enter a community of people that despised her kind without being armed. Since the laser was silent, Tara felt it was her best mode of defense.

They placed the basket containing the pie in the backseat of Reena's car—an old rusty two door with black interior. Tara hadn't ever seen such ancient vehicles, other than in pictures, and she grinned like a child when, unable to resist, she reached inside and turned the steering wheel one way then the other. Reena scolded her when she came out of the house, but Tara just continued grinning.

When the car hesitated to start, Tara volunteered to check under the hood and even consented to putting on her black gloves before lifting the hood.

Reena insisted it would not do to take her newfound niece into town with grease under her fingernails. "The cable to the battery is more than likely loose, yes," Reena said, from behind the wheel.

Tara stared at the motor in disbelief. If Patha could only see this! Once, he had shown her sketches of an ancient motor. But to think Gothman had recreated them and used them daily. Maybe this race had a bit more intelligence than she gave them credit for having.

"Okay, try it now." Tara smiled when the car lit to life, sputtering and shaking enough to send birds flying from the trees.

The gravel road leading away from Reena's house was uneven and tree branches overhead made it feel as if they drove through a tunnel. Tara noticed when they reached a stone paved road, that one would have to know specifically where the road to Reena's house was, or they would never find it.

The morning air was crisp, and Tara appreciated the knitted sweater Reena had given her before they left. She enjoyed the sweet smell of the pines and the variety of birds singing their morning songs. The road caught her attention as well. Flattened rocks, more than likely from the surrounding hills, varied in color, making the road as unique as the people who had created it.

Soon they reached the peaceful town of Bryton.

Reena told Tara that the town was once known as Smithton, but as long as Reena had been alive it had been called Bryton.

Merchants' stores soon appeared on either side of the street. The town itself was surrounded by rocky hills providing natural protection. Most of the buildings were made of a white stone and wood. Houses off the main road appeared to be made of the same stone as the hills.

Tara noticed a large residence on a hillside. Built at the opposite end of town from where she was riding, it was high enough to be visible above Bryton. Even from a distance, Tara could tell that it was very large. The thought of a stationary house, one that would never move and always be in the same place for the lifetime of a person, overwhelmed Tara. Patha told her these people would be different, but this amazed her.

Reena told her Lord Darius lived there with his mama and youngest brother, who was still a child. Lord Darius had another brother, Mikel, who served as his advisor. Mikel and his claim lived in Bryton with their children.

Reena put the vehicle in a designated stopping zone, offering a rather bored-looking guard several coins to park there. Mamas and their daughters were everywhere. The women stood in small groups, chatting, while small children ran up and down the sidewalk and older girls huddled, giggling, not too far from their mamas.

Tara slowly opened the door and stood, taking in her surroundings. Reena seemed oblivious to the sensation the Runner caused, but Tara grew alert when women and children whispered and stared with rapt attention. She couldn't help notice Reena holding her head high, as if proud, when they walked toward the stone structures. From what Tara had learned of the old lady's personality, she assumed Reena enjoyed this interest. But Tara avoided their curious glances and carefully kept her eyes down. She remembered Reena's instructions well.

"We'll go into the grocery store first. It's run by the Olgoods, an old family, they are. Once we introduce you to them, I daresay the whole community will get word of your being here. I'd say, they'll all know before the day is out." Reena headed toward double doors propped open with polished tree stumps.

"Ah, Reena, it's nice to see you, it is." A plump older woman standing behind the counter looked up and smiled when the two women entered.

A short man with gray whiskers and a potbelly remained sitting on a stool next to the counter. "And who might this young lass be?" He looked Tara over as if she were a side of beef he might purchase.

"Thelga, it's good to see you, it is, and Garg, you're looking well." Reena nodded her head to the couple. "I'd like you to meet my niece, Tara. She's come to stay with me just this other day, she has. I daresay she's quite an aid to an old lady."

Tara nodded her head to the couple, but kept quiet just as Reena had instructed before they had left the house.

"Ah, what a comfort for a woman with no children," Thelga said, clasping her hands over her large girth. "I daresay you'll have her claimed before the week is out. She's quite the looker, she is."

Garg grunted and then got up and walked toward the back of the store without a word of goodbye.

"To be certain, I know she is." Reena winked, apparently not daunted by Garg's departure. "Her Papa's a mite bit picky though, if you ask me. But who asks an old lady? Turned down a claim, he did. She's his only daughter, you know. So, now she's with me." Reena clucked to herself as she moved toward the fresh produce. She took a basket from a stack by the door and handed it to Tara.

Tara wandered past barrels of produce as she followed Reena, and watched with curiosity as the older woman poked and sniffed, pinched and shook each vegetable before selecting what she wanted. Evidently, it was quite a task for Reena to find produce that suited her needs, but finally she seemed satisfied with her choices, paid for the items, and nodded good day to the Olgoods.

"Well now, that's done," Reena said as she chuckled to herself. "Thelga'll be quite busy letting the town folk know of your arrival, she will. I swear to you now that half the town'll come down with some ailment or another just to come see old Reena's niece." She laughed out loud and wrapped her arm around Tara's. "You did mighty fine in the store, you did. Now I need to pick up some more yarn. Sirlah Maken's shop is just up the street. I'll be going in alone. It won't do to have them noticing your lack of seamstress skills. It'll be there that I tell them you'll help with the young ones at the quilting. I'll point out we have enough quilters and too many wee ones. It'll make sense, it will. You wander around, if you like."

Reena left Tara on the sidewalk and hurried down the street.

Tara was amused by how much Reena seemed to be enjoying herself. Left alone, she walked slowly down the street looking into each store window. She smiled as shyly as she could to anyone who saw her.

So *these* were the women she'd wondered so much about? They lived a life of domesticity, completely oblivious to anything outside their daily routine. They grew up, anxiously waiting to be claimed, and then fell into a role of servitude and inconsequential gossip. So far, she wasn't too impressed. How could these women go through life with no say in matters that involved them? How could they feel complete when they needed a man simply to exist?

Tara passed a gap between two of the stores. It was wide enough for a vehicle to move between them. The tall buildings cast shadows, and she realized this was not a place where the townsfolk walked. It was full of trashcans and the smell reflected that fact, along with the flying insects hovering over the bins.

Tara's keen eye caught the movement of several figures at the other end of the alley, and she stopped to watch them. Young boys obviously hoping not to be detected clung to the shadows. They were probably supposed to be in school. She started to look away, a smile creeping up on her face, when she spotted several other children entering the service road behind the first group.

"There they are!" one of the boys yelled.

She slipped easily enough behind a large trashcan and squatted unnoticed as she continued to watch the boys on the dark road.

"You'll be dealing with me now." A large youth of thirteen or fourteen winters walked with sureness toward the group Tara had first noticed. "Let's see if you can fight, Torgo." He was almost twice the size of the younger boy whom he addressed.

Tara realized quickly that the younger boy had very few fighting skills as he backed awkwardly down the alley.

His comrades spread away from him, the hope of escape obvious in their faces.

"Don't be telling me we have a coward here?" The large boy laughed, lunging at the younger one as he feigned a punch. "It couldn't be, I would think."

Torgo turned and made an attempt to run, but he was quickly overtaken and thrown to the ground. He tried to yell.

But the older boy sat on him and put one hand over Torgo's mouth. With the other, he started hitting Torgo. "Not only can you not fight, you would cry like a baby for help, would you?" The large boy laughed again; the other boys stood around watching.

Tara removed the small laser from her dress pocket and shot at a trashcan next to the group of boys. The metal can sliced into two pieces that flew down the alley in opposite directions. Its lid slammed against the wall. The pieces made a horrific sound, the screeching sound echoing off the buildings, which intensified the effect.

The frightened boys jumped and scattered down the side street.

Torgo tried to get up and run, but fell awkwardly back to the ground.

Tara rose from behind the trashcan and walked over to the boy.

"You know, son, often if you act like you're willing to take a challenge, a bully will back down, he will," Tara said, in her best Gothman accent. "Let me see you now." She held up his face and looked at the scratches that were starting to bleed. "It'll be hard to explain how you got those while studying in school." She smiled at the child.

He smiled back cautiously. "How did you do that?" Torgo sputtered.

"I'm not rightly sure. I threw a rock. I was trying to hit the boy that was pounding you. That trash can had to be rotted clear through." Tara rolled her eyes and the young boy laughed. She hoped no one inspected the destroyed can too closely.

His laughter stopped quickly as he looked past Tara toward the sidewalk.

Tara turned and saw a man sitting on a motorcycle, watching. Blond curls fell to his shirt. His expression revealed none of his thoughts, and dark, penetrating gray eyes stared at her without blinking. His appearance was rugged…distracting…but more than that.

He was captivating.

The man shifted his attention to the boy, then looked at Tara again with a bit more interest.

She returned the gaze with an equal amount of regard. She could tell by the size of the motorcycle he was straddling that he was fairly tall. He wore a dark plaid shirt with a brown leather jacket over it. It was unbuttoned and successfully displayed a broad, muscular chest. She noticed a crest embroidered on the sleeve of his jacket and the matching crest on his motorcycle.

"They challenged me. What was I to do?" Torgo stood as tall as his young body would allow as he spoke to the man.

"Back to school with you. We'll talk about this later, we will." The words were barely out of the man's mouth before the boy took off running as fast as his legs would take him.

Tara stood silently, continuing to watch the man's eyes as they surveyed her. She assumed the boy was his son, and she would never allow herself to show interest in a married man, but his look possessed her and it was hard to look away. After so long, she was finally standing face to face with a Gothman warrior...a gorgeous one at that.

"Who might you be, lass?" The man's voice was softer now. He studied her, as if memorizing her features, or perhaps trying to remember where he might have seen her before.

"I'm Reena's niece. My name's Tara." Tara finally remembered to lower her eyes and quickly did so. For some reason, her heart pounded, and she felt her palms grow damp.

"I haven't seen you before, that's for sure."

"I've just arrived and came into town with her today for the first time."

"I see. Well, Tara, Reena's niece, I'll be thanking you for breaking up the fight for my younger brother's sake."

Tara returned her gaze to his before she could stop herself. *Younger brother, not married?*

His expression didn't change nor did he bother to say who he was. He also gave no indication if he thought it odd that a Gothman woman prevented a fight. He looked at her a minute longer and then drove down the street.

Tara exhaled slowly, willing her heart to stop pounding as she walked to the sidewalk and stared after him. Had he said *thank you for breaking up the fight?* Had he seen her shoot the trashcan?

Reena walked down the sidewalk toward Tara, the older woman's attention moving from the departing man to her *niece*. "Well, child, don't it figure, your first day in town, and you've the honor of meeting Lord Darius himself." Reena sounded absolutely delighted.

"*That* was Lord Darius?" Tara asked quietly as she stole another glance at the handsome man disappearing down the stone road.

"Yes, my dear. What'd he say to you?" Reena handed the bags of yarn to Tara and started walking to the car. "Come now, tell an old lady everything. He hasn't claimed anyone yet, although I daresay the rumors are that he's been with each girl in this town, he has. Now he's seen you, maybe that will change. Ha, it's plain to see you are a mite prettier than any other girl this town has to offer."

"He said 'thank you'."

Reena turned to Tara, a puzzled look on her face. "A bit strange, but then he always has been odd, he has."

The two reached the car, and Tara put the bags on the floor behind the two seats. Her mind raced. What should she do if the ruler of this land *had* seen her with a laser that was more sophisticated than any Gothman had ever created? He had to be the same man who instigated a search for a Runner on his land the night before, and she credited the man as intelligent.

Eventually, he would put two and two together and uncover the identity of the Runner who had eluded the guards.

Letting out a gasp, Tara realized her next move in this community had better be carefully thought out if she were to stay alive.

Chapter Three

୧୦

"There were some children fighting in the alley. One of them was hurt and I was going to help the child when Lord Darius showed up and told the child to go back to school," Tara explained as Reena drove through the remainder of downtown. "I didn't know it was Lord Darius."

"Well, now you know who he is and he most certainly knows who you are, there'll be no mistaking that." Reena seemed quite pleased. "Imagine the lord, himself, taking a fancy to you. And I might add, I saw the way you were looking at him, I did." She nudged Tara with her elbow and let out a low chuckle.

"You act as you want me married, or claimed, as you call it."

"Well my dear, you can't very well experience our culture as a female if you're not claimed, that's for certain. There'd be nothing else to do with you at your age but to show you off for a claiming." Reena smiled at the young girl. "I'm an old lady, my dear. I daresay you've brought excitement to my life."

"I don't want to be claimed."

"Ach, shh, you better keep thoughts like that to yourself, love. You'd be suspected as odd for sure if you say thoughts like that out loud." Reena chuckled some more and glowed as she glanced at Tara.

The two were silent as Reena drove slowly through the town.

Tara looked out the window at the community, watching the people she saw on the streets. Young women worked in gardens with children running around them. The houses appeared clean and well kept, for the most part. She wondered at a lifestyle in which the people lived in a home all of their lives and raised children.

This was all so new to her. She'd spent months in one location before, but there was always a sense of excitement when it was announced that her clan would be moving to a new location. She couldn't imagine living in the same place all her life.

The thought wasn't too appealing.

"I daresay this must all seem so strange to you."

Reena brought Tara back from her thoughts. "I was just imagining what it must be like to live in one spot all your life."

"You'll probably never know that feeling, sweet child. You're a Runner, you are. I can dress you like a Gothman and teach you how to act like a Gothman, but the Runner is in your blood. You must forgive an old lady. I've spent the morning going on about my niece come to stay with me. It's a pleasant thought, and you're quite the young lady to be showing off, you are. I guess I'd say I got a bit carried away. I wouldn't know what to say if I weren't talking about getting you claimed. That's what we do with our young ladies, it is."

Reena had now driven through the town and was turning onto a paved road winding up a hill. Their next stop would be Lord Darius' house.

Tara wondered if he would be there. The man appeared strong, not only physically, but mentally as well. He ruled all of Gothman and hadn't been the designated heir. He had taken the right to rule. Tara imagined he would be intelligent, manipulative, and shrewd in his methods.

There were problems also. This man believed women didn't have the intelligence to do anything but birth babies and raise them. He was not a fair man. And hadn't she already determined that the warrior skills of his men were inferior to her own? Tara frowned as she chastised herself for her previous thoughts of finding him appealing. Obviously he had a lot to learn.

The road ran past beautifully landscaped scenery. The grass on the ground was cut short and tall pine trees were scattered through the yard.

As they approached the house, Tara was aware that Reena watched for her reaction. After all, Tara had grown up living in trailers, never having a piece of land to call her own. Reena would know that the Runners were proud of their nomadic existence, but

Tara sensed that the home she was about to visit might alter her perspective.

She was right. Perfectly nestled among the foliage, a large stone house stood proudly before them. A wide front porch wrapped around both sides of the front of the house. Porch swings hung on each end, and sharply carved stone stairs led down to a pebbled walkway that traveled out to greet the road. The house itself was several stories high with a large veranda off the third floor.

Tara studied the vantage point offered by the veranda, guessing that it enabled soldiers to survey the land and ensure its safety. Standing watch on that ledge was probably considered a significant achievement for Gothman warriors.

The two men on guard duty in the front yard walked to the car, and Reena slowed to a stop. "My apple pie as promised." She smiled to the large man leaning over, peering through the car window. Tara remembered seeing him at Reena's cabin the previous night. He had been one of the men looking for her.

"Who do you have here?" The man tossed a toothless smile at Tara. "I daresay his lordship will like this a mite bit more than your apple pie, he will."

"She is my niece," Reena said coolly. "Will you announce us or are you going to stand there with your jaw hanging?"

"How you've lived to be an old lady with that mouth of yours is a mystery to me." The man snarled and stood up to speak into his walkntalk.

* * * * *

Reena knew how she'd lived to be an old lady. She was protected. Her one and only love had seen to that. She wasn't sure if Lord Darius knew the history behind why his papa had declared her unavailable for a claim. He'd upheld his papa's wishes though, and for that she was grateful.

She looked at the beautiful young woman sitting next to her in the car, whose sapphire eyes made her appear too wise for her winters. Tara was watching the guard speak to the lord through his walkntalk. Reena wondered if Tara had ever seen the Gothman communication device before. This was a young lady who digested and analyzed everything she saw, and Reena could see qualities of a natural-born leader in Tara. All the Gothman attire in Nuworld wouldn't hide that quality in the lass.

Reena knew Lord Darius would claim Tara instantly. In fact, he might already have done so. A man didn't always tell a woman immediately after he claimed her. She would find out soon enough. Tara would fight it, but Reena knew it had to happen. They were meant to be together. Tara could help Lord Darius realize his potential.

* * * * *

Tara struggled to hear what the guard said into his walkntalk, wondering to whom he might be speaking, but the car motor made it impossible to hear. She watched with fascination as the man held the black box to his mouth, and his thumb moved to press a button on the side when he spoke.

A minute or two passed before the man returned to the car window. "Pull your car over to the side, Reena." The guard pointed to an area off to the left.

"Of all things I know where to park, I do." Reena waved the guard away and drove her car to the side of the house.

"Grab the basket out of the backseat, child," Reena instructed Tara as she stared toward the grand house. "You ever seen anything so magnificent?"

Tara reached for the basket then turned. "It looks so permanent."

The front door opened and a lady about the same age as Reena walked out onto the front porch. "Reena, I'll be, it's so good to see you again, my friend." The woman reached out and hugged Reena. "I daresay it takes the scare of a Runner intruder to bring you to my doors these days. What to think, I wonder."

"I stay quite busy with the way this town is populating itself," Reena said, and the two women laughed out loud.

"Ah, so here she is." The woman took Tara's chin in her hand and turned the girl's head from side to side. She glanced sideways at Reena and then wrinkled her brow. "She's the spitting image of you at her age, she is. And she's your niece, you say? Well now, you're definitely related, that much is true."

Tara smiled politely and glanced at Reena. She thought she saw a worried look on the old woman's face.

"I'm Hilda Bryton."

The lady either didn't notice the look on Reena's face or didn't pay attention to it. She was a large woman, taller than Reena. She wore a long loose frock flowing below her knees. Her silver-gray hair wrapped in a bun behind her head.

Tara pictured Hilda raising Darius and the young boy from the alley. She wondered how much influence the Gothman woman had in their upbringing, or had their papa controlled the way in which they were raised?

"My Lady," Tara said quietly with her eyes lowered as she offered a slight curtsy.

"I'm sure you know how the gossip flies through this town. I had heard she was quite the beauty, but the words do her no justice, that's for certain. You'll be mighty proud of this one, won't you?" Hilda patted Reena's arm.

"I hadn't seen her, myself, since she was a baby. Until this night past, of course. She's the beauty, she is."

"Ah, my manners, to entertain you on my porch, I am sure." Hilda laughed and opened the front door wide. "Please, do come in for a visit. Reena, when have we last sat and had a good talk of the goings on, I'm sure I don't remember."

Tara followed the two old women into the house. She gasped as they entered the foyer and caught her first glance at the magnificent home. At that moment, she figured if someone were looking for a Runner in disguise they would have immediately suspected her because she couldn't get over the vastness of this dwelling. Never before had she been inside such a structure. The most shelter she'd had from the elements throughout her life was the trailers Runners lived in while with their clan.

Tara wanted to run her hands along the walls. They had to be solid. This house had been built to stay right here on this land, never moving. Runners moved when the weather changed, when trade agreements improved in a different area, or when news of a dispute or challenge in another area came forth.

But not the people of Gothman.

They ignored Nuworld and focused only on themselves. And this house would be an excellent place to ignore the outside world. The arched ceilings allowed for a wide curving stairway to show all of its glory as it climbed in front of them to a second floor. Tara remembered seeing windows outside indicating more rooms on a third floor. She wondered where another staircase might be.

The hallway above could be seen from downstairs. Dark mahogany doors along the second floor hallway left Tara to imagine what might be on the other side of them. As they left the entryway and walked through two glass doors, Tara found herself in a large room with glossy wooden floors and a large area rug so thick she could feel her feet sink in it through the thin cotton material of her shoes.

This living room was as large as her entire trailer.

Beautifully carved wooden chairs had forest green cushions resting on them. There was a long sofa made out of the same dark green material. The wood on the tables on either side of the couch, as well as the oval one in front of it, were polished to the point that Tara could see her reflection in them. She almost did a double take at the strange-looking woman staring back. It wasn't often she gazed at her own reflection, let alone without her headscarf.

"So, sit down and tell me all your goings on, if you will," Hilda said.

Reena made herself comfortable in a tall, well-padded armchair. "Be a dear, Tara, and set the pie on the dining room table." Reena pointed to the room adjoining the one they were in.

Tara placed the pie on a long wooden table and walked over to one of the long glass windows. She could see a sprawling, well-groomed yard and gardens, and heard the muffled voices of two men working in the yard. They appeared to be getting something out of an old flatbed pickup truck. The cab of the vehicle faced Tara, so she wasn't able to see what it was they were trying to get off the bed.

Lord Darius walked across the yard toward the truck. Her gaze followed his every move. His long stride and tall features sent a warm sensation through Tara's body, and her stomach flip-flopped. It had been a long time since she'd seen a man so striking.

Her attention shifted from him to the truck.

The men struggled to lift something from the bed and set it on the ground—her motorcycle!

Tara groaned. They probably couldn't start it, since it was coded, but they'd found it and brought it here. A lot of good it was going to do her if it was stuck up here! She watched the men lift the bike and carry it to a shed before she turned to join the women. Those solid stone walls seemed to close in around her, trapping her and preventing her escape.

"Enjoying the scenery of my backyard, are you girl?" Hilda let out a deep chortle.

The men continued hollering instructions to each other, and their muffled sounds proved a disturbing distraction.

"I daresay it's my son you'd be admiring." She looked through the hallway at Tara and then turned to Reena. "They would make the most handsome claim in all the Gothman nation. Can you imagine, we would be sisters for real, you and me?"

"Just think of those gorgeous grandchildren to show off." Reena clasped her hands together as if it had just been finalized.

Tara glared at the two women as she joined them in the living room and sat on the end of the couch. Her future was ready and waiting for her. She had worked hard to deserve title of heir to rule all Runner clans, and no one would take that from her. Especially two scheming old women with nothing better to do than play mate-maker with two people who were strangers to each other.

The two women continued to chatter endlessly, talking about whatever came to their minds and laughing at each comment that was made.

Tara blocked out their conversation as she thought of her own predicament. For the time being, she was stranded. She hadn't given any thought to leaving in the near future, but now she couldn't if she wanted to, unless she revealed her identity and stole a Gothman motorcycle.

Tara didn't want to leave, she wanted to stay and learn about these people. But having the option of departing taken from her was annoying. An image of Darius appeared in her mind. She imagined how smug he must have felt to have found her bike, and Tara knew at that moment that she would get it back. She would not let Darius best her.

The men sounded like they were arguing outside, but try as she might she could not figure out what they were saying over the women's voices, or through the blasted thick Gothman walls. She finally gave up and turned her attention back to the women.

"So, you'll be staying for lunch then." Hilda smiled and got up. "I've some cold ham for sandwiches, boiled new potatoes and cheese rolls. That pie will go along famously, it will."

Reena and Hilda left the living room and walked through the dining room and back toward the kitchen.

Tara followed, noticing that the men were no longer in the backyard as she passed the large dining room windows.

"I had a girl to help with the house for a time. But Lord Darius didn't take a liking to her and sent her back to her parents. I will say this big house is too much for an old lady to manage, that much is certain." Hilda winked at Reena.

"I know what you're saying, I do at that," Reena sympathized. "My hands wear out long before the housework does these days I'm afraid. I've a liniment you might try. It does take the sting out."

"Tara, be a dear and go cut some of those flowers out back in the garden, will you?" Hilda opened a drawer and pulled out gloves and clippers. "Take these...ah...there you are. Use caution, girl. The thorns can bring blood faster than you may think, it's true."

* * * * *

Hilda watched Tara pass through the back doorway with deft agility. Never had she seen anyone move as Reena's niece did. It was as if the girl were one with the ground she stepped across. Quite captivating…and, it was more than outer beauty. There was something in the girl's eyes. She couldn't quite place it, but the girl seemed to put everything she saw and heard to memory. And Tara didn't look like one to forget.

* * * * *

Gloves and clippers in hand, Tara entered the backyard. There was no sign of the men, so she turned her attention to the different rose varieties growing bountifully along the side yard. She walked over to the flowerbeds and knelt so she could inhale their strong fragrance. She chose some yellow and white roses and began to cut the stems. Footsteps behind her alerted all her senses, and she jerked to a stand as she turned.

"Ah, lass, no reason to be so jumpy. I won't hurt you." A tall man with thick curly blond hair stood before her. He smiled and let his eyes roam over her body. His looks were less than appealing, and the grin on his face put Tara on her guard. "It's a mite bit strange to me that a lass as pretty as you hasn't been claimed. You're too pretty to be keeping to yourself." The man approached her, his hands open, palms up, in front of him.

Tara held the clippers out defensively.

"Now, that ain't fair. I just said I wasn't going to hurt you none, and here you are ready to hurt me. I daresay you're a wild one." The man laughed and started to grab the clippers from Tara.

She decided that he must have assumed he was dealing with a female who had no idea how to defend herself. *Boy! Was he in for a surprise!* Instinctively, she pulled the clippers back and punched him hard in the stomach with her other hand.

The man bent over for just a second and then stood again, the grin still on his face.

"Ah, nothing like a frisky one, I'll say." The man lunged forward, sending Tara to the ground.

He was heavy and the ground was hard beneath her.

Tara moved faster than the man anticipated, managing to avoid his full bulk on top of her. When he pushed to his knees, she brought her knee up hard in his groin and he howled loudly.

Tara was almost to a stand when he grabbed her foot and pulled hard enough for her to fall flat. The garden gloves protected her hands as they slapped the ground, but she groaned, knowing her rear end would be bruised later.

He crawled toward her and she turned around, nailing her fist against his jaw as hard as she could. The stunned man didn't move as she jumped up.

"You leave me alone," she growled through clenched teeth.

The man sat staring at her as she walked away. Tara felt satisfaction at his dumbfounded expression, although she knew she had acted out of character for a Gothman girl. Hopefully, the man had been so humiliated, he wouldn't comment on her ability to defend herself.

Tara began marching to the house, then paused. As an afterthought, she turned and grabbed the cut flowers lying on the ground where she'd dropped them. The women would question why she returned without the roses. And if they hadn't seen her escapade, she didn't want to have to tell them about it.

As she walked back to the house, she noticed Lord Darius staring through an opened upstairs window on the second floor. Adrenaline already pumped through her, but sudden panic made her heart race painfully. Her mouth went dry. The lord wasn't stupid. She didn't regret putting the ass in his place, but if she didn't watch herself around Lord Darius, her life could be lost.

He didn't hide his presence, and Tara couldn't pretend not to notice his appraisal of her. She stopped and studied the man who watched her for a moment, wondering what he thought. Tara believed she detected a slight grin on his face when she finally looked away to return to the women.

* * * * *

Lord Darius turned from his bedroom window. A sudden thought hit him like a punch to the gut, but he had to be wrong. His walkntalk chirped and he turned to grab it. "Your Runner bike is secure, my Lord," one of his guards said. Darius growled his response and tossed the contraption on his bed. It chirped again. He ignored it.

Someone tapped on his door, and his boots pounded the floor through the carpet as he crossed the room.

"Darius, how many you be wanting to join you for lunch today?"

His mama stood in the doorway, and he forced a blank expression so as not to unnerve the woman. "Hire more help, woman." He tried to sound calm. It wouldn't do to upset his mama. The last thing he needed right now was one of her fits. "You don't need to be climbing those stairs like common help, no."

His mama beamed. "Funny you should mention that, my son. We were just talking about that, we were."

Darius waited for the woman to continue.

"Reena has brought her niece to callin', she has."

"You want Reena's niece to help you around the house?"

"We had talked about it, yes."

"Have her start tomorrow, yes." Darius thought about the scene he had just witnessed in the yard. "And it'll be just the guards and me that will be eating, it will."

His mama looked very pleased with herself as she left the doorway and shuffled toward the steps.

Darius turned back to the window. He felt pleased, himself. Yes. He would have that woman under his roof. In fact, he would have that woman. What better way to determine how she could have obtained the abilities he had just witnessed?

* * * * *

"Ah, those flowers are beautiful, they are. Here, love, put them in this vase, and set them on the table. The men will come in hungry to be sure," Hilda said as she walked back in the room.

Tara followed her instructions.

Reena and Tara stayed through lunch, and Tara willingly helped to clean the dishes afterward. Hilda and Reena sat at the kitchen table and nibbled at the pie as Tara washed and dried each plate.

"Yes, I will say, enjoy her while you have her."

Tara saw Hilda smile as she turned to study the two women. She felt good about cleaning the kitchen. It was the least she could do considering how delightful the meal was.

She placed stacks of sliced meat on a plate on the counter for when the men came in to eat as Hilda had instructed her to do. Tara would have loved to listen to the conversation among Darius and his men, but she knew better than to think such an activity would impress these two older women.

Reena and Tara prepared to leave, and Hilda walked with them to Reena's car.

"Reena, I'll see you again soon now."

"You will. It'll be a day when your son lets you come visit me. The place is small, but we had our times up on that hill when we were younger, yes we did." Reena beamed and Hilda laughed in agreement.

Tara was quiet as the two drove through town and back up the hill to Reena's cottage. She entered the small house and started a fire while Reena sat and wiggled her feet.

"Hand me that bag of potatoes along the kitchen wall, child, and I will get started on a salad for our meal later, I will."

Tara brought the bag, then helped peel and slice the potatoes.

"Well, child, what do you think of Gothman now that you've had good exposure to us?"

Tara stared at the flames while the peeler dangled from her hand.

"I saw Lord Darius and two other men with my motorcycle. They put it in a shed behind the Bryton home."

"No! That's not good."

"I'm stranded for the time being." Tara turned and looked at Reena. Once again she felt the sensation of claustrophobia, and the feeling didn't settle well at all. "Not that I was planning on leaving any time soon, but now I can't. It'll be rather difficult to get it back unnoticed."

"Well, I don't know now." Reena was quiet for a moment. "Hilda and I had an interesting talk while you were out in the garden, we did. She'd like you to come live at the house, to help out with things, of course."

Tara blushed at the thought of living under the same roof with Lord Darius. She imagined sparring with the virile lord, and wondered if she would be able to fight with his hands on her. She looked up at Reena and saw a mischievous smile on the older woman's face.

"What were you two scheming? I'm not interested in marriage, Reena. Not to mention Lord Darius is not the most talkative man, and the men who work for him have no manners."

"I've no doubt you'll put them in their place, I'll be guessing. Did one of the guards get a bit fresh with you, child?"

"I had to fight one off when I went to cut the flowers for Hilda," Tara said.

Reena glared at Tara, but still had that mischievous look in her eye. "It's not like a lady to fight off a man."

"I'm not just going to lay there and play dumb so some brute can do what he will with me." Tara raised her voice and then more quietly added, "I just don't think I could do that."

"You know you remind me a lot of myself when I was your age." Reena smiled. "Granted, I was no trained warrior. But, I was loyal to one man. When he left, I'd have no other. So today, I am alone."

Tara thought for a moment, wondering what Reena would have been like as a young lady. She imagined her to have been quite beautiful, and Tara wondered what man had captured the older woman's heart.

For some reason, Tara couldn't see Reena falling hard for a man unless he proved himself better than the lot. Reena had a quiet dignity about her. Not for the first time, Tara could see why Patha had included the older woman in his stories.

"And you, you will be loyal to one man too. It's your nature, I believe." She chuckled and reached for her knitting. "So, you'll live in the Bryton home?" She paused and then added, "You'll be close to your motorcycle."

"I'll give it some thought."

* * * * *

Later that evening, Darius stood facing his bedroom window. Maps lay strewn on the bed next to him, and additional charts scattered across the long wooden table to the other side. It had been a long day, *hell*, it had been a long night.

His men weren't pleased when he ordered that the Runner not be brought down, but they were loyal and knew to follow his word. His Gothman instinct warred within him at his own order since his heritage ran so deep within his veins. His papa had never made an issue over Runners. If seen, they were killed. No questions asked.

The Runner race offered only danger.

This fact remained simple and clean, and no one questioned it. Runners didn't mingle with Gothman people. They weren't allowed in Bryton at all. Not once in Darius' lifetime had he ever known an exception to that rule.

Until now.

Darius left the window and paced to his open bedroom door, filling the doorway as he stared below into the open entryway. The young woman he'd watched take down one of his guards had acted like a Gothman woman the rest of her stay in his home. Her impression remained imprinted in his thoughts, distracting him. No. He would be honest. The lass more than distracted his thoughts. At the moment, she consumed them. Never had he seen a Gothman lass behave like that one did. Reacting like a warrior. She turned on his guard with the skill of a trained fighter. Too trained.

He turned and moved back to the open window, running his fingers absently through tangled curls. She offered too many signs that she could be a Runner. His men were in an outrage, and Darius was confused. Not that he would admit his confusion to a soul. The

Lord of Gothman offered no weaknesses. But damnit to hell, he couldn't figure this one out.

His papa, Lord Jovis, had never enlightened Darius on any of the thinking behind his decision making. The reasons for not doing that were obvious. Darius had not been the intended heir. In the past that had never bothered Darius. He didn't need any education from his papa to rule Gothman. Darius knew he possessed a strength his papa never had, nor his older brother. Dwelling on either of them was wasted thought. The only thing Darius wanted to know right now was why were Runners such a deadly enemy?

And why was one Runner in particular considered such a threat?

Nowhere in their history could he find one documented fact as to why Gothman hated the Runners. Darius knew next to nothing about the race. And he didn't like not having all the facts. Somehow he would have to learn about these people.

At this moment, he placed learning about Runners at the top of his priority list. He would learn how to operate that mysterious bike he had housed in his shed. He would learn what Runners had done to Gothman to earn such harsh laws implemented against them. And above all his other questions, he would learn why one incredibly beautiful Runner had entered Gothman without an escort...

...and what that Runner was doing in his house.

Chapter Four

∞

Tara felt thoroughly exhausted when she left the house where the quilting session had been held.

Reena had arranged for her to care for at least fifteen children. Tara had never obtained an accurate count of the kids running around the backyard, for she had spent the entire morning changing diapers, nursing scratches and pulling children out of trees when they cried for help. Although fun at first, after several hours she had been ready for Reena to rescue her.

It was hard to conceal her relief when Reena finally came out the back door of the house with several other women, and announced they were through with yet another quilt.

"Help me load everything, now be a dear, my girl," Reena said, as she dumped the contents from her arms into Tara's.

"What is all of this?" Tara adjusted the folded piles of material, trying not to drop anything.

Reena laughed and glanced over her shoulder as several of the women gathered children in the yard.

"To be certain child, it's the makings for the next quilt. I'm thinking anyone could see that." Reena didn't speak loud enough for anyone else to hear, and Tara got her point. A typical Gothman woman would grow up around this domestic life. Tara couldn't imagine such a thing and fought not to feel sorry for the suppressed existence. Yet, these women didn't look unhappy.

Tara managed to put all the materials in the back of the car in a somewhat orderly fashion. She watched Reena mingle with the other women, who now were chattering outside the house. From what Tara could hear, their conversation didn't appear to be about anything important. They discussed what someone had worn the other day, and a pregnancy that didn't appear to be normal. Tara knew she should listen and learn the ways of these women. After all, that is what a Runner did when entering a new community. But her thoughts continually strayed.

The image of a tall, powerful-looking lord kept consuming her thoughts. Although she knew the Gothman lord would view all women as docile and simple, it seemed to her that a woman like that would be boring. She could offer him more excitement than any of these women could.

"Are you about ready then?"

Reena's question startled Tara, and she chastised herself for the fantasy she had just created in her mind.

"I guess our next stop is the Bryton home."

Tara noticed this last comment immediately brought whispers from the remaining women, who were now openly studying Tara. She looked down and reached for the handle to get in the car. This time she wasn't practicing the humility of a Gothman woman, but trying to hide her embarrassment at the realization she would soon be the topic of the latest gossip.

"You aren't having second thoughts now, are you?" Reena asked once she sat in the car next to Tara.

Tara noticed worry in the older lady's tone. "No, of course not." Tara tried to reassure Reena with a smile. "We talked about this last night. Moving into the Bryton home and helping Hilda with the housework will be a wonderful opportunity to learn more about Gothman."

"Not to mention you will see much of Lord Darius, I'm thinking," Reena added with a chuckle.

"True." Tara couldn't deny she felt some sort of attraction for the man. But the smug look Reena gave her made her nervous. "He has my bike, Reena. That is why I want to keep an eye on him."

"Okay child, whatever you say." Reena's expression didn't change.

Tara knew she hadn't fooled the woman for a minute.

The two guards on duty in front of the Lord's house didn't pay any attention to Tara and Reena as they parked and ascended the porch stairs.

Hilda greeted the two of them with open arms and laughter.

"Reena, you are too good to an old woman to share such a fine young lady with me, you are." Tara was sure there were tears in Hilda's eyes. "You'll be treated quite fine, I will say. Do come inside, the both of you. Reena, you'll inspect the chambers to see if they don't suit her, won't you?"

Hilda and Reena entered the house. Tara followed them carrying the cloth bag Reena had given her. They climbed the wide, winding staircase and walked to the end of the hallway where Hilda inserted a key into a door.

"This is my wing of the house, it is." Hilda led the two women through the door. She pointed to a closed door. "These are my chambers, and you'll be next to me. As safe as can be, don't you think, Reena?"

Tara was curious about the question of her safety. Hilda seemed to be emphasizing this to Reena as if it was a concern. She smiled to herself at the thought of two old women worrying about her wellbeing.

Hilda then led the two to the farthest door at the end of the hallway. She took them into a beautifully arranged bedroom. The carpet on the floor was as thick as the carpet had been in the living room, except that it extended to the wall. A single bed had several comforters spread over the top, and an afghan was folded at its foot. A bureau and dresser were on one wall and a small couch was on the other. Two glass doors led to a balcony that looked over the backyard and provided an excellent view of the rocky hills spreading for miles beyond the back of the house.

Tara was certain she had never seen anything so magnificent in her entire life. This was to be her bedroom? A servant in a lord's house certainly lived well. No wonder Reena had encouraged her to live here. Tara walked over to the glass doors to survey the view and then turned to the two old ladies and smiled.

"I do believe she likes it," Reena said.

"You consider this your home," Hilda said. "Arrange the room as you please. You unpack your bag, and I'll see Reena to the door, I will. Come down when you're ready, and I'll show you what chores you'll be doing. It's a true pleasure to have you here, child, that it is."

Hilda walked out the door with Reena, and Tara could hear her say, "She'll bring life back to this house if she does anything, that much is certain."

"I know she was only with me a couple days, but I'm sure going to miss her," Reena replied.

"You're the one that brought her into town and went all about showing her off, you did." That was the last Tara heard as the door at the end of the hallway closed.

Tara set down her bag on the bed and looked around the room once again. She walked to the glass doors, opened them, and stepped onto the balcony.

Oh, if Patha could only see me now. Here she was, a Runner, living in the house of the Lord of the Gothman. She smiled again.

The Gothman were a tolerable people. They needed a lesson in equality, though. Again she wondered why these women put up with the way the men treated them. Tara knew she could never be the submissive person the females of this culture were. And she figured that surely if they were given a clue about the type of life they could have, they would give up this submissive lifestyle in a second.

What kind of thinking was this? Tara wondered about her thoughts. She wasn't here to change this culture, just observe it, *right?* So, when did her feelings change? Suddenly, Tara felt very confused. She was beginning to feel some type of attachment and loyalty to these people. *That* scared her.

For a minute she wondered if she shouldn't try to leave. It wouldn't be hard to get her motorcycle now. She'd seen the men put it out in the backyard, unattended and unguarded. Maybe she could sneak out after dark, be away from Gothman territory within the hour.

She mulled over the possibility as she stared at the beautiful hills rolling farther than the eye could see. The rocks jutting up from the earth added to the glory of the sight.

Far in the distance she saw someone on a motorcycle racing along side of a hill. The rider dodged the rock that sprang up from the earth with a skill equal to her own. Even from this distance, she could tell the person was accustomed to the terrain; she imagined the rider enjoyed the challenge of the path he'd chosen.

She yearned to be on her bike and take the same path. She wasn't familiar with the terrain, yet it called out for her to accept its challenge. Her hands itched with the temptation, and she rubbed them on the soft material of her dress. Remembering she was expected downstairs shortly, she turned from the tantalizing scene with a heavy sigh and reentered her new bedroom.

The bureau held ample space for the dresses Reena had given her. The older woman had spent a great deal of time over the past couple days creating this wardrobe. Tara gazed at her Runner clothing at the bottom of the bag. The black leather looked so appealing after having worn Gothman dresses. If anyone found the outfit, it could mean her death. But leaving it at Reena's would endanger the woman's life. Too many people moved through that house for Tara's liking.

She grinned as she recalled how she'd managed to pack the Runner outfit without Reena noticing. Tara stroked the silky headscarf and fingered the embroidered symbol of her clan, then wrapped her Runner clothing around the landlink from her bike. She grabbed the bundle and was looking around the room for an appropriate hiding place when she heard voices coming up the stairs. Quickly, she stuffed it back into her bag and put it under her bed. Then, she straightened and walked out of the room as if she hadn't a care in the world.

Hilda and Torgo were climbing the stairs; she went down the hallway to meet them.

"So, you're coming to live with me, now?" Torgo didn't hide his pleasure as he grinned from ear to ear. "Do you want to see my room?"

"Ah, all in good time, my child." Hilda patted the boy on the head. "Tara, have you met Torgo?"

"Only for a moment." Tara almost caught herself clasping her hands behind her back, the pose of a warrior. Instead, she relaxed her features and stared at innocent gray eyes. "We've not been properly introduced, though."

"Well, this is my youngest son, Torgo. He is quite the handful, he is." She hugged the boy and ruffled his hair. "Go play, child. Tara and I have work to do, we do."

"Will you spend time with me later?" Torgo asked Tara.

"I look forward to it." Tara winked at the boy and his face lit up before he took off running down the hallway.

"It's too bad for the boy, it is. He has no papa to teach him how to be a man. His mama might as well be his grandmama, and Darius is so busy he's no time for him, that's for certain." Hilda walked down the stairs with Tara. "He's a good boy, high-spirited like they all were at that age."

"Maybe I could spend some time with him," Tara said quietly.

"Ah, that would be nice, it would. It's the training of a man he needs though." Hilda led Tara to the kitchen and opened up a back pantry. "Well now, here are all the supplies. You'll be cleaning the house for now, you will. Over time, I'll teach you how to prepare Lord Darius' favorite dishes. Until then, I'll keep doing the cooking. I like to cook, I do." She laughed and patted her stomach. "I like to eat my cooking too. It wouldn't hurt you to eat my cooking either, you know." She laughed again, then turned as the kitchen back door opened.

Lord Darius entered the room, his hair tossed wildly. Tara concluded that he was the rider of the motorcycle in the hills.

"Glad to see your help has arrived," Darius said as he studied the young woman standing in his kitchen.

* * * * *

The light material of her dress made it easy for Darius to see how toned her body was. This woman hasn't birthed a child, he reasoned, and she sure doesn't look like she spent a lot of time sitting and chatting the day away like so many other Gothman women. He imagined her to be full of energy and always busying herself with one task or another.

He noticed the intelligence in blue eyes fighting not to return his stare. She struck him as someone with whom he could have a conversation. And from the spark in those sapphire eyes—that dared him to end his mental evaluation—he imagined she could get a bit feisty, as well.

He chuckled to himself. Whoever had taught her how to be a lady had failed. She didn't appear shy or humble in his presence, like all the other females he'd known since boyhood, and he found her demeanor refreshing. Darius smiled, having caught himself deciding a strong woman might prove welcome.

* * * * *

For the first time, Tara saw a genuine smile light up his face. The transformation of his already devastating looks was almost more than her heart could handle. She felt like her insides were melting from her toes upward, and an unaccustomed warmth climbed through her entire body. With the sudden onslaught of awakening desires, an electric current seemed to suddenly charge the very air around her. She licked her parched lips then blinked so she could focus on his wonderful face

"Reena just brought Tara to me, Milord." Hilda shut the pantry door, and gave her son her attention. "And where have ya been? Traipsing around the countryside alone again, I'd say."

"The hills called out to me. Besides, I needed to rest my brain, I did." He glanced from his mama back to Tara. "Have you ever been on a motorcycle, Tara, niece of Reena?"

The directness of his question took Tara aback for a second, and she had to bite her tongue to keep the defensive answer from betraying her fears. *Think* she demanded of herself, *think*. Don't give yourself away. True, she'd been on a motorcycle for as long as she could remember, probably longer if she knew Patha. But to admit *that* would surely risk her being found out.

So, how *did* she answer, and even more important, *why* would he ask such a question? Reena had explained to Tara that she and Hilda had thought of the idea of Tara staying in the Bryton home, but had Darius somehow put the thought in his mama's head? Tara glanced at Hilda and had to acknowledge that the woman would do whatever her son suggested. Hilda stood straight and tall, her focus centered on Darius. This was a woman proud of her son.

The only conclusion she could come to was that he suspected her true identity. That would explain his desire to bring her under his roof: he wanted to keep an eye on her. And he *certainly was* keeping an eye on her at the moment.

"For heaven's sake, Darius. Of course she hasn't been on a motorcycle before. Look at her, she couldn't possibly even get it to a standing position," Hilda said pointing to Tara's thin body.

* * * * *

Lord Darius didn't have to look. He'd already memorized her face, her figure, even though her curves were hidden tantalizingly beneath her thin shift, and he suddenly realized she drove him to feelings he hadn't experienced before. This Tara was unlike any woman he'd ever seen. He was a trained warrior, the leader of all Gothman, skilled at controlling his feelings, his emotions. But what he saw before him was a challenge. A challenge he meant to overcome. This had to be the Runner who had escaped them in the forest—he could feel it in his gut—and he would prove it...in time.

He covered his lapse in conversation by clearing his throat, then he answered his mama, "I'm looking at her, I am." Darius smiled, and decided it was time to start proving his theory as to who this woman really was. "Come with me, woman. I'll take you for a ride on a motorcycle."

"Darius!" Hilda protested. "I would think...we were just starting—"

"Ah, your housework can wait woman, it can." Darius put his hands on Tara's shoulders and quickly escorted her to the back door.

* * * * *

Tara almost turned on him when he grabbed her shoulder. Winters of training had her ready to defend against such a touch. Her body tightened before she could think, and she had to consciously make the effort to relax. Taking a deep breath, she turned to face the lord. *Big mistake.* Powerful gray eyes were devouring her, and she couldn't look away.

Up until that moment, Tara had worried she had given herself away by almost reacting in a hostile manner to the lord's touch. As she met his gaze, however, she realized that discovering her identity wasn't what was going through the lord's thoughts at all. Instead, Tara saw unbridled passion. She turned back around and stepped through the door. Fresh air helped clear Tara's thoughts, which enabled her to focus on the matter at hand.

As they walked through the yard, Lord Darius took his hand from her shoulder, and she stepped to the side a bit, giving herself a broader view of the man and his actions. He was very, very tall, and even broader through the shoulders. His golden hair capped his head in curls and she had the sudden urge to run her fingers through their softness.

"I've something to show you, I do." Darius walked in the direction of his bike, which was parked next to the shed. The very same shed which harbored her bike!

Tara fought the urge to rush forward and throw open the doors to check on her beloved cycle. Instead, she took the time to appraise his motorcycle. It was much larger than her bike, and was of Gothman style with its long narrow seat that came up in the back. She could tell it was not designed for speed. Instead it was large and sturdy—obviously made to handle the rough terrain it traveled each day.

Instead of showing her his motorcycle, Darius opened the shed door.

"Look at this, if you will, my Lady." He walked into the shed and pointed. "Have you ever seen anything like it?"

"Both are very nice. Are they yours?" Tara noticed the shed wasn't locked when he pulled the door open.

"It's a Runner's bike, it is."

Darius sounded proud as he ran his hand over the bike that Tara had cared for lovingly all these winters.

"Can we ride it?"

"Ah, I wish we could, I do." Darius looked at her. "It has some kind of lock on it. I haven't figured out how to start it yet, but I will. You can believe me on that one."

"I do believe you." Tara stroked her bike. She was glad to see it wasn't damaged during its ride on the truck. It didn't appear tampered with either. Her eyes did a mental inspection as she fought the urge to squat next to it and reassure herself that all was still in working order.

"Let's go." Darius walked out of the shed and shut the door after her.

Reluctantly she followed him to his bike. Tara turned to face the Gothman cycle and stifled a gasp when large hands encircled her waist and lifted her onto the bike.

"Goodness, girl, you're heavier than you look, you are. You're quite the thin one, I'd think you'd be light as a feather, but every muscle of yours is built up like a man's."

He looked at her with deep gray eyes, so unlike any eyes she'd ever seen before. They held her captive although she tried to look away. His hands still stayed around her waist, and Tara wriggled from the unaccustomed sensations his nearness was causing. When he dropped his hands to his sides, she almost wished he would put them back.

"I've worked hard all my life." Tara finally forced her gaze to the ground.

"I'd like to hear about that life sometime, I would," he spoke as he eased onto the bike in front of her.

Tara stifled a gasp as the smooth leather of his pants rubbed her inner thighs. The man didn't offer her a lot of room behind him, and her body was forced up against his backside. Her legs spread wide to accommodate him, which caused her dress to slide up, exposing a fair amount of leg. The position left her feeling incredible vulnerable, and she wasn't sure she liked that feeling. At the same time, being smashed up against this virile man's backside sent a rush of heat through her that she couldn't deny. She'd never been aroused while exposed in such a way before. She didn't have time to sit and evaluate her conflicting emotions however.

"Hold on tight, my Lady." Lord Darius started the bike and took off quickly...very quickly.

Tara's inner thighs locked against him, while her arms tried to squeeze the life from his chest.

* * * * *

He grinned and knew he would enjoy the mission of exposing this Runner. And yes, she had to be the Runner. Any Gothman woman would have fallen off the bike and landed flat on her back from his sudden acceleration. Yet she'd remained glued to him as his bike left the ground to fly over the uneven, rocky ground.

* * * * *

If Tara hadn't been an expert rider, he would have killed her right there on the spot.

She wondered for a moment if that wasn't what he had in mind. Her instincts took over as he raced over the first hill. She stayed close to his body, moving as he did, keeping her head down. Taut muscles rippled underneath her hands, and she fought not to stroke his chest.

They moved faster than she anticipated, almost as if racing into battle. The wind slapped her hair against her face and, when she tried to look up, made her eyes water. Lord Darius raced over the hills and around the rocks. She wrapped her hands tightly around his body and held on with all the skill that her many winters of riding had taught her.

After a half hour, Lord Darius slowed the bike and stopped. They were at the base of a very rocky hill, and a gutted path disappeared into the pines leading up the hillside.

Tara allowed her hands to move slowly down Darius' chest until she rested them on either side of his waist. His body was as fine tuned as the machine they sat on. She imagined him an incredible warrior...and an incredible lover. But she couldn't focus on that at the moment. A test of her abilities was at play here, and she planned to do her fair share of testing in return.

"You've been on a bike before, that much is true. I daresay you could ride one if you were so inclined.

Lord Darius turned his head, and she could feel his breath on her face. Her chin grazed his shoulder as she decided not to respond. A Runner wouldn't lie.

"Good thing then, are you ready for a climb?"

"I think so," Tara said quietly, but she was thoroughly excited about the fact that they were not through with the ride.

"Wrap those arms around tight now."

He didn't go as fast this time. He took the rocky path slowly and the bike groaned under their weight as he guided it up the forbidding path.

* * * * *

She didn't need to hold on to him for this climb. He'd already sensed her expertise as a rider. But Darius wouldn't deny enjoying the female body pressed against him. When she obliged, and wrapped her arms around his waist once again, he offered a boyish grin that he was happy she couldn't see. No woman had stirred him like this before. Not only did he want her body, for some reason he had a desire to know her reactions to his world.

"I'm going to show you my secret hideout. I've been coming here since I was a boy, I have. I hope you won't think less of me if I say I like to escape from ruling this land once in a while."

* * * * *

"No, my Lord, I won't think that." Tara also watched the road, if you could call the jagged path that. She didn't have to ride so close to him now and was able to focus more on her surroundings. While she didn't need to wrap her arms around him, holding on to this mass of power felt good, so she indulged herself.

He skillfully navigated the bike around each rock and protrusion without any instruction from her, although she did have to bite her tongue a time or two. Eventually, the path led them to a clearing on the side of the hill.

It was a small shady area of grass, completely surrounded by pine trees and hidden from the world. "Oh, it's beautiful," she said without thinking.

Tara again ran her hands down the side of his chest, and adjusted her legs, feeling him all the way from her inner thighs up to her crotch. This man overwhelmed every sensation she had.

And she knew then he would not make a good enemy. Not only was his physical strength twice that of hers, his body distracted her beyond what it should. Fire rushed through her wherever she touched him, the heat from his body tormenting her senses. Beyond that, his strength, the natural warrior blood that ran through him, his ability to connect what was around him—all of it attracted her to him more than it should. For no matter what, this man was her enemy.

Lord Darius stopped the bike and cut the engine. This time, Tara flipped her leg over the bike and hopped off before he could help her. She twisted and shook her hips to adjust her dress, and knew Darius watched. She turned to see his eyes on her rear end and felt a sense of power.

"So, when did you first ride on a motorcycle? I bet you can drive one, can't you?"

She sensed him watching her, those powerful gray eyes never leaving her while she walked across the small patch of grass to a large rock and sat down on it. Tara wrapped her arms around her legs, pulling the material of her dress so that she felt less exposed and looked at him as he climbed off his bike. He suspected her of something, of that there was no doubt. Did Darius know her true identify and simply toyed with her? There had to be a way to find out.

Tara had to be careful, very careful. If he killed her, Patha would have his revenge. If she killed him, it would start a war. Her instincts never failed her when caution was called for. This man could be a threat to her, but for some reason she felt no fear, nor had she since she met him.

By the look in his eyes it didn't appear that he had murder on his mind. His gaze was incredibly seductive yet, at the same time, very dangerous. She smiled at him and decided to take his comment as a joke. "Certainly I couldn't drive a motorcycle as big as that one." Tara attempted a shy smile, as she had seen some of the Gothman women do, and then asked out of curiosity, "Why did you bring me up here?"

"I want to know you better. I've seen your response to men's advances, and I sure don't want to be made the fool."

Tara looked down at the ground quickly, realizing he was talking about the actions she'd taken against his guard during her previous visit.

He walked over and sat down on the rock next to her. He didn't hesitate but put one arm around her back and rested his hand on her shoulder.

Tara's entire body tightened from his forwardness, and the urge to elbow him in the gut was almost as strong as the urge to turn and kiss him before he kissed her. These warring emotions clouded her ability to think clearly. She doubted many people ever told the man no. Be careful, her inner thoughts warned, be very careful.

He pointed at the hill across from them with his other hand. "There's a cliff up that way. You have to climb to it, but you can see all of Gothman from up there. That, my lady, is my favorite place of all." Darius pointed to some rocks further up the hill. "Are you up for the climb?"

"I don't think I could do that, my Lord." Now he was trying to test her abilities, and she felt safe to say a Gothman woman did very little rock climbing. "I would tear my dress for sure."

"Of course." Lord Darius leaned against the wall of rock behind them and stared at her. His hand moved from her shoulder to rub the center of her back. "You're very beautiful, Tara, you are. I know for a fact there's not a lady in all of Gothman that comes close to your looks."

He smiled and reached to stroke her hair softly. "I can't help but wonder if you'd attack me if I tried to kiss you." Darius looked at her, seeming amused at the thought. "And the way that body of yours is fine-tuned, I wouldn't be surprised if you'd have some luck at it."

Tara turned to look at him, but didn't answer. The thought of attacking him if he tried to kiss her brought a rush of warmth between her legs. His face was inches from hers and those gray eyes seemed capable of owning her every thought. She fought a grin when she imagined challenging him.

He must have noticed her slight change in expression because his eyebrows rose, as if anticipating her answer.

He did suspect her. She felt certain at that moment that she'd betrayed every secret she had by meeting his gaze. He would own her every thought if she didn't pull her eyes from his. He was reaching deep for her very soul.

She fought for control of her thoughts with every ounce of power she possessed. Just because the man suggested sensuality didn't mean she had to submit. He was accustomed to passive women and at that very moment she forgot all about the role she was supposed to be playing. She realized her defiance would probably prove an ugly taste for him. But the lord would throw her on the ground and have his way with her right here and now, unless she took charge of the situation.

Passive, be passive.

The voice in her head warned her against striking him, or worse yet, taking the initiative herself and having *her* way with him. Both thoughts entered her mind almost at the same time, although her rational side warned that she had to play the part of a Gothman woman, or risk giving her true identity away.

Tara studied Lord Darius, with those incredible gray eyes. The sunlight added color to his blond curls, some of them pale as corn silk, while others were darker than gold. His hair bordered a smooth face, shy of a small scar that interrupted an otherwise perfect jawline. She curled her hands into fists to prevent herself from reaching up to touch that scar, and trace it just to see if it would alter his expression. He had no wrinkles, no worry lines, nothing to indicate he was consumed or tortured by thought. His features were perfect.

Tara realized she had to face those dark gray eyes, otherwise she would have no indication of what he might do next. They defied the warrior in her to take a stand and put action to his words. She suspected Darius found her fighting him in lovemaking an appealing thought. That realization brought the heat in her tormented body to a boiling point. Self-control was her only weapon here.

"Would you have me fight you, my Lord?" she whispered the words and tried to remain still.

His lips parted, and he dropped his gaze to her mouth. "No woman has ever tried to stop me before."

"And you think I would have some success at it?"

His chuckle forced his Adam's apple up and down, and sent chills through her heated body. "I'm thinking you are like no other woman."

The laughter in his eyes when he returned her gaze was almost her undoing. She wanted to pounce on him, to slap him for his pompous attitude, and to kiss him just to show him she could overpower his supposed omnipotence.

"But no, my Lady, you would not be successful at it."

Tara jumped to her feet. She stood over him with her hands still balled in fists at her sides. Every bit of sense she had, along with winters of training to understand all types of attacks, prepared her to take the offensive. She towered over Darius, planting her feet firmly on the ground, and inhaling deeply to clear her thoughts.

"You think you could have me as you please, simply because you desire it?" Tara felt her desire shift to fury. The change of mood helped her to think clearly, so she worked to feed the anger.

"There is no doubt, my Lady."

"And if I don't wish it?"

"My lady," Lord Darius whispered, almost growled. "You do wish it."

Tara had never met a man more sexually sure of himself. He excited her while consuming her with outrage. She stared at him.

Darius appeared to relax under her study, and then crossed his arms across that broad chest. Her eyes watched the rope-like muscles twitch under his tanned forearm. He seemed at ease, as if allowing her time to accept the inevitable.

Tara narrowed her eyes. "You will not rape me," she hissed.

Darius laughed, and she took a step backwards. "My lady, I'm thinking that won't be necessary."

Darius straightened his legs, stretching them so that long corded muscles rippled underneath the brown leather of his pants.

She found herself standing between those long, powerful legs and realized he had needed to rearrange his position to allow room for his growing arousal. Tara stared at the hardened length now visible under the material below his belt. Beyond a doubt, she had never met a more pompous, self-righteous, and incredibly sexy man as the one who now seemed to surround her with his aura.

Tara turned to create distance, and Darius bent one leg, blocking her path. She didn't jump around him, or stumble over him, but merely stopped. "Is this how you take every lady who catches your eye, my Lord?"

"I've never waited this long before, no." Darius sounded amused. "But then any other lass would have submitted by now."

Tara almost said she wasn't any other lass. Those would have been her exact words to any other man, but Lord Darius wasn't any other man. No man had ever stimulated her emotions like this before, much less one who kept her guessing at the same time. Tara had a feeling she could enjoy this man, and that it would be a long time before she grew bored.

"Do they fall at your feet? Or do they simply strip in front of you?" Tara asked as she continued to stare at the leg blocking her path.

"Has it crossed your mind to do either?"

Tara sensed Darius' movement and turned as he leaned forward. "No," she stated, unable to do more as one large hand interlocked fingers with her smaller hand. Tara didn't oppose the touch, but studied his hand, which now held hers. Blond hairs tickled the tips of her fingers, while the rough heat from his grasp sent warmth up her arm at an amazing speed.

"I'll teach you to submit, I will." Darius didn't make the statement as a threat, but spoke the words gently, as a papa willing to show the child a new stunt.

When he pulled her to him, the only thing crossing Tara's mind was that likewise, she would teach him manners. The intensity of his gaze, those gray eyes, so unique in color, watching her while he brought her face to his, gave her the impression teaching him anything would be quite the chore. Stubborn and powerful, determined and ruthless, she saw the good and the bad while he watched her.

She wanted to look away, anything to distract her so she could keep her thoughts straight. But damnit if she didn't want to taste him and learn the source of the heat that flooded through her with just his touch.

His arms wrapped her into him, almost crushing her in their grip. And then he kissed her.

Tara couldn't stop herself. Placing her arms on his shoulders, then grabbing hair on either side of his head, she returned the kiss with an aggression she didn't know she possessed.

He slid her off the rock and onto the ground. His strength made her wild. All attempts to conceal her identity escaped her, a thick fog of lust consuming her senses. His body was strong, powerful, and dangerous. It excited her more than anything had before. Submission was forgotten. She found herself fighting to strip the pants away from the treasure that would be hers.

He was huge, hardened to stone. It was hard to move while she stared at his magnificence.

She climbed on and forced the penetration herself as he pulled her dress from her body. She felt him slide in deeply as he grasped to control the moment.

He pulled back as she rocked forward and then he lunged powerfully, almost choking her with the depth he reached.

She collapsed on him and before she could recover and clear the overwhelming desire to submit to him, his powerful arms wrapped around her body and he lunged again. Fighting to regain control, she dug her fingers into his chest and pushed, hard, forcing his body down. As his grip around her intensified, she took advantage of the preoccupation and thrust her hips down on him, consuming every inch of him inside of her, tightening around him, suffocating all life out of him. She had, at last, achieved control over him.

A muffled grunt, deep within him, rose to a howl as she forced his orgasm. Then, not willing to let him experience ecstasy without her, she thrust again and leaped to meet the intensity of his climax. Her muscles tightened, holding him inside her, while he stretched and filled her. Closing her eyes, she rode the waves of passion that rushed through her. Where she had tried to show the upper hand, she had instead received the privilege of being fucked good and hard, allowing her one orgasm and leaving her wanting more.

This was not lovemaking. There had been no foreplay. Pure and simply, it was a struggle of powers. A ruthless, dominating nation taking on another, equally powerful and equally dangerous. Through the act of sex, they'd tried to conquer each other—and failed. If they'd attempted to keep the act purely physical, playing the part of a skilled warrior, and not allowing emotions to interfere—again, they both failed.

* * * * *

Slowly, his grip around her eased. He sat up, still inside her, and stared deeply into that place he'd just experienced. There couldn't possibly be another woman like Tara on Nuworld. Sex had always been an act of pleasure, sometimes necessary, sometimes simply to amuse himself. It had never occurred to him how the pleasure could intensify with a willing, enthused partner. Darius enjoyed sex as a predatory act. Sometimes the look of fear, or submissive anticipation, excited him enough to pursue a lady who caught his eye. Tara had offered him neither, yet she had brought him to a hardened boil like none before.

What was it about this woman?

Intelligence mixed with her beauty in a way Darius hadn't thought possible. She wore the two qualities in a way that drew him. He wanted to know her. It dawned on Darius at that moment that he had never really cared to know any woman before Tara. Women served a purpose, but one of them wasn't companionship.

Tara made him want to learn more about what she thought, what ticked behind those sapphire eyes.

But there was something else. Darius wanted to make Tara his. This woman was no Gothman, but she was on his land, acting the part of a Gothman. There was mystery behind her, but that didn't bother him. All knowledge of her would be his in time. What fascinated him was the desire to possess her.

"How do you feel about the fact that with one word I could have you rule this land at my side?" Darius whispered into her ear.

"You know nothing about me. I may make a lousy ruler." She returned his gaze, snagging her fingers in his hair and then pulling them free. "I would think something like that should be a mutual decision, my Lord." She pushed herself off of him and looked around until she spotted her dress.

"I'm not surprised you'd answer like that, my Lady." He wasn't daunted by her boldness. "You're not like any lass I've met and I've known a few, that much is true. They're always polite and submissive, of course, and they say only what they think I want to hear, they do. You think for yourself. I like that. Why are you like that, Tara?"

"I guess I don't see why women have to be less than men." She looked at him quickly, as if checking his face for a reaction.

He didn't respond but instead, got up and picked up the pants Tara had managed to pull off him. Showing this woman how to submit would be more pleasure than he thought possible.

* * * * *

Tara couldn't help noticing that he appeared as if he could go another round. She liked that quality in a man. But there was more than his sexuality that impressed her. Darius appeared interested in her, but Tara didn't fool herself into believing his curiosity was drawn by affection.

She knew better.

Darius questioned her nature because he needed confirmation she was a Runner. His tactics were far more impressive than capture and torture. Tara also felt this approach showed that he might possibly consider the fact that she wasn't the enemy.

Gothman and Runners might have a bad history, but that history didn't affect her. In fact, Tara wasn't sure if there was reason for the two nations of people to despise each other. Ignorance had made them enemies. Tara wondered if knowledge could make them friends.

Tara pulled her dress over her head then twisted around until it hung properly. She walked to his motorcycle, assuming he wasn't pleased by her last comment and would probably take her back to the house. The man wanted her compliance.

Any Gothman woman would do well to be claimed by the Lord of Gothman.

But Tara wasn't Gothman, and he couldn't offer her anything that she wasn't able to obtain on her own. She guessed that since she didn't dance in appreciation to his suggestion, she had offended him, and possibly bruised that mighty ego.

"The Gothman culture has been the way it is for hundreds of winters, it has." Darius buttoned his pants.

She turned and then walked back to him. "Cultures can change, don't you think?"

Darius wasn't looking at her face.

She wondered if he even heard her when he didn't answer. He seemed more intent on studying her breasts. "And who better to start a change but the leader of the land? I've never known a man like you." Tara ran her hands up his chest, feeling the pounding of his heart under muscles that rippled from her touch. "Gothman is powerful, and that power comes from you. You alone could alter the state of women, and no one would stop you."

She watched her hands caress his chest, feeling the ironclad strength as well as his heat. The scent of their sex was intoxicating, her insides swelling, pulsating, aching for him to be inside her again.

Darius lifted her chin with one finger.

Those gray eyes captivated her. Did she see amusement?

"Now, how would I do a thing like that, girl?" Darius tapped her chin with his finger and then headed toward his bike, leaving her lightheaded standing alone. She forced her thoughts to clear, knowing a point should be made here.

"I've heard you're a great leader, Lord Darius. I'm sure you can do anything if you set your mind to it."

Darius got onto his bike and gave her a hard look, not offering to help her on board. She wasn't affected by the look but simply smiled at him and easily slid onto the bike behind him.

Tara hoped her expression appeared calm. Her body tingled in pure satisfaction, and snuggling behind him increased her desire to have him again. But her brain was in pure turmoil. She feared that she'd allowed him to learn more about her than she'd wanted to share.

He'd openly admitted that she was different from any woman he had been with. Tara had to acknowledge that his ability to keep her from knowing whether or not he knew she was a Runner was excellent strategy. It kept her alert and guessing.

* * * * *

Darius took his time returning to the house. His emotions were absolutely contorted beyond recognition. Tara was no Gothman. He had his Runner, of that much, he was certain. The woman stirred something within him. Oh, she'd moved him physically; there was no doubt about that. He would have her again, and soon. It was more than physical lust though. She'd challenged him.

His best advisors didn't question the laws and traditions of Gothman. No one did. Not while he'd been lord. Yet this female didn't hesitate to do so. Darius didn't feel a need to explain to her why women were kept the way they were. Conversation like that would have been a waste of his time. And really, it wasn't the issue she brought up to him, itself, but the fact that this female had enough spunk to speak to him in such a way. No woman, no person, had done that before.

He thought about the past few winters and how he'd taken whatever he'd wanted, and how no one, absolutely no one, had stood in his way. If they'd tried, they'd been killed. He felt no remorse. He'd not been heir to Gothman, but had known since he was a child that he was the one meant to rule. His older brother hadn't the backbone. His papa had known that, but was too traditional to allow the middle son to rule. So, Darius had taken matters into his own hands. He felt no regrets over his brother's death.

Over the past few winters he had taken everything he wanted. And that had included practically every available lass in Bryton. Not that any had objected. His mama had brought every young Gothman woman she could into the household. He'd slept with each one of them; at least he was pretty sure he had. But then, he'd lost interest. Each one had taken the edge off, fucking him when he went to them. But beyond that, they bored him. The Lord of Gothman needed a claim. He would push on thirty winters before long, and he knew the town anticipated he claim one of their available women. More than once he'd told himself to just claim one of them and be done with it. But the thought of having any of those women under his roof for the rest of his winters rubbed him to the point of irritation.

His younger brother, Mikel, frowned upon his promiscuity. Mikel was too much like their papa, Lord Jovis, and although Darius hadn't mourned his papa's death, he could only imagine what his papa would have said if he'd learned Darius just had sex with a Runner—something he definitely planned to do again.

In Darius' tenth or twelfth winter, his papa had engaged in a heated argument about Runners *with* a Runner. Darius hadn't witnessed the event, but he remembered his papa's tirade after it was over. And he had listened as the guards speculated over the results of the argument. What had stuck in Darius' mind over the winters was that, according to gossip, his papa relented to the Runner's wishes. He remembered thinking his papa was weak not to stand up to the Runner. It had also put a kind of awe in his young mind as to the type of man who could argue with the Lord of Gothman and survive to have his way.

It dawned on him suddenly that the argument had concerned Reena. And it was Reena who'd brought Tara to them.

Darius knew Reena associated with Runners from time to time. Word had reached him more than once that a passing clan would bring her gifts. In return, she allowed a lone Runner to spend a night in her secluded cabin before they continued on their way. He hadn't seen reason for concern. Technically, the woman lived outside the town proper, and so had no influence on others. She didn't gossip about her occasional visitor, and his guards never reported that the Runners caused problems.

But with Tara's coming, something had changed. She was the first Runner to enter Gothman land and then venture farther into the community.

As he pulled into the backyard behind his house, he decided that before long he would know the life story of this beautiful woman sitting way too close. He would know why she was here and what she wanted. He already knew what *he* wanted.

Tara hopped off the bike and started walking toward the house without saying anything.

Lord Darius grabbed her arm and stopped her. "I'll say it again, my lady. You're different from any woman I've met. And I'm curious about why you'd like to see Gothman culture change. Changing to be like whom, I'm wondering." He looked at her hard, but Tara remained silent, staring back with an expression so calm he couldn't help but think it had taken winters of training to master it.

Darius studied her tanned complexion, the brown hair that fell past her shoulders and was soft as silk. Her lips were full, and he ached with a sudden urgency to kiss them. He focused on her eyes, a blue that darkened with her emotions, as he was quickly discovering. Right now they were like a dark sapphire, showing no sign of submission.

He moved his attention to her breasts, perky and full, with nipples hardened to a tempting peak under the fabric of her dress. He released her arm and ran a finger over one nipple. She didn't flinch, which pleased him for a reason he couldn't identify. Darius pulled her close. "I enjoyed you, though. We'll do that again, soon."

* * * * *

Tara smiled, tingles rushing through her from his bold touch, but then pushed against Darius' chest, needing distance before she ripped that shirt free from him and begged him to do her again right there on his bike. She would have loved to escape to her room for a shower but Hilda was nearby, arguing with a teenage girl who appeared to have brought groceries.

"There you are, girl," Hilda said, smiling when she saw Tara.

Tara knew she must look rumpled and wondered if Hilda had correctly guessed what had occurred between her son and her new assistant.

She turned away from the older woman's speculative gaze and nodded to the teenage girl. The girl didn't nod back but curled her lip as she eyed Tara from head to toe. Tara felt her cheeks warm and slipped past them and hurried to the small room where she could wash her hands and face and brush her hair.

Torgo appeared to be glad to see her, too. He reminded her she'd said she would spend time with him.

Tara gave the boy a hug and promised she would do so as soon as his mama permitted.

Chapter Five

෨

Hilda insisted Tara was in their home to help with the household chores and not to be a playmate for Torgo. It took many days to convince her, but finally she consented to the two spending time together.

Tara knew Hilda didn't understand why she'd want to spend time playing with the boy when she could be inside baking and catching up on local gossip. It seemed to Tara that was all Gothman women did for entertainment. But she craved being outside. She felt too confined inside the large house, even with its many windows and high ceilings. Tara knew she had to be careful not to arouse suspicion in Hilda, but the woman seemed content with the knowledge that Tara had grown up with just a Papa and brothers, and so therefore had spent time outside playing the *boy* games as a younger girl.

Darius wouldn't be as easily fooled however.

Tara was relieved and frustrated that Darius didn't spend much time at the house. She ached to see him more, to touch him, and to experience his touch again. But the leader of Gothman appeared to be so busy that he was awake and gone often before sunrise, and seldom returned before late in the evening. Many nights Tara, after she had supposedly retired for the day, sat in her bedroom with the door open so she could hear when he came home. Then she would strain to hear what he did until he finally went to bed.

The man appeared preoccupied with the affairs of Gothman. Tara itched to know what politics distracted him, but knew no Gothman woman would think of asking the lord about his business. She wanted to join him in his office, ask him about his day, and exchange stories. She wished she could share experiences with him and learn more about how the man ticked. But to attempt to do any of that would spread suspicion. And that was something she couldn't do. As much as she ached to let Darius know her better, she knew that would be a fool's mission. So she sat alone in the dark of her bedroom every night, and wondered what Darius thought of her, and when he would seek her out next.

Tonight she had fallen asleep before he'd come home. Her eyes fluttered open at the sound of his boots on the stairs while he ascended them. Slow and steady, her heart raced with anticipation that he might be coming to her. With every breath, her breasts swelled, pressing against the covers while she listened to him move down the hallway.

A door opened, but didn't close. He had gone to his own room.

She ran her hands down her body, imagining Lord Darius touching her. A fever burned inside her, an ache for him grew with every moment that she lay in the dark, straining to hear what he might be doing. Her frustration peaked when his door finally closed, the house growing quiet once again. Embers smoldered while a fever she couldn't control made her insides throb for a man she knew she could never truly have.

* * * * *

"What will we do today?" Torgo asked, as he sat on the stool in the kitchen watching Tara clean breakfast dishes.

"Well now, I will have to check with your mama and see if there are any extra chores she has in mind for me. I have to earn my keep, you know." She smiled at his forlorn look.

"Mama will have you busy for hours, I'm sure," he said with disappointment.

"I don't know about hours, child." Hilda stood in the doorway. "I'll have you clean the first floor today. You'll get your own routine down soon enough, I'm sure, as long as his Lordship doesn't take you away from me again."

Tara blushed.

Hilda grinned and chuckled as she walked out of the room.

"Has my brother claimed you yet?" Torgo asked.

Tara was surprised at the question, but the look of innocence on his face reminded her that this was his culture. "No, child, he hasn't."

"When I get older, I'm going to claim a girl as pretty as you."

Torgo followed Tara around the house, talking to her as she dusted the rooms and cleaned the floors. The late morning air was brisk and a cool south breeze floated down from the hills as the young boy led Tara to the grassy meadow beyond the backyard.

"To be a strong warrior like your brother, you must start your lessons at a young age." She squatted to collect several small rocks.

"And what do you know about being a strong warrior?" Torgo laughed.

Tara squinted at the boy who stood next to her, silhouetted by the sun. "I grew up with brothers who all worked to be great warriors, I did."

Torgo accepted the explanation with a quick nod. Every Gothman boy dreamed of being a great warrior.

"Darius said he would teach me to ride a motorcycle when I was a little older." The boy put his hands on his hips and stood a little taller.

"Ah, that's good. Let's see how your aim is today. Do you see that tree over that way? Hit it with these rocks." She handed him the rocks.

Torgo hesitated. "It's too far away."

Tara held the rocks in one hand and with the other threw them, hitting the trunk of the tree each time. She bent down and gathered more rocks. "Now, you try."

Amazed, the boy took the rocks and threw them, missing the tree each time.

Tara agreed they could move closer.

After many attempts, Torgo finally started to hit the tree. His excitement showed through his young eyes and he hugged Tara joyfully. "They won't pick on me at school anymore." He attempted a jig as he jumped around in a circle.

"This is just the beginning of the many things a great warrior will need to know." They walked slowly back to the house together.

"Throwing rocks?" Torgo looked confused. "Is this something you did with your brothers?"

"Did you just learn to throw rocks today?" Tara eyed the young boy whose face showed his eagerness to learn.

"Yes. All I did *was* throw rocks." Torgo sounded confused.

"Ah, I think you learned several things today. Give it some thought. Meanwhile, practice on different targets. Maybe tomorrow we can get outside again. It sure is a nice break from my chores." To Tara's surprise, the young boy jumped at her and gave her a tight hug. He held on to her for a moment and she returned the hug.

* * * * *

Hilda worried about Tara working with Torgo after school. One or two walks after chores was okay, Hilda guessed. And Torgo escorting the girl did keep her safe from the guards. But the two of them traipsed off daily, and Hilda couldn't see the point in it.

Tara showed every sign of growing up without a mama. The girl had a bit of the wild side to her. Hilda felt obligated to her friend, Reena, to help the girl master the domestic skills she obviously lacked. Tara could clean well enough, but she seemed clueless about making many common meals. Hilda wondered more than once how Tara's brothers and Papa hadn't starved to death. Tara had no culinary skills whatsoever.

Hilda knew her son would not want a claim who couldn't run the household. What man would? Her son hadn't sent Tara packing yet, and that was a good sign. Granted he seemed busier than normal lately, but the Lord of Gothman needed a claim, and Hilda felt the two of them would do just fine together, if she could just get Tara to fine-tune some of her skills. And as long as she made sure Tara's little adventures occurred when her older son wasn't home, then no harm should come of it.

Hilda also noticed how happy her youngest son was with Tara in the house. The boy would run home eagerly each day, throw down his books, and call for Tara until he'd located her in one of the rooms of the large house.

* * * * *

"Remember you said we could hike along the creek today." Torgo leaned against the doorway, watching Tara put fresh sheets on his brother's bed.

"I remember." Tara grabbed the large comforter from the floor and threw it on to the bed. She couldn't help but wonder how many women the lord had brought to this bed. Her stomach tightened at the thought and she turned her attention to Torgo. "If I suggest something, could you keep it a secret?"

Torgo's gray eyes grew wide and he grinned. "Of course I can keep a secret. What is it?"

Tara glanced into the hallway. No one else appeared to be upstairs.

Torgo turned his attention there briefly before focusing again on Tara.

"It would be a lot easier to take a hike along the creek if I could wear some pants. Your mama is resting, and your brother isn't here. If you have a pair I could borrow, it would also keep my dress from getting dirty."

Torgo almost leapt for the hallway, and then grabbed the doorframe as he turned to face Tara. "I'm sure I have pants for you, I am," he whispered. "And you're right about your dress, you are. Mama would have a fit if you got all messy. We can't have that."

"No, we can't." Tara grinned as the boy hurried down the hall to his bedroom.

The pants Torgo offered fit her well enough with a belt. She observed herself for only a moment in the mirror in her bedroom, before joining Torgo in the hall. Halfway down the stairs however, Tara stopped and Torgo ran into her backside.

Darius stood talking to two of his guards in the living room.

Tara mentally chastised herself for not hearing them enter the house. She motioned with her hand and the two of them backed up the stairs. Tara cringed with every noisy footstep Torgo made. "Let's try the other staircase," Tara whispered and pointed toward the back of the house where the servant's staircase led to the kitchen.

They made it to the kitchen, and Tara reached for the doorknob on the back door, when a sound alerted her already electrified senses. Winters of training had her pushing Torgo behind her, as she turned and faced one of Lord Darius' guards.

"My Lord," the guard called, and at the same time pulled his oversized Gothman bang stick on Tara.

"What are you doing, man?" Darius frowned as he pushed past the guard and spotted Tara and Torgo. "Put that away, I say."

"But Milord, we have her in pants now. I daresay that says a lot."

"It tells me nothing," Darius' voice boomed. "Out with you and your man. I will meet with you in a moment."

He watched the man leave the kitchen.

Tara heard the front door open and close, but kept her gaze pinned on Darius' large backside. Muscles twitched under his shirt, which stretched over his broad shoulders. Large and dangerous. Her heart fluttered, missing a beat while she worked to keep her expression relaxed.

Darius turned and cocked his head as he studied Tara. "I do believe I like you better in dresses."

Tara focused on his eyes, once again forgetting to be submissive in his presence. His eyes were darker than a storm-filled sky.

Tara had no answer. She felt the room grow warmer as she quit looking at his face to take in the rest of him. The excitement she had felt moments before about hiking along the creek disappeared. Now she wanted to stay here and give this man all of her attention. Enemy or not, she wanted him. And she wanted him now.

"The pants are mine, Darius." Torgo stepped around Tara. "She didn't want to upset Mama by messing up her dress."

Tara rested a hand on Torgo's shoulder and smiled. She could feel the tension in the young boy. "It's okay, Torgo. We've done nothing wrong."

"I'm thinking I will be the judge of that," Darius scolded.

She gave him her full attention.

"Where is it that you are going dressed like this?"

"Torgo and I are going hiking along the creek." Tara worked to focus her thoughts on something other than the virile man standing in front of her. She risked suspicion and needed to put any questions to rest. "I thought it would be nice to give Hilda some peace and quiet so she could rest."

"I see." Darius sighed and waved a hand.

Torgo took that as a dismissal and pulled the door open before his plans were cancelled.

Tara turned to follow the boy who already ran across the backyard.

Darius grabbed her jaw before she could turn from him. He cupped the top of her neck and turned her to face him. Without a word, his mouth covered hers.

She gasped at the heat from his lips as her mouth opened to return the kiss. Her fingers eagerly slid under his leather jacket and traced the strong chest muscles under his shirt. The heat between her legs made her knees quiver, and she felt herself getting wet. She grabbed his shirt in her hands and held on.

"Be back within the hour, or I will be looking for you myself," Darius whispered.

Tara wanted to make him hunt for her, but she would be with Torgo, so she pushed that fantasy to the side.

He released her jaw, and let his hand slide to the nape of her neck.

She let go of his shirt and released a jagged sigh, before turning to leave.

"Be careful now, my lady."

Tara hurried to catch up with Torgo, but turned to give him a delighted smile. "You have nothing to worry about. We will be fine," she called.

* * * * *

Tara scrubbed windows the following morning as she watched Lord Darius secure a leather bag to the side of his bike. She still ached from waiting for him to seek her out the day before, but realized that the Lord of Gothman had many other responsibilities besides hunting her down. He hadn't returned until the early morning hours of this day, and Tara wondered what task kept him from her arms.

She watched the muscles in his shoulders work as he hunched over with his back to her. Finally, she had all she could take of cleaning and threw her rag to the floor. She stood, straightened her dress, and marched through the house to the back door. After their kiss the day before, she knew he was still interested. And she saw no problem with saying hello. Unfortunately, Hilda came down the stairs at that moment.

"I must say, you do make my old house sparkle." She smiled at Tara. "Have you cleaned most of the windows?"

"No, my lady, I've gotten as far as the living room and dining room." Tara stopped and leaned back to inspect her work. She hadn't cleaned many windows in her life, but this was the second time in almost a cycle that she'd cleaned these windows. They didn't look like they needed any more cleaning to her. "I'm glad my work pleases you."

"You're still here and that pleases me more than your work. But, I'll be needing you to take a break for now. I have a list of things I need from the grocery. These can wait 'til you get back." Hilda handed the list to Tara along with the keys to her car. "I'd go myself but my head hurts this morning. Be sure and get all the news from Thelga."

Tara returned the cleaning supplies to the pantry and paused to look longingly out the back door at Lord Darius. Several of his guards joined him and she watched them for a moment. They seemed to be in a rather serious discussion, and she wondered what they could be talking about. Unfortunately, Hilda's car was parked out front, and Tara had no reason to leave through the back door so she could hear their conversation.

Their voices grew louder, and the guard who had attacked Tara was telling the rest of them something. Whatever he said upset Lord Darius, and he lunged at the man. The man backed down but continued to growl. Tara simply couldn't make out what they were saying, even when she went to the back door and put her ear to it. She finally turned away and headed out the front door to the car.

The argument between Darius and his guards proved a good distraction, so no one noticed Tara teach herself how to drive Hilda's vehicle. Tara had read about cars, and she felt confident in her mechanical knowledge of them, but driving one proved a small challenge. The car lunged forward, and then the engine stopped with her first attempt. Tara killed the motor several more times before she was able to make the small contraption move slowly along the road.

The village was lively, with people going in and out of different shops. Children and dogs ran up and down the sidewalk, and the women and older girls gathered here and there catching up on the latest gossip. Tara parked the car in front of the grocery and smiled politely at four women standing outside the store. They smiled back and then returned to their conversation with more excitement than ever. She heard them say her name but didn't bother trying to overhear what they said. She could only imagine what gossip was being spread about her now that she was living in Lord Darius' house.

"Ah, good morning to you, girl." Thelga smiled broadly as Tara entered the store.

"And a good morning to you." Tara smiled in return and picked up a basket from the door.

"It's quite an honor you have done your old aunt, being claimed by his lordship, and all." Thelga clucked. "And you only being in our town for such a short time."

Tara grabbed her basket with her other hand to keep from dropping it. She looked at the old lady, quite stunned. "What are you saying?" Tara couldn't do more than whisper. "I have not been claimed by anyone."

"Oh, do you say, maybe you haven't been told. I'm sure I'm right, to be certain. It was my claim told me. He heard from the lord's guards, he did." Thelga leaned on the counter and her eyes twinkled, knowing she got to be the first to share the news. "It happened this way to my granddaughter, it did. She was claimed, and the menfolk had such a merry party over it they forgot to tell her." Thelga laughed at the thought. "I know for a fact there isn't a prettier girl in town than you. I'm sure the lord wouldn't have anyone else to take the likes of you." Thelga saw the look of shock on Tara's face and was trying to be reassuring. She reached over the counter and squeezed Tara's arm with her rough fingers. "There isn't a life a girl could ask for as nice as the one you'll have. Your sons'll be lords."

Tara was so surprised by what she'd just heard that she turned to walk back out of the store.

"Ah, my Lady, your list?"

"Oh, yes…here it is." Tara handed the list to Thelga and then just stood about. She wanted to give Thelga the third degree and find out every bit of information she knew about this claiming. A guard had told her claim? When had Thelga heard this? How long had she known? Tara kept her mouth closed however and stood awkwardly in the middle of the store while a young errand boy took the list and ran through the store gathering the items.

Two young women not much older than Tara entered the store and smiled politely at her. They moved over to the produce, and Tara could hear their conversation easily.

"My mama took a pie to her aunt the other day. The old lady said it was what they'd planned all along."

"I daresay she wasn't in town but a day when his Lordship claimed her. Imagine the likes, all of us having our hopes so high for so long. She comes along so merrily like, and he claims her right off, he does."

"Yeah, and I heard she can't cook, you know. It's her pleasures that sold her, that's for sure." The two girls laughed at this comment, and then realizing Tara could hear them, they started whispering.

Tara's blood started to boil. All of this was simply too much. Hearing that Reena had planned her claiming all along put Tara into a rage. Was it true Darius had claimed her before she'd even gone to live in the house? The only time he'd seen her prior to that was in the alley when she'd kept Torgo out of that fight. Did Reena know at that point and Hilda, too? The entire town seemed to know this casual bit of information and somehow had overlooked sharing it with her.

The young errand boy brought the basket to the counter with the items from the list. Thelga arranged the items in a brown paper sack and then smiled at Tara.

"Don't you worry yourself none about the comments of girls such as those." Thelga didn't move her lips much, trying to speak quietly. "They've all tried for his Lordship and failed. They're jealous, they are. You hold your head high. You should be proud, you should."

Tara thanked her and quickly walked out of the store and to the car. Her eyes burned with tears of anger, and her hands shook as she drove back to Lord Darius' house. Hilda's vehicle died so many times that Tara wanted to pull the circular handlebar from the inside of the car and hurl it out the window.

Darius had asked her about being claimed when they'd driven into the hills together. Had he already claimed her publicly by then? Could that be why she'd been brought to the house?

Tara remembered watching him ride toward his house from her bedroom window, remembered how quickly he'd driven through the hills. That had to be the reason why he had hurried home that morning almost a cycle ago. She had been made to believe she was hired help, yet the whole thing was a façade.

She drove the car up the hill to the house with such a vengeance that the tires skidded on the gravel road. Grabbing the groceries, Tara nearly ran into the house. Darius was in the living room with his guards, and she stormed past them into the kitchen.

"I don't see why you don't listen to reason, my Lord," the large guard who'd attacked her growled loud enough for her to hear.

"Judo, the reasoning isn't sound, it isn't. I'll not hear of it." Darius' growl chilled her blood.

"What's wrong with you? You won't even listen to reason when it comes to that girl there." Mikel, Lord Darius' younger brother, shouted.

"We won't be talking of that today." Darius had a tone in his voice Tara hadn't heard before. There was complete control mixed with anger. His baritone sounded very dangerous.

"Your brain isn't doing your thinking for you, my lord, it isn't. We found the bike, and you yourself have commented on her abilities. Her thighs are wrapped around you so tightly you can't see the truth. She's your Runner! You've let her into this house, and now she'll bring down your kingdom, she will."

Mikel, Tara had noticed, was a smaller build than his older brother, but that didn't appear to intimidate him in the slightest. "Our Papa would be disgraced if he knew what you were doing."

"That's enough!" Darius yelled so loudly that Tara actually jumped.

She quickly started to put away the groceries although her hands were trembling from her anger. She wasn't trying to bring down any kingdom and she sure wasn't going to be anyone's claim.

Tara fought to clear her thoughts. Darius' men knew her true identity. And, from the sound of it, wanted her taken down. Yet Darius hesitated. Her heart skipped a beat at the thought that he hesitated because of a mutual attraction. But her mind told her that the man ruled a very powerful nation. His hesitation could be for other reasons, and Tara needed a clear head to determine his thoughts.

How many men were in the living room? Three or four? Could she take them all on and escape the house to her bike?

The front door slammed, and the house grew silent.

Had they all left? Tara knew she couldn't possibly return to washing the windows right now. She needed time to think. In the past, when her temper threatened to get the best of her she'd usually taken off on her motorcycle and driven until the anger left. When that wasn't possible, she'd pick a fight with one of the others in her clan until she'd released all her anger on her poor victim.

The house still remained quiet, and Tara wandered cautiously out of the kitchen.

The living room was empty so she went upstairs. Hilda must have been asleep in her room, or at least resting. Tara couldn't imagine anyone being able to sleep through the tirade that had just occurred in the living room. Was the woman fearful that she had a Runner in her home?

Tara shuddered. She didn't have time to worry about that right now.

She wandered past the closed doors to her bedroom. The balcony seemed an appealing place to sort through all the thoughts she was having at the moment.

Tara had a compelling urge to leave Gothman and put as much distance between her and this nation as she could. Oddly enough, something just as strong was telling her to stay.

"Tara, you're back. Will you come down? I've waited for you forever, I have."

Tara looked down to see Torgo standing in the yard looking up to her.

He smiled and waved. "Hurry, I have a surprise. Oh, do hurry. Put on a pair of my pants if you will. But do hurry."

"Alright, boy. Calm down. I'll come down to you, I will." Tara went to the boy's room and quickly changed into a pair of his pants. She didn't care if any of the guards saw her like this. It would serve Darius right.

If he had indeed gone and claimed her after she said she wanted the claim to be mutual, then he could suffer the consequences. Or, worse, if he had claimed her before and then mentioned that he *could* claim her just to tease her, he had insulted her intelligence. She fumed as she ran down the stairs.

The blue pullover shirt and tight dark pants she borrowed from Torgo fit snugly, and Tara guessed she probably showed a bit more of her figure through the clinging material than she planned. But she could move easily in the outfit and that mattered more to her than appearance.

"You won't believe what I got." The boy danced around her when she entered the yard. "Look!"

Next to the shed was a motorcycle about the same size as Tara's.

Torgo ran to it and patted the seat. "It's mine." He glowed with pride. "Darius gave it to me just this morning." Torgo looked around and then said quietly, "You can ride. I know you can. I heard my brother talking with his men, I did. Will you teach me?

My brother isn't in a very good mood today. He gave it to me and said we would ride, but then he got some kind of news, he did."

"What kind of news did he get?" Tara asked. *And what else did you overhear your brother say?* Tara knew asking Torgo would be fruitless. The boy wasn't interested in conspiracies. He'd just received the most coveted thing a teenager could want—a motorcycle.

"Oh, I don't know, I'm sure. What I do know is I want to learn to ride. Darius learned to ride when he had twelve winters. He told me so. I almost have thirteen winters, and I don't know how yet. You'll teach me, won't you?" he begged, with gray eyes a softer version of his older brother's. "I know some of my brother's men think it's odd that you know how to fight. But I don't think it's strange at all. Your papa was smart to teach you all he did."

Tara wondered how the boy could be so open-minded when his older brother seemed so closed to new ideas. "Of course I will." Tara ran her hands over the small bike.

It was well designed, painted a clean metallic red. On the side of the body, the word *Bryton* was written in gold. The seat curving up in the back was of the familiar Gothman style. It was an impressive motorcycle. Tara was just about to straddle the bike but hesitated at the surprised look on Torgo's face.

She turned her head to see Darius walking around the shed coming toward them.

Torgo looked as if he just got caught with his hands in the cookie jar. "Uh, my lord, I was just letting her look at my new motorcycle." Torgo blushed and leaned on one foot then the other.

Darius stopped next to Tara. He stared down at her.

She noticed the undeniable lust in his eyes. Her insides quickened in response, but she still felt an outrage with the man and his claiming. She looked up at him and pretended not to notice, then looked back at the boy. "Torgo, a true warrior never lies." She looked directly into the youngster's eyes. "My papa said that to my brothers again and again, and I think there is truth in it, I do."

Torgo took a slow deep breath and squared his shoulders. "Tara was going to teach me how to ride because you're too busy."

Tara immediately felt very proud of him.

"Torgo, you'll make an incredible warrior some day." Darius gave away his feelings on the matter when a small, crooked smile appeared on his face. He was proud of his younger brother. "You'll have that lesson, but first I want to speak to Tara. Run on along now, boy."

Torgo looked at both of them and then slowly walked away from his bike.

Tara turned to face Darius. His shoulders seemed broad enough to block the sun. She felt he towered over her — emphasizing his domination. And that's when all the anger bottled up inside of Tara raced through her blood once again. If Darius noticed, he hid it well.

"Come here." He walked back towards the shed and opened it, pointed to the bike inside, then stared back at Tara. "A true warrior never lies, those are your words."

She stared at her cycle before looking at Darius, and instinctively her hands moved until they clasped behind her back — the stance of a warrior — as she awaited her next orders.

"Can you start this motorcycle?"

She met his gaze and returned it, unwavering. Damn, he had her trapped by her own words. Not to be outdone she issued a challenge. "And you?" Her words shot laser beams his way. "I've heard the people say you're a true warrior."

Darius walked over to her bike. "Ask me anything. I've no reason to lie." He leaned on the handlebars and stared into her eyes.

"You've already lied to me." She glared back at him, wanting to pounce on his pompous ass and wipe the smug look from his face.

Darius raised his eyebrows, looking surprised. Then his gaze narrowed and grew serious.

She could tell her look and words affected him. But she was the enemy here, on his land. She knew, as he did, that there was no way she could beat him in hand-to-hand combat, yet she'd still take him on if she had to. Her anger was genuine. She'd become involved with this culture and this family. *If* she became a part of this family, it would be her decision, not his. It would not be because some man who didn't even know her had taken a fancy to how she looked. They had experienced wonderful sex together, but sexual compatibility wasn't enough to build a relationship. He'd know her first. Of that she demanded. And she planned on him knowing her well, in every respect. Mind, body, emotions. She wanted him to know everything about her.

"You think you know what you need to about me, but you haven't asked me anything. You don't even talk to me." She grabbed on to the back of her bike with clenched fists, growing more outraged at the thought that he would claim her with so little prior knowledge of her wants, her desires.

"You're even more beautiful when you're mad." He smiled and reached for her face.

Tara smacked his hand, knocking it away with all the emotion in her heart. "I'm not unclaimed land to be taken without asking."

He pulled back his hand slowly and raised one eyebrow. He spoke quietly, almost in a reprimand. "If you're referring to the claiming, I've broken no laws. I've a right to any unclaimed lady in Gothman. There's no discussion required. That's been the law of the land since before my Papa was born, or his Papa before him. Are you trying to tell me you are not affected by the laws of this land?" He straightened and crossed his arms across his chest.

Tara watched his muscles twitch with the action. He stepped to the side of her bike with his face close to hers. She thought for a moment she saw amusement in his eyes. "It's a bad law," she whispered. "I'll not be claimed unless I say I'll be claimed."

Darius slowly moved his gaze from her face down to her breasts. The tip of his finger stroked the fuel tank on her bike. "Can you start it?" he asked softly.

The sultry whisper challenged and seduced her simultaneously. Tara took a step backward.

Darius grabbed her.

His touch sizzled her skin, and the smell of man and leather consumed her senses. But outrage overpowered her.

He must have surmised that his touch wouldn't cause her to swoon because his expression became serious. "This is your bike…" He wrapped his long fingers around her arms. "…And you are a Runner. Start this bike, and I'll never tell a soul. I'll say I started it.

At this point your only threat here is me, and my dear lady, I'm no threat at all."

He yanked quickly before she could react, and she fell against his chest. He let go of one arm, and placed his knuckle under her chin, then tilted her head back so he could meet her lip to lip. Touching her mouth with his, he growled, demanding a response when she did nothing.

Tara pushed away and gasped for air, trying to get her bearings. She studied his face and hoped she wasn't making a mistake. Darius had told her he was not a threat.

She would honor him as a warrior and trust his word.

Tara broke away from Darius' grasp and walked around him, and for some reason, he didn't stop her. Touching the bike, she ran her fingers over the handlebars for a moment, then grabbed it without looking up and rolled the bike into the sunlight.

He followed her with all the eagerness his younger brother had displayed a short time ago. "I'd love to ride it. It must possess a speed not known in Gothman." He watched her every move as she climbed aboard.

Tara looked around to ensure the yard was empty from any of Darius' guards. Immediately she took off with a jump, causing the bike to literally leave the ground.

"You can ride it if you can catch me," she yelled over her shoulder.

"Ah, you want to play, do you?"

Darius literally ran to his motorcycle, which was parked along the side of the shed.

Tara raced her bike to the edge of the backyard and then spun around and stopped. She would make her challenge a fair one. It would not do to beat him and have him say she had some kind of edge.

He quickly pulled his bike up beside hers and stopped, letting the motor of his cycle idle. "We both know your bike is designed to be faster than this one." There was fire in his eyes.

She could tell at that moment that he was indeed a true warrior. He was thrilled by her daring and excited to take her on in a physical activity other than the act of lovemaking. Tara smiled wickedly. "This bike may be faster, but you know the land like you know the gloves upon your hand. It'll be a fair race. Just name the destination."

"We'll race to the cliff I wanted you to climb. You're not in a dress today." He grinned as his gaze raked down her pant-clad body. "And, my lady, the claim stands."

Tara didn't respond but instead took off across the meadow with all the skills of her Runner heritage.

Darius was quickly at her side, dodging the rocks and ruts in the earth that opposed both of them.

The two sped so fast across the land that the naked eye had a hard time following.

Although Tara didn't know the terrain, she'd traveled at high speeds across many a land she hadn't known. She didn't look next to her to watch her competitor but instead kept her eyes ahead of her, soaring over the gullies in the land. She passed hill after hill, and when she spotted the crag with the rocky road outlining it, she added to her speed and easily left Darius behind.

The rock-strewn road was steep, and her bike was not designed for such travel. Tara decelerated, fearing the bike would literally slip out from under her. She crept up the hill aware that Darius quickly approached from behind. She knew the dust from the gravel impaired his vision and intentionally spun her tires on the road to further slow him down. A large rock came up on her before she could react, and Tara slid to the side of the road, scraping her leg. The sting in her leg intensified when she put her weight on it, but she would not allow an abrasion to cause her defeat.

She glanced down at Torgo's torn trousers and the scratched skin underneath. *You can handle it, warrior. It's no more than a scrape.*

Darius came up behind her and slowed his bike. "Are you okay?" His face showed concern.

Tara righted her bike and took off, yelling, "Gothman have never cared about Runners, why start now?" She placed a big smile on her face as she reached the patchy area surrounded by the pine trees where they'd had sex.

She looked at the rocks Darius suggested they climb and drove over to them, then parked. Knowing there was no way she would be able to ride up the jagged rocks to Darius' cliff, Tara jumped off her bike and lunged for the first group of rocks.

She'd rock climbed for sport as a child and from what she could see, the jutting wall offered little challenge. Nonetheless, her heart pounded as she grabbed the first tier of rocks and pulled herself up. When she anchored her foot against the next level up, the sting from her scrape raced up her side, letting her know the extent of damage she'd actually incurred. But more than anything, she wanted to beat Darius, to show him they were indeed equal.

When she glanced down, she realized the man was good, real good. Reaching the first ledge of rocks, she had turned and looked below. The tree-covered hillside, hiding a rocky ground strewn with protruding roots, hadn't slowed him in the least.

Darius had parked his bike next to hers and also jumped for the rocks. His skill at climbing obviously matched hers, as he appeared to crawl up the side of the cliff with little effort. She remembered now that he'd told her this was a place he'd come to since he was a boy.

The second set of rocks was more jagged, and she was forced to move around them since she had no gloves. Ahead of her, a good fifteen feet above, she could see what appeared to be a flat ledge. Ignoring the sharp jabs from the rough boulders, she hurried to reach the top. As she crested the rise, she looked out over the scene and was immediately overwhelmed by the view.

No wonder he'd chosen this place as his sanctuary. A leader could easily be reminded why he was willing to fight for his land when it was laid out before him in such a panoramic fashion. She pulled herself up to a stand and sucked in her breath as she witnessed the glory before her.

The countryside was beautiful, providing a view to the north as far as the eye could see. The rolling hills went on for miles, and although not visible on the horizon Tara could imagine the mountains that she already knew existed there. As a young child, growing up, she had traveled the land she now saw from a distance.

It seemed as if the sky was higher, spreading out farther than usual. It looked bigger to Tara than she knew it should. Very few clouds prevented the aqua color above from almost overwhelming the vast shades of green below. For a moment, its beauty transfixed her.

But she had a man to whom she needed to prove herself. With a quick glance around her, she reached for the next ledge and pulled herself up to lean on her elbows. That's when she saw the grassy flat, a small area secluded from the rest of the world. Tara relaxed her sore leg for a moment, before putting her weight back on it, and took a deep breath so she could judge the depth of her injuries. As she did, she noticed Darius pulling himself up from the other side of the plateau. He'd been behind her!

He pulled his body over the ledge with ease and sat on the ground, catching his breath for just a brief second. Then he moved over to her and reached to help her up.

"Get back, you!" she said through clenched teeth and pulled herself up. Tara didn't take defeat well. She cursed the time she'd wasted enjoying the view, knowing the victory would have been hers otherwise.

The smug grin on his face showed that he would enjoy gloating. "I won. You have to let me ride your bike now." Darius sat back on the ground and smiled broadly.

Tara sat next to him and pounded the ground with her fist as she scowled.

Darius leaned forward and brushed her hair away from her face.

She glanced at him out of the corner of her eye and then broke out laughing. She knew herself well. Not an hour ago, she was fuming with anger. The ride and the intensity of the rock climbing had freed her of all hostilities. Physical activity cleared her head every time. "You're lord of all this great land." Tara swung out her hand, gesturing to the magnificent view in front of them. "How can an invader of your country possibly stop you from riding that motorcycle?" She pointed to her bike parked next to his.

"You've done a good job of stopping me so far, you have." He laughed with her.

"So how long have you known I was a Runner?" She looked at him, serious now.

"Ever since you shot that trash can to prevent my little brother from getting the tar beat out of him. Although, I daresay, for skipping school, he should have had worse than that beaten out of him."

"I don't understand. Why didn't you capture me right then?"

"You had my curiosity going, you did. We were scouting the town, looking for a Runner, an enemy of our land. I didn't see an enemy. I saw a woman acting differently than other women. I saw a woman, beautiful beyond all measure that made my blood race in my veins. You appeared to be out of place, but not a threat." Darius blew out a breath and stared down at their bikes.

Tara could tell he was choosing his next words carefully and watched him while he thought.

"Runners don't enter Gothman, at least not since I was a child. Why are you here?"

"The need to explore is in a Runner's blood, my lord. I've heard the stories of Gothman, and they fascinated me. I wanted to see how a nation could be so powerful when half of its race had no clue how to fight or defend itself."

"And what have you concluded?"

"Why do you care what I think?" she answered sarcastically. "I didn't think it was my mind that impressed you."

Darius smiled and put his arm around her. He took her chin and lifted her face to his. "At first, that was true. You are so beautiful. There is more to you than that, there is. I didn't know women like you existed. I've yet to find a man that is my match, much less a woman. But you may be that exception, and not many have the nerve to be that way, no."

Darius looked so focused, yet his expression remained gentle. Tara felt something release inside, like a dam breaking—something she'd never felt before. He had made her so angry yet she felt such a longing to be right here by his side indefinitely. Patha described love to her once, when she asked. He told her that love was when you were content to be with one person no matter what you were doing. He had said that when you weren't with this person they were somewhere in your mind always. He had also told her that no matter how mad you may get at that person, true love never allowed you to stay mad for too long.

"And to be certain, my Lady, you've made it quite clear I can't do anything with you unless you say it's okay." He brushed his lips gently across hers. In one quick motion, he stood and pulled her with him then held her closely at his side. He pointed to the countryside that lay magnificently in front of them. "Look at it, Tara. We could rule this together, you and I. You must say that has some appeal to you."

"Darius, we're enemies," she stated, although she made no attempt to be released from his arms.

He turned her towards him and kissed her passionately.

She wrapped her arms around him and returned the kiss. Heat from their passion set her blood to boiling. Tara arched into him, pressing the length of her body against his. Every inch of him that touched her felt so hard and sent rushes of energy through her. She grabbed his arms and then let her hands slide up to his shoulders, clasping her fingers behind his neck. Tara felt his hands on her rear end, pulling her closer to him.

He nibbled her bottom lip and she gasped, heat rushing through her fast enough to make her dizzy. Darius tasted her, sending a trail of kisses to her neck as she let her head fall back. Darius maintained a tight grip, his touch fueling the fever within her. She realized through fogged senses that he interpreted her reaction to his passion as submission. He wanted to control her.

With a silent chuckle, Tara knew she would have to show him how Runner women expected to be treated. At that point, she decided to end the kiss on her own, just to show him she could and take the lead.

It took more effort than she figured it would.

"You're not my enemy," Darius said, once their lips parted. "You're my match in every way. I don't want the likes of you as an enemy."

She smiled at him and then went up on tiptoe and kissed him once again. "So, do you want to ride that motorcycle?"

"In a minute," he said and pulled her to him. His hands reached under her clothes, down into her pants, and clutched her rear end. He shoved her into him and set her on fire.

She fell back, pulling him onto her. She needed to feel skin, wanted to explore this virile body that had grown to be more than a distraction. She yanked at his shirt.

He assisted by putting enough distance between them to take off the offending material. He reached for his pants.

But she stopped him. "I want to do it." Her voice sounded husky, and he smiled. Tara pulled free the belt and then tugged down his pants. She placed kisses around the thick mass of hair that did nothing to hide his rock-hard arousal. She offered his erection no attention, but kissed her way down his legs as she pushed his pants to the ground.

Darius reached under her arms and pulled her back up along his naked and aroused body. He shocked her wherever he touched her, and the moisture between her legs soaked through all that she wore.

* * * * *

Darius didn't take as long to remove her clothes. She was naked within seconds, and he held her as he rolled to his side, then placed her on her back. He took her hands and laid them above her head. Then, slowly, he began to kiss her. And slowly, so slowly, he moved down her, kissing every inch along the way. His hands caressed and stroked as he continued his exploration of her body.

There was no rush this time. The newness from the first time was gone. He wanted to explore and get to know, very well, every inch of her. He spread her legs, and she didn't fight him. Instead she lifted her hips from the ground, and he let out a low chuckle as he blew soft air onto the downy hair between her legs. Tara gasped, and he enjoyed watching the quiver race through her body. He opened her up and could see the glistening moistness, proving how aroused she was. He kissed the moist area first, then ran his tongue up and down, tasting her.

Tara yelped and arched her hips further, grabbing the back of his head as she fought for release.

Darius smiled, knowing she was exactly where he wanted her to be. He licked his lips as he sat up, enjoying her taste on him.

Tara groaned and reached to pull him back to her.

He searched her fogged-over blue eyes as he situated himself above her, resting his erection on her saturated opening.

Tara arched again, as if trying to enclose herself around him.

His hardness felt engorged, and the blood racing through him wanted to slam into that heat. But he teased for a moment, until her blue eyes widened, and her mouth opened in a silent protest.

As she was ready to explode, he entered her. He moved with a steady pace, pushing into her heat until he felt intoxicated, and then pulling back as his body shook with need to return to the center of her heat. When he knew neither of them could handle the pressure built from his motions, he thrust hard, aggressively, and brought them to climax simultaneously.

She stared at him, breathing fast.

He'd controlled her, and he knew it.

* * * * *

Tara dressed in silence, almost disbelieving of the sex she had just experienced. No man had ever done to her body what Darius had just done. She felt numb, more than satisfied, and almost in awe. Her thoughts still floated in a fog of aftermath, and she couldn't interpret how she felt.

Darius dressed and then pulled her close for a minute as they stared out at the beautiful land. It felt good being in his arms. He was strong, powerful, and still very dangerous. All of it excited her.

"I'll ride that bike of yours now." He got up finally and moved to the edge of the ledge they were on and shimmied down to the first set of rocks. He reached his hands up to help her down as well.

She laughed at him. "Didn't you just say I was your match in every way?" She sat down as well and scooted down the rocks without his assistance.

Within seconds they were back at the motorcycles, and he eagerly climbed onto her bike.

She showed him the order in which to push the buttons on her handlebar to start the bike, and he watched eagerly. She could tell he looked a bit worried as his contented smile turned to a frown when she climbed onto his bike.

"Are you sure it's not too big for you, my lady?"

"My papa's bike is at least this big, and I have ridden it a time or two, my lord." She stressed his title, sarcastically implying his superiority over her.

Side by side, they rode down the rocky road and back out to the meadow.

Tara enjoyed riding the big, noisy, cumbersome motorcycle. There was something raw and untamed about it, although it would be difficult to use in battle, she thought. However, the nature of the Gothman wasn't to sneak up and attack their opponent but to roar into battle with screams and confidence in their victory; this bike suited their nature just fine. If anything, she felt she understood Lord Darius and his people just a little bit better after riding on the large bike that took each rut in the earth with a vengeance of superiority.

She wondered if Darius was concluding anything about her nature from riding her bike.

After winding past the first group of hills, he slowed her bike to a stop.

She pulled up next to him.

"Park my bike here and climb on behind me. I'll come get it shortly. It'll make it a bit easier to justify the story I'm planning to tell if we are seen, it will. When we're back, you may take Torgo out to the field and give him his lesson. I daresay he's quite eager, and there's no reason to disappoint the boy."

Tara obeyed and climbed on behind him. Her bike was not designed to carry two easily, but she enjoyed being as close to him as was required for them to ride together. She wrapped her hands around his waist and locked her fingers together. He held her two hands in his and skillfully drove her bike back to the shed with his other hand.

Chapter Six

ઝ૭

A couple weeks of riding lessons proved very effective for Torgo, and Tara awoke one morning to the sounds of his bike cruising around in the meadow. She lay in her bed for a while listening to the rumble of the teenager's motorcycle and remembering her first experiences on one. She'd felt so mature and independent to be riding by herself, free to go wherever she pleased. She knew the glory Torgo must be experiencing without even getting up to look out the balcony to confirm her thoughts. He had worked hard to get to the point where he could master the machine and ride alone.

She showered and dressed and was absolutely ravenous as she went down the stairs to help prepare breakfast. Hilda and Darius were in the kitchen talking about something, and she could tell by Hilda's quiet tone that the woman was not pleased.

"I just don't understand. It was you yourself that said it was final, you did." Hilda wrung her hands then placed them on the counter nervously when Tara entered.

"I know, and it is. I have matters of ruling a country, Mama. It's just not a good time."

"But, son, the community expects this, there'll be talk, there will." Hilda reached for her son.

"Oh blast it all with your talk, woman," Darius barked.

"Good morning." She looked at the two of them questioningly.

"Tara, certainly you want..." Hilda looked at Tara as if relieved that she would side with her on whatever issue the two of them were talking about.

"Mama!" Darius interrupted her with a firm tone in his voice. "Tara, walk with me to my bike."

Darius grabbed a bag from the counter and turned to look at his mama.

Tara watched Hilda grab a dishtowel and twist it in her hands. She seemed very upset.

His tone softened when he spoke again, "I'll be back by tomorrow, I'm sure. Don't you worry yourself, none, my lady." He patted his mama's hand as he spoke, but it didn't appear to be soothing her much. "The Lord of Gothman must protect his country, I have my duties."

"That's right, son, you do at that." Hilda looked up at her son and spoke quietly, as if she were making one final attempt to reason with him over whatever point it was they were discussing. "You have the duty to uphold tradition in this land and be an example to your people."

Tara suddenly had the strongest sensation that their discussion had something to do with Darius and her. She stood quietly at the kitchen door and tried her best to keep her facial expression blank yet pleasant.

"You think I don't know that?" Darius didn't yell, but he was very close to it. He turned and headed for the back door. "Tara!"

She took that as her cue to follow. She glanced at Hilda who had crossed her arms across her ample middle and tightened her lips into a thin, straight line. She met Tara's gaze without changing expression, but then focused again on her son. Grabbing a glazed roll from a plate as she passed, Tara followed Darius into the backyard. He walked quickly to his motorcycle, and Tara almost had to run to catch up with him. There were more guards than usual in the yard, all sitting on their motorcycles, as if they had been waiting.

"I'll meet you out front." He waved his hand at them, indicating they should go.

None of them said a word, although most took a good look at Tara before slowly driving down the driveway to the front of the house.

"What's going on?" Tara tried to sound casual and indifferent knowing she felt anything but that. The conversation in the kitchen had spurred her curiosity. Now, the presence of the guards really had her interest piqued. The men on the bikes were armed with the long black bang sticks that made so much noise. She wondered what Darius was leaving to do. She also wondered if he would ever confide in her...that is, if she decided to stay with him.

Darius waited until all the men had moved to the other side of the house, then placed his hand on the back of Tara's neck and guided her to the backside of the shed.

"You'll tell my mama that you're a Runner."

"Why?" By the expression that quickly came over his face, she sensed he was not accustomed to having his commands questioned. His mama had exasperated him, and now she was questioning him.

"I don't have time to explain everything to her. She's asking questions, and the lady has a right to the answers, she does."

"Where are you going?" Tara sensed some type of military excursion was about to occur and wasn't accustomed to being left out of such things. "Your men are dressed for battle."

"There are some rumors." He twisted a strand of her hair between his gloved fingers. "Mind you, they haven't been confirmed now. But possibly, the Sea People are preparing an attack." He smiled and tightened his grip on her hair. "Ah, I see your eyes dancing, I do. You're a wild one now."

Tara didn't smile though. She didn't need to be *protected* from the harsh realities of whatever was going on. She felt that was what he was doing and realized she needed to be persistent. "What are the rumors?"

"Just that their armies are moving close to the Gothman borders. I intend to find out if this is true or not, I do."

"I don't think I could sit by and not fight if you're invaded." Tara showed all signs of the true warrior that she was.

Darius saw more than that. "I daresay, my lady, I do believe you're showing loyalty to the Gothman." He leaned down and kissed her. "Be a good lass for now. Go talk to my mama. I'll be back soon."

He got on his motorcycle and drove off and Tara walked back to the kitchen.

An idea came to her as she entered the kitchen, and she approached Hilda with enthusiasm. "My lady, if I'm quick with my chores this morning, could we invite Reena over for the afternoon? I haven't seen her in awhile, and I have something I want to tell you. I would like her to be here for it." Tara hoped the old woman would be agreeable.

She didn't have to worry.

The old lady's face lit up. "Ah, a splendid idea, that one is." Hilda grinned broadly and then opened the pantry to inspect the shelves. "While you're doing your morning chores, I'll drive to the grocer's and pick up a few things. Ah, and the blueberries are good and fresh. We'll have some of those, and I'll whip some cream. Cold cuts will work well, don't you think? Ah, and set some potatoes to boil. I'll make a hot potato salad to go with the sandwiches. You might want to pick some fresh flowers for the vases, I'd think."

Tara smiled as the old woman hurried upstairs to change for her trip into town. It felt good to know she'd made the old woman happy. She grabbed a walkntalk and placed the call to Reena who also thought the idea was splendid.

Tara sat in the kitchen by herself and decided to have another frosted roll for breakfast before starting her housework. She felt bad about not telling Reena she'd only been invited for moral support. Mulling over in her head the speech she would give to Hilda, Tara remembered that she hadn't asked Darius what questions his mama had been posing. Seeing the guards had completely distracted her. She thought about the fact that Darius was out in some field going over military tactics while she sat here preparing for a luncheon. The irony made her chuckle. Her life had changed so much since she'd come here.

But that was why she came, right? Tara nodded to herself. She had yearned to experience a different way of living, a different kind of lifestyle. To immerse herself in new societies in order to see how they lived. Firsthand. Yet, had she planned on changing her life forever? She knew for a fact that she definitely had not when she started on this adventure. She merely wanted to come into the civilization and observe.

Tara smiled as she realized she'd done a lousy job of that. Here she'd been prepared to remain an outside observer, and instead she'd fallen in love. She was sure of that now. As she thought about it, goose bumps traveled across her body.

Jumping up, she quickly cleaned the kitchen and then moved to the other rooms of the house. Energy soared through her, and she didn't question its source. Her thoughts focused on each room as she entered it, wiping down woodwork and making sure glass sparkled. Tara had never lived in a structure like this. Although its newness had worn off a bit over the past cycle, the place's magnificence still hung in the air. She would make the place look absolutely immaculate for Reena. She wanted Hilda to be proud too. Both women had taken her in and allowed her to explore their people, even though Hilda hadn't realized that was what she had done. And Tara knew a clean house meant something to both of them. She hummed an old Runner tune as she worked.

The house began to sparkle, but Tara's thoughts remained a tangled mess. She couldn't change who she was. She was proud of being a Runner. How could she live here with Darius and maintain the heritage that ran thick through her blood?

Hilda came home and interrupted her thoughts. She'd taken her frustrations out on the house until it was spotless. Hilda was pleased with her work and told her so.

Torgo entered the house, instinctively knowing that food was being prepared.

"What's for lunch?" he asked, as he hovered around in the kitchen and sampled the blueberries and cold meat as it was laid out on the serving dishes.

"With that appetite, you will be as big as your brother before the new winter." Tara laughed and poked the boy in the stomach. "Why don't we let him eat now, so he isn't bored with the conversation during lunch?" Tara didn't want him there when she explained herself to Hilda.

Hilda nodded her agreement. "I'll fix you a plate, my boy." She smiled, showing a mama's love, as she grabbed one of the porcelain plates from the cabinet and began assembling his meal. "And mind you, give us peace while we have our repast. I won't have you chattering and underfoot while I enjoy the gossip."

Reena showed up punctually, carrying one of her wonderful pies. The three women sat to a table of scrumptious food.

Tara listened as the two chatted away about mutual friends. Tara cleared the dishes from the table as the two women continued to chat and knew the time for her revelations had come. She wasn't sure how to steer the conversation, and was almost relieved when Hilda suddenly changed the subject as Tara entered the room after moving the dirty dishes to the kitchen.

"Ah, my dear, this was a grand idea of yours, it was." She sat back and patted her large stomach. "I'm full to the brim, I am. Now then, you said there was something you wanted to tell me. Plans on the claiming, I'm thinking." The old lady smiled and looked at Reena.

Reena looked up at Tara with curious eyes.

"Well, in a way, you could say that." Tara hesitated. "If you'll excuse me, I will be right back. I think if I show you something, it will be easier."

Tara ran up the stairs, forgetting the ladylike manners that had almost become instinctive. In her room, she reached under her bed for the bag Reena had given her and pulled out her Runner clothing. For a moment she just sat there, holding the articles. She hadn't seen them in over a cycle. She could smell the leather. The embroidered symbol of her clan made her feel warm inside. This is who she was and that would not change.

Reena's mouth fell open as Tara entered the room with the clothes in her hands. "Child, what are you doing?" she whispered in amazement.

"What do you have there, girl?" Hilda looked up, not seeing the expression on Reena's face.

"Lord Darius asked me to do this." She laid the clothing on the table and spread them out.

Reena immediately recognized them. The embroidered symbol of the clan stood out plainly to see.

Hilda gasped in horror. "Where did you get those clothes?" She stood up quickly, and her hand went to her heart.

"Hilda, they're my clothes. I'm a Runner."

Hilda gasped.

Reena and Tara quickly were at her side and helped her back to the chair.

She stared at the clothing as if it would bite her if she dared look away. After a minute, she looked at Tara. "What is this you're saying?"

Tara sat next to Hilda, and Reena took her seat.

"I came to this land to see what the Gothman were really like. I heard the stories of a proud, large race of people, so different from my own. All I wanted was to see how you lived. I didn't expect to become so involved with your family," Tara said the last sentence quietly, almost to herself.

"Ah, so now you have a lord who's gone and claimed you. I daresay he can't figure out how to get out of this mess, and so he's sent you to me, he has. Tell me if I'm not right." Hilda tossed her hands up into the air.

"Well, my lady, I didn't know he claimed me when I moved in here." She glared at Reena.

Reena just stared back. She was leaning back in her chair with her arms crossed.

Tara could swear the look on her face was one of amusement. "He did finally tell me that he'd announced a claiming. But it was after I found out from Thelga at the grocery store. I was furious and ready to run from this land right then. I told his lordship that no one could claim me unless I said they could."

Reena couldn't help a giggle at this comment.

"I don't see what's so funny about this. To be sure, we have a problem on our hands, we do. The Lord of Gothman can't claim a Runner." Hilda looked at Reena.

At that moment, a change came over Hilda's face, and she looked as if she was about to say something. She looked at Reena with disbelief and alarm. Then, she looked from Reena to Tara and back again. Her mouth fell open as if she would say something.

The look on Reena's face changed as well, and Tara was sure she saw her shake her head ever so slightly.

Hilda closed her mouth.

"Do you love Lord Darius, child?" Reena asked Tara as she quickly turned her attention away from Hilda.

"I think I might."

"I've seen the two of them," Hilda said to Reena. Her tone had changed, and she sounded like she shared knowledge of a crime committed by Darius and Tara. "They act like they were made to be together, they do. You knew about this didn't you, old lady? I daresay you planned the whole thing!"

"Ah, she came to me the night she arrived." Reena waved her hand in front of her as if knocking Hilda's accusations out of the way. "She wanted to know the life of Gothman, she did. I didn't know she was coming."

"Reena, Runners are our enemy. You know as well as I do, she won't stay here. It's not her nature to stay put. She'll yearn for her old ways and…"

"My lady, I'm not your enemy." Tara put her hand on Hilda's. "I don't understand why our people consider each other enemies. We aren't a threat to each other."

"Ah, and you think you can change how Gothman feel about Runners, do you?" Hilda shook her head and clucked with her tongue.

"If she's claimed to the Lord of Gothman, it would be a good start." Reena was quick with her argument.

"You'd like it if that happened, wouldn't you?" Hilda stood up glaring at Reena. She looked at Tara, and her hands went to her wide girth. "His lordship must not have known you were a Runner when he made the claim. I don't know how he'll save face with his people. He has promise to be one of our greatest leaders."

"He did know I was a Runner. He knew all along." Tara wanted to jump up and stamp her foot. Why was she defending him?

"Did he really?" Reena was smiling again. "Hilda, he knew and he still claimed her. Maybe they were meant to be together."

"Ah, what a day that would be for you, wouldn't it my old friend? I'm not so old myself that I don't remember what happened over twenty winters ago." Hilda snapped her finger in the air. "My claim knew of your goings on with the Runners. Maybe he should've been rougher with you."

"Ah, old woman, but he wasn't. Then was not the time for Runners to be among us. But now! Times are changing. The Runners have not opposed the Gothman for many a winter. This generation has a fear of a people, but they know not why. You said it yourself. These two are in love. Tara will challenge him, that much I can guess now. Imagine it, Hilda. She could only make his kingdom stronger. For sure, I've heard you say a time or two that behind a good man is a good woman. What a match they will be, don't you think?"

Hilda was quiet. She looked at the clothes and then pushed her chair away from the table to stand.

Tara watched her move over to the clothes and pick up the cloth with the embroidered emblem on it.

Her chubby fingers traced the circle with the red drop of blood centered in the middle. "What is this?"

"It is the symbol of my clan."

"And what is the name of your clan?"

"The Blood Circle Clan."

"Ah, and who are your parents?"

"Patha is my papa, but not by birth. He found me as a toddler and brought me into his clan to be raised."

Hilda started to stomp out of the room, then stopped and turned around just as quickly. Crossing her arms, she glared at Reena. "Did you know she was coming to you?"

"No, Hilda, I told you already." Reena remained in her chair, but her lips narrowed to a fine line.

An animosity of some kind appeared between the two women, as if some old wound had suddenly been opened. "She caused quite a ruckus in the pines that night. The guards were out thick looking for her. She dodged them and made it to my house. I saw her for the first time when she came out of the woods."

Hilda stood there for a minute, thinking. Then, she picked up the clothes and handed them to Tara. "Put these on. I want to see you in them."

Tara took the clothes and looked at Hilda confused.

"You've been with us for over a cycle now. You've lived like a Gothman, but you're a Runner. My heritage means a lot to me, and I daresay your heritage means a lot to you, it does. Put those on and feel your heritage. Do it now, girl." Hilda's voice shook with emotion.

Tara left the room to change her clothes. She trotted up the stairs, feeling queasy from the excitement of being able to wear her Runner clothing again. A tightening in her gut also existed, because she didn't understand the undercurrent between Hilda and Reena. There was something the two of them weren't telling her.

The leather felt so good next to her skin. Her feet rejoiced to be in her boots again. She wrapped the cloth around her face and went back in to the dining room. Her soft boots were quiet on the floor, and the two women did not hear her return.

"I want her to be able to tell me she'll not have my grandchildren and then leave in the night, I do. Those clothes will bring back reality to her, I daresay. She's been pretending, and she'll come to her senses if she faces who she is, she will."

"You want her to leave," Reena's voice sounded strained.

"And you can't make her stay anymore than you could make her papa stay." There was a sting in Hilda's voice.

"You'll not speak of that. I have your promise!"

"She can't continue to deny who she is and where her place is."

"I am not pretending, my lady. I've known who I was the entire time I was here." The two women looked up as the Runner entered the room.

Hilda gasped.

"I've taught your youngest son to ride a motorcycle and have raced his lord through the hills on my motorcycle. Lord Darius had it brought here. It's in the shed right now. I've not been able to suppress my heritage, although, at first, I'll admit I tried. If I stay here, I'll stay as a Runner, and Darius knows this."

Tara proudly stood in front of the two women. She wished she could live among these people openly wearing the symbol of her clan but she knew that wouldn't come to pass…at least not yet.

"Ah, I see. Well Darius asked you to tell me and so you have. Now I know. It's done. I'm an old lady, I am. If his Lordship is asking for my blessing, he knows how I feel about you. That has not changed, no. You have a good heart, lass." Hilda sat back down and looked exasperated.

Tara moved to the old lady, bent, and kissed her on the cheek. She then did the same to Reena. "I don't know your reasons, but you are a responsible party to all of this and I mean to find out why," she whispered in Reena's ear.

"Well, child, you best get back out of those clothes before someone thinks you are attacking us instead of kissing us, yes." Hilda grabbed her cloth napkin and dabbed her cheeks and neck. "Go now."

Tara noticed the woman's hand shook, then ran upstairs, changed, and returned her clothes to the bag under her bed. She came back down in time to see Reena gathering her things and preparing to leave. Tara followed Hilda and Reena on to the front porch.

"I'll be seeing an announcement to a claiming party before long, I expect." Reena walked across the yard to her car. "We'll have to make her a dress for certain, old woman. Goodness knows she can't sew a stitch."

"I wonder why she's so anxious to see me claimed to your son." Tara watched Reena drive away and then turned to face the plump older woman.

"Now, child, I can't go and tell you her thoughts, I can't. She'll have to do that herself." Hilda headed upstairs, claiming exhaustion and the need for a nap.

* * * * *

Lord Darius returned the next afternoon and was greeted in the yard by his younger brother.

"I'll help fight if you need me." Torgo sounded delighted at the thought.

"Ahh, will you now?" Darius didn't look at his brother but slid off his bike and stretched.

"I can ride my motorcycle pretty well," Torgo continued. "And I could run errands, or do anything you wanted."

Tara couldn't help but smile as Torgo tried to receive his brother's approval. She'd been walking through the pines at the edge of the meadow, and her heart jumped when she heard Darius' motorcycle pulling into the backyard. She wanted to run and greet him and let him know how she had missed him. Instead, she stood, sheltered by the branches surrounding her, and watched the strong man push his bike around the back of the shed, amusement on his face as he listened to Torgo ramble.

Torgo finally ran to get water and rags so Darius could clean the mud from his bike and returned just as his older brother was opening the shed. The young boy disappeared inside along with Darius. She wished desperately to hear what the two were talking about, but since that wasn't possible, she continued walking across the backyard toward them.

Torgo saw her first and ran to greet her.

Darius turned and watched as she moved toward them. Their eyes met, and there was a look on his face she had not yet seen. He looked exhausted and very serious.

Guilt ran through her blood as she thought of him creating strategies and hearing reports from his scouts while she sat and dined with old women. She felt she should have been at his side. She had knowledge of the Sea People. She had heard many stories and had briefly encountered them herself.

Tara wanted to draw his bath for him, and rub the exhaustion from his body, as he told her the stories he'd experienced. She had grown up watching men and women greet their warrior spouses after a conflict. Much romance occurred after the return of troops. But Darius wasn't to the point where he would share his experience with her, she feared.

If the rumors of the pending invasion proved true, she intended to share her knowledge. She knew the Sea People to be an untrusting lot, greedy and paranoid. They sought only what would suit their own needs. They were a people not to be trusted. Many of the stories she heard said they were a race addicted to some type of opiate drug, and that was how their ruler kept them in line. She found such stories extraordinary and had a hard time believing them. If they were true, she knew their actions would be hard to predict in battle.

As she neared the shed, Torgo grabbed towels to clean the bike, and Darius reached for her.

"I raced some of the other boys after school," Torgo said.

But Tara hardly heard him.

Darius stroked her cheek, but then slipped his arm around her when she walked into him for a hug. "I will be…" he whispered in her ear, but wasn't able to finish.

"Tara, oh my dear, there you are. Come at once, the walkntalk made its noise, it did." Hilda waved her arm toward the house.

Darius broke off what he was about to say, instead looking at his Mama.

"And I do fear there is some importance to it, yes." Hilda's tone was strained, and the pair hurried to the house.

They entered the kitchen and found Hilda rushing about, a distracted look on her face, but she didn't offer an immediate explanation for her behavior. As she moved items around on the pantry shelves, they heard her mutter to herself, "I'm losing my mind, I am. There aren't good times ahead, no."

"Woman! Have you gone batty?" Darius spoke from behind Tara.

"My Lordship, son of mine, I answered the walkntalk."

"You said that already. What is so incredible about the walkntalk, woman?" Darius' frustration sounded in his tone.

"Oh dear. Tara, Reena called and asked for you at once. She said, uh, there are," Hilda began, but then turned in the pantry doorway with several small jars in her plump hands. Her pallor didn't look good. "I mean, she has company, yes. She said some of your, uh," she paused as Torgo slipped into the kitchen eyeing a plate of food on the counter. "Your family has arrived. She needs you to take these herbs to her. I know they are used for medicinal reasons, so someone must be hurt."

Tara didn't wait to hear more. She rushed from the kitchen and up the stairs to her bedroom.

"Tara!" Darius' bark echoed off the walls.

She ignored him as she ran to her closet and quickly flipped through her dresses until she found one more practical than the frilly thing she had on at the moment. It was made from a knitted material that moved easily with her body and would allow her freedom of movement to help in whatever way she could.

"What are you doing?" Darius appeared in her doorway. He leaned against the doorjamb and watched her.

Tara glanced up and realized she'd forgotten to shut the door. Already having taken off one dress to put the other on, she worked desperately to get the zipper in back to close. "Would you help me with this zipper?"

He walked toward her, turned her around, and zipped her dress. "You'll take the herbs and come right back."

"I'll be back as soon as I find out why there are Runners at Reena's." She squatted down on all fours and reached under her bed.

"There are Sea People ready to attack Gothman. I'll not have you running around the countryside."

Tara ignored him. She took her Runner clothing out of the bag and set them on the bed. She slid the flat softened leather boots on her feet.

* * * * *

Darius watched her in fascination; this was the first he'd seen of her Runner clothing. More curious to him though were the several guns she'd pulled out of an inner sleeve in the bag and how she checked their ammunition like a seasoned professional. One weapon in particular caught his attention. Darius leaned over and picked up the small laser to look at it. "This is what you used to shoot the trash can that day, isn't it?"

"Yes." She continued to get herself ready.

He put down the laser, then picked up the largest of the three guns and strode over to the balcony. He opened the doors, aimed the gun at a group of trees outlining the edge of the meadow, and pulled the trigger. A branch of a tree a good half-mile away fell to the ground. Darius grunted as he scrutinized the weapon closely.

Tara reached into the bag and pulled out a small case. She quickly opened it and removed a small flat disc. It was more minute than any coin and as flat as a piece of paper. She placed the disc on the edge of her finger and walked up behind the tall lord.

"I like this one." He held up the large weapon.

"It has four more shots on this cartridge." She reached around him and pointed to the attachment on the side. "It works best at a distance. If it's used at close range, it emits a large explosion. You may keep it. I'll do with these."

Lord Darius put his arm around her waist and pulled her close to him with some roughness. She lost her breath when he flattened her to him with a possessive grip. He continued to hold the powerful weapon in one hand that fell to his side. But with his other arm, he held her in a death grip.

She put both hands up around his neck and gently stuck the small disc to the back of his neck. The disc held its place under Darius' curls, and she prayed he wouldn't detect it. She had never applied the device in such an intimate fashion and managed to keep a neutral expression at her success. Darius didn't notice what she had done.

"It's important that you listen to me, now. Gothman is going to be attacked sooner than I anticipated. I want you to be safe." Darius searched her face with his eyes as he spoke.

Tara pushed away and slipped a harness over her dress into which she slid two guns. "What do you know of the Sea People? Have you had contact with them before?"

* * * * *

He saw something in her he hadn't noticed before. She was preparing for battle, and he realized it would take many guards and locks and chains to keep this woman at home. The woman was a Runner, though, and staying put wasn't her nature. He wondered if he would ever be able to calm that trait in her. An emotion washed through him that he couldn't readily identify. Tara appealed to him because she was wild, untamed, outspoken and beyond sexy. Would taming any of those qualities make her less appealing? He worried the answer to that was yes.

"This is the first time they've come this close to Gothman, it is. I'll not stand for their threats, though."

"They've communicated with you?"

"I've received messages saying the Gothman have grown too large and are pushing against their borders."

"That isn't true. The Gothman borders run into the Freelands. Darius, have you never been out of Gothman?"

He narrowed his eyebrows and his gray eyes darkened. He wasn't pleased that she questioned his knowledge or worldliness. "Are you saying I can't rule this land because I've never been outside its borders?" He scowled. "My papa didn't need the help of outsiders and neither do I."

"Knowing your enemy helps to defeat them."

"So now you are telling me how to rule." He looked fierce, but then he smiled and stroked her cheek. He didn't have time to get riled at her right now. "You worry about getting back here safely."

* * * * *

Tara put her black leather jacket over the dress and folded the clothes she had on a minute ago. Grabbing the bag, now empty and ready for Hilda's herbs, she headed for the door.

He followed her quickly and grabbed her arm. "I expect you home within the hour, I do." He kissed her firmly on the lips.

"I'll be fine." She returned his kiss and looked into his eyes. "You'll hear from me. You need me."

She reached up and pulled a band off his leather jacket sleeve that bore the seal of the Gothman and shoved it in to her bag.

"I'll represent two nations today." She smiled and kissed him again.

"Tell your people the Gothman would appreciate it if the Runners would stand with them in battle against the Sea People."

She looked at him with surprise before she pulled away and left the room. Her leather boots were silent as she ran down the stairs.

Hilda looked at Tara's outfit as the girl reached the bottom step, but didn't say anything. She saw her son standing at the top of the stairs with the large Runner gun in his hand. Her mouth opened, but she closed it and quietly handed the keys to her car and the herbs to Tara.

Hilda's car moved a lot faster than Reena's, but it still seemed to Tara that it took her forever to get through the town and up the hill toward Reena's house. Two Runner motorcycles were parked in front of Reena's house when she pulled up. Tara immediately recognized one of them to be Patha's. She got out of the car and ran to the house.

There was no one in the living room area, and the house seemed very quiet. Instinctively, she pulled out the small laser and held it in front of her as she silently moved toward the hallway.

The door to Reena's bedroom was open, and she pointed the gun at the empty room. She walked to the window opening to the backyard, but she didn't see anyone. A group of five pictures on the dresser next to the window caught her eye.

The first picture she saw was of a small child picking flowers in a meadow. Others depicted the same girl at different ages.

The last picture was of a girl in her adolescence sitting on a small motorcycle. Tara cocked her head sideways in puzzlement. The motorcycle looked very familiar. She looked back at the other pictures again.

They were all of her!

Tara's heart raced, and she wiped her suddenly damp palms down her hips while staring at the pictures. What in the name of all of the heavens was Reena doing with pictures of her at different ages? She hadn't even known they had been taken.

"Tara?"

She jumped at the sound of her name coming from the other room. She heard the front door close, and it sounded like several people were entering the house. Tara walked to the doorway, gun in one hand and pictures in the other.

Reena called out again. "Tara?"

"I'm here." Tara took in the scene greeting her.

Reena stood in the middle of the room while Patha and one of his guards struggled to help a Runner she didn't recognize to the couch.

"Did you bring the herbs?" Reena asked.

Tara nodded and pointed to her bag on the edge of the couch as she ran to the large old man, setting the gun and pictures on the table beside her. "Patha! It's so good to see you."

After settling the Runner onto the couch, Patha reached his arms out as she literally jumped into them. He picked her up off the ground and hugged her so tightly she lost her breath. When he put her down, she felt dizzy for a moment and had to steady herself on the back of the couch before she could smile up at the man she called Papa.

"What brings you this far from home?" She looked from one Runner to the other and then at Patha.

"Reena's the best doctor in the area, and we needed her." Patha squeezed her wrists with powerfully large hands. "Look at you, child. You look mighty sharp in that dress." He held her hands out in front of her and took a good look. "I do believe she's put on a little weight." Patha looked at Reena for confirmation. "What do you think?"

"Maybe Gothman suits her." Reena had mixed together a salve from the herbs and coated the Runner's wounded leg. She finished by tying a bandage around it then stood and moved to stand by Patha. "Your man should be fine. Mind you, those wild boar lashes can get infected, but I've got him good and cleaned up, I do."

"We're closer to you than the clansite right now," Patha said. "I knew you could take good care of him."

"Tara, what have you brought here?" Reena picked up the pictures from the side table and flipped through them quickly.

"I found them on your dresser when I was looking for you. They're pictures of me. What are you doing with them?" Tara watched Reena glance up at Patha and she studied both their faces. Her papa hid his thoughts well, but he was definitely concerned about something. Then, as if in silent communication, the two older adults turned their gazes to her. She narrowed her eyes. "What's going on here?"

Reena looked at her patient, ignoring Tara's question. "How does that bandage feel?"

"I'll make it," the Runner answered and reached for the other man, who helped him to his feet and allowed the Runner to use him as a crutch.

"Let's put him in the bedroom on the right, yes," Reena instructed. "I'll watch him for a bit, I will, make sure no infection sets in."

"Reena, you didn't answer me," Tara persisted, after the two men had entered the bedroom.

Reena kept her back to Tara as she stared at the hallway and the open bedroom door where the two Runners were. "Tara, I'm your mama." Reena spoke the words barely above a whisper, and she didn't turn to face Tara.

"What?" Tara gasped, certain she had misheard. "It sounded like you just said—"

"I did," Reena interrupted and turned to face Tara. "I am your mama."

Tara reached for the back of the couch to steady herself. Her mouth fell open without her noticing and the room suddenly began spinning. "My...mama?" She could barely utter the words.

"Come outside with us, child." Patha pulled Tara to him and placed his other hand gently on Reena's shoulder. "It's time you knew the truth."

The uninjured Runner appeared from the hallway, and Reena turned to him. "Slice some pie for you two," she said, gesturing toward her kitchen.

Tara noticed Reena's hand shaking and turned to the kitchen, thinking she could help make the Runner feel more at home.

"I can handle it." The Runner smiled at Tara and waved the group toward the door. "Go share your stories. If there is pie in the kitchen, I will find it."

Patha chuckled and again placed his hands on the two women, guiding them to the door.

Tara followed them onto the front porch in a dazed stupor. She settled on the steps while the two of them sat in the porch swing together, Patha's large fingers around Reena's small hand.

Her gaze strayed to their intertwined fingers. "I thought my mama died and that you never knew her name. I never guessed…I mean, I never dreamed." She shook her head, all the while keeping her gaze on their clasped hands.

"Child, I don't know where to begin." Reena's eyes welled with tears. Oh, how she'd waited for this day. "Patha and I have known each other for a very long time. He would come see me from time to time, but staying for too long was not his way, it wasn't. I'd been established as the doctor of these parts, and Lord Jovis would not permit me to leave."

Reena took a deep breath.

Patha patted her hand. "Lord Jovis had a fine time looking the other way, when I continued to come see you," Patha chuckled, and Reena nodded, both silent for a moment as they relived the memory.

"When I found out I was pregnant I was so happy. I had a part of Patha that would stay with me, and I was free of the claiming forever, I was. For a while, I entertained the thought of Patha settling down with me here, yes. Ah, but Lord Jovis would not hear of it, and Patha was not the settling down type. I kept you until you were about three, I did. Ah, you were beautiful even then."

"Why didn't you keep me?" Tara pulled her knees to her chest, forgetting the Gothman dress she wore. She turned on the porch steps, so she sat facing her Mama.

"Lord Jovis wanted to have you claimed to his son, his first-born son that is, with you both being just children, yes. Tara, it wasn't the life I wanted for you. I wanted you educated, free to make your own choices, I did. It wasn't the life you would have in Gothman. The next time Patha came through we talked about it, and he agreed to take you with him and make you part of his clan." Reena wiped a tear off her cheek. Another one immediately replaced it. "My dear child, it was the hardest thing I ever done in my whole life, it was. I just about couldn't hold my emotions when you told me who you were the night you arrived here. Oh dear girl, you're everything I hoped you'd be, you are." Several streams of tears traced paths down her cheeks now, and Tara moved over quickly and sat at her feet.

"I had no idea." Tara was completely overwhelmed. Her throat felt thick, and she realized she was shaking. "Patha, why didn't you tell me? You really are my papa? I wish you would have told me."

"Reena didn't want you to feel any obligation to visit her. She was afraid you'd be claimed once Lord Jovis knew you were back. He wanted you for his son almost before you were born. The man felt you came from good blood, I guess." Patha chuckled and wrapped his arm around Reena. "As you grew and became more beautiful, we both knew the second you were on Gothman territory, the first man who saw you would have you. When you told me you were leaving to do some exploring, it didn't surprise me when I got word you were here. I knew no man would mess with you if you didn't want it. You are a trained warrior now, not the helpless child you once were." Patha shook his head at his daughter. "I would actually pity the man who would take you on. You've two very stubborn parents, child. And you are an incredible warrior."

"Thank you, Patha. It's an honor to hear that from you." Tara couldn't stop the tears any longer. She let them fall as she absorbed this incredible news. She sniffed loudly and wiped her teary face on her sleeve.

"So, suddenly I'm no longer an orphan. This is too much to have in my head right now. I need to focus on other things." Tara took a deep breath and turned to look at the tall pines surrounding the house.

Patha had told Tara that her mama's dying wish was that he raise her as his own. Well, her mama wasn't dead, the woman had sent her away. Tara figured she should feel abandoned, but had to admit she was grateful to be the person she was and not a Gothman female, living in ignorant suppression.

Tara realized she would be able to know her mama better if she stayed here. She would be a Runner in Gothman territory, which was exactly as it should be.

She shook her head to clear it, then stood, and stared at the watery-eyed woman who looked up at her. Tara saw concern suddenly cross Reena's face. The woman worried Tara would hate her for the choice she had made. Maybe she'd lived with that worry for winters. She'd made an incredible sacrifice so that Tara could have a life of opportunity. And now Tara stood before her mama, heir to the leader of all Runner clans. Tara straightened and smiled.

"Hello, Mama." Tara couldn't keep her voice from cracking as she held her arms out to Reena.

"Oh, Tara," Reena cried, and fresh tears streamed down her face as she got up and hugged her daughter.

"I have so much I want to talk to you about," Tara said. "But now isn't the time."

Tara looked over Reena's shoulder at Patha, who smiled at the two women in front of him. "Patha, there is about to be war, I fear."

"You refer to the Sea People." Patha's smile disappeared.

"I'll join the Gothman and fight. Lord Darius will have the Runners stand with him if they're willing. Patha, he needs us. That man has no knowledge of the world outside of his kingdom. He doesn't even know what he's fighting. I gave him an Eliminator, but he'll need much more than that."

A look of surprise came over Patha's face, and he looked at Reena. "So, the son of Lord Jovis is not narrow-minded and full of hatred?"

For winters, Patha despised Jovis for keeping him from the woman he loved. Tara never had a whole family to love her because of the man. Patha could have taken Reena from Gothman, but Jovis would have viewed it as an act of aggression. Patha couldn't risk an attack on the Runners because of his personal feelings. He and Reena had suffered their loss quietly. But now Jovis was gone, and the son wanted his daughter. Patha wouldn't put Tara through the pain he'd lived with if she wanted this man. "Do you love him?"

"Yes, Patha, I believe I do. He's a good man. He claimed me, but I told him I wouldn't be claimed until I was ready. He knew I was a Runner; he could have arrested me, but he didn't." Tara realized she'd officially stated her love for Darius and that declaration made her feel very warm inside. Tara still had her arms wrapped around Reena, and gave the woman a slight squeeze.

Reena returned the affection and hugged her daughter.

"And are you ready to accept his claim?" Patha searched her eyes for more of an answer than she could give him with words.

"Gothman don't feel a need for their women to accept a claim," Tara said. "But yes, I think I am ready to accept it."

"Does he know this?"

"I haven't told him yet."

A small smile appeared on Patha's face, and then he quickly grew serious. "I'll have a thousand Runners here in a couple of days. Right now we have about fifty, but don't worry, the rest will come." Patha nodded authoritatively. "Where's his army?"

"I believe the Gothman armies are preparing to head south."

"Why are they heading in that direction?" Patha looked surprised.

"He told me his scouts saw the Sea People heading in from the south."

"There are no Sea People there. We've been south of here within the past few days when we traded with the River People. It was when we came around the edges of Gothman territory to the west and then to the north that the Sea People became more abundant. They are traveling with tanks and heavy artillery from the reports I've received. For the most part, we were able to avoid them. Some of the clans coming down from the north to meet us weren't as successful. I've heard through our landlink transmissions that there have been many deaths."

"Patha, this doesn't make sense." Tara's stomach fisted into worried knots. If Darius took his army to the south, Gothman would be very vulnerable from the north and an easy target. She distinctly remembered he'd told her his scouts said they saw Sea

People to the South. "Patha, somehow Darius has some bad information. I need to warn him!"

Tara released Reena, and before the old man could say anything further, she ran into the house and grabbed her bag. She pulled out the flat landlink and punched keys with a vengeance. The tracer she'd put on Darius' neck quickly told her he'd left his home and was headed south.

"Patha, Darius has already left." Tara looked at Reena, noticing the worried expression on her face. Her mama had entered the house with Patha behind her, and now Reena moved to the stove and reached for the kettle. "Reena, I'd like to send Hilda and Torgo to stay with you for the time being. I believe they'd be safer here. If the Sea People target the area, they would go after Darius' home. This place is isolated, and we could post guards to protect you. Will you have them?"

Patha gestured to the Runner who sat on the couch with a landlink on his lap. "I can leave Glib here with you for the time being. He can monitor the area."

"Of course, child, they can stay here." Reena walked around the counter and put her hands on Tara's waist. "I know you will go to battle with Lord Darius, yes."

"Oh yes," Tara said. "I'd be of no help staying in hiding with the women."

Reena smiled but looked serious, almost sad. "My daughter finally knows me, and she could be going to war."

"Reena, don't worry. I'll be back."

"Tara, you're with child. Did you know that?"

Tara and Patha both looked at her with amazement.

"How could I be?" Tara was ready to disagree.

"There's only one way." Reena smiled.

Tara looked down quickly.

"I'd say four or five weeks. I know the look and I've never been wrong, no. You take very good care of yourself and my grandchild, you hear?"

Tara stared at Patha and Reena but didn't say anything. Instead she grabbed her bag, turned slowly, and left the cottage.

That last bit of information was one piece of news too much. She was too bewildered to form her thoughts.

* * * * *

Reena watched as Tara drove down the hill in Hilda's car. "Tell me all of this is a good thing." She looked up into Patha's face for reassurance.

"I'll let you know after I meet this Darius person. What do you know about him?"

"He has a lot of power but no experience, I'd say. People that get in his way have a tendency to fall into bad luck, so to speak. I don't know whether or not he's good enough for our daughter. But I daresay I'm hoping Tara will stay here. I'd like get to know my daughter, and she can live here as a Runner." Reena pursed her lips.

Patha wrapped his large arms around Reena's petite frame. "It will be tough on her at first, living here, but their union would make the most powerful nation in Nuworld."

Reena stared at the spot where Tara had disappeared down the road. With that one statement, she understood Patha's thoughts. He was more concerned about how powerful they'd be if the two were claimed. She was more concerned about her daughter's happiness.

And Reena hoped the challenges Gothman would bring Tara would satisfy her.

Chapter Seven

%

Tara pulled up in front of the Bryton house, ran up the porch stairs, and called for Hilda and Torgo. The two of them appeared after several minutes. "I'm going to send you two to stay with Reena."

"Certainly Darius wouldn't leave us here if he didn't think we were safe." Hilda crossed her fleshy arms over her bosom and stared at Tara. "We should stay right here, I'm thinking."

"Darius doesn't realize the number of Sea People surrounding Gothman right now. But there are Runners here now, and with our equipment we can help Gothman. These Sea People have attacked and killed many of us, but they'll be no match for our two armies combined. We'll have them defeated in no time," Tara reassured the two worried faces staring at her.

"You talked to Runners?" Torgo's eyes grew large.

"Yes, child," she smiled and ruffled his hair. "It'll be quite a great story when I tell it to you."

She realized at that moment she loved more than Darius. With Hilda and Torgo standing there in the living room looking helpless and worried, she felt a need to protect them from harm.

Hilda had taken Tara into her home. Given a stranger the room right next to hers: *where a girl would be safe*. She'd taught Tara how to cook...very patiently...and Tara knew she wasn't the best of pupils. Torgo had immediately taken to her. He eagerly learned everything she offered to teach him. He'd been so excited when he first successfully hit a target. The look on his face when he first rode his motorcycle without her sitting behind him wasn't something she'd soon forget. These two had taken her in as family. She loved both of them as well as feeling love for Darius. Now she had two parents as well. Tara never would have expected her life to turn out like this several cycles ago.

"Now quickly, go get some clothes for the next few days." She followed them up the stairs.

"I still don't like the idea of being sent away from my own home," Hilda grumbled. "And by a Runner no less."

Tara decided not to comment since the woman moved to her room and closed the door. Once in her own room, she'd quickly changed into her Runner clothing. Completely dressed for battle, she sat down on the bed and pulled out the little landlink from her black bag she had taken to Reena's. Scanning for a minute, she looked for a local server to which she could tie in. It didn't take long; soon she was communicating with some of the Runners on the edge of Gothman.

It felt good to be connected with a transmission again. Ever since she'd been in Gothman her link had been down. There'd been no main server close enough for her to stay connected. Now that a Runner clan had moved close to Gothman, she'd be able to communicate with her people.

"This is Tara of the Blood Circle Clan," Tara whispered the words as she typed. "Requesting any known information on Sea People in the area."

Tara sent the message to the two clans she'd managed to locate. She would check back soon for a response.

"Come on, let's go!" she yelled as she left her room and headed down the stairs.

"Whoa!" Torgo came down the steps and froze as he saw Tara fully dressed as a Runner sitting on the couch with her landlink on her lap. "Tara, is that you?"

"Torgo, never fear a Runner." She beckoned him. "A Runner will never attack someone unless attacked first."

"I wasn't scared. You look cool!" Torgo sat next to Tara and stared at the flat screen. "And I guessed you were a Runner all along."

Tara didn't know whether to believe the boy or not, but ruffled his already tousled curls, and then pointed to her screen. "I'm linked now. I can communicate with any Runner in the world this way." She pointed to the map displayed on the screen. "I can also tell where Lord Darius and his army are."

"You're kidding. How do you do that?"

"It's Oldworld knowledge. It's easy enough though. It won't take long to teach you."

Torgo was leaning over looking at the screen when Hilda came down the stairs.

"So, you're a Runner now, are you?" She looked at Tara almost disapprovingly.

"Hilda, I've always been a Runner." In the older woman, Tara could see some of the prejudice that had obviously kept her son ignorant of other races. "Now go, both of you. Reena is expecting you. Remember, if you see any Runners at her place, they're not your enemy."

"Can't I stay with you and fight, Tara?" Torgo asked. "Why are you sending me away with the women? I'm not a child anymore, you know."

"I know." Tara faced Torgo, snapped her heels together, and clasped her hands behind her back. "Stand at attention, and let me give you your orders."

Torgo imitated her stance and grew serious with wide gray eyes glowing in excitement.

"These women need protection, and right now I have no soldiers to send with them. You will escort your mama to Reena's. And you will stay there, guarding them with your life. Understood?"

"Yes. Understood." Torgo broke out in a grin, and before Tara had time to react he reached for her and gave her a quick hug. "Be careful, okay?"

Tara smiled when Torgo released her. "I always am."

Torgo hopped out the front door ready for the adventure. Hilda did not look at Tara as she left.

As soon as the front door shut, Tara jumped up and ran to the shed out back. There was a lock on the door. Tara sighed and looked around the yard to see who might be watching. No one was in sight. She pulled out her laser, and a small blast caused the lock to fall to the ground. Within seconds, she rolled her bike out of the shed and snapped her landlink on it.

Tara narrowed in on Darius' signal. He was south of town and from what she could tell, twenty or so others were with him. She scanned for local roads and was pleased to find a current map. She took off at top speed.

Who would have led Darius to believe he should go south? This was now the question at hand.

Tara considered the matter. The Sea People approached from the northwest, which made sense since their home was to the west. Darius would be protected from any attacks if he was in the southern region, but Gothman would not. Who would want to place Gothman in such a predicament?

Within a quarter mile of the signal, Tara slowed to a stop and scanned for Gothman communication. It wasn't hard for her landlink to pick up their simplex form of transmitting, although static crackled on her multiplex system. Her equipment wasn't accustomed to such antiquated forms of communication. She tapped into the Gothman conversation and clicked on her speakers, which she usually kept off. The audio was poor but leaning forward she heard conversation through the small, attached speakers on either side of her landlink.

"He'll be within sight in a few minutes. Be ready now."

"Have you had any further communication?"

"I have. They're coming across Runners."

"Is that a problem?"

"It's a passing clan, it shouldn't be."

Tara eased her bike forward into the forest and slowed to a stop. There, up in the tree, a Gothman was lodged between two branches talking on a walkntalk. Tara killed the motor and sat silently, waiting to see what would be there within a few minutes.

She heard voices and saw movement through the trees ahead.

So did the Gothman in the tree. He pulled a gun from his jacket and aimed at the group approaching.

Tara watched the Gothman focus on his target, and realized with horror who the man planned to kill. One of the voices was Darius'. He barked orders, and the booming sound of his voice sent a tightness through her insides. Tara slid off her bike without a sound, moved to the tree, hoisted herself up and pulled the man to the ground. Before he could yell out, she shot him in the back. Grabbing the walkntalk she crept behind some nearby bushes and hunted for the dead man's companion.

"What is that smell, my lord?"

Tara froze, with the walkntalk held out in front of her and watched as Darius approached with a group of his men.

"I smell it too. I daresay it smells like something's burned," another guard answered.

Darius passed by without seeing her. "That it does." Darius stopped within feet of her.

She focused on the back of his boots from her hiding place in the bushes.

"It smells like flesh burning."

"Should we search the area, my lord?"

The group of men stopped with Darius, and the sound of their boots shuffling over the undergrowth showed Tara they weren't concerned about concealing their whereabouts.

Could she communicate with him on this thing? She didn't know how to switch channels or to make sure a channel was private. Before she could act, however, the box crackled and a voice came through the walkntalk. Tara knew if the guards hadn't been so noisy, they would have heard the walkntalk she held.

"Why didn't you get him?" a voice said. "Mikel will be furious."

Tara frowned. Mikel was Darius' brother.

There was movement in a tree farther in the woods. She ran forward, and someone jumped from the tree and shot at her.

"Who is firing?" one of Darius' men yelled.

"Over there!" Darius barked the command. "I see movement."

"You're a Runner," hissed the man who had tried to gun her down. He aimed his gun directly at her chest.

"And you're a dead man," Tara whispered through clenched teeth. The whistling sound of the weapon pierced the air, and the man fell to the ground.

It was the guard who had tried to attack her. Now, why didn't that surprise her?

"It's that smell again." Lord Darius and his men were soon surrounding the dead man's body. They coughed and covered their mouths with gloved hands as they stared at the man who had been sliced wide open by the laser.

"What was Judo doing back here?" one of Lord Darius' soldiers asked, as he stared at the charred body.

Tara watched Darius as he studied the dead man. She guessed he'd never seen a man killed by a laser before. Yet his expression remained blank. If his emotions were that much in check, then he was a better warrior than she. Her emotions swarmed around her, making it hard to concentrate. Darius needed protection. Gothman could be attacked in the near future. And for some reason, it appeared Darius had an internal problem.

"I thought he was down with the other troops, my lord," a guard standing next to Darius said. "Maybe he was trying to get word to us about who ever shot at him."

"We've been all across this land, and there's no indication that any Sea People have been here. If he wanted to tell me something, I'd think he could've talked through the walkntalk. It's right here." Lord Darius squatted to take the walkntalk off the dead man and then studied the laser wound on the side of his body. He searched the foliage and was silent for a moment.

Tara knew he realized a Gothman gun couldn't have killed in that fashion. She pushed the button on the walkntalk in her hand. "I need to talk to you alone," she whispered into the little box. She took a chance contacting him in that manner, but it made sense that the walkntalk by the corpse and the one she'd taken from the other dead man would be on the same channel. After all, it appeared as if these two, now dead men, had been collaborating on a scheme with Mikel.

* * * * *

Lord Darius quickly looked around him. His men hadn't heard Tara's transmission. Where was she?

An intense desire to wrap his fingers around her Runner neck overwhelmed his thoughts momentarily. Tara was risking her life out here, and not knowing where she was at this precise moment brought his blood to a boil. His scowl slowly changed to a small smile as he realized he was going to enjoy the challenge of taming his Runner claim.

"Let's head back to camp." He stood and kept a wary eye on his surroundings. "Something's not right here. I want to confirm that the Sea People are south of Gothman, I do. Grab Judo and haul him back."

He stood in the forest watching and listening as his men slowly dragged the body toward the bikes. Tara was somewhere in the woods. He didn't like the fact that she was here, but he couldn't do anything about it.

What was she up to? He thought about all the stories he'd heard about Runners over the winters. They were rumored to be better soldiers than Gothman. While he questioned that, there was no doubt Tara's body was tuned into a well-oiled machine. He knew that first-hand...the toned thighs she wrapped around him with the strength of someone twice her size...the way she hung onto him... He shook his head. What was he doing? Now was not the time to get lost in the remembered pleasures of her body.

Closing his eyes, Darius listened. Concentrate, man, he told himself. *Don't let a Runner outperform your skills.* He squinted to see better and looked in the direction where he thought he'd just heard something. There! Through the bushes! Something in black. He moved through the trees quickly and silently.

He had her in sight as she reached her bike and straddled it. He approached her from behind, wrapping his arms around her with blinding speed and cupping his hand over her mouth.

Instantly, her body lurched backward off the bike. She shoved herself into her aggressor. Her body had more pack to it than he might have guessed. She pulled her legs up and slammed her heels into his knees. He felt excruciating pain, but determination prevailed.

He decided she must know it was him and was trying to convince him she could fight. She twisted her body and thrashed against his. He tightened the arm around her chest until he was afraid he would smash her rib cage if she didn't succumb.

Darius was impressed by her fight and struggled to keep his balance. He tightened his grip on her just slightly until she was gasping for breath. She stopped thrashing her legs. "What are you doing here?" he whispered into her ear.

* * * * *

Tara struggled to turn far enough within the constraining arms to verify that it was indeed Darius holding her. She relaxed as he slowly removed his hand from her mouth and slid it sensuously around her neck.

"You've been fed wrong information," she whispered. "Hopefully, your spies are dead. I don't detect any other Gothman in the area other than those behind us and about twenty or so down the hill." She stopped and gasped for breath.

"What are you talking about?" He turned her around quickly and gripped her arms.

"The Sea People are north and northwest of Gothman. They're heavily armed and coming in tanks. You need to move your troops quickly." She paused for a moment, confirming they were alone by listening to the sounds around them. She pulled her shirt down, straightening it. "I do believe Mikel fed you false information to get you out here and kill you."

A look Tara couldn't identify crossed Lord Darius' face. "I didn't know he was warrior enough to try such a stunt."

"I heard your men talking on their walkntalk." She paused, trying to read his reaction to what she was telling him. "There'll be a thousand Runners meeting you at the northern border in about two days. Your defense needs to be strong to hold the Sea People off until then." Tara attached her landlink and began punching keys. She searched for a moment, then smiled. "Patha's on line. He's verified reinforcement."

"Patha of the Blood Circle Clan?" He frowned. "How do you know Patha?"

"He's my papa."

"I see."

Tara realized that his lack of reaction meant he already knew about her heritage. That or he didn't trust her answers.

He murmured, "My papa knew him."

"So I've heard."

"I will confirm your information." He started to walk away and then turned to look at her. "I'd hate to think of what might have happened if you hadn't interfered."

"I'm not interfering."

Darius saw her smile through her headscarf.

"What are you going to do about Mikel?"

"He'll be taken care of." His voice was quiet, and his gray eyes melted her insides as he looked down at her. He tried to kiss her, but she pulled her bike to the side and started it.

She rolled the bike forward, its engine almost too quiet to hear. "I've made my decision. I'll let your claim stand." She didn't wait for a response, but accelerated and left him standing there.

Arriving back at the house, she set up camp in her bedroom. She propped the landlink on the desk and opened the balcony doors so she could better hear any arrivals. Confirming she was still on line, she then searched for Runners in the area.

"This is Tara, of the Blood Circle Clan," she typed, after detecting one of the clan leaders on line.

"Greetings. This is Jaree, wife to the leader of the Red Star Clan."

Before long, she was deep in conversation explaining to Jaree what to expect when her clan arrived at the north Gothman border.

"The Red Star Clan is loyal to Patha and the Blood Circle Clan." Jaree's typed message appeared on Tara's screen. "You can count on our help if you need us."

Tara worked into the night, briefing clan after clan that had either heard from Patha or from another clan leader. She joined a transmission with several other clan leaders, including Patha who was on his landlink at Reena's house, and argued the pros and cons of a Runner and Gothman union.

"I see you claim two titles now," Patha typed a side message to Tara, while both of them continued to discuss political issues in a group transmission. "You are not only my heir, but now you claim the title of claim to the Lord of Gothman?"

"I need to show that I am dedicated to helping Gothman." Tara felt her fingers cramp as she hurried to express her point to Patha, while continuing to comment in the group transmission. "This is the first any Runner has heard of our teaming with Gothman. Sharing news of my claim will help strengthen the alliance."

As the evening wore on, news traveled of the union between the Runners and the Gothman.

"Is it true?" One of her friends sent a transmission that popped up on her screen. "How have you become the claim to the Lord of Gothman?"

The questions from Tara's clan members were justified. She typed and typed until her fingers ached and her eyes could no longer focus on the screen. But Tara knew the Runners needed reassurance that Gothman, who had always been their enemy, would now be an ally.

Tara fell asleep before Darius returned that night and woke up with the cool morning breeze coming through the open balcony doors. She was starving and the walkntalk beeped next to her. Getting up quickly, Tara experienced a wave of nausea. She suddenly realized that Reena could be right; she was showing all the signs of pregnancy.

"Tara?" It was Hilda's voice. Then, the older woman's voice became muffled as if she was speaking to someone in the room with her. "It's Tara. She's there, she is."

Reena's voice came through in the background. "Are you okay?"

"Yes. I'm fine. What time is it?"

"Oh, for heaven's sake. We woke her up." It was Hilda again, apparently speaking back and forth between Reena and Tara. "Reena thinks you're pregnant, she does. Is that true?"

Tara rolled her eyes at the thought of those two old women having gossiped through the night.

"I don't know, Hilda. What did you want?"

"She wants to know what we want," Hilda said to the background again, then spoke into the walkntalk. "Now what do you think we would want? We want to make sure you're okay. Is my son there? Did he send you home?"

Tara wasn't in the mood to answer Hilda's questions. "Your son is out with his troops defending Gothman as he should be. I'm fine. I don't want you to leave that house. Do you have enough food?"

"The Runner, um, Patha, is here. And yes, my dear, I daresay we have plenty of food—even for Torgo."

Tara hung up, amused by the thought of Patha putting up with the two old women.

She searched for something to eat and settled on some crackers and juice. She then returned to her landlink and planned her strategy for the day. She remembered the walkntalk and pulled it out of her coat pocket. Could she reach Darius on it?

Tara might not have knowledge of such antiquated devices, but she was sure they were not a secured means of communication. How had a nation become so large on such primitive equipment?

What information she had obtained last night led her to believe the Sea People were slowly obtaining more sophisticated equipment. The Gothman would have to be armed with better tools and weapons than this if they were to survive. Tara made a note to do something about it immediately. She prayed Darius wouldn't grow stubborn and challenge her for taking these matters into her own hands.

Tara decided the walkntalk was more suitable as a child's toy than a communication device and put it back into her pocket. The landlink was much better.

Now, where was that man? She opened the program monitoring the disc on Darius' neck. A map appeared on her screen, and a red dot blinked, indicating his location. He was close to the northern border of Gothman.

Tara closed her landlink and carried it out of the house to her bike. The few guards on duty were alongside the house gossiping, much like the Gothman women did. Tara could tell these people weren't accustomed to combat. They didn't know how to react to the threat of attack. Darius would have to work to train his troops better. But for the moment, she was glad they didn't notice her climb onto her bike and disappear around the other side of the house.

The morning air was cool and the sky, a magnificent blue. She traveled north on an obviously seldom-used rocky road heading for the location indicated on her screen. Half an hour later, she noticed several black trailers coming across the meadow to her west. Within minutes, many motorcycles became visible as well. It was a Runner clan and a rather large one at that. The scouts leading the clan approached her first, and she slowed to greet them.

"Identify yourself, Runner." The voice was female although the headscarf and large jacket gave no indication of gender.

"I'm Tara of the Blood Circle Clan." She scanned the open area as more motorcycles came into view.

The Runner spoke into a microphone clipped around her ear and extending to her mouth. The comm was used by most clans, proving the easiest way to communication while on a bike. Tara knew that one of the black trailers contained the clan's base unit, and the female Runner was informing those inside the van of her contact.

"I'm to tell you that Redo of the Red Star clan greets you. He's received your communication and has brought his clan to assist."

"I'm very grateful to all of your clan for your willingness to help with the Sea People. I'm on my way to meet Lord Darius of Gothman. Will you all ride with me?"

The woman spoke into her comm again and then quickly responded, "Lead the way."

Tara's screen indicated that Darius' exact location was beyond the oncoming hills. She and the clan began making their way toward him, slowing their pace over the rough ground so the trailers would be able to keep up with them.

Pride in her heritage surged through Tara as she rode with a scout on either side of her, the remaining members of the clan behind them. She was well aware that she and her fellow Runners were creating history with every passing moment. The noise of their approaching motorcycles—several hundred in all—roared through the hills like thunder, louder than a tornado, sending tremors through the ground like an earthquake.

One of the scouts pointed to a large number of bikes, and scores of tents being assembled. They'd arrived at the Gothman camp. As the Gothman became aware of the approaching Runner clan, all hands dropped what they were doing. But while a commotion stirred in the camp, Tara could tell it had been notified of the Runners' impending arrival since no shots were fired. Nevertheless, Gothman guards at the edge of the camp pulled their guns and stood alert.

A line of scouts now drove in unison, leading the clan, and Tara alerted them to slow down. She stopped the clan within twenty feet of the Gothman guards. It would appear to any bystander to be quite a standoff, with Runners lined up along a quarter mile area and Gothman guards on alert in a similar formation.

"Halt your clan and wait for my instructions," Tara told one of the scouts.

She drove slowly to the guard that wore the armband of highest rank.

"I'm Tara of the Blood Circle Clan. This is the Red Star clan, here to assist the Gothman. Inform Lord Darius we await his instructions."

He yelled to another guard who was standing next to him, and that man turned and ran into the camp toward one of the tents.

Tara didn't move, and the Red Star clan sat perfectly still with the Gothman watching them. Over five hundred people stood firm in the meadow. Their silence was dreadful. Tara wondered if they could put aside their prejudices long enough to fight this battle together.

Suddenly, Tara heard rumbling behind her; she turned to look back toward the Red Star clan. Behind them, at the bottom of the hill, another clan approached.

Tara shouted to the Gothman warrior, "Tell your men to hold their position, and I will see what clan this is."

She drove back to the Runner scout and told the woman to communicate with the other clan, have them identify themselves, and then ask them to hold their ground until they received further instructions.

Tara turned back to the Gothman at the sound of an approaching motorcycle. She breathed a sigh of relief at the sight of Darius.

"Lower your weapons, Gothman!" He barked with enough ferocity that his men turned on a dime to face him. "The Runners are here to assist us. Get back to work and get this camp in order!"

The guards returned to assembling the tents and preparing the camp for battle, although many kept their eyes on the arriving Runners. Darius drove his bike around the Gothman guards and pulled up alongside Tara.

"How many Runners are here?" Darius' tone was quiet, authoritative.

Tara recognized the warrior chain of command. He addressed her as a leader would another leader, and not as a female he wished to control. "I don't have a count, yet. I'll get one."

She left him and slowly drove up to the scout. "Lord Darius wants a count of Runners. How many are there in the Red Star clan?"

"We are two hundred and fifty," the scout responded. "Two weeks ago, our clan numbered over seven hundred. The Sea People attacked us because they thought we were destroying a field where some opiate plants grow. We were all but destroyed by them. It's an honor for us to join the other clans and the Gothman and return the Sea People to their place. They are a no good race of drug addicts, and we would all do better without them."

Tara could see the anger in the woman's eyes as she spoke.

"The Blood Circle Clan is behind us. They number twelve hundred, and Patha sends his greeting to you, Tara." The woman smiled through her headscarf.

Tara's face lit up. Her people had come. This in itself was a moment in history to remember, as far as Tara was concerned. She started to turn back toward Darius when the woman raised her hand.

"Wait," she said. "Patha is coming forward. His clan will maintain their location until further orders, as will ours. Patha says no further action is to occur until he meets with Lord Darius."

It was well known among the Runners that the Blood Circle Clan was the largest and Patha the leader of them all. He'd established the large networking system existing among the Runners when he was a very young man. It was due to Patha's ingenuity that the Runners were able to communicate with each other no matter how far away they were from their clans. He'd encouraged complete equality among the clans, insisting all Runners would work to their maximum ability if they were treated with the same respect.

Tara was proud of Patha, her papa. She watched eagerly as she noticed a man on a motorcycle approaching the front line of the Runners. She glanced at Darius, and he too watched the figure approach.

She returned to his side. "It's Patha. He'll want to speak privately."

* * * * *

Darius watched her as she looked on at the large man approaching. Completely covered by her Runner attire, it was still very obvious how beautiful, she was. He wondered what made her more desirable, her incredible good looks, or the power she possessed with her clan.

He said, "Of course. My personal tent is ready." Darius quickly looked at Tara. "*Our* personal tent is ready."

Darius sat on his bike studying Patha as the Runner leader drove toward them. He was impressive in his black clothing, a large leather jacket and thick black gloves. The Blood Circle Clan emblem was embroidered on a sash that crossed his chest. Several other pins of achievements were attached to the sash as well.

Darius acknowledged the great warrior, and sat proudly on his bike, his face expressionless.

"Patha, I'm so glad you've arrived." Tara sat tall and proud as well. "I would like to present Lord Darius."

Darius noticed Patha's eyes travel from his Gothman warrior clothing to the Gothman seal wrapped around Tara's arm.

Looking at Tara, Patha said, "I'll speak with you two privately."

Chapter Eight

ဢ

The Gothman camp appeared large and well-organized. All around the edges of the encampment stood Gothman soldiers. A row of tanks had been parked along the northern boundary. Tara saw two towers constructed from wood logs with a ladder rising to a platform where a soldier was posted. From that vantage point, Gothman could see far past the hill they were on. Toward the middle of the camp stood a large circle of tents with their entrances facing each other. Each tent stood well over six-foot tall and had to be fifteen by twenty feet in diameter.

Tara guessed the Gothman soldiers were organized into groups of fifty or so. Tara, Darius, and Patha passed by each group of soldiers on their way to the tents. She noted how the soldiers ceased their target practice to study the two Runners driving by them. She wondered what these individual men thought of their presence here. How many now knew she was claimed to their lord? Did they know it was this union that brought the Runners in to fight the Sea People? She also couldn't help but wonder if they knew they wouldn't stand a chance in this war if the Runners weren't here.

Darius pulled his bike alongside the tents and parked it. The two Runners followed as he made his way to the largest tent in the circle.

"So, Tara has asked you to come, and you've agreed, I see," Darius said after they were inside.

Two large screened windows allowed sunlight to fill the interior. A drape divided the tent into two rooms. The one they currently occupied contained a large table in the center. Maps and outlines spread across it. Several chairs surrounded the table, and Darius sat in one while waving his hand for the other two to sit also.

Tara couldn't see what was in the other room, although curiosity had her wondering if it were the bedroom, and if so, how big the bed was.

"You're the son of Lord Jovis." Patha sat back in the chair and rested his hands on his large stomach. He stared at the young Gothman warrior. "I had dealings with your papa many winters ago. He didn't care much for Runners. I see you don't share those feelings."

Tara sat very still in her chair and was glad for her headscarf so neither of the men could see her blush at Patha's implication. Obviously, Darius liked Runners very much.

She wondered what Patha intended to say. She hoped he would keep the conversation on the topics of the pending war and not on her relationship with Lord Darius. It suddenly dawned on her that he might mention Reena's belief that Tara was pregnant. That was certainly not something she wanted brought up right now. She knew both men would quickly agree that war was no place for a pregnant lady.

"I'm aware of your associations with my papa." Darius looked very relaxed. "That was a long time ago. I know you're Tara's papa, and Reena is her mama."

Tara stared, certain shock clearly registered on her face regardless of the scarf. How long had he known this?

He continued, "All soldiers in this camp have families. They keep their personal issues at home and are here to fight a war. There's no room for thoughts other than the strategies we need to prepare." Darius leaned back in his chair, crossed his arms, and stared at Patha. Darius didn't want to discuss his personal life with the Runner leader. Patha would accept him as a warrior. That was all that mattered at the moment.

"If there are no thoughts other than strategy and combat, you turn your warriors into machines," Patha commented.

"They would become machines if they quit thinking," Darius countered. "And machines break down."

"Very true." Patha rubbed his chin and focused on the floor while he gathered his thoughts. He returned his gaze to Darius. "So, you allow for emotions and personal feelings to be integrated into your strategy?"

"We fight for Gothman. Our nation is powerful, and we are proud of who we are. That is an emotion." Although Darius sounded as if he spoke from his heart, his expression remained neutral and controlled. "And as for personal feelings, a good warrior is always affected by war. I wouldn't fight next to a man who wasn't affected by the blood and death around him."

A slow smile crossed Patha's face. He stood and walked around the tent, looking out the windows. Turning, he removed his scarf from his head and gestured for Tara to do the same. "Very good, young man. We'll review your strategies. I will have one thing made clear first."

Darius did not change his position or even bat an eye.

Tara had no idea what could be going on in his head at that moment. She was impressed by his manner, though, and hoped Patha was as well.

"Do you want the Runners' help in this war?" Patha walked to the table and leaned his fists against it.

"Patha, I will accept your assistance in defeating the Sea People." Darius leaned forward and looked Patha straight in the eye. "Now, I'll ask *you* a question." Darius got up and moved behind the chair on which Tara sat.

Tara froze, wondering what the question would be. She couldn't be sure, but she thought she saw a hint of amusement in Patha's eyes. Tara guessed her papa enjoyed the way Darius reacted to Patha, as if they were equals. Patha didn't have many people who made that assumption around him. But Tara would have to agree that by rank, the two men were equal.

Darius put his hands on the chair.

She could feel his fingers on the back of her neck.

"What's your opinion of the Gothman, Patha?"

Patha looked the young man square in the eye. "I've worked most of my life to incorporate a belief that a person should be judged by their actions and not by their race. We are all of Nuworld, Lord Darius. I see before me a man who rules a race of people, but has little knowledge of the world around him. There's a law in this land stating if Runners enter Gothman territory, they are to be shot on sight. You intentionally broke your own law. I believe you had a glimpse at the world outside your own through Tara and it intrigued you."

Patha paused, looking from Tara to Darius. He had their undivided attention.

Tara could guess Darius wasn't missing a word.

With a sigh, Patha sat back down and rubbed his forehead. "Tara has shared her feelings with me, now I must hear yours. What are your intentions here?"

Tara suddenly realized how old he looked.

Darius placed his hands on Tara's shoulders. "Patha, I love your daughter."

Tara trembled inside. She felt a quiver go through her body and wondered if Darius felt it too. He'd just said he loved her. Did he mean it, or was he saying what Patha wanted to hear? She had seen affection in his eyes, but she would have been inclined to think of it as possession more than love. Maybe, this was his culture showing through. After all, claiming a woman and owning her without concern to her thoughts or beliefs was the only way of life he'd ever known.

"I hope the two of you have the same meaning of love." Patha smiled gently at his daughter. "I'll accept that answer. Now, when you unite, you'll bring together two cultures. It'll be hard on both of you. I want this uniting to be more official than a marriage, or claim, as the Gothman call it."

Patha reached inside his jacket and pulled out some papers that were clipped together. He dropped the papers on the table and looked at Lord Darius.

"This is a treaty of peace between the Gothman and the Runners. It will state officially to Nuworld that our two races have united. There will be no race stronger, or larger in numbers, once our signatures appear on this treaty. It states that you'll continue to rule Gothman, and I'll rule the Runners. When I die, Tara is my next in line. She'll be leader of the Runners and the Blood Circle Clan. The two of you will rule almost half of Nuworld. While I am alive at least, that rule will be a fair one. Read through this treaty carefully. The Runners will not help you with this war until this treaty is signed." Patha got up and headed to the entrance of the tent. "I'll be waiting for your response."

He pulled a comm out of his pocket and handed it to Tara. "Contact me when it's signed."

Patha walked out of the tent, leaving Tara and Darius alone. She turned and looked up at him.

He returned her look, moving his hands to her head and stroking her hair.

"How long have you known Patha and Reena were my parents?" She didn't know why that was the first thing out of her mouth with all the issues at hand.

"A good ruler must know what is going on in his kingdom." He smiled at her. "I remember hearing about it when I was a boy. My papa was furious when Patha took you. You were claimed to my brother, did you know that? I didn't know you were the girl I'd heard about as a child until you told me your papa was Patha."

"I just found out myself. It appears I'm only half-Runner." She suddenly felt very serious—the rush of excitement was gone.

Darius grinned. "When did you find out that I loved you?"

"Just now."

He laughed and pulled her out of her chair, sat and set her on his lap. He wrapped his arms around her and hugged her so tightly, all air was forced from her lungs. She felt very lightheaded as he released his grasp and stared into her eyes.

What a man he was! She was proud of his conversation with Patha. He'd been put on trial as a leader during that brief conversation. Patha had tested Lord Darius' knowledge, and all the answers had been delivered without hesitation. She hadn't known how excellent a leader he was until that moment.

"My lady, we're meant for each other. You took me on by the horns, you did. I thought I could break you at first, but then I found I didn't want to. It's the excitement in your eyes when you're challenged that I love, yes. I wouldn't be happy with a passive woman. I tried to make myself think I would, but as they were presented to me, they disgusted me. Then, you came along.

"Oh, I knew you were a Runner. Patha was right. I broke my own laws. There was no way I could let you go, though. We're an excellent team, you and I. What do you say to that?"

She smiled. "I'll challenge you, that's for sure, Darius. We're equals, and I have no problem with accepting the challenge of teaching you that. Neither of us surpasses the other in any way I can see. I'll say this much, you proved your worthiness to lead this country to Patha. He was impressed, and so was I." Tara wrapped her arms around him and kissed him passionately.

He picked her up and carried her toward the adjoining room. A blanket served as a door, and he pulled it to the side so they could pass. There were no windows in this room, and when the blanket fell, the room became dark.

Tara's eyes adjusted and she could see a large down mattress on the floor with several quilts thrown over it.

"If there were time, I would ravish you right now," Darius growled as his arms slipped around her. He began slow kisses up her neck toward her ear.

"If there were time," Tara began and ran her hands up his chest until she clasped them behind his neck. She stood on tiptoe, leaning her head and allowing him room to continue his path of kisses. "I would demand you satisfy the fire you've lit in me."

Darius chuckled.

She could feel his body tremor.

"And if I refused?" he asked.

"I would have to take you by force," she whispered and then captured his mouth when he turned to look at her with pure amusement on his face.

Darius growled and deepened the kiss, until Tara was mad with need. But now wasn't the time. Troops waited outside, and both of them had work to do. She sighed and loosened her grip.

Darius kissed the tip of her nose before releasing her. "I do want to know when you planned on telling me that you're pregnant." He walked out of the room.

"What?" Tara yanked the blanket to the side and stormed after him.

Darius sat at the table, the treaty in his hands. He glanced up with a mischievous grin on his face.

She glared as she slammed down her fist on the table. "How could you possibly know if I am pregnant?" She snapped at him so hard that he raised his eyebrows in surprise.

"I told you I know everything that goes on in Gothman." He was still smiling but quickly looked back down at the treaty.

She walked over and pulled the treaty out of his hands. "I don't know that I am pregnant and nor does anyone else." She had begun yelling but quickly lowered her voice to a snarl.

He leaned back in the chair and looked at her. "I know that a true warrior eagerly takes on the challenge of battle. The look in your eyes over the thought of defeating the Sea People matches the feeling in my soul. Our battle will begin soon, and the satisfaction of their blood on our hands will be yours as well as mine. You're an outstanding warrior. You've proven your abilities, and I need your skills. As a good warrior, I know you respect the chain of command. But the plain simple truth is, I outrank you. I am lord, you are not. Therefore, I assure you, my lady, the second you start to show signs of carrying our child, the future ruler of the greatest nation on this planet, I will see to it that you are taken from the battle."

His voice was so low and calm, she knew there was no way she could argue. His was a very sensible statement. If she knew one of her warriors were pregnant, Tara would remove her from the line as well.

Suddenly, she was outraged. Hilda or Reena had obviously gotten word to him, there was no other way he would have this knowledge. No proof her pregnancy existed other than a *look* noticed by an old woman.

Tara turned and stormed toward the bedroom, then turned as if to leave the tent. The thought of not being in control of her own body, of something else taking over, was new. She was not one to be owned, and she viewed this as a loss of her freedom. Having a child wasn't a top priority for her, but then, neither was falling in love. She was a warrior!

She stormed outside and plucked her landlink from the bike, then returned to the inside of the tent and flung herself into a chair at the table, desperately trying to discipline her thoughts. She couldn't and slammed down her fists on the table, causing everything on it to bounce.

Darius knew the temper of a warrior should be treated with its due respect. He thought his words out carefully and spoke very gently. "My lady, do you not want this child?"

She glared, not softened by the gentle look. "Darius, how could you possibly understand?" She didn't completely understand herself. "Now's not the time for this. There's so much to do. The crisis before us is great, and we must be careful in order to win the day. This...pregnancy...would only be a distraction. It can't be true. There's no proof. We can't rely on some woman's *knowledge* about a *supposed* pregnancy."

"Time will be proof enough, it will. I'm sure there are doctors in your camp that could ease your mind, if you wish." He smiled and cautiously covered her hand with his. He was seeing a side of her that was new. Tara had an incredible temper.

"I have faith in Gothman doctors and their ways, my lady. I know some Runner ways are different from ours. I've heard stories of how Runners try to control when they have a baby, yes. And there are even tales told how you will decide not to be pregnant, even after you are that way. If you don't want this right now..." he paused and looked at her, knowing the seriousness of what he said was written on his face. "This time, I will allow you to choose not to be pregnant, I will. But hear me, I won't allow it a second time, no."

* * * * *

Tara knew what he was implying, and she gave him an odd look. This wasn't the way of his culture, to consent to abort the pregnancy—if there was one. She leaned back in the chair and stared, studying the radiant gray eyes and the curly dark blond locks that surrounded his face. He was quite easily the most handsome man she'd ever laid eyes on. What appealed to her most was what she saw in his eyes. He possessed something she'd not seen in other Gothman. He didn't take things for granted because of tradition. Darius challenged life. Laws and social expectations didn't faze him. The man existed by what he saw as right in his heart.

Tara saw a lot of herself in him. It tied their spirits in a bond she knew could not be reversed.

"No, if I am pregnant, I will stay that way. Such things won't be reversed, if they do in fact exist." Tara knew a pregnancy would bind them together more so than a Gothman claim could. She felt her stomach tighten at the thought.

"I knew that would be your answer, but the choice exists for Runners, and I will not deny you your heritage." He squeezed her hand, and she looked up quickly. "We conceived the first time we were together, I'm sure of it! We were meant to be together, my lady." He leaned over and kissed her gently.

"Promise me our child will know no prejudice, not over race or sex. If there is a child." She needed to add this one last point.

"I'll do my best, my lady."

He took the treaty out of her hands and pulled her chair next to his. With his arm wrapped about Tara, he set the treaty in front of them. The two read it together.

Patha put a lot of thought into the papers. It was full of the necessity of equality among all men and women. It emphasized that the Runners and the Gothman were setting a standard they hoped the rest of the world would meet. Nuworld would need to become one united nation. It stated this would be the only way all war and hostility could end. The treaty stated all cultures should always be honored and respected for their diversity. No race should ever be asked to give up its traditions or religious beliefs to adhere to the beliefs of another race. If two cultures chose to unite, it would be their responsibility to peacefully combine their cultures.

The treaty was very idealistic, Tara thought, after having read through it. What a wonderful world it would be if it could actually be enforced to the last letter. However, she feared that when Runners and Gothman started to follow its instruction, it would be a difficult paper to honor.

Darius shared her concern as they mulled over different sentences and argued certain points. The day was well over when they finally emerged from the tent.

"Here." Tara stopped him outside of the tent and put the comm around his ear. "You will need to learn how to use one of these." She adjusted the device so it would reach his mouth then secured it.

"What is it?"

"It's similar to your walkntalks. You can choose who you wish to talk to, however, and the main landlink will secure your line. We call them 'comms'."

He felt the mouthpiece and blew into it.

"There's a switch right here." Tara showed him. "Flip it on and tell the landlink you want to speak to Patha. You don't have to speak loudly. Its microphone is very sensitive. A whisper can be detected."

Darius pushed the switch and requested to speak to Patha.

Tara watched the look of fascination on his face as he listened.

"We will go down to the Blood Circle Clan and meet him there," Darius stated after he'd finished talking with Patha. "Do you think we can get more of these?"

"I'd think they should be supplied to all the Gothman army. I can confirm with Patha, but I'm fairly sure we have an ample supply. It would be difficult to fight a war without them." Tara climbed onto her bike. "I guess we're already incorporating part of that treaty. Our cultures are uniting."

* * * * *

"Our cultures are still very different." He stared across the meadow at his army as the men prepared for nightfall. Yes, very different. He had found the woman for him who came from a very different culture, and he was willing for their cultures to learn and grow together. But Darius had to admit to himself that he wasn't willing for their relationship to become a bonding of cultures. He thought about his own urges to demand obedience from Tara. She'd accepted his claim, was pregnant with his child, and it was all happening so fast. He needed time to assume control over her.

"We'll have to be the example of equality in a couple," Tara said, as if she sensed his thoughts and wanted to differ with them.

The two drove slowly through the camp and observed the men, who appeared quite ready for battle. Campfires were lit, and talking and laughter could be heard. Cheers and whoops, and just a few catcalls rang out as Darius and Tara moved among the men huddled in groups around the fires.

* * * * *

The small Runner clan they approached next was much quieter. Trailers and vans were parked in a circle with motorcycles parked around the edge. The Runners watched with curiosity as Tara and the Gothman lord drove through the camp. Tara knew that through transmissions circulated among them, the Runners probably already knew of the treaty. Patha would have made an announcement about it upon his return.

Darius saluted the Runners they passed, and the Runners acknowledged the deference with raised arms of greetings.

This was promising, Tara thought, although she knew the Runners would face less change with the treaty than the Gothman. The Runners were not opposed to change. Their nomadic heritage had provided much opportunity for them to adapt over the winters.

The next clan they approached—the Blood Circle Clan—stood and cheered the second Tara and Darius were spotted, outdoing the noise the Gothman had made. Several of the younger Runners ran beside the motorcycles encouraging the two along. Tara pulled up alongside a large trailer and got off her bike.

"Well, Tara, you sure have brought the crowd out tonight." The pair turned to see a young woman approaching them. Her Runner outfit showed every curve of her female body, and the black headscarf didn't conceal a sneer.

"Tasha, I didn't know you'd returned."

"How could you when you were off playing house with some Gothman lord? Although why you chose such a primitive race is beyond me. I never took you to be the submissive type." The young lady eyed Darius and flashed a flirtatious smile. "So tell me, did you have to beat her terribly to get her to obey?"

"Not terribly." Darius let his gaze wander over the young Runner.

"Lord Darius, I would like you to meet my sister, Tasha."

"No, she wouldn't like you to meet me." Tasha sashayed in a circle around Darius before coming back around to face him. "But, I wouldn't miss this for the world. From what I hear, it sounds like the two of you are trying to rule Nuworld."

"Come on." Tara took Darius' hand. "Patha is waiting."

"I'll say this," Tasha continued as they walked away. "He's much better looking than Kuro was."

"Who's Kuro?" Darius growled.

"He's a guy I dated when I was a teenager." She waved her hand, dismissing the comment her sister had made. "Tasha's trying to start trouble. It's her nature. You aren't jealous, are you?" She looked up to see if she could read his thoughts.

His face was expressionless, and he looked straight ahead.

They spent several hours with Patha, going over the details of the treaty, discussing military strategy, and explaining the comm along with other military equipment that the Runners were willing to supply to the Gothman. When finally the two left the trailer, it was quite dark, and the Runner camp had settled. All was quiet.

When they returned to the Gothman camp, Darius informed the guards he wanted his men assembled so he could speak to them. Thirty minutes later, the soldiers gathered in the meadow, looking curiously at Tara as she stood next to their lord.

Tara listened quietly, with her eyes on the crowd of men as Darius explained the treaty and the new equipment to be provided by the Runners.

"Today is a great day in Gothman history, it is." Darius' voice boomed through the speaker. "The Runners presented a treaty to me today, asking Gothman to form a truce with them, and to exist as their allies. I daresay Runners are a race different from many since they have no land, and move about from place to place to support themselves. They have learned about many races on Nuworld and know Gothman are the strongest and most powerful, yes. So, they come to us seeking allegiance, and I have granted it.

This is an excellent move for Gothman, it is, since the Runners have obtained knowledge that will now be readily available to Gothman. We go down in history today for discovering this race and seeing the abilities they can offer us."

His speech was moving and the Gothman cheered loudly when he was done.

"Very soon you will all receive a new communication device." Darius held the comm up in the air. "The Runners call it a comm. You will be instructed in its use. It will become your principal way to contact others, it will."

Darius took it upon himself to show those leaders who reported to him, how to wear the comm and how it worked. Not once did he ask Tara for assistance. She stood next to him silently. When he was done with the demonstration, he walked to his tent.

She followed. "You were rather impressive out there." She secured the tent flap once they were inside.

He sat in one of the chairs and kicked off his boots. "I have to be confident in front of the men or they'll have doubts, they will. You know that. Your equipment may be different than ours, but it's not complicated to understand, no. I agree all our forces should be using the same means of communication." He leaned back in his chair and stared. "You may think we're more primitive than you, you may, because we don't use these landlinks or have your advanced technology. But just because we are different doesn't make one of our races better then the other, no. I have a tight rule over those men out there. I know how to speak to them, yes. This war will be won, and Gothman will remain strong because of its leadership." He paused and studied her face.

"Don't let the words of my sister affect you. Just because she referred to you as primitive, don't take it personally. She was out of line, as she usually is." Tara sat next to him and took off her boots as well. "She doesn't speak for the other Runners, or they wouldn't be here."

She draped her long legs across his and leaned back in her chair. "You best believe she doesn't speak for me, or I sure wouldn't be here."

Darius stared at her legs, while running his hand along her inner thigh in a stimulating caress, then without comment he moved her legs, got up and went into the other room.

She sat there, leaning back in the chair completely exhausted. She had almost fallen asleep right there in the chair when he returned to the room. She opened her eyes and saw him standing in front of her. His shirt was off, and his bare chest distracted her out of her sleep.

Tara moaned as she studied the different shades of golden curls that covered hardened chest muscles. She didn't bother to wake up enough to talk, nor did she see reason to lift her eyes to his face. The view she had at the moment pleased her, and she allowed her eyes to follow the chest hair down to the top of his drawstring pants.

Darius must have noticed that she enjoyed the view, because he didn't move.

After a minute, Tara looked to his face and met his gaze. She noticed the interest in his eyes and smiled slyly.

He said, "I have something for you. Come here."

"What?" She followed him and then stopped as she noticed a small box sitting on one of the pillows of the bed. "What have you done?"

She opened the small box and pulled out a delicate chain with a small gold circle on it. In the middle of the circle, a tear-shaped ruby was fused to the side. The deep crimson of the ruby glittered in the dim light.

"It's the symbol of my clan." Tara smiled brightly and turned to look at him. Tears welled in her eyes, and she quickly looked down. She couldn't remember the last time she'd cried for any reason.

He sat next to her and lifted her face, wiping the tears and smiling gently. "I had it made for you shortly after I first saw you in town. I tell you, my lady, it was love at first sight. You and I were meant to live this life together."

Her tears flowed freely.

He laid her back on the bed, wrapping his arms around her. He slid off her coat and lifted her shirt over her head. She slid out of her pants and he quickly slid out of his clothes. He gently laid down on top of her naked body, and his flesh on top of hers excited her so much she could hardly contain herself. She wrapped her arms and legs around him, and he leaned on his elbows and stared into her face for a moment.

His kisses were soft and caressing. Once again, he moved slowly and passionately. Several times she tried to roll over and take charge of the lovemaking, but he pinned her and continued to make love slowly to every inch of her body.

She fought to control her soaring passions, but he controlled her destiny. He entered her, and she attempted to thrust upwards and bring him to a climax. He reached down for her legs and carried them upwards until he was able to rest her feet on his shoulders. She refrained from screaming as he penetrated deeper than he had before.

He seemed quite pleased with himself as he watched her face and slowly brought them to a mutual orgasm.

She rolled over on top of him and dared him to make love to her again.

His smile filled her heart with warmth, and he sat up with her facing him on his lap. "We've affairs of a nation to tend to, my lady. We need the rest." His hands caressed her back. "I'll accept that challenge later."

He laid her back down, then stretched his body out beside her. "Sleep well, my lady."

With a kiss to the tip of her nose, he pulled their bodies close, and they fell asleep.

Chapter Nine

✂

Several cycles passed with no indication of an attack by the Sea People. But, they were out there. Landlinks detected them in vast quantities just beyond Gothman borders. But since their arrival almost four cycles ago, the Sea People lingered.

Darius sensed the uneasiness in his soldiers. They did not like sitting and waiting when they were geared up to fight. He'd agreed to send scouts out to visually detect the Sea People using viewers, a long cylindrical tube that magnified items in the distance. They had been provided by the Runners.

After waiting so long for an attack, the Gothman began circulating rumors doubting the accuracy of Runner landlinks. Still, scouts verified thousands of Sea People with large amounts of artillery. No one could say for certain why the Sea People just sat there, apparently doing nothing.

"I wouldn't be surprised if the Sea People have discovered the Runner's presence and are waiting for reinforcements," Tara spoke to a small group of men assembled around the table in Patha's trailer.

"And who would they be waiting on?" Geeves, Darius' personal assistant, stared at the Gothman map spread over the table and didn't glance up at Tara.

She finished slicing a block of cheese, although she didn't take it to the table. She would be damned if she would wait on these men. She left the sliced cheese on the counter and plopped a piece in her mouth as she moved to stand behind Darius.

"They could just be waiting for more Sea People to arrive," she offered.

"I say we attack now, I do." Darius hit the table with his fist, and Geeves grunted his approval. "Gothman won't tolerate our borders lined with Sea People, no."

"Runners do not attack unless attacked first." Patha didn't raise his voice and glanced at Darius as he spoke.

"Tension builds among the men, my Lord," one of Darius' commanders spoke from behind Tara as he leaned against a wall by the trailer door. "They are ready to fight, they are, and we have them sit like women."

Tara cleared her voice, to show the commander she didn't like his comment.

"I can't justify leading any Runner clan into combat at the moment." Patha paid no attention to his daughter. "The Sea People sit on Freelander land. They are not in violation by being there. Everyone knows the Freelanders allow anyone free rein to their land."

"So Gothman will sit and do nothing?" The same commander behind Tara raised his voice a bit with the question.

"I don't like it anymore than you do." Darius pushed his seat from the table, almost backing into Tara. She moved toward the counter as Darius faced his commander. "But I daresay in all of Gothman history, no attack has occurred before the enemy crossed Gothman borders."

"We shall wait for the Sea People to make the first move." Patha didn't bother to stand.

Both Darius and his commander turned to study the Runner leader.

The commander released a few expletives, apparently feeling Tara's presence didn't prohibit such language, and left the trailer, not bothering to shut the door.

Tara chewed her lip as she followed Darius from Patha's trailer. She felt irritated that the men couldn't agree, and frustrated because she wanted more of the cheese and had left it on the counter. Needless to say, her mood was as sour as Darius'.

One morning, Tara lay on her mat working to pull her pants over her hardened belly. This had become a routine, trying to get her clothes to fit, but this particular morning she realized the pants just weren't going to go on without her making the conscious decision not to breathe. She absolutely could not fasten her pants.

Runner women often wore black, loose-fitting dresses over leggings when they were pregnant.

Tara groaned at the thought that she might have to concede to wearing such clothes. She stared at the ceiling of her tent, her hands still gripping button and button hole of her pants, and her fingers burning from trying to pull the material together over the growing bulge of her baby. She'd be forced to obtain some temporary clothing while her child grew within her, even though such articles would hamper her ability to climb on a bike and perform military maneuvers.

Tara decided to drive over to the Blood Circle Clan site and say hello to Balbo, her stepbrother. She'd been too busy with planning and training to have visited him before. Now that Darius and Patha had decided to create a better fighting mechanism by having the two cultures—Gothman and Runner—learn from each other, Darius had gone out daily with a party of scouts comprised of both groups. This left her the opportunity to leave the camp without any questions. Besides which, Balbo might be able to help her with the clothing issue.

Patha had had two wives although Tara only knew one. His first had died in battle. His second wife, Cloya, raised Tara but died giving birth to twins when Tara had seen fourteen winters. One of the twins died with Cloya, and the other twin was sent to Cloya's family to be raised. Tara also had a half-sister, Tasha, and Balbo, a stepbrother. Balbo was Patha's son by marriage—a son of his second wife. He was older than Tara, but since he was not of Patha's blood, was not heir to Patha's clan. Balbo was a good man, though, and had always been someone Tara could confide in. Right now she needed a favor.

Balbo hugged and kissed his sister on the cheek as she entered his trailer. Then, looked confused as he listened to her request. "You want what?"

"I need a pair of pants, mine don't fit anymore." She privately begged that he wouldn't ask why.

"Eating to much of that Gothman food, are you?" He laughed and then looked at her closely. "Tara, your face is gaunt. And why are there dark shadows under your eyes? Have you been to a doctor recently?"

"No, and I feel fine. I just need a larger pair of pants."

Balbo left the room for a moment, returning with a pair of pants. As he handed them to her, he gave her that brotherly look she had hoped not to see. "Tara, I've never interfered with your life, and I won't start now. But, what's the harm in stopping in and seeing Dr. Digo while you're here?"

"We'll see." She hugged her brother and thanked him for the pants. "I wanted to say hello to a few people I haven't seen in awhile. Maybe, I can see the doc, too."

Tara no longer had any doubts as to her condition, but she decided to pay heed to her brother's advice and see if Dr. Digo was busy. He'd been her doctor all her life, or as long as she could remember. He'd tended her first laser wound and set more bones than she cared to remember. He was a good man, and she didn't mind stopping in to hear the latest stories.

"Tara, child, how you've grown. Why, you're not even a child any more, but a beautiful woman. I've heard the stories about you…how you started a revolution. Doesn't surprise me a bit. Here, have a seat, tell me a good story." The old man patted the chair that was reserved for his patients and assumed his doctorly position, leaning on the examination table.

"Okay, here's a story." She squirmed in her seat. "This young girl has reached the *Age of Searching* and is drawn to places she's never been. She enters into a culture unlike any she'd experienced. Doctor, I tell you, she is exposed to a way of life she had only heard about in many exaggerated stories. An old lady takes her in and teaches her about the culture and provides her with clothes so she will look like one of them. It was harder to give up her way of life than the girl thought it would be. Then, one of the men in this culture takes an interest in her. He knows her for what she is, but she doesn't know this. She thinks she has him fooled. She comes to discover later that he not only knows her for what she is, but he knows more about her than she knows herself. I guess it was inevitable, fate some may call it, but she falls in love with this guy."

"And, this man, does he love her too?" Dr. Digo looked interested.

"Yes, he tells her this, and then proves it by his actions again and again. It's just that their cultures are so different. She's not sure they define love the same way."

"So, what happens next?"

The old doctor had already moved over to the cabinets along side the wall of his trailer and started opening drawers.

She ached from the tight pants she wore and tightened her grip on the pants in her lap. "I don't know."

Dr. Digo pulled a syringe out of the cabinet and moved over next to Tara. "Shall we find out?"

Tara didn't answer but took off her jacket and pulled up her shirtsleeve.

Dr. Digo smiled as he drew the blood. He'd seen this look of concern and worry on many young women's faces. They always approached him with the obvious staring him in the face and telling him they didn't know. He never argued and always let them be the first to know or to admit it out loud.

Tara remained quiet as the doctor took the blood over to the equipment on the table.

He turned the monitor so Tara could see the results as soon as they were available.

"Tara, you're definitely pregnant. Would you like an examination?"

She consented and it was done.

* * * * *

She left the office wearing the pants her brother had given her. They fit much better but she knew they wouldn't work for long. Dr. Digo told her she'd have a baby in five cycles, right before the New Winter. Only five cycles before her entire life would change—she would be a mama!

She drove away slowly, lost in thought, which is probably why she didn't pay much attention to the young Runner standing outside Dr. Digo's trailer.

The young boy leaned along the backside of the trailer watching her as she mounted her bike and disappeared into the camp. As soon as she was gone, the boy reached up and turned on his comm.

"I found her. She just left Dr. Digo's trailer."

* * * * *

As Tara entered the Gothman camp, mulling over how she would handle a pregnancy, a war, and being claimed by a Gothman, Darius and Patha slowly pulled up in front of Dr. Digo's trailer.

"Come in, Patha, you're not hurt, are you?" The doctor's smile lessened as Lord Darius entered the trailer behind Patha. He looked at the tall blond man, as the lord stood expressionless, returning the gaze.

"Digo, my friend, I'm not hurt." Patha accepted Digo's extended hand and shook it with both of his. "I'd like you to meet the Lord of Gothman. Lord Darius, this is Dr. Digo. He's cared for my family as long as I've had one."

Darius appraised the stocky older man, guessing his age to be closer to Patha's than his. And the doctor was definitely nervous. Darius decided he didn't really care as long as the doctor told them what they wanted to know.

"Digo, we won't take up much of your time. I imagine you're quite busy." Patha crossed the room and sat in the chair behind Digo's desk.

Dr. Digo stood to the side as Darius moved as far as the middle of the room. He could sense the doctor studying him, but could only wonder what Tara had just told the man.

"We're here to talk to you about Tara, we are." Darius didn't want to waste time on civilities. He wanted to know what happened between the doctor and Tara.

"Patha, you're an old friend, but you know I can't talk to you about my patients."

"As Patha said," Darius interrupted, looking down at the doctor. He didn't like speaking to the doctor and then having the doctor address the answers to Patha. "We won't take much of your time."

"What can I do for you?" The doctor looked nervous, but held his ground and continued to focus on Patha.

"What did you find out while Tara visited you?" Darius used his tone that had a quiet, unquestionable authority.

"I can't tell you that." The doctor rubbed his hand through his hair and sighed deeply. "This is a very sensitive situation."

"How pregnant is she?" Darius knew in his heart that the child was his, but he had to hear it from the doctor. He had to make sure Tara didn't arrive in Gothman already pregnant.

"Answer the question," Patha ordered when the doctor hesitated.

"About four cycles," the doctor sighed again. "She'll give birth before the New Winter."

"Thank you," Patha said and stood.

Darius knew it had been a good idea to pay the Runner lad to follow Tara after one of his men had reported that his claim had left camp. Tara would learn soon enough that the Lord of Gothman's claim would always be watched. She may view a claiming as demeaning, but to Gothman, she was a valued woman.

When the lad reported that Tara had gone to the Runner doctor, Patha had told Darius he would go with him when he learned why the Gothman lord wanted to see the doctor. Darius had accepted Patha's offer, knowing the Runner leader would play diplomat. Still, Darius guessed the older man wouldn't have wasted words if the doctor had shown reluctance in offering what Darius wanted to know.

Dr. Digo showed Darius he did have a backbone when he turned and gave the lord his attention. "She shouldn't be in this environment. It's not good for the baby." He then turned and looked at Patha. "While Tara has always been good about ordering ladies in her command to step down when field maneuvers become dangerous for the unborn child, I detect confusion in her. I fear you will have to remind her it's time to remove herself from the battlefield."

Patha and Darius looked at each other and left the trailer. Neither one looked forward to implementing the doctor's advice.

* * * * *

Tara awakened the following morning and realized Darius was not next to her. They'd made love most of the night, and she'd overslept. She had hesitated the night before in telling Darius about her visit to the doctor. And he'd appeared to be preoccupied. Now, he had left without waking her, and she had no idea where he had gone.

She lay there a moment trying to convince herself to get up. She felt absolutely exhausted and merely wanted to sleep several more hours. Tara knew the time had come to remove herself from the battlefield, but she had responsibilities here. Of course, several good candidates existed to take over her duties. But damnit, she wanted to be amidst the action.

Tara jumped to her feet when a sudden large explosion rent the air, causing the very ground beneath her to quake. Screams and the sound of running footsteps permeated her tent from every side. Instinct took over, and Tara dressed in a flash, hobbling to the entry as she shoved the second boot on her raised foot. Another explosion rocked the ground before she got out of the doorway.

"Darius," Tara shouted, struggling to wrap her comm around her ear. "Where are you?" She left the tent and jumped on her bike. "Shit," she howled as another explosion shook the ground.

Tara slowed her bike when she reached the middle of camp, joining several soldiers squatting behind large barrels of water. "Report!" she yelled through the noise and understood when none of her Runners looked at her. Their eyes were on the sky.

Tara's comm beeped, and she slapped at the small button to activate it. "Yes," she yelled over the dim.

"The Sea People sent five aircraft out about twenty minutes ago," one of Tara's commanders shouted in her ear. "We got one of them, but the others should be flying over you within minutes."

"I can see two now." Tara squinted at the dark gray cylindrical objects in the sky. She didn't see the other two.

"They're coming back around," the Runner next to her yelled, as she jumped behind the Gothman who squatted with an Eliminator resting on his shoulder. Both Gothman and Runner soldiers were equipped with the powerful Runner weapon, which was more than capable of destroying the aircraft flying overhead.

"On my mark, fire," Tara ordered. She quickly moved aside to give the Gothman space, knowing what kind of kick the Eliminator had. She waited for the two planes to come within range.

"Fire!" Tara yelled.

The Gothman pushed the large button on the side of the Eliminator, and then fell backwards as a zinging sound pierced the air. Tara didn't focus on the Gothman, but turned her attention to the sky and the two dark gray crafts now shadowing the ground.

"Take cover! Take cover!" Someone screamed, but the advice wasn't needed.

"It's a direct hit!" The Gothman next to her let out a whoop of excitement then immediately ducked.

"Excellent," Tara whispered as one of the crafts suddenly rippled with fire, distorting as she watched. Burning fragments separated from the craft and began twirling to the ground. The second plane wasn't hit, and it fired on the camp.

The ground exploded around them.

Tara grabbed the Eliminator from the Gothman, who had let it go limp in his arm and aimed at the craft as it hovered over them. She fired and the plane exploded. She couldn't tell if there were more planes — the flames and smoke from the multiple explosions around her made it difficult to breathe and see.

"Tara! What's going on?" Darius' voice came through her comm.

"Two crafts are destroyed. Where the hell are you?" Tara coughed as charred metal hit the ground burning, and black smoke filled the air.

"Help!" someone screamed.

Tara stood quickly and then balanced herself as a wave of dizziness consumed her. *This is no place for a woman in your condition*, a little voice chided her. She couldn't do anything about that now. Runners with spray packs on their backs began hosing down the isolated fires. The water turned the black smoke to gray as it filled the air.

"Where are you?" She put her hand over her mouth and nose as waves of smoke consumed her.

"We're at the edge of the Blood Circle camp. The Sea People have attacked down here, but we're holding our ground, we are. But what about you, woman? Patha tells me the landlink shows you took some hits. I don't want you in the middle of that, no."

"We brought down two crafts. All is under control. And I'm fine. But what about you? Are you okay?" Tara coughed again and ignored the curses she heard through her comm.

Her comm beeped again, and she reached for the thin wire that ran along her cheek from her ear to her mouth. "Stand by Darius," she said.

"What?" he barked. "Like hell—"

But she cut him off with a sigh, regretting that when she saw him next his first words would be a reprimand. "Tara here," she said as she acknowledged the new call.

"Frig here, Tara," one of the Runner soldiers she had known since childhood responded. "We'll have these fires out in no time. I've got a medic team reporting only three wounded."

"Thanks, Frig."

The attack only lasted a few minutes, but it seemed as though hours had passed. Even though casualties had been few, the soldiers were shaken, and the campsite was partially burned, but functional.

"Darius, were you hit hard?" Tara waited a long minute before his deep baritone swam through her senses. She wanted to know if he was injured, and if Patha was okay, along with the rest of her family. Darius would view that as a sign of weakness, however. So Tara kept her comments pertaining to the issue at hand.

"A few casualties. Prepare yourselves. More crafts have been spotted!" He sounded stressed.

Tara could guess that any warrior would be anxious under pending attack, but she couldn't help but hope he wanted to be at her side as much as she wished she were with him. "Acknowledged," she said simply and shut off her comm after hearing the termination on Darius' end.

Tara left the minimal protection offered by the water barrels and moved her way through the active camp. She tapped her comm again and addressed Frig. While she could see him instructing several Gothman, he stood too far away to hear her without the device. "We have more crafts headed our way."

Frig indicated he understood, and she watched him gesture to several soldiers surrounding him. "Several of my best warriors are armed with Eliminators," he told her. "We'll have the Sea People out of the sky before they are able to attack this time."

"Make sure of it." Tara felt a wave of energy surge through her from the enthusiasm in Frig's tone. Well-trained warriors lived for the battle. They fought for a just cause, and Runners and Gothman would be triumphant. Tara held her head high as she continued working her way through the camp toward her bike.

Daylight could not penetrate the smoke and dust swirling around them. By mid-afternoon, the sky remained a dark gray, and black clouds created from burnt rubble and campfire smoke, hung heavily.

Visibility was so poor, Tara could barely distinguish forms of the people around her. The trees outlining the camp were completely obscured. She was forced to guide the soldiers' movements with the aid of her landlink, which she'd found in her tent, unharmed and lying on tossed bedding. Absentmindedly, she'd noted that although the tent interior remained dark, she could see about the space with far more clarity than she could see outside.

Tara spotted a group of Gothman soldiers through the murk and approached their leader. "What are your orders?"

"Preparing to search the surrounding area, them's the orders." The Gothman only half-turned to acknowledge Tara, an act to which she'd grown accustomed with many of the Gothman.

"The area surrounding the camp?" Tara wondered if someone had picked up movement, and she hadn't yet been told. "Who gave you your orders?"

"Lord Darius." This time the Gothman didn't even turn when he answered, but instead signaled his men to begin their search.

"Darius?" Tara asked after tapping her comm.

"What do you need?" Are you okay?" The concerned sound in his tone made Tara want to tell him she would be better if she were at his side.

"Have you spotted movement surrounding the camp? Why wasn't I notified?" She heard mumbling through her comm and surmised Darius was speaking to someone with him.

"Your landlinks show no activity," Darius said after he finished talking to whomever he was with.

"Then why did you order men to search the area?" Tara waved at the Gothman leader to halt his men.

He only appeared mildly interested in her gesture, and didn't stop his men.

"To make sure the area is secure."

"Tara, we've spotted the crafts!" Frig waved frantically from several tents' distance, and then turned to acknowledge several soldiers approaching him.

Tara's comm beeped in her ear. "Darius, order your Gothman soldiers to cease their search. It's a waste of manpower." Tara barked the order, suddenly frustrated with the man for not trusting Runner equipment and belittling her authority by issuing commands she didn't know about.

She hit the small button on the silver stem of the comm to acknowledge the next call, cutting Darius off in mid-rebuttal.

"Eliminators are ready," a Gothman yelled in her ear.

Tara ran back to her bike, ignoring the stitch that ran from her lower abdomen down her leg. She started the bike with one hand and moved it slowly while attaching her landlink to the handlebars. "When you have them in target, fire," she ordered, deciding to monitor the attack inside one of the nearby Runner trailers.

An explosion shook the ground, and people flew from a location not too far from Tara's right.

"One of the crafts has a different type of artillery on it," one of her commander's reported through Tara's comm.

"Get those blasted things out of the air!" Tara yelled over the growing confusion around her.

Another explosion shook the ground.

Tara was forced to stop her bike when several Gothman bolted in front of her. Then she heard the zinging sound of an Eliminator. "Yes!" she hissed, eyes riveted to the sky as one of the crafts rippled and burst into flames.

She moved around barricades and soldiers issuing orders until she reached the spot where two warriors stood next to each other, aiming Eliminators at the second craft. Tara stopped again, jumping off her bike to stand as close as she dared to the marksmen, watching the sky the whole time.

The second craft turned to flame.

"I want a report of damages," Tara continued issuing orders through her comm as she mounted her bike and headed with more speed to the nearest trailer. The ground explosions billowed smoke, and the stench of burning metal, rubber and human flesh turned her stomach. "Get this camp in order and prepare for any further attacks."

Over the next few weeks, the Sea People challenged the Gothman borders, but Gothman and Runners managed to keep them at bay. Tara remained in charge of the Gothman camp, even though many still challenged her command.

Patha and Darius began to bond, as Patha assumed the role of mentor. Tara knew Patha looked ahead to a time after his death, when she and Darius would rule both races. To this end, Patha considered it his highest priority to train Darius, to help him understand the Runner way.

It was late in the evening when Tara ventured to the front line to see Patha and Darius. The rocky ground jostled her bike, and when she stood after riding, mild stitches shot down her legs from her pelvis. Knowing the discomfort came from overworking the muscles holding her baby in place, she stood still until the bits of pain subsided and she could walk without discomfort.

As she glanced about her at the busy clan site, now turned into a military operation on the front line, Tara saw Patha and waved. Idly, she noticed that he appeared to stop speaking into his comm as soon as he saw her.

Flicking off the device, he waved back, and after saying something to the Runner he was with, began walking toward her, smiling. His smile warmed her.

She narrowed the distance between them as quickly as she could, taking care not to jolt her body as she stepped on uneven ground.

"It appears we've a break in the action. The report I received this morning showed the Sea People have regrouped and returned to their camp." Patha looked tired as he greeted his daughter.

"And how are you doing?" She slid her arm around his and walked into the camp.

"I'm fine Tara-girl, just fine." Patha chuckled and patted her arm. "Darius and I plan on preparing our next method of attack today. You're just in time. Come to my trailer."

* * * * *

Patha had noticed how his daughter's pregnancy had progressed when he'd first spotted her. Tara's rounded tummy stuck out, noticeable from her otherwise thin frame. Even with her jacket on and her face covered by her headscarf, he could tell she was feeling the stress of the growing child inside her. She stepped gingerly over the rough ground. He didn't think she noticed how he supported her over the small ditches that had been created from the heavy jeeps driving over the ground daily.

"We've three more clans arriving from the east, we do," Darius said, without looking up as Patha and Tara entered the newly converted main headquarters.

* * * * *

Darius sat at the landlink reviewing incoming transmissions from his commanders and a newly arrived clan, the Kill Water clan. He responded with orders, telling the clan where to set up camp. Then he turned to look at Tara. As she tossed her jacket on the back of a chair, he immediately noticed bones showing at the top of her shoulders. He stood and removed her headscarf without asking.

She smiled and stared into his face, and he watched her blue eyes search his features before meeting his gaze. Dark, puffy circles rimmed her eyes in a gaunt face. Her skin looked gray, partially from lack of sleep and partially from dirt and campfire smoke. She smelled of the smoke and anti-inflammatory powder. There was also the familiar stench of dirty clothes, body odor, blood and wet dirt; common smells of warriors during battle.

It struck Darius that he still found her incredibly beautiful. He reminded himself of his promise to relieve her from duty. A promise that now had to be carried out.

"Sit, Tara, have something to eat." Patha guided her into a chair at the round table, which sat to one side of the spacious living area.

* * * * *

Tara complied and felt a wave of exhaustion ripple over her. Holding up her head with her hands, she ran fingers through her hair. She was not thinking clearly and guessed fatigue was taking over quickly. A few hours' sleep and a hot shower and she was sure she would be good as new.

"I can help." Tara stood again. She started to move toward Patha, who pulled food from the small cold box where perishables were stored.

"Sit." Darius stopped her with a hand to her shoulder and guided her back to her seat.

"This looks so good." Tara eyed the sliced meat, smoked boar with the fat trimmed, and cold duck legs. Several chunks of cheese were still wrapped in a thin, almost transparent cloth. She reached for a vine of grapes when Patha put a bowl of fruit on the table.

She ate the food put in front of her with a vengeance.

"The Blue Horn clan reports all units are ready for battle," Darius said with his mouth full and a duck leg in his hand.

"Good. I want all clans to report in before the end of the day." Patha used the silver utensils he'd brought to the table and sliced his boar, then added a chunk of cheese. "Something to drink, Tara-girl?"

Patha leaned back to a wooden counter with stone top, which divided the living area from the kitchen. He grabbed a ceramic pitcher, then poured iced grape juice into a mug.

"Thank you," Tara said between bites. She took the mug and sliced a thick chunk of cheese from the block Patha had unwrapped.

* * * * *

Darius still pondered how to bring up the conversation he needed to have with Tara. He was not looking forward to the fight he would have on his hands when he relieved her from duty. And he'd had time to think about it. Patha had broached the subject when he contacted Darius upon seeing Tara arrive at camp earlier. He'd told Darius it was his duty to take her out of the fighting and made it clear he needed to do it now.

Darius felt he'd learned more from this old man than his papa had ever taught him. Indeed, Lord Jovis had never instructed him in much of anything. In return for his tutelage, Patha demanded a loyalty that he was glad to give. Now, the old man had more or less given him a direct order, and it was not a pleasant one.

"Don't let those clans dawdle in getting their updates to you." Patha waved his silver eating tool, a gift Tara had given him when she'd been a child, and then he pointed it at Darius. Its silver tip, similar in style to a knitting needle but with a sharper end, had remnants of cheese on it. "If all clans haven't reported in within the next few hours, send them notice they need to have all pertinent info relayed before sundown, or they'll receive the last available slots when I position everyone for battle."

Patha slid his chair from the table, then stood and patted his belly.

"Are you leaving? I'll walk with you," she said, grabbing a vine of grapes and starting to stand.

Patha chuckled. "Not this time, girl. I can tell you aren't done eating. And when you're done, enjoy a shower. I know living out of that tent you've been in all this time has denied you such luxuries."

* * * * *

"A shower would be nice." Tara relaxed and plopped a grape in her mouth. She took several more bites after Patha left and then stopped when she noticed Darius staring.

"I'll put this food away." She grabbed what was left of the meat and cheeses and wrapped them. Darius followed as she moved around the counter to the cold box. "Your Gothman leaders still have trouble acknowledging my authority."

Tara didn't understand why she suddenly felt shy. She was alone with the man she had dreamed of being with every night since they had parted for battle.

"It will take them time, it will. I daresay a culture doesn't change overnight, no." Darius slid her hair across her shoulders and kissed the back of her neck. "Go enjoy that shower now, my lady," he whispered, sending chills through her body.

She walked down the hallway, noticing it seemed narrower than it had in the past. The water was hot as she stood in the small cubicle surrounded halfway by a white plastic cover, and Tara let it spray over her body, praying it would revitalize her enough to impress her claim when she was done. She hurriedly scrubbed off the dirt, knowing water was rationed and not wanting to use all of it for her own comfort.

Tara stepped out of the shower long before she wanted to and wrapped herself in a large towel. There was no way she could talk herself into putting on the clothes she'd removed to shower. They were stained, and they smelled. She would have to send for fresh clothes. The large bulky towel wrapped around her accentuated the size of her growing tummy.

"You've got to come out sooner or later." Darius leaned patiently against the wall at the end of the short hallway as Tara opened the bathroom door and turned the other direction. Nothing but that white towel separated her from Darius.

She couldn't rid herself of shyness, although she had a feeling that being alone with her claim made that towel an endangered species. She gripped it around her growing breasts and padded away from the eyes she felt sure devoured her.

Patha's trailer had three bedrooms. She knew the first door led to Patha's bedroom and behind the second door were supplies he might need on his journeys. The third door led to a spare bedroom, although before Tara had her own trailer, this had been her bedroom. She opened this door and saw Darius' clothes hanging in the closet.

So, Darius had moved into her old room.

She was pleased that even though she hadn't been able to see Darius for less than a cycle, he had slept in her old room every night. It made her feel she had been close to him after all, although, she thought with an audible grunt, Darius probably hadn't given a thought to the fact that she had slept in the same bed many nights.

* * * * *

Darius came up behind her. As she turned to face him, he grabbed the towel and pulled it off her.

"Woman, you're so beautiful." He gazed at the growing bulge between her quickly disappearing hipbones. "Look at you, I should have you at home, with plenty of servants to see to your needs, yes."

He stroked her hair, pulled her to him, and rubbed her stretched tummy. His child grew within her. And that child would be healthy and strong if his mama didn't carry him through battle. She must return home, to a safe environment, nurturing the babe so his strength would be assured.

* * * * *

"We're warriors, I don't need to be taken care of," Tara said, but she made no attempt to move away from his strong hands. She did want him by her side, helping her through this strange transformation she was experiencing.

"I love you, and our child," he whispered in her ear as he picked her up and shut the door with his foot.

He laid her on the bed and caressed every sore muscle.

Darius kissed each bruise with lips that seared her skin. She found strength in her weary limbs to reach up and run her fingers across his muscular chest. She barely touched him, allowing only her fingertips to experience the pleasure of his virile skin.

She had no idea how her gentle exploration drove him to a state of madness, but simply enjoyed the sensation of feeling him, exploring the body she had dreamed about, and letting the downy hair on his chest tickle her sensations.

As exhausted as she was, she felt her body kindle with excitement when Darius lifted and spread her legs as he kissed her inner thighs. The heat between her legs grew unbearable, and the slight contraction as she lifted her hips to meet his lips seemed oddly pleasant when surge after surge of orgasm followed.

When Darius entered her, she felt the velvety roundness and long shaft as her soaked muscles clung to him and saturated him with greeting. She did not want their lovemaking to end. But after she'd hit that point of ecstasy to which he carried her with little effort, she collapsed.

* * * * *

Darius leaned on his arm next to her, enjoying the half-smile on her face and the glow in her sapphire eyes.

She'd let him have her, going limp and not instigating a thing. Her body slowly relaxed as he watched. Contented peace of mind crossed her face, an expression that hadn't been there before. This is how he wanted Tara; satisfied with his love for her, and looking relaxed instead of stressed and overworked as she had appeared when she'd entered the trailer. He wouldn't have his claim seen in public again showing such extreme signs of battle fatigue, no. This beautiful woman would carry his child and glow in satisfaction that she belonged to him, needing nothing and not entangled with worries.

"What?" Tara asked, trying to suppress a small delighted grin at the attention he was giving her. "Why are you staring?"

"You're glowing. Pregnancy suits you very well. We should have lots of children." Darius traced his index finger along her cheekbone and down to her mouth, allowing her to suck on it while her wide blue eyes stared up at him.

Tara pushed his finger out of her mouth with her tongue. "Oh right, that way you can order me to my room as soon as I start to show."

"Tara, you know you can't stay here. I don't need to tell you that, no." He lay next to her and tightened his grip when she tried to pull away. "I'm going to reassign you—but your skills won't go to waste, I think. The Sea People have attacked Bryton as well. They flew over and have caused fires and much confusion.

"I have warriors assigned there, but I daresay I don't have to tell you there's mostly women and children in the town, there is. I need someone to take charge of the men in Bryton, I do. You'll stay at the house and set up camp there. Hilda and Reena can see to your needs, yes, as well as any other lass you wish to have help you, I'm thinking. I've stationed soldiers around the house, but I need someone for them to report to who's there, yes.

"So far they've answered to me, but they need a constant presence to keep them in line. I'm thinking you can do that and then report to me directly, yes. You'll keep me informed of any potential attacks on the town, you will."

"How long did it take for you to think up that one?" She smiled at him, pleased she would still have responsibilities, although she'd be out of the heart of battle.

He didn't return the smile, but his eyes twinkled.

"I'll leave in the morning," she said. She snuggled up next to him, as she began thinking how she would have the entire town of Bryton under her control. She would organize the armies and make sure the women worked to supply the troops with food and clean blankets. Her mind tried to churn with the many tasks that would be under her power, but sleep overwhelmed her.

* * * * *

Darius listened to Tara's gentle breathing. Life couldn't be this good if he'd planned it. He ran his finger up and down her outer thigh. She'd been so submissive during their lovemaking. Agreeable even when he reassigned her to home, where she could rest and let the warriors tend to the duties of battle.

Just thinking about how she'd obeyed his orders caused him to harden again. Maybe she'd realized that he could direct her activities and offer her a life where she could do as she pleased, and not have to work so hard. Could it possibly be that she'd accepted the fact that he was in charge, sooner and not later? If he succeeded in convincing her to submit to him completely, he'd rule Gothman *and* all the Runner clans.

He ran his hand up her body and fondled one of her exposed breasts. She was so exciting. Darius knew that Tara wanted to be in charge, too. But, there could be only one leader. She would advise at his side, and he would control both nations. Darius smiled at the thought as he played with her nipple and delighted in her quickened breathing even though she remained sound asleep. He'd captured a beautiful Runner, and now she walked proudly at his side. He would keep her there. He'd see to that.

* * * * *

When Tara awakened, she was once again alone. She got up and noticed an outfit folded on the chair next to the bed. It was a Runner's maternity dress. Tara held the dress in front of her for a moment, then pulled it over her head. It slid down her body with such ease, she smiled, already liking the fact that she didn't have to struggle to make her clothes fit and then feel cramped in them. She ran her hands down the black material and then turned to the full-length mirror that still hung next to her door from when she was a child.

Tara wrinkled her nose at her knees and bare feet. She turned and searched the room and then noticed black leggings which had been folded underneath the dress. Of course, she had seen women dressed like this many times. The leggings were easy to slip into, and Tara decided the end result was tolerable. She slipped her laser into her pocket and decided to find food.

A plate of sweet rolls and fruit sat on the living room table. Tara relished the easy movement allowed her by the new clothes as she grabbed her landlink from where she had left it on the counter the day before. She sat and ate while clicking through the screens, catching up on communications and strategies she had missed. After saving several maneuvers to review later, she began consuming a second roll. Suddenly, she heard a jeep outside the trailer.

She waited to see who would come through the door, assuming one of Patha or Darius' commanders had arrived with news or questions, but instead she heard the sound of a motorcycle being started. Tara stood and opened the door, curious as to why no one came to the door, and noticed one of the soldiers sitting on her motorcycle. No one touched her bike without prior consent.

"I'd get off of that right now and find your own," she said, walking out of the door with her laser pointed.

The soldier froze and slowly moved off the bike. "Look, I'm just following—"

"I can see what you're doing." She shot the gun at the ground next to the soldier's feet, and he jumped off the bike before running like his life depended on it. Good thing too, since she was a crack shot.

Laughter caused Tara to turn quickly and there stood Patha and Darius. The longer Patha stood there, the harder he laughed until he was holding on to Darius' shoulder to keep from falling over. Darius' baritone chuckle only annoyed her further.

"The poor lad." Patha shook his head as he wiped his eyes.

"What's so funny about someone trying to steal my bike?" Tara turned her attention to both men and glared, wanting nothing more at the moment than to slap the large grins off both their faces.

"My lady, the man was following orders." Darius must have sensed her anger, because his smile disappeared, although slowly. "We asked him to drive your bike up to the shed behind the house."

"Why?"

"You'll drive this jeep." He walked over to the jeep parked next to her bike.

"You're taking away my bike?"

"It's doctor's orders, girl." Patha still smiled as he walked over to her although he tried to stifle it when he saw her expression.

"And you asked the man to bring the jeep to me?" Tara was quiet for a moment and then smiled at her own mistake. "That poor man will never come near me again."

Tara slipped her laser into her dress pocket and patted her bike. When Darius approached her, she smacked his chest. "Well, what are you waiting for, man? I can't very well drive both of these into town. You need to get someone over here to drive my bike to the house."

Darius moved before she could stop him and wrapped an arm around her, pulling her back against his chest. "Is that an order, my lady?"

"You bet it is," Tara said, as all anger disappeared, and she fought to suppress a giggle. "Now let me go. I've got a town to organize."

Darius watched his claim drive away from the campsite and hoped his town would survive her onslaught.

Chapter Ten

ॐ

"She's here," Reena yelled from the living room. "Oh, goodness, old woman, hurry up. She is here, she is!"

"I'm coming." Hilda waddled down the stairs as fast as her plump legs would carry her.

Torgo galloped past his mama and flung open the front door. "Wow, you look pregnant, you do!" He ran down the front porch stairs to greet Tara.

"And hello to you, too." She smiled at the young boy as she got out of the jeep. He greeted her with a big hug and a smile that went from ear to ear. "Miss me, did you?"

"It was awful boring with two old women picking on me all the time, it was." Torgo peered into the back of the jeep at all of the landlink equipment. "Especially with a war going on. What's all that for?"

"I'm in charge of the soldiers in town. I need this equipment to help me survey what the enemy is doing. I'll set up camp in my bedroom."

"Look at you, will you?" Reena stood on the porch. "Not going to come in and say hello?"

"Oh, Reena, look how big she is." Hilda clasped her hands to her mouth.

"Of course she's big, she'll have that baby in a couple cycles, she will." Reena sounded sure of herself.

"I wish I had only a couple cycles to go," Tara said with a laugh as she kissed the woman on the cheek. "But the baby won't be here until around the New Winter."

Tara hugged both women and instructed the guards standing in the driveway to unload the equipment and take it up to her room. She was forced to indulge in social chitchat with the two women before politely excusing herself so she could get to work. She begged forgiveness as she told them the guards would get lazy with a *woman in command* if she didn't show them her intention of running a tight ship.

"I'll be wanting to do a thorough exam, lass." Reena rubbed her chin as she studied Tara's belly. "I'm wondering about that fancy doctor of yours, I am."

Tara doubted it would do her any good to argue. "I'll make sure you get to do your exam."

"And soon," Reena said, and wagged her finger. "Don't be putting me off."

"As soon as I have everything in order with the troops," Tara promised.

The women hovered a bit longer, but bored quickly when Tara began arranging her landlink and left her to her business with promises of a warm meal as soon as she was settled.

"Can I help you?" Torgo stepped to the side as the women left, and then hovered in Tara's doorway. "Or I could just watch if you'll let me."

"Come on." Tara smiled at the young boy and he joyfully leapt to her side.

"I'm a quick learner, you'll see." He watched her plug in cords and attach adapters.

"You watch and see what you can figure out. Once I know all is in order, we might have time for a lesson."

Torgo learned quickly. Over the next few days, Tara organized shifts for the soldiers, established military tactics, created a layout of the town on the landlink, and discussed procedures with Patha and Darius. Since the schools were closed for the safety of the children, Torgo had plenty of time to learn. He was careful not to get in the way, and although Tara didn't say so, she enjoyed his company and eagerness.

"Tomorrow morning I'm going to drive into town and take a look at the damages." Tara leaned back and scratched her stretched-out belly.

* * * * *

She was one of the most unfeminine women Torgo had ever seen, and he decided that was what he liked about her. She didn't snap at him to sit up straight or tuck in his shirt. In fact, she didn't even seem to notice when he plopped down in her room with dirty shoes or food on his face.

"I can show you exactly where the bombs hit." He wanted so much to be part of it all. "Some of the buildings downtown are all the way gone, they are."

"Did many families lose their homes?"

"Uh, I'm not sure, my mama won't let me wander too much. I saw the buildings downtown though, they're rubble on the ground, they are. That's why Mama says I have to stay near the house." Torgo looked at her, hoping she wouldn't make him stay home too. "Please, can't I go with you?"

"I guess that would be up to Hilda."

* * * * *

Needless to say, there was an argument at the breakfast table the next morning. Not only did Hilda not want Torgo to go, neither Hilda nor Reena thought *Tara* should go.

Reena mentioned she still wanted to give Tara an examination. She wasn't convinced the Runner doctor was right about the due date. Tara was getting very big, and Reena was convinced she would have the baby in the next two cycles. To make matters worse, the first snow had fallen the night before. Tara felt awkward enough walking on the uneven ground and knew she would have a difficult time maintaining balance in the snow. There was a bitter wind, and both women ganged up against Tara, saying it was not wise to tempt a cold in her condition.

Torgo looked at Tara helplessly as the two women sounded triumphant with their argument.

"Are the two of you quite through?" Tara leaned back in her chair and calmly surveyed the women. "I'll be driving into town today. I've spent many days in much colder weather than this, and

I'll be fine. I think it might be a good idea to take Torgo with me. Look at it as a compromise. He can be my chaperone. I assure you, I'll keep him from harm."

Hilda threw up her hands in the air. "I don't have the fight to keep up with you, girl. I daresay there probably aren't many people who do."

"How's this," Reena suggested. "You take the boy, but when you get back, I do the examination. Will that suit you, Hilda?"

Hilda looked at Tara.

Tara couldn't tell if it was a disapproving look or not.

"I reckon it suits me. It's man's work inspecting what's left of those buildings, it is, and he'll be a man soon enough, he will."

"Great!" Torgo jumped up from the table. "When do we leave?"

"After I eat." Tara helped herself to more bacon.

"That's right. Sit, boy." Reena smiled. "She's eating for two now."

"Dr. Digo says that's the type of thinking that makes women fat," Tara said in between bites.

"Ah, and this same man says you're due in four cycles as well, huh?" Reena shook her head and scooped more food onto Tara's plate.

Tara finished eating quickly, and soon after, she and Torgo were out the door. Downtown looked so different than it had before. Tara remembered coming to the stores for the first time with Reena. As she parked the jeep and walked down the sidewalk with Torgo, very few people were visible, unlike before when merchants bustled about and the streets filled with chattering women and children. The grocery store was open, but most of the other shops were closed.

Tara pointed to the side street where she'd first met Torgo. The two buildings no longer bordered the service road. One side of the street was simply a mound of bricks and boards. They walked past the rubble. She watched two women hurry across the street with long coats pulled tightly around them to block the cold. Neither one of them looked their way—unlike Gothman women who would eagerly welcome gossip about how the lord's claim looked good and pregnant.

"We should organize a team to clean this up. These people need hope. They're not accustomed to being challenged with the hardships of battle, and I fear morale is low. This war won't last forever, and the town will have to be rebuilt sooner or later. I think if we have a crew start on clean up now, self-esteem in the town will return to normal."

"None of the men are here to do it," Torgo pointed out.

"What's wrong with the women, and all of you young people too young to fight, doing it? There's no reason why you can't help. You've nothing else to occupy your time since Darius closed the schools until further notice. It'll keep the kids out of trouble. And I'm sure the women want to help, too. That way, when the men do come home, they can focus on rebuilding."

"I'm game, but I don't think many of the women around here would help. We aren't like you, Tara. If the men came home and found their women had been doing their work, I don't think they'd like it much, I don't."

Tara thought for a moment and then looked up smiling. "I have an idea, come on." She walked quickly back to the jeep.

"What are you thinking?"

Tara pulled out of the parking spot and headed toward the camps. Torgo held on as she bounced over the rough road. She looked at him and saw the excited look on his face as he realized where they were going.

"My brother is going to be mad, he is." He was still grinning.

"Don't you worry about your brother, I can handle him."

She drove in to the Blood Circle Clan's camp and slowed the jeep.

"I've never seen so many Runners," Torgo almost whispered and watched people walking around him who were indifferent to his presence.

"They're people just like you." She pulled up in front of Balbo's trailer and got out of the jeep. She didn't see her brother, but his daughter came out and greeted her. Syra had fourteen winters and was of age to wear the full Runner clothing. The young girl bounced down the trailer steps to greet them, wearing her headscarf, which Tara guessed she had put on when she noticed she had company. Tara remembered reaching the age when she could finally don full Runner garb, and how anxious she had been to wear it at every opportunity.

Tara noticed the looks Torgo and Syra gave each other. They were the same age, and although she knew Torgo had not shown any interest in girls yet, he appeared to be appraising Tara's niece with interest.

"Where's your papa, Syra?"

"They should be returning soon. I just got word from him." The young girl shyly watched the boy in the jeep with eyes that appeared bright through her mask.

"Where is he?"

"He went down to the front with the other men last night."

"If he returns before I do, let him know I wish to talk to him, okay?" Tara got back into the jeep and headed to the battle site, which was also the same direction as Patha's trailer. She got as far as the side of the trailer when she saw Patha and Darius riding their bikes toward her. She was delighted that she was able to see Darius while here. A week without him made her heart ache. Torgo, however, slouched down in his seat.

"You are about to meet my papa, who is also the leader of this clan." Tara looked at the boy as they pulled up in front of the trailer and climbed out of the jeep. "Be sure to show all signs of your warrior training, understand?"

"Yes." He straightened.

"What in the world are you doing here?" Patha got off his bike and approached them with long strides.

"Patha, I'd like you to meet Torgo, younger brother of Lord Darius." Tara ignored the question and instead offered the introduction.

There was a slight smile on Darius' face as the young boy stood alert, did not smile, and saluted with all the signs of a great future Gothman warrior.

Patha acknowledged the salute and treated Torgo like a man by returning the salute, as he would one of his soldiers.

"I've come to recruit several young people to take care of some work I want done in town." Tara looked from one man to the other.

"What work is that?" Darius dismounted his bike and reached Tara's side within the next second, pulling her into his arms.

"Several of the buildings downtown are nothing more than rubble."

"Which buildings?" Darius frowned at the news.

Torgo looked as if he was ready to respond to the question, but a quick look from Tara reminded him of the training she'd given him. A young warrior doesn't speak to a superior unless spoken to directly.

"The building next to the grocery store is gone. It'll need to be rebuilt. The pride of the Gothman people in town has been affected, as is normal during war. If we show signs of preparing to rebuild, it'll boost their spirits. They need to see that life as they knew it will return soon."

"That doesn't sound like work for children," Patha frowned.

"The Gothman women won't do such work. I want some of the young people too young for fighting to work. The school's been closed, and they need something to do. I need several Runner children, as well as Gothman children, to start hauling this rubble. It'll allow them to get to know each other. And if the Gothman girls are allowed to work also, it will help them start to learn how to work alongside men, doing the same task."

"Could you do this work?" Darius now addressed Torgo.

"Yes, I could." Torgo stood tall as he spoke.

"And what do you think the mamas of these children will say when you tell them you want their children to do a man's job?" Darius stroked Tara's arm as he held her firmly next to him.

"I know what I would like to tell them. I've seen the kind of work these women do around the town. They could rebuild the buildings themselves with instruction. My first thought was to have the women do the work. It was Torgo who said they would fear what their claims would say when they returned. That's when I thought of the children."

* * * * *

"You can't change the ways of a nation overnight, my lady. Whether they can do the work or not isn't the point." Darius rested his chin on the top of Tara's head and moved his hand over her growing belly. She looked so pregnant. He was sure she'd almost doubled in size in the one week since he'd last seen her.

There was a folding chair by the trailer, and he set it next to Tara. Placing his hand gently on her shoulder, he made it clear she was to sit. "There are things in life that are simply viewed as men's work," he said with a smile. "Some of them I don't believe you'd argue with. They are part of your culture too, they are. I've seen them now. A man will carry heavy items while the woman takes care of the children, yes. Your women may be warriors, but they don't mind the chivalry of a man."

Tara smiled and accepted the chair. "I still want the children."

"Stubborn as they come," Darius said to Patha, who nodded and walked into the trailer.

"The town people won't go for it, Tara."

"They will if you tell them to."

"Could we ask your niece to help?" Torgo spoke up, forgetting about not speaking unless addressed.

"What?" Darius turned a foul expression on his younger brother.

"Nothing."

Tara gave Torgo a sharp look. "The people will do what you say, Darius." She was not going to give up. "They follow you blindly."

Darius turned from her and walked toward the jeep, deep in thought.

"It's true," Tara said. "I mean nobody will even mention your brother Juro."

He couldn't believe she had just mentioned his dead brother's name. There was a damn good reason why he was never mentioned. No one would be allowed to question why his brother had died, giving Darius right to lead Gothman. He wouldn't have it.

He turned quickly as anger surged through him, then looked at Torgo and felt the emotion fade away. "Fine. I'll issue the order."

Darius scrutinized Tara for a second. She still looked tired, but she was clean and there was more color in her face. Her eyes glowed, and she seemed pleased with her victory, but he was looking deeper. He wanted to see some type of satisfaction with her oncoming mamahood. He knew she loved the life of a warrior. Would she love the life of mamahood as well? He wanted her to…desperately. The thought of her raising their child kept him going in this dreary and tiresome war, a war he wished would end.

"When's your next doctor's visit?"

"As soon as I get home."

"Good. I expect a raving report." He kissed her affectionately. "The Sea People are showing signs of weakening. This war should be over soon, it should."

* * * * *

Tara was glad he approved her plan. She would have implemented it even if he had said no; she'd already made her mind up about that. It wouldn't have been hard to tell the people he'd given a command. They wouldn't have found out otherwise, not until the deed had been done. But going behind Darius' back wasn't how she wanted to do things. The two of them needed to be a team, not working against each other.

Balbo agreed to send his daughter to town; several other Runners also agreed to send their children. That was the easy part. Back in town, Tara took Torgo's suggestions on which houses to approach. The women who answered the doors were reluctant at first, but realizing it was an order, they also agreed. The next morning, the young people would meet downtown and begin work.

As far as Tara was concerned, approaching the Gothman women was the easy part of the day. Reena's exam awaited her, and

Tara didn't look forward to it. Driving back to the house, she felt tired and in need of a nap. It was not part of her nature to admit fatigue, and she kept her attitude positive and cheery in an effort not to show it.

Reena was ready for her and scooted Torgo out of the house, telling him he could return after the exam ended, but she wouldn't have a man under the roof while examining a woman.

"Now then, I am going to see if your cervix is softening, I am." Reena waited as Tara got comfortable on her bed and Hilda looked on.

The examination was uncomfortable but, regardless of what any doctor may say, there's no way to examine female organs without some discomfort. Tara put all her attention into keeping her face expressionless. She'd handled gunshot wounds, broken bones and other injuries with dignity, but the unusual pressure she felt as Reena probed her with fingers made Tara want to yell and pull away.

Reena poked and prodded and pushed on Tara's tummy. She would stand back and look at Tara and then continue with the prodding.

"That's interesting," she said once. "Well, I'll be," was another response.

Tara watched her and strained her neck to see what Reena was doing, although it was difficult with her big tummy in the way.

Finally, Reena stepped back and washed her hands.

Hilda handed Reena a dry towel and studied her friend's face, then turned and patted Tara's shoulder.

"Do you want anything, dear?" Reena asked.

"No." Tara put her legs together and then began to sit.

"Stay there then. I'll be right back, I will."

Hilda followed Reena out of the room.

Tara strained to hear their words as they walked down the hall.

"Why?" Hilda asked.

Tara thought she sounded irritated. Why what, Tara wondered, but all she could hear were the two women descending the stairs.

She must have drifted to sleep, because Tara awakened to the sound of voices in her room. But they sounded so far away...she was content to ignore them. Slowly, she opened her eyes and was rather surprised to see Dr. Digo standing there looking at her with Reena and Hilda at his side.

"You needed that sleep, didn't you, dear?" Reena smiled at her daughter.

"How long was I out?" Tara tried to sit up, but a cramp slowed her down. This was something she experienced often. She didn't bat an eye at it, but slowed down until it had passed and then relaxed again on her bed.

"Do you cramp often?" Dr. Digo put on a pair of sterile gloves and unloaded the contents of a bag onto her dresser.

"I guess so. I don't give it much thought."

He lifted a suitcase she hadn't noticed until then and opened it to display a portable landlink.

"How can I help?" Reena looked at the foreign equipment.

"A bowl of very hot water might help. This ointment is always cold for some reason. It would be nice if we could warm it up." Hilda quickly left the room before Reena could.

It was obvious she was bothered about something and that alerted Tara.

"What's going on, Doc?"

"I'm going to do a sonogram. Ever had one of those?"

Tara allowed Reena to adjust the sheets so just Tara's protruding belly showed.

"No, but I've heard of them. Can you tell me if my baby is a boy or a girl?" Tara wasn't sure why Reena sent for Dr. Digo, but she thought both women looked a bit worried. "Is everything okay?"

"I'm sure all is fine, but we'll take a look to make sure. If you want, while we're checking, we can tell if you are going to have a son or daughter." He smiled at her and accepted the hot water as Hilda returned.

After plugging in cords to the machine, Dr. Digo spread the ointment over Tara's tummy. The women watched as he turned on the machine, then placed a flat disc attached by a bunch of chords to Tara's stomach.

"That won't hurt the baby, will it?" Hilda looked more nervous than a cat.

"Goodness, no, ma'am." Dr. Digo tried not to smile at the ignorance of the question. "Look at the monitor, and you'll be able to see what's inside Tara's uterus."

"For heaven's sake," Hilda breathed.

Tara couldn't tell if Hilda's response was a result of the extraordinary equipment or at the doctor mentioning a female reproductive organ so casually.

"I can't tell what I'm looking at." Tara watched the movement of the black and white picture on the screen.

"You were right," Dr. Digo told Reena.

"I knew it." Reena clapped her hands to her mouth.

"Knew what?" Tara looked at each adult hovering over her, confusion and fear settling hard in her gut. "Is everything okay?"

It hadn't crossed her mind until that moment that anything could possibly go wrong with the pregnancy. She'd seen her fair share of pregnant women in the clan. Other than getting bigger, they never acted any different and continued with their lives just as before.

"I'll tell you that in a minute. What I can say now is that Reena discovered you are carrying two babies."

"Twins?" Tara let her head drop to the pillow in disbelief. "Are you sure?"

"Carrying two babies is a lot harder than carrying one." Dr. Digo turned his attention to Reena and Hilda. "She is going to need to keep her activities to a bare minimum from here on out."

"Oh no! I can't do that." Tara tried to sit up and cursed when her large belly stopped her, not only with its size, but with shooting pains that captured her breath momentarily.

* * * * *

Reena noticed the look of defiance she'd grown accustomed to seeing. "Now we know…and you'll not go anywhere until these babies are born." Reena let her daughter see where she got some of her stubbornness.

Tara opened her mouth to rebut.

Reena lifted her hand to make it final. "Her cervix is a lot thinner than I expected it to be. She shows all signs of a woman preparing for birth in a cycle. But I'm thinkin' we don't want those babies coming before they are done." Reena spoke to the doctor, but caressed her daughter's head, letting Tara hear the reality of what could happen if she disobeyed this order to rest. Reena might be conferring with the doctor, but she still watched him warily. She wasn't comfortable with the idea of a man giving her daughter such a personal examination.

"Well, these babies are not ready to be born yet. We need to do everything we can to keep them in her for at least another cycle and a half. The longer, the better. I don't have very good equipment to handle premature babies." Dr. Digo leaned back against the dresser, aware of the fact that he would not be able to do an internal exam with the two old ladies present. "Tara, you're not going to like this, but I want you to stay in bed as much as you can. If you move out of that bed, it should be to a chair. Do as little walking as possible. The more you move, the more those babies will move around in you, and the thinner that cervix will get. Now they haven't turned yet, and that's a good sign."

* * * * *

Tara lay on the bed, not quite willing to let it all sink in. Everything had been fine this morning, and now her body was on red alert. Sitting still was not something she did well. She was glad to hear the babies were okay, but staying put for the next cycle and a half? She wasn't sure she could do it.

Dr. Digo told them one of her babies was a boy, but he said the other was being bashful and he couldn't tell its sex. As Dr. Digo packed up, the women stood anxiously watching him and helping to organize his things. Tara could tell they couldn't wait to get out of the room and share the most exciting piece of gossip they'd come by in quite awhile. She was sure every soul in town would know before the day was out. She also knew they would not leave the room before the doctor did, for it simply wouldn't be proper for the man to be in her bedroom unattended.

After assuring all three parties she would stay put and call if she needed anything, Tara found herself alone. She slowly got up and moved over to her desk where all her landlink equipment sat. The homing device was surprisingly still on the back of Darius' neck, and she was able to locate him without difficulty. He was at Patha's trailer. She reached for her comm to see if he'd respond. "Darius?"

No answer.

She resorted to the landlink and sent him a message to see if he was on one of the transmissions.

Patha answered the message and told her Darius was in the shower.

She told her papa to send him to her at once indicating it was very important. She could not go through this pregnancy alone and needed to talk to him personally.

Patha said he would send him.

Tara logged off the landlink. She stared out the window, not seeing the beautiful view for the first time. She'd grown accustomed to the thought of having a baby to raise by the New Winter, which was still two cycles away. She was familiar with the amount of work involved. She'd helped with the younger children in her clan as she grew up. But two babies...double the work...she'd not once entertained that thought. It was so overwhelming. Suddenly, she was scared of parenthood all over again.

She needed to hear Darius tell her he'd help her with the babies. She'd known in her mind all along that when the baby came she'd do most of the raising. The thought hadn't actually bothered her too much. He would rule the nation with her guidance, and she would raise the child with his guidance. By the time she became ruler of the Runner clans, this child, uh, children would be much older.

Now, with two babies, she needed to know he would help feed them, change them, and get up when they cried at night. But she didn't want anyone else to assume responsibility of her armies. Tara had worked hard to gain Patha's respect—her *papa's* respect—so that he would give her all the responsibility she now had. Her days already were full with overseeing all the commanders, not to mention the tasks that she would need to undertake once this war ended. How could she possibly handle working all day with her clan and being the mama to two babies? Tara let her thoughts absorb her and after a bit laid her head down on the desk and started to cry.

"Tara?"

Tara lifted her head at the sound of his voice and smiled at Darius, then wiped her eyes to clear her blurred vision.

"I'm so glad you're here," she whispered and pushed herself to her feet before falling into his arms when he moved across the room. "I've just found out that we're going to have twins, Darius. How are we going to handle two babies?"

"We're going to have twins?" Darius sounded pleased.

Tara looked up at him and frowned. "That isn't good news," Tara said and pushed away. "That means twice as much work. I've got responsibilities, and so do you. How will we handle twins?"

"Together, my lady." Darius pulled her to him again. "We will handle them together. I'm not that ignorant to the raising of a child, you know. You forget that Torgo came along when I was old enough to help, he did. Papa didn't have much of a hand in raising him, but I did."

"You helped with Torgo when he was a baby?" Tara's voice cracked through her tears, and she walked over to her dresser and pulled out one of her handkerchiefs, then blew her nose.

"Yes, my Lady. My papa wasn't around too much, and the lad often put my mama at her wit's end." Darius sat on her bed, and patted the spot next to him. "I know my share about changing diapers and feeding time, I do. You and I will do just fine, we will."

Tara smiled and hugged him. The man said exactly what she needed to hear, and now she felt like crying again, because she was so lucky to have him.

"It doesn't seem right that it takes two people to make the baby," he stroked her blotchy cheeks, smiling gently, "but just one is expected to raise the baby."

"I can't believe you just said that," she whispered as he pulled her close. "Do you really mean that?"

"Having you in my life has brought out what I already believed in my soul, it has." He pulled away far enough to be able to look deep into her eyes with those penetrating gray ones of his. "We can't have you all upset like this, now can we? You'll rest now, you will."

Had he truly meant all those things he'd just said? She knew only time would tell—and she hated that she would have to wait and see Darius in action to find out if he spoke the truth.

* * * * *

Darius smiled to himself as he closed her bedroom door. He'd calmed her and appeased her worries nicely, he told himself. They would need to hire servants, especially with twins. He thought about some of the pretty young Gothman women he'd noticed over the past few cycles.

There were several that were exceptionally enticing that brought food and other services to the Gothman warriors out on the battlefield. He'd declined their offers. After all, he had just claimed a woman of his own. And, there was no way he would risk the union of Gothman and the Runners by enjoying the pleasures of a whore. No, it would be better to hire plain-looking servants to help with the children after they were born.

* * * * *

The next few weeks moved along uneventfully. Tara moved from room to room, changing her environment, so she wouldn't go stir crazy being in her room all the time, and she went outside a few times—although the oncoming winter made it easier to stay inside. She wasn't exactly bored. There was plenty to think about.

Especially since Reena had returned from town a few days before with news. Rumors in town claimed the war was all but over.

"We finished clearing the last of the rubble today." Torgo joined Tara at the table, carrying a hot bowl of soup he'd brought from the kitchen. "I think several of the womenfolk are going to have a gathering for everyone who helped."

"That sounds great." Tara sipped at her own soup and smiled when Torgo offered her a slice of bread from the platter in the center of the table. He'd smeared butter on it, and she took a bite.

"I think some of the Runner kids are going to be there." He wasn't sure why, but he decided not to mention his friendship with Syra. He'd never hung out with a girl before, but she was cool.

"You're experiencing history in the making." Tara smiled in between bites. "Already our cultures are accepting each other."

Torgo slurped his soup just as Hilda entered the room.

She slapped the back of his head. "Reena should be here soon." Hilda sat at the opposite end of the table from Tara and placed a large cloth bag in front of her so Tara couldn't see her face. "I wanted to show you some of the material we will use on the baby quilts."

Ladies in town gathered once a week to work on quilts for the expected twins. Tara had seen so many different materials for the quilts; she couldn't keep straight what they'd look like when they were done. She humored the woman though and watched attentively.

The front door opened, and Reena entered the room in the next minute, bringing a gust of cold air with her. "I daresay that one is my favorite." Reena ran her hand over a flowery print Hilda had just pulled from the bag.

"I'm going to join some of the kids in town to play." Torgo stood, grabbing his empty bowl. "All this quilting talk is for ladies."

"You behave now, boy," Hilda scolded, but smiled and then turned to see Tara's reaction to the material.

"I have to agree with Reena." Tara dunked the crust of her bread into her soup. "I like that pattern too."

Hilda seemed pleased and folded the material before placing it back in the bag. "Now are you sure you'll be okay left alone for a time?"

The pair appeared anxious to go, and Tara hurried to reassure them. "I'll be fine. Get going you two. We'll be needing those quilts soon, I expect." Tara stood and walked around the table, then made a feeble attempt to hug the two women. She watched as they left the house.

Soon after that, Tara headed out the back door to enjoy a walk through the snow. The weather was crisp, and she felt her lungs freeze with her first gulp of air. A path was shoveled through the snow, and Tara stuck to it. It led through the yard to the driveway, which had also been shoveled. Small mountains of snow towered on either side of her. Snow from the path rested on the pristine, sparkling white yard.

Tara desperately wanted to wade into the snow to reach the shed and the backfield. There, she could truly enjoy the winter's beauty, but she behaved and stayed in the cleared area. She reached the end of the path and began walking toward the front of the house along the driveway.

Suddenly, she stopped in her tracks. A red spot soiled the ground in front of her. The ruby liquid covered a two-foot area, and from it something had been dragged through the huge pile of snow to the other side. Tara moved closer and recognized the mark as blood. One touch told her the liquid was still warm.

Tara pulled her comm out of her pocket and hooked it around her ear. "Darius," she said quietly as she looked around her warily.

"Yes?"

"There's something wrong at the house."

"What is it?"

"I don't know. There's blood in the driveway. I think one of the guards has been dragged off. Darius, I'm outside and I'm not armed," she whispered as she moved closer to the house.

"We'll be there in a minute. Who's there with you?"

"I'm here alone." Tara could hear the mouthpiece go dead as soon as she'd spoken those words. She wondered where Darius was and how long it would take him to get there. She was in no condition to fight unarmed, and her laser was in her other coat pocket, which was lying on her bed.

She looked toward the back of the house and then to the front. Four guards were supposed to be stationed out here. She saw no sign of them.

Tara moved as fast as she dared along the slick surface of the driveway and reentered the back of the house. There was no way to tell if anyone was in the house, due to its size. She moved up the stairs to her bedroom as quickly and quietly as she could. The laser was still in her coat pocket. Grabbing it, she headed back down the stairs.

No sign of life was evident through the windows, and from the front porch she noted the snow was undisturbed except for the footprints along the driveway. Then she saw it—more blood along the snow in the front yard and indications that someone had been dragged.

Whoever did this was still nearby.

An icy breeze caused Tara to shiver, and icicles shattered to the ground from a nearby tree. Tara stepped carefully to the bloodstained snow and looked off into the direction where crushed snow appeared to form a path. The snow was deep, and she had to move slowly to insure her balance. A hard fall to the ground would possibly send her into labor.

"Isn't it inappropriate for someone in your condition to be out in this weather?" Tara turned quickly to face a Runner standing on the path by the house. She didn't recognize the man through his headscarf, and something was strange about his voice.

"Who are you?" She wrapped her fingers around the laser in her pocket.

"This is rather a shame," he stated, ignoring her question. "It's not really you I'm after, although I guess you should die as well."

Tara listened to the voice carefully. It was Gothman.

Just then, the sounds of motorcycles quickly approaching could be heard. The Gothman in Runner clothing pulled out a laser from his pocket and aimed it straight at Tara.

"Drop it, now!" Darius pulled his bike to a stop and aimed his gun straight at the Runner.

"Oh, what perfect timing. And how heroic. Don't tell me you came alone." The intruder turned his laser on Darius.

Tara pointed her weapon at the stranger and approached slowly. "Hold it right there."

The intruder pulled a second gun from his pocket and aimed this one at Tara. "I won't let this continue."

"You won't let what continue?" Tara took another step toward the stranger, feeling the snow crunch under her boots.

The stranger didn't acknowledge her question, although the laser remained pointed at her. He looked at Darius. "You've destroyed the Bryton blood line. You have no respect for anything but your power. To think how many bastards you have running around out there. That was bad enough."

"What bastards? Darius, who is this?" Tara didn't take her eyes from the man, and his laser didn't waver from her.

"Who knows when someone might show up claiming his right to be Lord of Gothman?" The man continued as if she hadn't spoken. "But then, you go and do something like this." The man waved his laser at Tara.

One of her hands instinctively went to her belly, although she realized with hideous clarity that her hand hardly offered an ample shield for her babies.

"You'll allow a half-breed to be our heir? Darius, that is unacceptable!" The man continued his rantings.

"Mikel, put down the gun." Darius spoke with a calmness that the other man didn't possess.

Tara's mouth fell open in disbelief. This masked stranger — the one holding a laser to her heart, dressed in the garb of people he claimed to despise — was Darius' brother.

"I may die, brother, but so shall you." Mikel raised both of his hands and wrapped his fingers around each trigger. "You murdered Juro, I can prove that, you know. That alone gives me the right to kill you. What do you think our papa would say about this?" He gestured his gun at Tara. "You disgust me, Darius."

Darius' shot rang through the air with a high-pitched whistle.

Mikel was thrown backwards from the close impact of the laser. As he slammed into the side of the house, both of his lasers went off, one into the air and one straight toward Tara.

Instinctively, she threw herself to the ground, feeling the loss of air in her lungs. She turned to land on her side, holding her belly with both hands, as her laser fell into the powdery snow next to her. The ground came fast and hard, and the pain was so intense she wasn't sure if she'd been shot or not.

Darius was by her side instantly.

The discomfort and pain racking her body overwhelmed Tara. She fought to stay conscious. "I fear I've thrown myself into labor, my lord."

"Shh. Be still." Darius lifted her into his arms and was up the porch stairs and into the house within seconds. He seemed completely disinterested in his dead brother lying out front, focusing only on Tara's condition. He took the wide stairs three at a time and had her on the bed before she realized it.

"What about your brother? You can't leave him here." Tara watched Darius as his hands went over her body, as if searching to see if anything had broken.

"Don't worry about him right now, my lady. It's you I am concerned about."

A sharp pain riveted through Tara's body, starting somewhere in her middle and ending halfway down her leg. Tara caught her breath and then exhaled when the pain subsided.

"How do you feel?" He stroked her hair and looked calm yet concerned for her wellbeing.

"Am I shot?" She wanted to ask if his brother was dead.

Darius was talking into his mouthpiece. "Patha, I need Dr. Digo sent to the house immediately." He was silent for a second and then flipped the mouthpiece off. "Where's Reena?" he asked her gently.

"She's working on the quilts with the other ladies." Suddenly, Tara was confused. "Darius, I think I'm okay. I guess I knocked the wind out of me." She attempted to sit, and a sudden pain flashed through her gut and down her legs.

Darius eased her back down.

She grabbed his hand with both of hers and squeezed harder than she'd ever squeezed before. The pain subsided as she lay back down, and she eased her grip.

Darius' face was expressionless. He tapped his comm. "Send someone to find Reena. I believe she is at one of those quilting meetings, I do."

Tara felt another wave of pain, and Darius offered his hand again, which she squeezed without mercy. She yelped with the intensity of the pain this time, and watched Darius' mouth move, but couldn't quite make out his words.

"And I don't want a trace of blood visible," she thought she heard him say, but another wave of pain hit her before the last one completely ended.

It seemed like hours passed before Dr. Digo appeared. Not long after, Reena arrived. Tara could hear Hilda's excited voice although she didn't see her. Whenever she opened her eyes, it was Darius' face she saw.

He watched her, his expression assuring her everything would be all right. Her claim stroked her head with a damp cloth, which felt better at that moment than she could have imagined. Then she felt his cheek brush hers, as he placed gentle kisses on her forehead. She focused on his touch, as wave after wave violated her body.

She turned her head to see the activity in the room. Everyone around her seemed surreal. Reena appeared to be bouncing from one side of the bed to the other. Dr. Digo placed a needle in her arm, and everyone suddenly seemed very far away.

Tara understood the conversation but had a hard time focusing on it. Her thoughts kept going inward. She vaguely paid attention as her legs were lifted and placed on cold metal. She blindly obeyed when Reena stood between her legs and instructed her to push.

"Tara," someone was speaking to her and there was cold water dripping slowly down the side of her forehead. She reached up with her hand and brushed the water off. "Tara, girl, open your eyes."

"Say hello to your son, my lady." Darius stood by the bed holding a bundle of blankets.

Tara focused on him and realized he was holding a baby in his arms. She had done it. It impressed Tara how easily she was able to sit up, and she looked around the room at her exhausted audience. Tara knew she should feel as tired as they looked, but a sense of exhilaration flooded her and she felt overwhelmed with happiness.

"Where are my babies?" Her throat was dry, and her voice cracked. She blinked several times to clear her thoughts.

Darius sat next to her and placed the bundle of blankets in her arms. Hilda approached with another bundle.

Tara wrapped her arms around the two babies and looked down into their squishy pink faces.

"We have a boy and a girl." Darius ran his fingers through her hair and lifted her face to his. "You were quite impressive, I must say." He leaned forward and kissed her gently.

She smiled. "I want to name them Andru and Ana."

Later that night, Darius crept into the dark room where Tara lay, cradling her sleeping babies. She smiled as he leaned down to kiss her.

"I wanted to wish you good night," he whispered. "But I fear I woke you, I did."

"I've been sleeping on and off, I guess. But I'm glad you are here."

"You were wonderful birthing our children, my lady." And when he kissed her again, she smiled against his mouth and returned the kiss until he backed away a few inches to study her.

"I'm sorry about your brother," she whispered.

He looked at her seriously. "I only have one brother, and he knows nothing of my papa's philosophies."

"Darius?" She looked up anxiously as he turned to leave and he stopped in the doorway. "Do you have any other children?"

"No."

The door closed, and the room became completely dark again.

Chapter Eleven

ঙ

"Come on, you can do ten more." Tara was dripping with sweat.

"Can't we take a break?" Torgo dropped to the ground. "If I do one more pushup, my arms will break."

"Okay, a little break." Tara laughed and fell to the ground as well. She was exhausted and it felt really good. "You don't know how happy I am to have my figure back."

"You do have it back at that, my lady." Lord Darius walked out to the backyard and looked at the two lying on the ground. "Duty calls, however, the cherubs are up from their nap."

Tara jumped to her feet and straightened her shirt. "I guess we'll continue your training later."

Torgo didn't mind a bit. He had a hard time keeping up with the new mama, and he didn't want to admit it.

Tara went upstairs to greet her beautiful children. Each lay in his and her own cradle and smiled at the sight of their mama. She'd grown accustomed to picking them both up and laying them at opposite ends of the diaper-changing table. The two children would kick at each other's feet and giggle while she blew on their tummies, changed diapers, and dressed them.

"I can't believe how much you two are growing." She kissed fingers and toes. "You're six cycles old today, did you know that?"

"Oh, good, they're awake now." Hilda entered the nursery with a bag in her hands. "I bought these while I was in town this morning, I did. They were such cute outfits I couldn't resist. Don't you agree?"

The two outfits were made from blue denim. One was a pair of overalls and the other a dress with the straps like overalls. Hilda also produced a white blouse to go with the dress and a white shirt for the overalls. The two women struggled to get the lively children into their new outfits then placed them on the floor.

Tara laughed as Andru tried to inspect the shiny buttons on his sister's outfit. Ana slapped at his hands for his efforts.

"I heard news in town this morning, you know—catching up on the gossip so to speak."

"Oh?" Tara never appeared interested in any of the goings on of the community, but Hilda was determined to teach her daughter-in-law the fine art of gossiping.

"Ah, yes, I did. I heard Patha is planning to head south for a few cycles. It was Gertrude's daughter who told me, you know the baker's claim?"

Tara was less interested in the source of the gossip than the news itself. "Patha is leaving? I just saw him the other day, and he didn't mention it. Do you know when?"

"Now that I don't know, but here is the kicker." Hilda lowered her voice as if someone might be listening. "He has asked Reena to go with him, he has."

"What did she say?"

"Well, I would think she would say no." Hilda thought the question absurd.

Tara picked up the babies and walked into the large adjoining bedroom she now shared with Darius.

"Where are you going?"

"I'm going to say goodbye to my papa." Tara pulled a clean headscarf from her top dresser drawer.

"You're taking the babies?"

"Can you tend them?"

Hilda looked at her watch and shook her head. "I'm having tea with some of the ladies over at Roga's in an hour. You really should hire one of the girls in town to be a nanny, you should." The old lady scurried off to prepare for her outing.

Tara was left alone with her babies. She thought about asking Torgo or Darius to go with her, but neither was in sight as she loaded the babies into the back of the jeep. The weather appeared conducive to the activity, so she pulled the top off the jeep hoping the babies would enjoy the fresh air.

"It will get you accustomed to riding on a bike." She watched them look up at the endless blue sky.

There were signs that many of the clan members were preparing to leave. Doors stood open as trailer interiors were dismantled. Breakable items were being boxed before being placed in compartments under the trailer. It was summer and the best time to travel the country.

Tara suddenly felt a longing to be going. It surprised her. She'd been so busy with the babies and so wrapped up with her love for Darius that she hadn't even thought about the summer journeys.

The clan would move around for the next four to five cycles and then settle down again when the weather turned bad. The alliance built with Gothman enabled the Runners to leave some of their possessions on the land, with Darius promising protection. Patha and Darius agreed that the acreage on top of the hills just to the west of Gothman would be Blood Circle Clan property. The townsfolk had grown accustomed to Runners entering their stores. Tara had even heard business owners speak favorably of the race since the Runners had begun stocking up on supplies for their journeys.

"Hi, Syra." Tara pulled up to Patha's trailer and smiled at her niece. "What are you doing?"

"Nothing." Syra's tone was sulky.

Tara was about to ask her what was wrong when Patha and Balbo came around the other side of the trailer.

"I heard you were leaving," Tara greeted her papa as she reached for her children.

"In the morning." The old man smiled and went to look at his grandbabies. "These babies will be walking by the time I get back."

Tara handed Andru to his Grandpapa and held Ana in her arms. "What's wrong with Syra?"

"Believe it or not, she doesn't want to go." Balbo shrugged his shoulders at his daughter's behavior. "I don't understand her lately."

"Why not let her stay with me? I need a nanny for the children. I could pay her, and she could have her own room. It would help her save money for her first bike. She's about ready for one, you know."

Patha looked at Balbo, who showed his approval of the suggestion.

"She's growing up so fast." Balbo shook his head. "Nothing I do is right for her anymore. Are you sure she would be a help with the babies?"

"I was caring for babies at her age if not younger. Besides, Balbo, it might make it easier to find another wife. Syra is quite the young lady, and another woman might think she has competition with her around."

"Don't try to argue with her, Balbo." Patha laughed. "Sounds like she has her mind made up."

"Okay. I'll speak to her. That is, if she'll talk to me." He walked over to the sulking girl.

Tara watched her own papa play with her son. "I'll miss you. You better stay in touch with me."

"Don't you long to travel, yourself?"

"I hadn't thought about it to be honest with you. The twins keep me so busy; there is little time to think of anything but tending them." Tara squinted from the sun, as she looked around the clansite. Runners loaded bags onto their bikes and locked down trailers. "Coming out here does put the yearning into a person, though."

Patha looked at her, but instead of saying anything he reached out and tickled his granddaughter.

She noticed the look of concern in Patha's eyes. "Don't worry about me. I am happy. Really I am. I've found a good man."

"Good. You have an obligation here. The Runners have never had land like this before, and a lot of that is due to you, my dear."

"I know." Tara was aware the Runners viewed her as being responsible for a pivotal turn in their history. She received more respect from them due to the Lord of Gothman claiming her, than she did from the Gothman.

Balbo and Syra walked up to them, and Tara noticed the young girl was all smiles.

"Can I really stay with you?" Syra looked from one twin to the other but her smile didn't waver.

"You can work for me." Tara caught the girl's eye. "You'll be in charge of the babies, and you'll go to school. It won't be fun and games."

Tara knew the teenager had had exposure to young children. But Tara was concerned because Syra would be one of the few girls in her class. She knew Syra could handle herself and would not be bullied by anyone. Still, she was breaking the mold by attending school while Gothman girls were discouraged from going. The Gothman believed their girls could learn what they needed to know staying home and helping with housework. Tara had done her best to encourage the girls to attend, but it was a slow process.

The Runners had been allowed to enroll their children in the Gothman school by a new law Darius had passed. That was a slow process too, encouraging Runners to take advantage of the Gothman schools instead of home-schooling their children, as had been the custom.

"I won't let you down." Syra seemed excited as she ran to get her things.

* * * * *

Syra couldn't believe her luck. She would be staying with Tara and could see Torgo every day. This sure beat spending the next several cycles cooped up with her papa. Torgo would be a lot more fun to be with. He was so cute and so tall. Ever since they'd finished the project of clearing rubble for the Gothman, she hadn't seen much of him. This change of events was too good to be true.

"I'm ready." Syra ran back to Tara who was still talking to Patha and Balbo. She took Ana from Tara to show she could handle the work.

* * * * *

"The River people at the southern edge of Trueland are trying to form a new government, and I thought we would start by going there," Patha said. "I want to make sure they know the Gothman and Runners have united. We'll show our respects to their new government and see if they'll welcome our union by letting Runners enjoy their community."

Tara knew there was oil in the land down there and realized Patha and Darius had probably discussed this. Natural resources in Gothman land were limited, and the people would need to augment their supplies soon. She vowed to keep in touch with Patha and couldn't wait to hear the stories from his journey.

Syra had loaded the babies and her bags into the back of the jeep and was sitting in the passenger seat waiting for Tara. Hugs were exchanged one last time, then Tara and Syra headed back to town.

"I can't believe it. The house is so big." Syra watched in awe as Tara drove along the gravel driveway toward the Bryton home.

"Let's get you settled first." Tara parked behind the house. Tara gave Syra a quick tour of the home and showed her where her bedroom would be. She gave her old room to the girl, knowing Hilda wouldn't mind. After Syra seemed somewhat familiar with her surroundings, Tara decided to put her to the test and announced she was going to take a short ride and would be back in a few hours.

Her bike felt so good underneath her. She leaned forward and took off with enthusiasm. She had decided she would go look for Darius. It had entered her mind, while she was showing Syra around, that she would now be able to spend more time with him. She wasn't sure where he was at the moment and hadn't taken time before leaving the house to track him on her landlink. After driving through the town looking for him, she wondered if he was out joyriding, too.

Tara drove through some of the hills surrounding the town, slowly taking in the aroma of blooming flowers. It was fun driving through the trees, weaving in and out of the brush. Once she hit the open meadow, she pushed her bike and flew at speeds she'd only dreamed about over the past winter.

Instinctively she headed for the back hills, to the cliff where Darius had taken her on their first motorcycle ride, where the twins had been conceived. Now, it was her favorite spot, as well. She imagined her Darius sitting on the edge of the cliff overlooking his reign, lost in thought. She would sneak up on him, giving her Runner skills some much-needed practice.

Tara smiled, deciding she would take him right there and passionately make love to him. Their lovemaking was often interrupted or hurried since their children had been born. They were way past due for some incredible foreplay and heated sex. She drove faster, skillfully dodging the ruts in the earth, dwelling on her thoughts.

She bypassed the rugged rocky road leading up the hill, knowing the motorcycle would make too much noise going over the rocks. It was a slow climb driving through the jagged rocks and tall grass alongside the road, but she enjoyed it. Her heart leapt as she saw Darius' bike in the grassy meadow. She parked a fair distance before the trees ended and quietly dismounted.

Tara crept through the trees, but the excited pounding of her heart soon changed as she heard voices.

"Why must you always bring me here, my lord?" a female voice said. "Just once it would be nice if you would have me in a bed."

Tara almost tripped over a loose branch before she dropped to the ground and crawled through the grass. She couldn't believe what she just heard. Images of Darius' face, so full of love and concern throughout her labor, appeared in her mind. She could feel his tender caresses when another memory came to her—he was holding her, telling her she was beautiful even though she was pregnant with the twins.

The man had told her that he loved her. The pain she felt as she watched her claim through the trees shadowed all pain she had ever experienced in her life.

"Shouldn't a lord's mistress enjoy some of the fruits of his success?"

Tara could see the woman now. Darius' profile faced her, and she could tell he was looking toward the cliff.

Her heart seemed to stop beating. She couldn't breathe. The air had turned to poison.

Tara sucked in breaths trying to gain control of herself so she could make sense of what she saw in front of her.

He was with another woman.

How could this be? He'd given no indication he was having an affair. The blood boiled inside Tara as she listened to the conversation.

"Don't presume you're anything that merits a title," Darius said.

Tara could see the woman's face, or better yet, the girl's face, no...the *whore's* face! She was young...too young...more than likely not even twenty winters. Her long reddish-blonde hair fell in a mass of curls down her back. Tara was sure she would vomit at the beauty of the little tramp.

Tara watched in disbelief as the girl slowly undressed in front of Darius. She was experienced; Tara guessed she'd undressed in front of men before, seducing them with a toss of her long hair. And the way she played with each button before releasing it! She let her dress fall to the ground, then reached for Darius' shirt.

Tara was horrified. Her body began to shake. She couldn't seem to stop it.

The whore placed her hand on Darius, and he didn't stop her. The man showed no apparent emotion, but he let the whore touch him and didn't make a move to prevent her. His gaze appeared to rest somewhere other than the whore's face.

Tara squeezed her eyes closed, momentarily refusing to accept the fact that Darius, her man, her claim, allowed the whore to playfully pull at his shirt until it released from his pants.

He placed his hands on her breasts.

Tara grew livid.

"You'll have me, my Lord, won't you?" The whore ran her hands up Darius' chest underneath his loosened shirt.

"No, he will not." Tara walked into the open.

Every muscle in her body spasmed; she feared she might collapse in front of Darius and the female who still had her wicked hand on his chest. Tara's legs felt mechanical, but they didn't fail her. She pulled her small laser out and aimed it at the woman. The woman screamed and tried to cover her naked body with her arms.

Completely taken off guard, Darius dropped his hands from the woman's breasts and stepped back.

"Get dressed and get out of here," Tara ordered, her laser still aimed at the girl.

Darius put his hands out in front of him, his palms facing Tara. "Tara, don't do anything you'll regret."

"Why not? You have."

The blood boiling in her veins showed right through her eyes. Tara could see red dots popping in her vision. There was more anger in her than she'd ever experienced before. She shot a venomous look at the whore who was frantically trying to get her dress back on. Tara felt a warped satisfaction that her body shook so violently she could hardly step into her clothes.

"Don't bother with the dress, bitch." The snarl coming out of Tara was absolutely evil. "Just run. Run naked, and let the whole world see you for the fucking whore you are."

The woman froze and stared at Tara in absolute horror.

Darius started moving slowly to Tara.

"Run!" Tara screamed and raised her gun to the woman's head.

Now the woman screamed and with dress in hand took off toward the trees.

Tara's body didn't move when she fired the laser, sending the whore's naked body flying into the trees.

Darius lunged at Tara.

She dodged away from his attack and then turned the gun on him, forcing him to a dead stop.

"Tara! Put it down."

"Don't speak to me. I don't need words to add to the scene I just witnessed." She pointed the gun at his head.

"Put down the gun. It's done."

"You won't get out of this that easily." Tara breathed in gulps of air, as if she'd just run up the side of the hill.

He looked at her, not saying a word.

She stood there thinking for a minute. The silver weapon didn't budge from its target.

"Please then, my lady, put down the gun."

Tara noticed something she hadn't seen in Darius before: fear. The recognition of the emotion seemed to also bear witness to every other fault the man possessed. She cocked her head and studied Darius, as if truly seeing him for the first time. She lowered the gun.

Darius exhaled noticeably.

Tara watched him. She saw Darius with painful clarity at that moment—as if every trait, character defect, every emotion that made the man who he was, had been labeled clearly on him for her appraisal. Tara didn't see good looks, she didn't see sex appeal, and there was no hint of the magnificent warrior. What she saw was a man, impure and tainted, and she wasn't impressed.

Intentionally and with premeditation, Tara raised her laser again and felt a calming satisfaction as his eyes widened, and his lips parted. Then without hesitating, she shot him in the foot.

He went down on one knee and grabbed the bleeding foot with both hands.

"I am no longer your lady." She turned and walked away. Bile churned within her, and the spasms made her muscles quiver, but she managed composure. Darius wouldn't see her break from his deed. She wouldn't give him the satisfaction of seeing how he had affected her.

"Tara, where are you going? Come back here."

She could feel the pain in his voice, but wasn't sure if it was from being shot, having been caught, or having heard her last words. There was so much anger and pain racking her entire body that she could no longer speak. She passed his bike and headed to the forest. On impulse, she turned and shot the gas tank out of his bike.

"Tara, you can't leave."

That was the last she heard him say. She ran. Reaching her bike, she climbed on and destroyed the ground and most of the foliage surrounding it as she spun around and tore out of the forest.

Her fury surpassed the pain she was feeling at that moment. She could not get out of her head what she'd seen in the clearing. How he had betrayed her! Shit, the woman was no more than a girl. How could he have done something like this to her, to them, to the twins, their new family? He'd brought that tramp to their magical spot. How could he be so callous?

As she drove back toward the house, she began to wonder how long he'd been unfaithful. She remembered the words Mikel had spoken before Darius had killed him. They haunted her.

Anger so intense she could barely stand it coursed through her. She couldn't go back to the house in this condition.

She drove to the Blood Circle Clan, intent upon talking to Patha. She would leave with him. There was no way she could stay here. Darius had been unfaithful, and he had destroyed trust in their relationship.

Tears burned her eyes as she drove. No, he was no longer a lord, not in her eyes. He did not deserve any title of respect. He was Darius, a Gothman, and she'd been fooled into believing he actually thought more of her than he would a Gothman woman.

Her bike slid to a stop in front of Patha's trailer. She jumped off and pulled open the trailer door with a force fueled by the fury reeking havoc inside her body.

Patha was sitting at the table talking to Reena and stood with a start as the door to his trailer flew open.

Tara noticed his surprised expression and knew no one entered his trailer without knocking. She stood in front of the two of them and quickly shut the door behind her. She was shaking and knew her face was stained from splattering dirt and tears.

"Child, what's wrong?" Reena spoke first as she too jumped up and quickly moved around the table.

Tara's body now shook uncontrollably, and the tears fell from her eyes so rapidly she could barely see her parents standing in front of her. She opened her mouth to talk, but instead savage sobs came out. She gave up and fell into the nearest chair, holding her head in her hands as she cried hysterically.

"Tara, control yourself." Reena wrapped her arms around Tara. "What has happened? How can we help if you don't talk to us?"

Patha sat in the chair next to them.

"Oh god…it's awful. Awful. I just…just can't believe it."

"What? Has someone been hurt? The children? Lord Darius?" Patha asked each question with alarm deepening his voice.

"I found," Tara tried to say the words that would only cause her more pain. "I mean I saw—" She stopped talking and took a deep breath.

Now that she was here, with both her parents looking on with incredible worry, she wasn't so sure she could actually form the sentences. She'd have to describe what she'd witnessed and renew her shame of betrayal. Tara didn't think she could handle that right now.

"Say it quickly, child." Reena saw the pain in her daughter's face and no matter how much she wiped the tears, more followed.

"I found Darius with another woman." She quit crying and felt an incredible numbing sensation ooze over her. "I heard them talking…and she was…she was naked. Darius has taken a mistress."

"Oh child, no." Reena wrapped her arms around Tara. "I'm so sorry."

Patha leaned back in the chair and crossed his arms, but didn't speak.

Tara wanted more of a reaction, and decided to keep talking since she'd been able to get out the ugliest of the words.

"I went out looking for him." Her eyes moved from one to the other. "I found him all right. The son of a bitch was with the whore." Anger replaced her tears, and her temper raged once again.

Patha frowned. "Tara, what did you do?"

"I killed his precious mistress, if that's what you're wondering." She stood and walked to the door, then turned and looked at the two of them. "I will get the children, and we'll be back. We're going with you." She reached for the door.

Patha grabbed her arm. "Tara, where is Darius?"

"He's where I found him."

Patha looked her in the eyes, studying her as if seeking an answer he hadn't heard yet. "You didn't kill him, did you?"

Tara yanked her arms from his grasp and turned her rage on him.

Reena gasped as her eyes shifted from papa to daughter.

Patha, on the other hand, didn't look away from Tara. He crossed his arms, waiting for her answer. He appeared to Tara as he had over so many winters—the patient, but stern gaze that awaited her confession of the truth. Never had she been able to lie to the man, and in truth she had never tried to. She saw no reason to change that pattern now.

"How dare you show more concern for that man's wellbeing than mine? I have been wronged, and you care if the man is alive or dead?" Tara's voice shook from the anger she was experiencing. "He's been having sex with another woman. Who knows how many women he's been with? He's a liar and a cheat!"

"You're a strong woman, Tara. You can straighten him out."

"I'm not going to do anything with him. He's broken my trust and that can't be restored." Tara still glared at Patha. "There will be no second chance."

"Tara, this is bigger than simply your emotions." Patha was straightforward. "The two of you have an obligation to two different races. You must stay and work it out with him. You're under contract. It's as simple as that. These people need your strength."

"I'm not the one who broke the contract." Tara opened the door and ran from the trailer.

Chapter Twelve

ഔ

Tara's mind raced as she drove back to the house. Patha was going to try and stop her. It would only be a matter of time before Darius would communicate with him. She knew he wouldn't contact anyone with a lower rank and risk humiliation and gossip. Patha would go get him. All either one of them cared about were the nations they controlled, and no thought was given to the feelings of those around them.

Her anger escalated, as it became clear to her that to Patha her claim was an arrangement of convenience...a merger to unite two nations. It was no more than a business deal to him. He would have her continue without love or feeling toward Darius, just to keep the two races together. She didn't have the ability to do that. It was her love for Darius that had motivated her actions and without it; she was of no use here.

She lifted the microphone on her landlink and called the house.

Syra answered the phone, which was the first thing that had gone right since she'd left. It would be easier to get the babies out of the house if Hilda weren't involved.

"Syra, I need you to do something for me." Tara concentrated on making her voice sound as calm and pleasant as possible.

"Hi, the babies are fine." Syra assumed Tara was checking up on her.

"Great, I knew you could handle it. Now, I need you to load the babies into the jeep for me. Pack a bag with several of their outfits and a blanket or two. I'll also need a basket with some food in it. Can you do that for me?"

"Sure. Where are we going?"

"I thought I'd give you the rest of the afternoon off. The babies and I are going to say goodbye to several people before they leave," Tara lied. "I'll be there in a minute."

Syra was loading the jeep when Tara pulled up. She slowly guided her bike onto a flat trailer parked nearby. Syra started to watch with curiosity, but left to get the babies, who were still in the house.

Tara backed the jeep up to the hitch and attached the trailer to the back of the vehicle. She then went inside and hugged her babies before running upstairs to grab a few things. Once in her bedroom, she flew through the closet, hurriedly pulling out several outfits and throwing them into her bag. She turned to leave the room and then on second thought stopped and walked over to Darius' dresser. There was a small box buried under his clothes in the bottom drawer. Opening it, she saw several small bags filled with gold coins and a few priceless jewels. She hesitated and then dumped the contents into her bag. He'd robbed her, and now she was robbing him. She would need money and Gothman dollars would do her no good outside of Gothman.

Syra was talking to Hilda, who'd just returned when Tara went back downstairs. Tara quickly thought of what she would say to the obvious questions as she approached the old lady.

"Did you have a nice time?" Tara asked as she walked past Hilda to go out the back door.

"Ah, it was nice to see everyone, it was." Hilda followed Tara. "I see you took my advice on the nanny."

"Yes, it was a good idea." Tara turned and smiled calmly at Hilda.

"Where are you going?"

"We're going to go say goodbye to several of the Runners before they leave. I'll be gone most of the day. I'm leaving Syra here, if you don't mind. I told her she could have the afternoon off, but I don't see why you can't put her to work if you like." Tara checked to see that she had everything she needed.

"Have fun, my lady. I'll spend the time getting to know the girl, I will." Hilda waved as Tara slowly drove down the driveway.

She followed the road to town until she was sure anyone watching from the house could no longer see her. She then pulled off and started heading for a back lane that would turn south. There was no doubt she'd be followed, and all measures would be made to stop her. Her load was heavy, and she would not be able to travel quickly. She turned to look at Andru and Ana who were turning their heads to watch the surroundings move past them. Her stomach was tied in knots, and she knew it would stay that way until she was out of Gothman territory.

The first hour passed peacefully. She drove through the meadows on the backside of the hills. It seemed ironic that if Darius had been up on the cliff he would have seen her movements, but Tara felt safe assuming he'd not been able to climb up the cliff in his present condition. She actually started to enjoy the beautiful day and forced all thoughts of what had happened out of her head.

The landlink next to her started blinking as someone tried to reach her. There was little doubt as to what the message might say, and without looking to see who could be transmitting, she hit delete.

It wasn't much longer before she heard the sound of motorcycles behind her. She'd expected this. Gothman would not let her go without a fight. There was no way she could outrun the bikes, and she knew this. She drove with one hand and opened the suitcase on the floor of the jeep with the other. Inside were several hand bombs and two Eliminators.

She pulled an Eliminator out and set it on the seat next to her. She covered her babies with Runner blankets made out of the same black material as her clothing; they were bulletproof and would protect the children if things got really ugly.

Several of the bikes were close enough that she could see the guards' faces. She detonated one of the hand bombs and threw it. The three motorcycles skidded sideways across the field. Turning to focus her attention on her driving, she glanced at her babies, making sure the blanket remained secure.

"We'll be through this part soon, my dears," Tara said and hoped her voice calmed her wide-eyed children. She placed her flat palm on one child's head, and then the other, reassuring herself that they were securely belted in, so that the rough ride jostled them as little as possible.

She heard the other motorcycles in pursuit slow at the explosion. All she could do was continue to drive.

Gothman territory ended just several miles ahead and then she would be in Freeland territory. Briefly, she wondered if they'd continue their pursuit over the border. She didn't have long to wonder as she watched the remaining guards close in behind her. Darius probably assumed he could chase her to the borders of Trueland, and no one would dare to stop him—the pompous ass.

Tara counted four Gothman as they increased speed in an attempt to pass and force her to stop the jeep.

"Damn," she hissed, as one of the bikes swerved dangerously close to a front tire.

Tara knew she couldn't make any sharp turns with the trailer hitched behind her. And she couldn't fire at all four of them at once. "But I can take you out one at a time," she yelled through the wind, as she leaned past the windshield and shot the rider who had attempted to drive into her.

Tara noticed none of them had drawn their weapons. Obviously, they had instructions not to shoot her. Another guard pulled to the other side of her, while the third pulled alongside the trailer behind her. Tara swiveled her head back and forth in an attempt to keep tabs on what both men were doing. The jeep bounced over a small gully in the ground, and Tara cursed. Andru howled in protest, and Ana's tiny fists shot forward, knocking the blanket down to the babies' waists.

"We are going to make it through this," Tara said more to herself than to her children. She gripped the steering wheel with one fist, fought to secure the blanket with her free hand, and dared to turn the jeep just enough to delay either guard from boarding her.

Tara wouldn't risk shooting behind her, but had no problem eliminating the guard next to her. Now there were only two guards. She didn't see others pursuing her and was a little put out that this was all the fight Darius would make for her.

"You really didn't know me that well, Darius, did you?" Tara spoke into the air as her gaze darted from the two mirrors on either side, allowing her to see behind her, and to the side of the jeep, where one of the Gothman drove in plain view. "Not only did you think I could easily be deceived, but you think four of your guards are all it takes to capture me."

The guard behind her boarded the trailer and began climbing toward the jeep. She wasn't sure where he thought he was going to go, but if he crawled any closer, he'd be on top of the children. The second guard also mounted the trailer, letting his bike slide on its side to a stop. He successfully detached the trailer from the jeep and held on as the trailer slowed to a stop. Had Darius given orders to retrieve her bike if they couldn't retrieve her?

She was able to move a lot easier without the trailer attached and curved the jeep around quickly. The guard hanging on to the back of the jeep slid as she spun the vehicle around. When he was on the side of the jeep, she aimed her small laser, and the man propelled from the jeep, rolling along the ground for quite a distance.

"I think we might have pulled this off." Tara smiled at her children, who both acknowledged her voice with frowns. Ana let out a shriek, which Andru quickly imitated. "Just a little bit longer, sweethearts," Tara reassured them.

Now for her bike. She drove head on toward the remaining guard, who was struggling to start her bike. The bike was still strapped to the trailer, and he used it as a shield while he watched her approach. If he guessed she would not shoot at her bike, he was right. She stopped the jeep within shouting distance from the bike and got out, carrying her laser by her side. "What are your orders, Gothman?" she asked as she walked toward him.

"You need to come back with me, my Lady." His voice was shaking as he spoke.

Tara could tell he was young. "You won't be successful today in capturing me. Do you realize that?"

The guard peeked at her from behind her bike.

"Are more coming?" Tara pointed her gun straight at his head. He ducked down again behind her bike. She was close enough that she could hear his breathing. "I'll give you only one more chance to save your life, Gothman. Are more coming?"

"My lady, if we aren't back in an hour, Lord Darius will send out the next group of guards."

"I see. Well, if you start running now, you should be seen by them before it gets dark." Tara altered her aim by a fraction, and laser fire bounced over the field, causing several large rocks to fly.

The Gothman shouted his surprise and then hunched farther behind her bike.

She walked up to the bike and stood over the guard.

The guard backed away from her and slowly stood up. He quickly raised his gun.

She shot the gun out of his hand while hardly moving a muscle in her body, then she cocked her head and gave him a small smile.

The guard turned and ran back toward Gothman territory.

Tara let out a laugh as she let the man go. "Well, my loves, I think we might have won round one."

Andru and Ana must have realized there was a break in the action, because both of them simultaneously let out screams of protest over the experience they had just been forced to endure.

"It's okay, babies," Tara cooed as she climbed over the seat and grinned at their outraged expressions.

Both children wanted out of their car seats and reached for her as she spoke to them.

"Are both of you okay?" Tara pulled the blanket from their squirming bodies, which resulted in tiny legs kicking even harder. "It appears so," Tara said with a laugh, feeling almost shaky as adrenaline pumped through her.

Tara reached behind the seats securing her children and pulled a cloth bag free. "We don't have time to get out and play right now, my dears, but how about a snack while I get us ready for another ride."

The children fussed, showing their disapproval, but calmed a bit when she produced crackers and an apple, which she peeled and diced before giving them their portions.

It took a long time for Tara to hook the trailer back up to the jeep. The children were fussy and wanted to be held, but Tara knew she couldn't waste time preparing them to drive again.

Tara took each child from their seat and checked diapers then calmed them with bottles after re-securing them. Darkness approached when she finally resumed her trip. While the jeep and the trailer left an easy trail in the tall grass for someone to follow, it was soon obscured by darkness as night fell.

If Tara had known the turmoil going on at home, she might have been calmed.

* * * * *

Patha's comm beeped as he parked his bike.

"The less gossip about this matter, the better, I'm thinking," Darius said as Patha listened through his comm. "We've accomplished a lot in bringing our two nations together, and if word spreads, it will reverse everything we've tried to achieve, it will."

"Agreed." Patha decided he could wait until later to lecture the man. "I will come get you."

He left Reena at the house and took off toward the back hills.

"Make sure Hilda is quiet about this," Patha instructed Reena, before he left her at the Bryton house and headed south to gather his son-in-law.

* * * * *

"Hilda, are you here?" Reena let herself in the back door and moved through the quiet house.

"Hello?" Syra walked into the kitchen with a white rag in her hands.

"Ah, it's a good thing you're here, it is. Call your papa, child. He's worried about you."

"He knows I'm here."

Torgo walked through the back door at that moment and froze in mid-step.

Reena ignored the boy's reaction and persisted with Syra. "Tara has left, child. Your papa was scared you went with her, he was. Call him now."

"I still don't understand why I have to check in with him every few hours." She stomped over to the landlink set up in the corner of the living room.

"What do you mean, Tara has left?" Torgo walked over to the counter, and grabbed a cookie from a plate that had several more on it. He watched Syra as he stuffed the entire cookie in his mouth.

"I think Lord Darius should explain the situation. All I can say is that Tara and the babies are gone."

"They went out to say goodbye to some of the Runners." Syra said, her tone indicating she thought the old lady was confused.

"Is Hilda upstairs?" Reena wasn't going to explain anything to the children. She didn't feel it was her place, and she knew Lord Darius would be quite angry if he came home to a household apprised of the situation.

"Hilda, may I come in?" Reena tapped on her friend's bedroom door.

"Reena?" Hilda was working on a sampler for her grandchildren's bedroom wall. "Is something wrong?"

Reena entered the bedroom and shut the door. "I do believe Tara has left Darius, I do." Reena pursed her lips.

Hilda let her sewing fall to the floor. "What?" Hilda asked in disbelief. "Why would you say such a thing?"

"She caught him, Hilda. I daresay he should have known Tara wouldn't stand for that behavior, no."

Hilda gathered her sewing and then stood to face her lifetime friend. "How do you know she is gone? Where are the babies?"

Reena kept her tone to a whisper as she told Reena about Tara's visit. She stopped talking every time she heard a noise from somewhere in the house, and both women would look toward the closed door.

"And I'm thinkin' she took our grandbabies with her, I'm sure," Reena concluded. "Patha went to get his Lordship. I daresay they will be here soon."

Hilda just looked at her friend. "My son has more power than he can handle, I fear. His actions have surprised me more than once, they have." Her words sounded strained, and Reena knew she referred to her two dead sons.

* * * * *

Torgo and Syra tried to talk to each other in the kitchen, awkwardness threatening to overwhelm them, oblivious to the conversation taking place upstairs.

"So after my clan leaves, I will be staying here and helping Tara with the babies." Syra leaned against the counter and studied the golden hair on Torgo's arm. "Of course, I'm sure I will have plenty of time for other things, too."

Torgo had just put another cookie in his mouth and almost choked on it. "Like what?" he asked with his mouth full and then slapped at the crumbs that he spit on the counter.

Syra shrugged. "What do you do around here for fun?"

Torgo had a hard time looking at her face and not her rather large breasts. She looked soft and curvy. He wasn't too sure what he'd do, exactly, if he had a chance to be alone with her...really alone. The opportunity to find out might be nice, though.

"I dunno." He shrugged. Torgo tried desperately to think of one thing he did at his house, just so he could impress Syra. But his mind saw breasts, his groin hardened, and he knew he couldn't move from where he leaned over the counter. "I could do something with you...uhh...I mean, maybe I could show you around..."

Torgo jumped as Patha and Lord Darius walked through the back door, wondering if he'd permanently injured himself when his hardened dick banged against the cupboard door beneath the counter.

"Tell Reena to come here." Patha's tone implied that he didn't care which teenager jumped to his request.

Syra ran from the room.

Torgo looked at the blood on his older brother. "What happened to you?"

"Not now." Darius waved his hand for Torgo to come to him. "Help me get upstairs."

One look at his brother and all thoughts of large breasts and personal injuries left Torgo as he became a human crutch for his older brother.

Once Darius was in his room, Reena had Syra on the run gathering necessary items to mend his wound.

Torgo loitered in the hallway, catching bits and pieces of the very alarming news.

"Send out four of your fastest riders," Patha said into his comm, as he shut Darius' bedroom door behind him. "She's not to be hurt, you understand? Those babies are with her, and I want them all back here before nightfall."

"I can't believe she didn't take me with her," Syra whined several hours later as she joined Torgo. The house had settled a bit, and they stood in the upstairs hallway, leaning over the banister that opened below into the front entryway. Torgo wanted to suggest they go to his room, but didn't have the nerve and couldn't imagine what he would say to her once they got there. At least she was talking to him, so all he had to do was nod and watch her. "My clan is leaving. Now Tara's left, and I'll be stuck here."

"I don't mind you being stuck here." Torgo blushed so deeply he looked down at the ground. He was grateful for the deep shadows in the hallway. "I mean, I get really bored most of the time. It'll be nice to have someone my age to talk to, uh, sometimes." *Great, now he was talking like a bumbling idiot.* He glanced sideways at her, hoping she hadn't noticed. Just being near her raised his body temperature.

* * * * *

Syra guessed from Torgo's actions that he hadn't been around many girls. *Boy, could she teach him a thing or two.* It brought a smile to her face that she could make him blush and feel awkward. He was so cute, already pretty developed. And, he was a lot taller than she was—that in itself was a bonus—especially since she was taller than most boys her own age. "My papa and I travel around a lot, and there aren't many people my age to hang out with either." There were boys her age in the clan, but she didn't want Torgo to think she'd been with a whole bunch of them. And she hadn't, really, just a few.

"He's really lucky she just shot him in the foot," Syra continued, dropping her tone so as not to be overheard. She wanted to keep their conversation going.

"I know. If she shot his foot, that is what she was aiming for."

They were quiet for another minute or two, trying to figure out what to say to each other.

"Maybe you could show me," Syra began, but stopped talking when footsteps sounded on the stairs.

Patha approached them and passed, not seeming to notice they were there as he entered Darius' room. It was easy to overhear the conversation beyond the partially open door. "They found her, but she easily got away from them," Patha said.

"I'm not surprised. She isn't going to get caught unless she wants to. Still, I can't let her get away from me like this."

"You've made a mess for yourself, son."

"No lectures, please. Things are bad enough as they are."

"I suggest you let me look for her when we leave tomorrow. We know she headed south, and she'll probably pass through one of the towns to restock. I'll be able to find her."

"Ah, but will you be able to bring her back?"

"Son, you're going to have to do that. You've made a terrible mistake, and she'll not forgive you easily. I'll find her for you, but you'll have to do the convincing."

Patha came out of the room, and Syra and Torgo tried to look as if they hadn't been eavesdropping. Patha still seemed uninterested in them, but he paused and turned to address them before he reached the stairs. "Syra, I guess you should come with me, and I'll take you back to your papa. There's no reason for you to stay here." He disappeared down the stairs.

"Great, more time alone with my papa," Syra groaned. "I wish I could have gone with her. This isn't fair." She stamped her foot on the ground before following Patha.

They didn't leave right away, however. Hilda insisted Patha and Reena stay for supper, as it was about ready. Darius hobbled downstairs with his wrapped foot and endured the looks his mama gave him as she set the table.

She finally started to cry over the loss of her grandchildren and the woman who had taken them. Torgo didn't want to hear his brother yell at his mama, so he slipped out into the backyard. His brother had made his mama cry one too many times, and it was more than he could handle right now.

When Syra saw the opportunity, she followed him.

"You know, you're complaining that you have to leave, and I wish I didn't have to stay." Torgo leaned against the shed staring at the star-filled sky. He switched his gaze to her as she approached him.

"Is this yours?" Syra ran her hand over his bike.

"Yeah, and it was Tara who taught me to ride."

"That's why I was here, to earn money to buy my first bike."

The two were silent for a minute then Syra had an idea. It was really awful, and she didn't want Torgo to get the wrong impression if she brought it up. He'd started shining his handlebars with his shirt. His blond hair was a mass of tousled curls and his gray eyes were lighter, and not as deadly as his older brother's. He'd be nice to have as a boyfriend, she decided.

"Don't take this the wrong way or anything," she began and looked back toward the house to make sure no one else had come out. "Why don't we go find her ourselves?"

"What?" Torgo whispered the word. "There's no way we could get out of Gothman. Both of us together don't have half the skills Tara has."

"It's not like they are going to hurt us if they catch us. It would be an adventure, and I'm going to be bored to death if I have to spend another minute with my papa." Syra looked at Torgo slyly. "Are you scared?"

"Of course not!" he declared. "I'm just not going to take off running without a plan. Let me think about it. We also shouldn't leave before supper."

"Can you get out of the house tonight?" Her mind was already scheming.

"I guess so."

"I'm sure I'll have to leave after supper with Patha and Reena. Leave half an hour after we do and meet me at the edge of the clansite, on the west side. I bet we could be gone for at least an hour before anyone missed us. Maybe longer." She smiled at him to see what he thought.

Torgo couldn't think of anything better. He nodded and headed toward the house. There was no way he would back out or give her any indication, but he was scared to death to take off on his own. He'd never been outside Gothman territory, and the stories he'd heard did not make him want to leave.

Syra left with Patha and Reena and headed back to the Runner's camp. She didn't speak to either of them, but then she never did very much. They were so old and never understood! Instead of sulking however, her mind was making a list of things she would need. She walked back to her trailer with her bag that already had her clothes in it. Quite convenient, she thought.

"Ah, there you are, my girl," Balbo said, as Syra entered their trailer. "Hard to believe you could be missed after being gone only a day."

"No one to show you how you are always wrong?" Syra rolled her eyes at her papa, but couldn't help smiling.

"I felt lost without anyone to argue with." Her papa returned her smile and reached to pull at her headscarf.

She ducked past him and headed for her room. Syra grabbed the portable landlink her dad had given her a few cycles before. Stuffing it into her bag, she thought about how she would get food.

"Syra, I'll be back shortly."

"Okay, Papa." This was perfect.

In the kitchen, she took things she thought would not be missed immediately if her papa were to look. She did most of the cooking, so she hoped he didn't know what was there. She filled a bag with food, grabbed her bag of clothes, and left the trailer.

Torgo was on the west side of the clan when she got there, looking nervous as he sat on his bike. He had side bags into which she stuffed her belongings. Then she climbed on behind him. Her heart jumped as she edged her legs along his and then slowly inched her hands around his waist.

"I thought you'd never get here." He slowly drove them away from the clan.

Chapter Thirteen

ഔ

"This isn't on the map." Tara clicked from screen to screen on her landlink as she spoke aloud to herself. She'd driven all night and halfway through the next day. The babies were grouchy and so was she.

The Runners weren't familiar with the southern part of Trueland. They knew of scattered towns, but that was it. All morning long she'd been traveling through uncharted land, having already crossed the prairie of the Freelands. Now, a wide river blocked her path.

The river flowed from the west and curved in front of her, heading south as far as she could see. Shrugging, she determined that her only choice was to ride alongside it. There wasn't any way to cross. She added the river to the landlink map, taking it upon herself to chart the area.

After traveling for more than an hour, Tara spotted a barge moored at a small port. Several buildings stood next to the river, and she saw a handful of people. She pulled up to one of the buildings and parked.

Tara put Andru into the back carrier then shrugged into the shoulder straps. She lifted Ana into her arms, and the three walked to the dock. A large man ambled off the dock and tossed several bags onto the ground. He didn't look at her until she cleared her throat.

"Where does this ferry go?"

"South all the way to the border, if you have money." He took a good look at Tara and her babies. "Been travelin' a while, have you?"

"Long enough. How much does it cost?"

"Six Dorsels a person, no matter their age." He eyed the babies.

"I have gold."

"Change it over at the building, that way." The large man rubbed his hand over his unshaven face and studied Tara. He couldn't quite figure out her accent but knew he'd heard it before. She'd been traveling awhile...and so pretty...odd she didn't have a man with her. Those two babies would turn most men away, but with her looks...he scratched his whiskers some more.

"I need Dorsels," Tara said, dropping several pieces of gold on the counter in front of a small wiry man.

He handed her a stack of paper and she studied it, not familiar with the currency. The sheets were thin, dyed red, and there was a numeral two in each corner of the rectangular shape. She counted the papers by two and came up with twenty.

"Are you sure this is right?" She looked as if she expected him to shortchange her.

The man grunted and handed her three more pieces of paper.

"How much to haul a jeep and bike?"

"Ten apiece."

"How far will you take me?"

"To the border. The ferry don't go past the border." The wiry man tapped the counter with a bony finger. "You pay to come back, too."

"And meals? They're included with this outrageous price, I assume."

"Yeah, but I don't know that the cook will be fixing food they can eat." He aimed his longer finger at the babies.

Tara gave the man the gold he needed and took the Dorsels. She returned to the large unshaven man now loading bags onto the ferry.

"Where you heading?" He took her money and rubbed his whiskers as he stared at the jeep and bike Tara pointed to.

"South."

"There's a lot to see down that way."

"Have you been south of the border?" Tara could stand for some good stories, and as unappealing as this man was, he was the first adult to whom she'd spoken in over twenty-four hours.

* * * * *

Taffley studied her once again. She was quite browned from the sun and in dire need of a shower. Her hair was stringy from sweat, and her dress hung on her. She was beautiful, though. In fact, she was quite sexy. He liked dirty women.

He didn't entertain too much hope of catching her eye. Women like her seldom had much of an interest in men like him.

His thoughts returned to her accent. It bothered him when he couldn't tell what race a person was. You knew a lot about a person when you knew where they were from and what their people were. Then he noticed a necklace around her neck. It was a circle with a very nice looking ruby in the middle of it.

"Yeah, I've been to a town or two south of the border." He looked at the necklace one more time, and then it dawned on him. Panic attacked his entire body. "You can take the cabin on the left side of the hall." Taffley spoke quickly, unable to look at her and afraid his fear would register through his words.

Runners could smell fear.

* * * * *

The man who owned the ferry seemed nervous about something, but Tara was too worn out to worry about him. She walked onto the ferry and down a hall with several doors on each side. The farthest door on the left was slightly open. She peeked in and saw a bed sprawled in one corner. A table with two chairs pushed under it filled the other corner. An old dresser stood next to the door. One half-open window provided dim light blanketing the wooden floor and walls. She left her bags in the room and carried her children out to watch the crew bring her jeep and bike on board.

* * * * *

Taffley drove the jeep with attached trailer up a large plank and parked them on the back of the ferry. His hands shook as he worked. That sexpot he'd been drooling over was a Runner. He recognized the symbol of the Blood Circle Clan. The motorcycle matched the clan as well. The most dangerous race in the world. That clan called themselves that because they didn't hesitate to draw blood. He'd heard all the stories.

Why was she dressed like that? This was not the way a Runner traveled. For some reason, she didn't want anyone to know who she was, he guessed. This bothered him even more. No doubt about it, she definitely had to be trouble.

He looked at Tara briefly and walked off the ferry, muttering something about being right back.

A few moments later, he entered the wooden building. "Saffle, d'you see that lady that come this way with those babies?" Taffley spoke to the wiry man.

"Yeah, she had gold."

"She's a Runner."

"Taffley, you're going daft, she wasn't dressed like no Runner."

"I tell you she's a Runner. I know that accent, and she had the sign of the Blood Circle Clan around her neck." He scratched his whiskers and turned to look at his ferry.

"If what you say's true, you've a problem on your hands." Saffle pulled a piece of paper from under his desk. "This came through with all the mail today. They've been passing 'em out, from what I hear."

Taffley took a wrinkled piece of paper from Saffle's bony hand. His face fell as he looked at the contents of the paper. The top of the page said *REWARD* and a description followed. Oddly enough, it was Gothman writing, and the reward was Gothman currency. It was large: ten thousand Gothman gold coins offered for the whereabouts or return of a lady and two babies. The woman was described as a Runner, but it was said she might not appear in Runner clothing. The babies were twins, a boy and a girl, seven cycles old.

"That's a lot of money." Taffley scratched his beard.

"What are you going to do?"

"I'm going to take her to the border. She's a Runner. I'm not going to cross her." Taffley smiled. "You put a wire through and let them know our destination and where they can pick her up. You say I expect payment in full before I turn her over."

* * * * *

Inside her room, Tara pushed the table in front of the door and began exploring. She found a small, connecting bathing room — with only one door. Relieved, she realized she wouldn't have to share the facilities with another passenger.

Fatigue was taking over, so she decided to wash herself and the babies, and change clothes. Perhaps the activities would revive her. She left her gun on the bathroom counter and began filling the tub.

The children splashed the water as Tara scrubbed the dirt and grime from all of them, using a washcloth and soap she'd brought along. She rinsed herself after cleaning the babies, letting the water cascade over her head and back.

Suddenly, the water in the tub splashed to one side and her babies slid off kilter. She grabbed them as she realized the barge had just pushed off from the dock. The ferry rocked as it slipped into the river currents. Tara held her infants close to her body until the movement slowed.

After dressing the rambunctious babes in matching one-piece outfits, she put on a clean dress. A bell sounded, and the large man she'd encountered earlier yelled that supper was ready.

A long table was set up in the open area of the ferry. Tara was obviously his only passenger. There was a chair set at each end of the table and to her delight, two highchairs were set on either side of one end of the table. The menu consisted of fried fish, new potatoes, and a leafy green vegetable on each plate.

"I don't really have food for the babies." Taffley sat at his end of the table. "I found some bread and squash. You can feed them that, if you want."

"Thank you." She sat after putting the babies in the highchairs. She quietly smashed the squash on two plates and tore tiny bits of bread to feed Andru and Ana.

The babies made a mess, and the man ate loudly. Tara didn't mind either. The hot food gave her energy. She enjoyed every bite and willingly accepted a second helping of fish. The babies also ate well and contentedly sucked on bottles of juice after the meal was over. Tara sat back as the man lit several torches and cleared the table. The large wheel rotating under the ferry made a soft swooshing sound in the water. It was peaceful, and Tara began to relax for the first time since she'd left Gothman.

Later, she sat on the edge of the bed rocking her two children until their bodies grew limp in her arms. She'd taken two of the drawers out of the dresser and filled them with blankets. Her babies looked beautiful, as they lay asleep in their makeshift cradles. She admired them in the moonlight, and for a moment, her mind went to Darius.

A noise on deck forced her to push him out of her thoughts. She reached for her laser and held it low as she walked down the hallway.

Creaking boards told her someone was there. She stood very still using the shadows in the dark hallway to hide her position. Taffley was leaning over the front of the ferry, apparently fishing, as a pole extended out over the water. She heard another creak coming from above the doorway which set her instincts to humming. Whoever was there chose that moment to jump down onto the main floor with his back to her.

The noise startled Taffley, who turned around as the intruder raised a gun.

Tara didn't hesitate, she shot the intruder in the back. The sound of a yelp followed by a splash alerted Tara to the presence of another, much less brave, attacker. She chuckled when she thought of his shock when he hit the cold water. Tara stepped out of the shadows.

The large man approached the dead body. He reached down, picked up the limp figure and dumped it overboard. "Much obliged." He looked wide-eyed at her as he walked to the other end of the boat, evidently making certain no one else was in the water. "Damn thieves."

Tara walked to the edge of the ferry and listened. She was satisfied they were now alone and turned to look at the man.

He didn't say anything, but sat at the end of the table, leaning over to stir a fire burning in an iron stove.

Tara turned to go back to her cabin.

"Stay." It was more of a suggestion than a command.

She turned and looked at him.

"I won't hurt you. Heavens knows I'm no match. I'll admit you scare me to death." He smiled and showed off dirty teeth and several dark holes where teeth had once been. "Name's Taffley. Sit and tell one of your stories."

"One of my stories?"

"Come now, all Runners have stories. I've heard some good ones in my time."

"What makes you think I'm a Runner?"

"Several things, lass. You wear the Blood Circle Clan symbol around your neck. Your motorcycle is a Runner's bike, and you've just shown me the skills of a Runner." He pointed to the chair she'd used during dinner. "Sit."

Tara did so and looked up at the stars. Her fingers instinctively played with the telltale necklace. Why hadn't she taken it off? She watched as the man got up and went over to a cabinet built into the wall of the ferry.

He opened it and pulled out a large bottle and two clay cups. He poured some of the contents into each cup, then set one in front of Tara. "The Sea People make an excellent wine. It's become quite rare lately. Their economy's crashed, you know." He offered the information as if it were common knowledge and leaned back down in his chair.

"You said you'd been south of the border." She took a sip of the wine.

"Yeah, Southland." He took a large drink and made a face, then took another drink and set the cup on the table. "Why d'you want to go there?"

"I haven't been there."

"A true Runner response." He laughed and then drank the rest of his wine. He offered Tara more after pouring some in his own cup, but she shook her head. "What's your name?"

"Tara. Tell me what the people are like down there. Are they warriors?"

"Well now, some of them are. None to match you Runners, that's for sure. They were doing pretty well for themselves, had lots of money to spend, 'til the Sea People started that war up north. From what I've heard, they lost pretty badly. They didn't know them Gothman would go and hitch up with you all Runners. Strange people the Sea People are." Taffley stopped to wet his mouth. "Ever met one?"

"No, not personally." Tara wanted to hear about the south, not the north, but she decided she'd have to be patient.

"They come across nice enough, gave me a fair bit of business there for awhile. Not very trusting people, though. Southland is real good for growin' this opiate plant. All I did for the longest time was haul the harvests across the border. That's all done now. The towns down there are hurting pretty bad. No reason to grow their crops, because there's no one to buy them."

"The Sea People don't want it anymore?"

"I'm sure they want it. They just can't pay for it. They're broke, you see. Plenty of money they owe me." Taffley poured more wine into their glasses.

"What should I expect when I get to the border?" She swooshed the purple liquid around in the cup but didn't take a drink. "How far to the closest town?"

* * * * *

Taffley thought about how to answer. He imagined what she would see when they got to the border. Saffle had sent that wire, and she would be picked up the second she got off the ferry. A twinge of guilt ran through him. She'd saved his life, and now he was turning her in for the money. He focused on the reward. It would clear all the debts he'd created when he still thought the Sea People would pay him for his services.

"The first town is Semore. It's about ten miles from the border. There's Pixley, which is about fifteen miles in, but you have to drive a little west to get to it. And there aren't any roads nearby. The roads starting at the border go to Semore. After Semore are Highton and New Hanger. All those towns are under the same government and use the same money. They've got some good ideas down there. It makes sense to have the same rules and money. I guess you'd have to see how they live to understand." Taffley wondered if she would ever be able to go there.

* * * * *

"Are they all the same people?" Tara tried to picture what he'd described. Her excitement grew at the thought of being the first Runner to explore a new land. "Who's their ruler?"

"Well now, that's where they are real different. They don't have a ruler."

"What? That would be complete chaos!" She took a drink of her wine and pulled her legs up, getting comfortable in her chair.

"You'd think, but it's not. They have a bunch of people in charge. I can't remember what they call it, but all the people get together every five winters and vote on who the people in charge are going to be." Taffley got up and pulled a blanket out, shook it, then walked over and wrapped it around Tara. "Can't let it be said one of my passengers got sick on my ferry."

"People say who their leader is going to be?" Tara adjusted the blanket around her, pondering the concept. "Who is in charge right now?"

"The main guy is Gowsky, I think. Never met him. Don't have cause to, you see. He's got a mess on his hands. They were all accustomed to money coming in, you see. Except now, there is none. Money I mean."

Tara sat quietly for a minute. She'd never thought how their war could affect so much of the world. People who didn't know her were struggling to keep their towns going because of decisions she and Darius had made.

Tara suddenly came to the conclusion that a ruler would indeed be great if he or she were aware of all of the people around him or her, and not just familiar with a little corner of Nuworld. Darius had never been out of Gothman. Would he ever know what life was like outside his kingdom?

"What you thinking, Tara?" Taffley cocked his whiskery face at her.

"About everything you've just said. I look forward to meeting these people. It sounds like they need help getting back on their feet."

"Well now, how would you help them?" Taffley sounded curious.

"I don't know. It sounds like they're farmers. You said they grew something the Sea People needed. Maybe there is something else they could grow that someone else could use." Tara was anxious now to continue her journey and meet these people. "Like I said, I don't know. I'll have to wait and see what their land is like and what they're like. What do they think of strangers?"

"Anyone can come and go through their towns. That's something everyone knows. Though I don't know what they'd think of a Runner. They kind of blame you all for their turn of fate, you see. People say the Sea People could've beat Gothman if it weren't for the Runners. I've heard that the Gothman king got tricked…"

* * * * *

Taffley stopped talking, and his mouth fell open. Now, he'd never been accused of being a real bright man. He liked what he did and tried to keep peace with everyone with whom he did business. Still, he'd learned many things sitting at this table with his passengers. He'd almost said that he'd heard about a beautiful woman, who turned out to be a Runner, and had tricked the Gothman king. That's what he was about to say, but then he figured something out.

"You're the one, aren't you? No wonder there's so much money on your head!" Taffley quickly covered his mouth, knowing he'd said too much.

"What did you say?"

"Oh, I'm as bad as an old woman." Taffley hung his head and pulled a piece of paper from his shirt pocket. He tossed the paper across the table.

Tara picked it up and held it by the lantern. A look of shock crossed her face.

Chapter Fourteen

∞

"I can't believe this. The notice makes it sound like I'm his property." Tara began to fume all over again.

"Gothman women are property." Taffley said with a shrug.

"I'm not Gothman!" Tara slammed her fist on the table.

Taffley jumped and realized he'd hit a nerve. Had he made the right move by showing the paper to her? It crossed his mind that if this made her angry, what would she do when she realized she was being led into a trap?

A loud shot caused Taffley to jump again. One hand went to his heart and the other grabbed his bottle of wine.

Another loud shot rang through the air.

* * * * *

Tara adjusted her laser to scan for life-signs. She pointed the laser toward the woods along the river, judging that was where the shot had come from. She could hear people yelling, and although the red beam on the laser targeted the attackers, she didn't need it. She could have detected them from the noise they were making.

Taffley was on top of the ferry, and he had started shooting.

The darn fool was going to get killed. He'd made himself an easy target. She quickly shot at three individuals on the bank. A splash in the water and a howl let her know one of them had fallen in. She saw another fall from a tree. The third jumped in the water of his own accord and started swimming toward them.

Taffley aimed his gun at the person in the water, and a loud bang ran through the air. The man in the water let out a bloodcurdling scream. His arm floated away from his body.

Taffley's gun had such a kick she could see him lurch back after firing. For a second, she envisioned Taffley falling down the stairs, but he steadied himself and looked around at the now calm waters.

"Sure are a lot of thieves lately," he muttered as he came back down the stairs. "We live in a land of no laws. Take care of your own, that's the River People's law. I've learned to protect my property. Keeps one on his toes. They say a government will stop all this but I don't see it happening."

Tara could hear the babies beginning to cry and hurried to them.

Taffley walked to the edge of the hallway, but respecting her privacy, talked to her without coming to her door. "I'll keep a watch tonight. You don't worry none about them babies. I'll keep them safe. Ain't no thief going to board my boat tonight."

Tara doubted Taffley's ability to keep them safe, but she thanked him and pulled the children up on the bed. Within moments, the three of them were sound asleep.

It seemed like just minutes later when Tara opened her eyes to see the sun streaming through the open window of her room. Ana lay cuddled next to her, sleeping soundly, while Andru played with his feet. He smiled broadly at her when she looked at him. The smile looked just like his papa's.

Tara lay there, holding both of them tightly, feeling pain from the loss of the only man she'd ever loved. Tears came to her eyes and she let them flow.

It wasn't long before both babies were fully awake and ready to play. Tara had to put her own thoughts aside and focus on her children. As she sat on the floor of the small room, tickling and playing with the babies, she could hear Taffley walking around on the main deck preparing breakfast. Every now and then he groaned; she imagined he might be hung over from the wine.

The bell announcing that food was ready came shortly, and Tara picked up the babies and headed out to the table. She was surprised to feel how warm it was outside.

"We've had someone following us through those trees over there," Taffley said as Tara secured the babies into the highchairs. "If you want to eat in your room, I can set the table in there."

Tara looked over to the trees and could hear the low sound of a motorcycle. She squinted from the sun and was able to tell two people rode on the bike. They were matching the pace of the ferry and staying just out of view through the trees.

"If you'd help me push the highchairs to my room, I'd appreciate it." She walked back to the room, pushing Ana in the chair. Taffley followed with Andru, who talked gibberish all the way.

She could see the bike through her window as she fed the babies their breakfast. Why wasn't its rider attacking like the others? Still, she had to acknowledge it was a strategy she would use to flush out her prey: wear their defenses down by stalking them. Then bring them out in the open and nail them. It was a Runner strategy, but that wasn't a Runner bike.

"Tara?" A voice shouted her name.

She jumped, startled, and moved quietly to the window. "I don't believe it!" She ran out of the room and onto the deck.

"Stop the ferry," the voice called.

"Not on your life." Taffley raised his gun to fire.

"Taffley, no!" Tara yelled, but it was too late.

Taffley fell to the ground as laser fire shot across the water and knocked him off the deck. He yelled loudly and looked at his smoking leg. Dark blood started soaking through the torn material of his pants.

"Put that laser down now!" Tara yelled to the shore.

She ran over to Taffley and propped him up against the deck.

"Tara, you've got to make him stop the ferry," Torgo's voice yelled to her. He and Syra were now visible on the shore of the river.

"Who are they?" Taffley was grimacing from the pain.

"A couple of kids. What they're doing here is the question!" Tara looked back at the two sitting on Torgo's bike.

"Tara, can you hear me?" Torgo yelled.

"Yes, I can hear you."

"You're floating into a trap. There's a mob down there just waiting for you. They'll turn you in for the price on your head."

Tara looked at Taffley, who kept his eyes pinned to the deck. "How do we stop this thing?"

He got up slowly. Holding onto his bleeding leg, he limped to the back of the ferry. It took him a few minutes to climb the stairs.

All the while, the babies wailed. As Tara listened to their fussing, she realized that this was no life for them. They deserved warm cribs and their own bedroom, not this swaying barge.

Taffley called down, "Better get back to your room and hold onto those little ones. When the anchor catches, it will cause quite a lurch."

She returned to her quarters and sank into a chair between the two high chairs. The twins sobbed loudly as they reached for their mama. She quickly gave them each a small piece of banana, which they simultaneously put into their mouths. She gripped the sides of the highchairs and braced her feet as the ferry lunged to a stop.

The paddle wheel became silent, and it was very quiet on the ferry for a second.

Tara tore up more banana. Then, she grabbed a first aid kit and returned to the deck.

"Word is traveling all over the place that you are on a ferry headed to the border," Torgo yelled to her.

"I wonder how they found out." Tara looked at Taffley.

"I'm sorry, Tara. All I knew was that you were a Runner. People 'round here's scared of Runners. I'd already let you on my ferry when I saw the reward being offered." Taffley looked sincerely forlorn as she stared at him. "I don't know why you're wanted, but I can't imagine whatever you did was all that bad."

"I didn't do anything wrong."

Taffley looked at the two kids sitting on the bike on the shore. He nodded in their direction. "If things are as bad as those two say, the thieves attacked us to get to you." He shook his head. "There'll be more. Probably soon. You'd stand a better chance if you get off on the other side of the river."

Tara studied the water. The river was wide, and she could see a few sandbars ahead of them. "How far to the border?"

"Half a day, if you drive. We'll get there tonight on the ferry. If you drive straight south, you'll cross the desert. After several hours, head west and you'll hit the road."

"We need to get the jeep and my bike off this thing." She started yelling instructions to Torgo and Syra, "Cross the river up there by the sandbars. Torgo, give it some speed when you hit the water."

Taffley was obviously feeling the pain from his wound, and he moved slowly.

Tara loaded the babies into their car seats in the back of the jeep, much to their dismay. They hadn't gotten over being in them all yesterday and immediately started to cry. She hugged and kissed them and reassured them the running would stop soon. She only wished she could believe it. She now understood why Runner families had trailers. As bored as she had been at times growing up and traveling across country, she'd at least been able to move around in a trailer, instead of being confined to a car seat.

"What can we do to help?" Torgo lifted himself out of the water onto the deck. He'd parked his bike on the shore after driving to the other side, then the two had swum out to the ferry.

"You can start by telling me what the hell you're doing here." Tara showed her rage. "This isn't a game."

"You promised me a job." Syra shrugged with despicable arrogance as she wrung water from her hair.

"You can't stay with me. You'll both get killed." Tara wasn't in the mood for a mouthy teenager.

"You're not so great you couldn't get killed yourself." Syra's eyes flared. "Especially with two babies. You need help."

"I can make it to where I'm going," Tara responded. "Your papa would never stop tracking me if I brought you along."

Torgo spoke up. "My brother isn't going to stop looking for you, or his children, no matter where you go."

"'Scuse me. I hate to break up this family feud, but are you all getting off my boat or not?" Taffley shifted his gaze from the dripping teenagers to the irate Runner.

"Yes, we are." Tara continued to glare at both of them. "Okay, you want to work? You got it. Syra, take the bike off the trailer. It will lighten the load when we drive the jeep through the water. Torgo, you help Taffley lower the ramp."

Everyone got to work, and within minutes Tara was in the jeep, going through the water. The splashing on either side of the vehicle quieted the babies as they watched the spectacle with awe.

"Be careful, Taffley," Tara said after they'd secured the trailer to the back of the jeep.

"It won't be a welcome committee when I get to the border, that's for sure." Taffley let out a laugh. "Do me a favor, though. If it's ever brought up, tell them you shot me while escaping. I don't think I could live it down if they knew I got shot by some kid girl."

"Deal!" Tara smiled. "I'll ask a favor in return. From now on, you be friendly to Runners. We're good people, and no Runner will attack you unless you attack first."

"Deal!" Taffley waved, then started the paddle wheel. The ferry slowly glided down the river.

"Let's get a move on. You can drive with me at least as far as the border." Tara was anxious.

Syra walked over to join Torgo on his bike.

"You'll ride with me," Tara spoke over her shoulder as she climbed into the jeep.

"Why? I want to ride with Torgo."

"I can see that." Tara gave Torgo a hard look, and he quickly stared at the ground. It dawned on her that the two of them had more than likely been together all night. "You want to work for me, then get in the jeep."

* * * * *

Syra sulked as she climbed into the passenger seat. She knew her aunt would be justified to lecture her. She'd left without telling anyone. She was with Torgo. And, she'd followed Tara, who had every bounty hunter in Trueland after her.

Syra glanced back at Torgo who followed closely behind the jeep. He smiled and she faced front. So far, this was the best adventure she'd ever had. It was actually disappointing that they'd found Tara already. Riding with Torgo all morning, rubbing against his body, her arms wrapped around his youthful muscles...her mind drifted to the night before.

They'd driven south, following the only map she could find on her landlink. They knew they were driving south but that was about it. Once they'd found tracks that resembled those a jeep and trailer would leave, they'd followed them to the river.

After driving for five hours or so, they'd decided to take a break.

She remembered Torgo kissing her. The moonlight had made everything mystical. When she'd unbuttoned his shirt and slipped it off his shoulders, every one of his chest muscles were outlined with moonlight. His hands had been all over her. He never even hesitated with his exploring. Maybe he wasn't as inexperienced as she'd thought. Everywhere he'd touched her had set her on fire. She couldn't remember how they'd moved from standing to lying. They'd rolled around on the ground and greeted each other's bodies with excitement and anticipation. While she hadn't been aware of hurting herself at the time, the bruises on her body indicated they'd gotten carried away with their exploring.

And then there had been the...thing she'd done to Torgo. Syra never would have known to do it, except she'd caught her aunt doing it to another clansman one night. They hadn't realized she'd caught them. But, she'd never forget it. It looked like fun, so she'd tried it last night with Torgo. He'd seemed so surprised when, after making him hard as a rock with her hand, she'd put him inside her mouth.

It was bigger than she'd expected, and she wasn't able to make much of it fit; not like her aunt had. She'd done something right though. Torgo had almost flipped her when suddenly he'd arched his back and howled. She'd held on tight and was surprised when he'd soaked her face with his white fluid. It had been salty, but she liked the taste.

Torgo had then laid her down and spread her legs so far apart she'd thought he'd split her in two. When his tongue entered her soft sensitive folds, she'd gone over the edge, lust spreading through her like a wildfire. He'd sucked, nibbled, licked and kissed. It was more than she'd ever dreamed it would be, and he'd brought her to an orgasm so quickly she was dizzy for the next twenty minutes or so. Thinking about it burned her crotch. After another quick glance at Torgo, she shoved the thoughts out of her head.

* * * * *

It wasn't easy driving through the trees with the jeep and attached trailer. Every time Tara thought they were coming to a clearing, they would run into another group of trees.

"It would be a lot easier if we ditched the trailer, and you let me ride your bike," Syra suggested after driving for a while in silence.

"Syra, I can't let you go with me. Believe me, I wish I could. You're right, I could use the help. But, I just don't have the right to take either one of you from your parents."

Syra reached down, opened Tara's landlink and started to log on.

"What do you think you're doing?" Tara grabbed the landlink from Syra's lap.

"My papa said I could work for you over the summer," Syra started to explain.

Tara tried to stay calm and took a deep breath before she spoke, "If you log on with my landlink, it will instantly tell anyone who is watching exactly where I am. Trust me, they're watching. I've got the heirs of the Gothman and Runner nations on board."

"Okay. I'm sorry."

Tara was startled by the sincerity of Syra's apology.

Syra met her gaze and her youthful energy pulsated in her green eyes. "Did you love him, Tara?"

Tara didn't answer, but she fought the stinging in her eyes from tears that wanted to come. *Had* she loved him? She *still* loved him.

She needed to keep herself alert and thinking about this would get her nowhere. She turned her attention back to the direction they traveled and still didn't answer.

They drove on in silence for quite awhile. Tara was growing frustrated with their inability to pick up speed due to the terrain. Andru and Ana both watched with wide gray eyes as objects passed the jeep, and she praised them mentally for being such good babies.

Several hours passed, and still nothing but forest around them.

"We should have hit desert by now, according to what Taffley told us." Tara looked up at the sun. "We're definitely driving due south. Something is wrong."

"Could we use my landlink to see if there's anywhere to log on?"

"You brought your landlink?"

"Yes, it's on Torgo's bike."

"I'm willing to give it a try. For all I know, we could have already passed the border." Tara stopped the jeep, and Torgo pulled up alongside her. Syra jumped out and brought her landlink to Tara.

"Why don't you get the babies out and let them crawl around in the backseat?" Tara felt sorry for her confined children. "Hopefully, this won't take too long."

Tara searched for a local connection, and the landlink found one within a matter of minutes.

"Well, there's life out there somewhere," Tara commented as she started to explore the transmission she'd just found. "I found a map. Here it is. There are several cities that appear to be twenty miles or so from the border. And I see two roads…one of them leads all the way to the border. We must be farther east than we thought. According to this, if we head west, we should pull out of this forest faster than if we continue south." She studied the foreign screen providing this information and wondered what culture shared the technology.

"Sounds good to me." Torgo squinted toward the west.

"Let's keep moving. Syra, why don't you explore what these cities have to offer while you're back there, and I'll drive. Whatever you do, don't change connections. Hopefully, no one will be searching for us on this link." Tara started the jeep, and they began heading west.

The drive continued to be difficult as the trees grew closer together and cliffs and rocks appeared. The terrain almost appeared mountainous, and Tara noticed some of the rock formations appeared to lead into caves. At times, Tara would turn her head and listen, or quickly glance behind her. No one would stop them, she would see to it. Determination pumped through her, the success of their journey riding on her warrior skills.

* * * * *

Torgo noticed this and although he would look in the same direction as she did, he never saw anything out of the ordinary. The more time passed, the more often Tara checked their surroundings. Her actions began to spook Torgo. Although nothing around him appeared to be out of the ordinary, Torgo began believing they were being watched or followed, just by Tara's actions.

After driving for a time, Tara stopped. While the two teenagers watched, she got out of the jeep and stood, listening. She walked a short distance away from them and then returned quickly. "Syra, I want you to turn this jeep around and take it back to one of those caves." She reached down to the floor of the jeep and grabbed her suitcase along with her landlink. "Take these and put them on." She handed comms to both teenagers. "Set them to channel three."

"What's going on?" Syra looked confused as she watched Tara guide her bike off the trailer.

"Get this thing turned around, and go hide in one of those caves we just passed until I tell you it's okay to come out."

"Why?" Syra persisted.

"We've driven into an ambush. Head back toward those caves, and you and the babies will be safe." Tara's tone froze the expressions on both teenagers' faces. "Now move."

Syra's eyes widened. She obeyed and drove off in the jeep.

"Torgo, a good warrior always knows when he's outnumbered." Tara flipped open her landlink and turned it on. "I'd say at the moment we are grossly outnumbered."

"Tara, I don't see anyone anywhere, I don't."

"Trust me."

"I do." He looked around nervously.

Tara fastened the landlink to her handlebars, pulled out her Eliminator, and hooked it to a strap on the side of her bike. "Do you have a gun?"

"Of course." He pulled out one of the nicer Gothman guns he'd used for target practice.

She tossed one of her small laser guns at him. "You might need this too. It's a little more accurate. Aim it the same way you do yours. Let's go."

* * * * *

They took off, picking up speed as they darted around trees and rocks. The terrain was slightly similar to Gothman, and Torgo kept up with her nicely. She knew the loudness of the boy's bike would draw attention to her quickly. Glancing repeatedly down at her screen while navigating her bike, Tara quickly logged onto the main Runner screen.

Help was nearby—Patha and the Blood Circle Clan were less than a mile away.

The first shot ringing through the air came from behind them. Tara continued to drive at high speed but turned and shot at a vehicle closing in from behind.

Torgo did the same.

She saw an old car crash into a tree out of the corner of her eye and knew they'd hit their target. She faced forward and quickly sent a message.

"What are you doing?" Torgo spoke through his comm.

"We're too outnumbered. I'm detecting fifteen to twenty people to the north of us, about ten people behind us and there are three coming straight at us. We'll see them here in a minute. We need help, or we won't make it."

Three men in a jeep appeared in front of them. As one of them drove, the other two leaned out, hanging onto the bars. They aimed large guns at Tara and Torgo.

Tara pulled the Eliminator faster than Torgo could even react.

The first shot coming her way caused a tree to fall in front of her. She could hear the men whooping and yelling in the excitement of almost hitting her.

Did that reward announcement say *dead or alive*? She wished now that she'd read it a bit closer. From the sheer numbers around her, she could tell enough people had gotten wind of her location to turn the situation into a crazed hunt. There was no way she and Torgo could take on this many opponents. Who was to say how many more were on their way?

And they were River People—a crude people with no laws. That was the worst kind of adversary to take on in battle. There would be no pattern, no order, no way of predicting their next move.

Tara aimed the Eliminator and shot the jeep. The explosion caused several surrounding trees to catch fire. If there was any fool out there who was not exactly sure where she was, they certainly knew now.

"Help," was all she was able to type without crashing into a burning tree limb directly ahead of her.

"I've got you on my scanner." Tara saw the response to her plea and sighed with relief. She would deal with the wrath of Patha after all of this was over. Right now, she knew her clan would not let her down. She hadn't done them wrong, and they knew it.

Tara and Torgo continued to drive as fast as they could through the woods. A shot from the north exploded through the air, and Tara turned her head in time to see Torgo's bike slide.

She slowed down quickly and turned around. If the boy got hurt, she'd never forgive herself. Relief surged through her as she approached Torgo and saw that only the tire had been blown out.

He had slid through the brush and was getting up slowly from underneath the bike.

"Climb on." She pulled up next to him. "Tell me you're okay."

"My bike." He looked forlornly at his prize lying on the ground.

"Casualty of war, son. It's what you get for following me." She grinned at Torgo as he held on to her tightly and pulled his leg over her bike. They both noticed blood on his leg at the same time.

"I'm okay."

Tara took off again, but was not able to go far. At least ten men on motorcycles were driving straight at them. They were well-armed, Tara noted as they spread out and around her, forcing her to stop.

One of the riders in the middle, obviously their leader, had been gesturing to the others. Now, he spoke. "Okay, lady. I know you're a Runner, and I'm sure you're well-armed. Slowly, and I do mean slowly, I want you to get off that bike."

He raised his gun and pointed it at her head, just in case she didn't think he was serious. He was very nervous, Tara observed. This man was no warrior. A simple diversion would send all of them into a panic. She could tell they had a plan by the glances they kept giving their leader, as if waiting for a signal, but she guessed there was no backup plan.

She slowly got off the bike. She could easily pull the Eliminator and take out at least half of them. But, it would take just one of them to fire back, and she or Torgo could be hurt. Or worse. There would be no brave attempt to escape this time. Her babies needed a mama, and she would not risk Torgo's life.

"I can take the guys on the right, and you take those on the left," Torgo whispered at her shoulder.

"No. A good warrior knows when he's outnumbered. I told you that already. There's always time to escape. Right now isn't the time."

"Silence!" The leader on the motorcycle sounded worried. "Be careful, boys. Runners are sadistic warriors. They keep a calm look on their faces, but their minds are scheming your death."

He gestured at Tara as if he were using her as an example while teaching young warriors. "Get away from the bike!" He curled his lip as if her looks repulsed him.

Tara complied, walking several steps toward him. She seriously hoped Patha would arrive very soon. He couldn't possibly be that far behind all these goons. She took several more steps, and every gun instantly bristled in her direction. She was less than a man's length away from the leader.

"Let the boy go." She looked straight at him. "There's no price on his head." She paused. "Let him go and then fight me like a true warrior. I'll show you how a Runner does it. Then you won't have to make up stories."

She glared at the leader and tried her best to let the fury in her eyes shine through. He was scared, and she knew it. All she needed was one small distraction.

He responded, "The boy is Gothman. I'm sure their leader will pay for him just as he will pay for you. The way they treat their women, I'm sure he wouldn't care if we had a little fun with you first." The leader laughed, and the men around him joined in.

This was all the distraction Tara needed. As she raised her Eliminator to fire, the singing of lasers resounded through the woods in all directions.

She shot the leader.

Lasers fired from the woods, taking out the other men before they knew what hit them.

Chapter Fifteen

෨

Tara turned quickly and got back on her bike. Torgo scrambled to climb on behind her, tripping several times before Tara grabbed his arm and almost pulled him onto the seat behind her.

He held on tightly as she bolted from the circle of dead men. "What happened?" Torgo's voice shook.

Tara felt his legs shake against her body. "We had help. I would like to think Patha has arrived, but we aren't going to take any chances." She spoke calmly, knowing good and well how scared Torgo was.

"Syra, are you okay?" Tara spoke into her mouthpiece.

"We're fine. Can we come out yet?"

"I'll let you know in a minute." Tara paused, suddenly aware that more motorcycles approached. She pulled her gun and aimed it toward the oncoming bikes.

Torgo pulled his gun out as well. His hand was shaking as he held the gun and he pulled it back, bracing it against his body.

Tara pretended she didn't notice.

There were four bikes driving toward them and three coming from the side.

This time, Tara pulled behind a group of trees and jumped off her bike. She leaned over a low branch and aimed her gun at the closest bike.

A familiar laugh caused her to lower her gun.

"Is that any way to thank an old man who just saved your hide?" Patha pulled up in front of the tree.

The other Runners pulled up alongside Patha.

Tara came out from behind the tree to greet them. "I could have handled the situation." She tossed her hair and tried to hide her smile of gratitude.

"Ah now, there's appreciation for you." The old man laughed again as he looked at the other Runners.

Tara recognized all of them, most of whom she'd grown up with. Balbo was also among the group. They joined in the laughter. Tara looked at each in turn, smiling broadly at their grinning faces. "Thank you." She bowed gallantly.

"Where's my daughter?" Balbo's smile disappeared.

Torgo sheepishly came out from behind the tree, and he looked downright fearful of the oncoming punishment as Balbo glared.

"She's a mile or so back, in a cave with the babies." Tara flipped the switch on her mouthpiece. "Syra, we're coming to get you. Flash the lights on the jeep when you see the Runner bikes."

* * * * *

"I must say, this will be the best story for quite a long time. I can't think of many Runners that could have made it as far as you did, Tara-girl." Patha sat with his grandchildren around the fire later that evening. "And you did it with two babies as well."

Tara accepted another piece of apple pie from Reena, who was smiling at her.

"I'm just glad you're all alive and okay, I am." Reena sat next to Patha and took Ana from him. "This is no life for my grandbabies, it isn't."

"My grandchildren, too." Patha bounced Andru on his lap. "She's right though, Tara. What are your plans?"

"I know. You're both right." Tara looked at her babies as they giggled in their grandparents' arms. "Patha, there are five towns south of the border. I've heard some things about them, and they sound fascinating." She proceeded to tell her parents about the governmental structure and elections held in the towns.

"Who'd have thought of such a thing, I'd say?" Reena looked up from the pie she was feeding to Ana, appearing to be sincerely surprised.

"Yes, the Neurian government. I've heard of them," Patha nodded. "Gowsky is the head of their council. He's a young man with lots of ambition. I believe he's just been reelected by his people."

Tara was surprised. Patha seemed to know everything.

"Did you know their main export was a crop to the Sea People? When we won the war over the Sea People, this Neurian government lost its main form of income."

"Oh, so you want to go down there and help these people, do you?" Patha looked at his daughter.

"Yes. That's exactly what I'm going to do."

"How do you propose to do this, child?" Patha looked at her seriously. "You don't know these people. They are nothing like any of the nations on our land. They live a very different life. You won't be able to waltz into their country, change your clothes, and fit into their culture."

Tara smiled at Reena, remembering her first days at Gothman. "I realize that, Patha. But I'm going to try to do exactly that. It's time I find a new life for myself."

Both Patha and Reena looked up at her quickly as she said this.

"Tara, I..." Patha started.

But Tara lifted her hand. "No, Patha, please, I can't go back to Gothman. Darius isn't going to change. His definition of love is very different from mine. There's no way we could be compatible. I won't put my children through a life in which their parents don't love each other."

"It's a little late to be coming to these conclusions." Patha studied his daughter's face. "You can't walk away from your problems. They will still be there when you come back. You need to place a time limit on this adventure of yours."

"I don't know how long I'll be gone. Now that I've heard about these people, I've got to check them out. They live so differently from anything I've ever seen—and apparently they're doing it well; or they were until the war ended their lifestyle."

"She's living her culture, Patha," Reena pointed out. "She's doing what Runners do: she is seeing Nuworld."

Patha looked grave. "Is there a message you'd like to send to Darius?"

"I would think he would have a message to send to me."

Patha shook his head. "I believe he's sent you messages, but it appears they are deleted before they're read. I'm sure he's sorry."

"Sorry means you won't do it again. Tell him to call off this hunt. I won't have my children chased around the world." Tara picked up Andru, who had been sleeping in Patha's arms.

Reena got up with Ana, who was also asleep. She followed Tara into Patha's trailer to put the babies to bed.

"I'm not accustomed to offering motherly advice, Tara. And I know your mind is set. But I want to say something to you." Reena paused until the children were down. "Lord Darius has done you wrong. I don't blame you for your reaction, I don't. In fact, I will say, I look up to you. There are many women who would forgive and do their best to forget, yes."

"I know. And they would look the other way when it happened again and again. I can't do that, Reena. I would kill him."

"I believe you." Reena smiled, but it didn't cover the sadness in her eyes. "I think what Patha wants you to see, and what I want you to see as well, is that you started something in Gothman. It was you who brought Runners and Gothman together, it was. You're the one who insisted women should have rights. You've started something and have walked away without finishing it, you have."

"That's not fair." Tara sounded wounded. "I was willing to walk with Darius and lead his country with him. He said things to me, made promises. He lied to me. I can't make those changes without him, and he can't be trusted. He's the one who quit without finishing, not me."

Reena looked down without saying anything.

Tara watched her. For some reason it dawned on her how much she wanted Reena's support. She sat at the table across from Reena and waited for the older woman to say something, anything.

Reena opened her mouth to speak and then shut it again. Finally, she spoke. "Tara, I'm Gothman, I am. I always will be. I have no choice but to be loyal to his lordship." She lowered her voice and continued. "I can't help but say that I feel you're more of a man than he is, so to speak. You might just have to make the first move, I fear."

"I don't know that I could ever trust him again." Tara felt defeated.

"How long will you be gone?"

"I don't know." Tara got up and moved to the door. "Patha said he'd let Torgo sleep in the spare room tonight. I'll fetch the boy so he can go to bed." She paused in the doorway. "You know, that child has been loyal to me. He would make a great lord. But I doubt he'll ever have the opportunity to prove that." She sighed. "I'm leaving tomorrow, Reena. Tonight, I look forward to lying under the stars. It's beautiful out there, and I think sleeping in the night air might help my outlook. Good night, Reena."

"Goodnight Tara-girl." Reena hugged her daughter. "Don't you worry yourself none about those babies. If they wake in the night, I'll be tending to them, I will."

A short time later, Tara threw her bedroll on the ground next to the fire by Patha's trailer. The stars glowed larger than usual and filled the sky. She didn't have a chance to enjoy them, though. Sleep overcame her the second her head hit the pillow.

It was barely light when Tara opened her eyes. A good night's sleep was just what she'd needed. She was anxious to get herself organized and hit the road.

The trailer was still quiet when she entered. Tara was gazing at her sleeping beauties when Patha came out of his room.

"Good morning, Tara-girl." The old man looked over her shoulder at the two babies. "You've sure done a good job with those two."

"Thanks. They'll be great warriors, Patha. I promise."

"How could they not be? Look at their bloodline." Patha gently took Tara's arm. "Come with me. I've something to show you."

Tara followed Patha out the trailer and across the meadow to another trailer. He unlocked the door and the two of them went inside.

"This is for you."

"What do you mean?" Tara looked around at a place larger than Patha's trailer. A kitchenette, table, and small couch furnished the living room. An extensive landlink system caught Tara's eye, and she walked over to it.

"This trailer. It's for you." The old man grinned.

"It's mine?"

"Can't have my grandchildren running around without a roof over their heads." Patha walked to the door. "I'll see that your belongings are brought to you."

Tara was left alone in the living room. She walked down the hallway and opened the first bedroom door. A nice sized bed and a tall dresser furnished the room. There were shelves in the closet as well as a bar on which to hang clothes. The second bedroom contained a small bed and another dresser. She gasped when she opened the third bedroom. Inside were the babies' cradles from the house. She walked up to them in disbelief. Who had brought them here? Their dressers lined the wall; all their clothes were in them.

Tara stood in the little room, stunned by what she was seeing. What could all this mean? If Darius was giving her all of the baby things, did that mean he didn't want them to come back? A wave of panic ran through Tara's body. It had never occurred to her that he might decide he didn't want them to come home. She ran her fingers over a cradle, and her eyes welled with tears.

He wasn't willing to change for her. He'd made the decision and sent her these things. Tara imagined that the empty nursery had been more than he could bear. The man had no use for baby articles with no babies in the house. And maybe he thought sending her the items would make her react just the way she had. Darius could have sent her everything to scare her into thinking he didn't want her — a bluff to lure her home.

Tara wouldn't put an act like that past the man. But on the other hand, she *had* left to teach him a lesson. She *wanted* Darius to know she had zero tolerance for his behavior. Tara would not live with a man, continuously wondering where he was, and with whom.

As her finger traced the cribs' carvings, she suddenly realized that was exactly what she was doing right now. Oh, how she missed him. Maybe she should have stayed and battled it out.

She shook herself, trying to get her thoughts back to reality. She never could have lived with a man who did not respect her. Tara quickly walked out of the room.

The landlink in the living room was logged on. She hadn't noticed that a second ago. The screen indicated there was a message waiting for her response. Someone had taken the time to program this landlink to use her pass code. She tapped the screen and realized the message was indeed for her. She thought for a moment, trying to figure out who would know her pass code. Darius? She tried to remember if she'd shown it to him, but she wasn't sure. Curiosity got the best of her, and she opened the message.

"Hello, Tara. This is my third attempt to contact you, it is. I hope you'll not delete this message. It's not possible for me to right a wrong when you'll not return to allow me to do so. I hope this trailer will show you that my intentions toward you are genuine. I've made every attempt to bring you back. I am now made to understand that you still do not plan to return, and instead will enter Southland. Tara, your place is here. We've united two nations, and it is your duty to rule over them with me, it is. You, too, are failing your duty, just as you say I have. Return within one week, or I'll sever all relations with the Runners, disowning all of you. I don't want to do this. My love for you is strong, it is. Return to me now. Darius."

Tara read the message twice. Her blood boiled, and she wondered if Patha knew of this threat. She slammed her fist on the table and turned to leave the trailer. As she opened the door, Syra greeted her.

"Have you heard the news?" Syra was grinning. She had a bag in each hand as she entered the trailer. "I get to go with you. My papa said it would keep me away from Torgo. What an adventure. Which one is my room?"

Tara stood there speechless. She quickly regrouped her thoughts. No one must know about the message from Darius. She walked back to the landlink and deleted it. She would not bother to acknowledge such an insult. He didn't control everybody's life.

"You want me to go with you, don't you?" Syra apparently misread Tara's silence and looked worried. "I could be a big help with the babies."

"Of course, you can go with me." Tara smiled, quickly forcing her thoughts to the future.

Just then a jeep pulled up to the trailer. Patha and Balbo entered and began to bring Tara's things into the room. They spent the next hour organizing clothes and saying goodbyes.

Tara watched Patha closely. If her papa knew of Darius' threat, he gave no indication. He spoke only of his concern that Tara stay in touch with him and let him know what the people of Southland were like.

"Let me know when you are safely in Semore." Patha hugged his daughter soundly. His eyes looked moist when he pulled away.

"And take care of my daughter," Balbo added.

"I will." Tara held her hands out to both of them. She hugged Reena and Torgo then climbed into the driver's seat.

The rocky road led down a cliff and took a long time to navigate. The attached trailer with the bike on it swerved from side to side, and Tara crawled along, fearing it would fall off the edge of the road. She was glad when they finally came to the road at the bottom, and she was able to gain speed.

The town of Semore was unlike anything Tara had ever seen. It had been built around ruins from the Oldworld. There weren't many ruins like these in Trueland. Small flat buildings made out of white bricks lined each side of the road. People walked along sidewalks. Tara saw more cars than she'd ever seen at any one time. After trial and error, she figured out that the tall poles with lights at intersections, indicated to drivers where they could stop or go depending upon the color light displayed at any given time. What a concept.

Her attention was drawn to oil pumps slowly moving up and down at the edge of town. Oil was something Runners and Gothman needed.

Ahead on the right, Tara spied a sign saying, *"Rooms Available."* She pulled the trailer into a parking area covered with small red gravel.

A dark-skinned, white-haired older man with black eyes and bushy white eyebrows told her about a small boarding house at the edge of town where she might be able to park her trailer. He gave her such an odd look; she decided not to ask him if she could pay with gold pieces.

She drove to the place he'd specified—an older house set back off the road. It had a flat-roofed porch covering the front of the white clay building. The structure was longer than it was wide. Beyond it, the land stretched endlessly.

"Hello," she said to a young woman leaning against a counter just inside the house. "I need a place to park my trailer for a short time."

The young lady looked past Tara out the window at the trailer. She studied it for a minute and then looked back at Tara and studied her. The woman's hair was black as coal. She had it twisted in the back in several braids. Her skin was also as dark as night and her inky black eyes looked curiously at Tara. "Where are you from?"

"North of here."

"North? There isn't much north of here. You live in that trailer?"

The girl's dialect was not like anything Tara had heard before. She liked it. The girl's words ran together, sounding almost melodic. Tara listened carefully to understand what the girl said.

"I do for right now." Tara smiled, knowing her voice must sound very foreign to the young girl as well. "I have a couple of babies. We're looking for a new life, so to speak."

"So, you come to Semore?" This seemed to surprise the girl. "Things aren't good around here right now. I mean, if you're looking for work, I don't know if you'll find any."

"I'd like to try. Could I park the trailer for just a few days?"

"I guess we can't turn away a mama with babies. Pull it around back and I'll bring out the paperwork."

Tara thanked her and parked the trailer in the indicated spot. The young girl came out the back door within minutes. She handed the paperwork to Tara and peeked past the open door of the trailer at Syra and the babies inside.

"I've never seen such blond curly hair before," the girl commented. "Where did you say you were from?"

Tara was saved from answering by two men who appeared in the building's doorway. Both were tall, with dark skin and hair. One of the men, however, caught her off guard. He had long black hair falling to his waist. He was thin with broad shoulders and his black eyes glistened as he looked at her. The other man gestured for the girl to come to him, and the three disappeared into the building, leaving Tara alone to fill out the papers.

The young girl appeared again before long and smiled shyly as she walked toward Tara. "My husband wants to know if someone is going to come after you?"

"I don't think so."

"Do you have money?"

"I have gold. I'll exchange it if you tell me where I can do that."

She shook her head. "That won't be necessary."

The girl took three gold pieces and told her it would cost her the same amount for each day she was there. "You're welcome to join us for a midday meal shortly. You'll hear the bell ring when it's ready." The girl took the papers and disappeared into the building.

Tara watched her walk away and couldn't help but wonder which of the two men was her husband. She thought of Darius, then the dark man, and then she pushed both images out of her head and went to her children.

The food was not identifiable, but it was good. The couple served the meals, but didn't eat with them. In fact, over the next several days, Tara and Syra were not sought out by any of the town folk. Nor did anyone pay much attention to them, although their fair skin and sandy brown hair made them conspicuous among the dark-skinned Neurians. Even Tara's attempts at conversation in the food market went unheeded.

The landlink system in the community was quite elaborate. Semore was connected to nearby towns, and Tara studied everything she could about them and their residents. She discovered that a number identified every citizen on the landlink system. Everything in the town was on the landlink. She was able to obtain a guest number and visit many of the local merchants through their networking system. Her frustration grew, however, when a message continually appeared on the screen saying her "guest status" did not allow her to view her selection. She was prevented from viewing anything about their government.

Every morning, Tara walked down the street to buy one of the newspapers sold in the town. It primarily covered the town's current events, but Tara found a few political news items, as well.

They'd been in Semore a week. Tara was lonely and thinking of Darius as she walked back to her trailer. The time frame he'd given her to return had expired. She'd spoken to Patha every day, but he had never indicated whether or not he knew about Darius' threat. Darius hadn't sent her any more messages, and she wondered if he really would disown her, as he'd put it.

She walked slowly along the street, reading the paper, and looking for possible work. If she were home, there would be plenty of work to do. But here, there wasn't much call for overseeing military training, or resolving conflicts among clan members.

Briefly, she wondered who had assumed her tasks among the Runners. Darius had learned a lot about them—had he taken on her responsibilities? If so, how would members react to Darius mediating a clan dispute?

Tara stubbed her toe and let out a curse. Thinking of Darius would not help her right now. Maybe Patha had been right. He'd said she wouldn't be able to fit into this community easily.

As she half-heartedly scanned the paper, a new ad caught her eye. An assistant was needed in one of the government offices to do some landlink work. This was exactly what she'd been looking for. Excited, Tara read the ad closely. She was startled when she walked into something. Looking up, she realized she'd walked right into a man coming toward her.

"I'm so sorry." The man looked up from a landlink printout, obviously thinking it was he who had not been paying attention. He seemed to contemplate saying something else.

"No, it's my fault," she began.

"You just arrived in Semore, didn't you?" he asked after some hesitation. He glanced around the street as if to see if there was anyone watching. "Follow me."

Tara followed out of curiosity as he led her through a nearby door and down a poorly lit hallway. He was possibly five to ten winters older than she, very thin, with black straight hair that fell to his shoulders.

He turned toward a closed door at the end of the hall, tapped on it, and then opened the door slowly.

Tara tapped her pocket, reassured by the hard metal of her laser.

The dark man glanced at her and moved through the doorway.

She followed. Tara faced three men. The one she'd followed, along with two others who sat by a desk in what appeared to be an office. One of the seated men was quite heavy; the other had long silver hair pulled back into a ponytail. The silver-haired man looked older than Patha.

They all stared.

She returned their stare, noticing that they seemed nervous.

"We, uh..." The man standing by her began speaking, stopped, and looked at his friends. "That is, um, we know who you are."

"That's nice. But I don't know who you are." She forced herself to appear unconcerned.

"Fleeders," the tall man pointed to himself then to his friends. "Snith and Tilk. We, uh, work here."

The room was well lit with an overhead light and a lamp next to the landlink. There was another desk in the room with a landlink on it as well. The shelves lining the walls were filled with landlink parts and discs. After she'd studied the contents of the room, she turned to stare to Fleeders. "Why'd you bring me here?"

"To talk to you," Tilk, the old man spoke up, and the other two looked at him with worried glances. "We've been monitoring your communications."

"You've been what?"

"It's our job," Fleeders said quickly. "We understand that you're not happy about this. But, we monitor all landlink activity."

"Gowsky has us do it." Snith wiped sweat from his upper lip. "It's not really common knowledge, but we've been through bad times."

"We know you're Tara, daughter of Patha, leader of the Blood Circle Clan. You joined with the leader of the Gothman, and you defeated the Sea People," Fleeders said awkwardly. He added quickly, "We know you're not here to hurt anyone."

There was a chair next to the empty desk, and Tara sat in it, spreading her long legs out in front of her and crossing her feet. A small smile crossed her face. These men were scared to death— apparently of her!

As they should be. She could kill all three of them in this small office and return to the street without anyone realizing it. For some reason, they'd decided to speak to her. It had been a sacrifice for them, since they were obviously terrified by her presence.

"So why am I here?"

Tilk and Snith looked at Fleeders. So did Tara. He cleared his throat again, something he'd done often in the short time Tara had been in his presence.

"Gowsky found out you were here several days ago. Maybe he's known longer, I'm not sure. He's convinced you're here to start some kind of revolution—take over the Neurian Government. We were asked to monitor your communications and give him a report at the end of the week."

Tara listened closely as Fleeders spoke. She still wasn't accustomed to their singsong accents. "So you've monitored my communication. And…?"

"We don't think you're here to start anything," Snith said.

"We think you're here out of curiosity," Tilk said. "And to get even with your husband." He added this last sentence quickly and quietly.

"You did make one comment about our oil." Fleeders looked at his friends, instead of her.

"So you know all about me." Tara twisted in her chair and looked at the landlink next to her. It was a lot bulkier than the Runner landlink. The three men didn't say anything as she brought up the screen. It displayed a directory the main landlink offered to every Neurian. Tara had already accessed this on her landlink and was somewhat familiar with its contents.

"You use a similar binary code in your programs." She turned and looked at the trio. "So what will your report say to Gowsky?"

"That's just it," Fleeders lowered his voice just a little. "That is why we brought you here, or I should say, decided to try to get you to come here."

Tara looked up curiously.

Fleeders continued. "Gowsky stopped by yesterday and told us to infect your landlink so you could no longer communicate with your people."

Tilk interrupted. "He told us he was going to pick you up and charge you with—"

"Charge me with what?" Tara interrupted as she leaned forward in her chair and slapped her hands on her knees so hard the three men jumped.

"It's just what we've been told," Tilk said, sounding apologetic. "Charge you with conspiring to start a war."

"I see." Tara stood and began pacing while her thoughts raced. "Any defense I come up with will likely be shot down in your government. I could leave right now, but I would have accomplished nothing." She stopped and stared at the men.

They looked at her glumly.

"Why have you told me all this?"

"Neurians have been devastated by the loss of trade with the Sea People. We could rebuild if we could ship out our oil. We've researched you and your Runners since we had access to your landlink system while you were talking with your papa. You're an advanced race. More advanced than Neurians think you are. We'll try to explain all this to Gowsky, but I don't think it will make any difference. He wants you brought to him." Fleeders shrugged and sincerely looked sorry. "We're telling you this so you know the Neurian government is watching you."

"We don't know what you want to do with this information," Tilk added. "Now you know what's going to happen."

"I know exactly what I'm going to do." Tara walked to the door.

Chapter Sixteen

✂

Tara froze as she heard loud voices at the end of the hallway. It sounded like several men headed in her direction.

"It's the police." Fleeders looked nervously at the door.

"Is there another way out of here?" Tara looked around the room.

A small window was the only other option. Not waiting for an answer, she ran past the three men, jumped onto the desk and lifted the window. She was out of the office and in an alley within seconds. She heard the window shut behind her as she ran down the alley. She slowed to a walk and headed down the sidewalk toward her trailer. No one stopped her on the street, and she wasn't followed.

"You forgot the paper." Syra looked up when Tara walked into the trailer and plopped down on the floor next to her children.

They immediately dropped their toys and climbed onto their mama. She hugged and tickled them, but she was distracted. "Sorry. I guess I did."

"Well, can I go get one?" Syra stood up and stretched. "I sure could stand to get out of here for awhile."

Tara had been so caught up by her thoughts; she'd barely heard the desperate plea. At once, she focused on Syra. It's true, the youngster had been cooped up with the babies pretty much since their arrival at Semore, and it wasn't fair. "Go ahead. Make sure you take a comm. Call me right away if you have any problems." She looked at the long sundress Syra had on. "Girls here wear pants, though."

"When it's cold, they want me in dresses. And when it's hot, they want me in pants," Syra mumbled as she walked back to her room to change.

The children napped while Syra explored the town, leaving Tara time to reflect on what Fleeders had told her about Gowsky. Here was a man, a council, paranoid after having been stripped of the commerce upon which they relied. These people hadn't anticipated that their main income would disappear. Their opium was ample. It didn't run out. It was their buyers who had deserted them. Now they were frustrated, desperate, and not thinking clearly. On the other hand, the Neurians' precious oil was important to Runners and Gothman. It made sense they would want to discuss this with her.

Tara decided she must speak with Gowsky, which shouldn't be difficult since he wanted her brought in. The question was, should she let them capture her? It probably wouldn't be long before his police showed up at the trailer. Or should she seek him out on her own, maybe tonight after the babies were asleep? Could Gowsky be the man she'd seen her first day here?

She decided to take a walk with the babies. The children squealed in delight as she pushed them in the wagon across the sand and tiny stones behind the trailer. The heat from the sun made the horizon appear wavy in the distance. It was a good sun though — warm and refreshing on her skin.

Tara moved on, slowly trudging across the desert that lay south of the town. She passed several large tree-like plants with leaves the texture of rubber. They were quite beautiful and provided an abundance of shade from the hot sun.

Movement out of the corner of her eye caught her attention. Tara squatted down next to her children, talking to them quietly, as she surveyed the area.

"What do you think it was?" Tara smiled at Andru as he squinted his eyes to look with her. Andru smiled and giggled, and Ana kicked at him and also giggled.

"Look, there it is," Tara whispered to her children and pointed to an animal crossing the field. It looked like a large dog of sorts: dark brown with thick hair and a long tail, walking on all fours. It moved toward them slowly.

Tara knew from experience that most wild animals were not aggressive unless provoked. If she were threatened, her laser would easily kill the animal. She remained squatting next to her children as they pointed with curiosity at the animal.

As the dog moved closer, the heat rising from the ground distorted its features. The waves drifted up, making the creature appear to be walking on only two legs. As the distance between then lessened, Tara realized it *was* walking on only two legs. What she thought had been a dog was now a person. Her eyesight was strong and she questioned what she'd just seen. Had the creature transformed from beast to human?

To be more exact, the creature approaching her was an old woman. She walked hunched over, slowly, a deeply creased leathery face with large dark brown eyes focusing on Tara. Her darkened skin, a shade more orange than the Neurians, was covered with a loose animal skin dress. Her boots were made of the same material, laced up to her knees.

"A blessing to you, child," the old woman's voice cracked as if from lack of use.

"Hello." Tara squinted up at the old woman who now was no more than five feet in front of her.

"Why are you here?"

"I'm taking my children for a walk."

The old woman came closer and reached out to touch Ana. Tara's body tightened and the old woman noticed her uneasiness. She pulled her hand away from Ana's head and instead placed her deformed fingers on Andru's head. She glanced at Tara with each move to assure her that no harm would be done.

"The children will see and learn a lot. But why are you here?"

Was this old woman crazy? Tara looked at her, and the old woman stared back with dark, glassy eyes.

"Do you mean why am I here with these people?"

The old woman continued her glazed stare and didn't respond.

"We need a new life. We've moved here from the north." Tara tried to change the subject. "Do you live around here?"

"You aren't through with your old life. You still have much to do."

Now it was Tara's turn to stare. The old woman was out of her head, she decided. Old age and the heat of the desert had done her in.

"Crator knows your fears and your pride. You must put that aside. There's no time for it. You have so much to do. None of it will happen without you. Do you realize that?" The old woman's eyes were glassier than before and they seemed to penetrate through Tara. It was almost as if they were focusing on the ground behind her.

"I don't understand what you're saying."

"That is your fear. Crator knows you're strong. Overcome it."

Tara didn't know how to pursue conversation with the old woman. She felt sorry for a people who didn't take care of their elderly. The woman was delusional and possibly lost out here. But what she said *did* apply to Tara's life. Was that delusional? She reached into the wagon for a bag of bread pieces and fruit she'd brought for the children.

"Would you like to have a snack with us?" Tara pulled the food from the bag and then looked back to offer it to the old woman. With a shock, she saw nothing except a large dog running away from her across the field. She watched until it was out of sight.

"There you are." Syra smiled at Tara and immediately got up from the table to help with the children as Tara entered the trailer. "I wondered where you went."

"We took a walk," Tara said, deciding not to mention the lady in the desert.

"Well, that's what I did, too." Syra slid Ana into the toddler seat, attached to the table with clamps, and then struggled to strap her in while the child pulled her hair. "Folks here aren't too friendly, are they?"

"We look a lot different than they do." Tara managed to get Andru into his seat, and then walked to the cold box for two bottles. "Maybe in time they will warm to us."

"Maybe." Syra shrugged and began dicing cheese and apples for the children. "I got a paper and read a few stories in it while you

278

were gone. Sounds like they have an organized government here." Syra commented on a few of the stories in the paper.

Tara didn't hear much of the conversation. The old woman occupied her thoughts. Who was she? What had she meant by her words? Was she simply a disillusioned old lady? And who was Crator?

After supper, Syra bathed the babies and prepared them for bed.

Tara sat at the landlink and decided to see if the Neurian network said anything about a Crator. She wasn't connected for long when a message flashed across her screen. "Why are you looking for Crator?"

She panicked for a second, but a few clicks told her the message was from Fleeders.

"Can I talk to you?" she typed.

"This line isn't secure. Log off."

Tara wondered why anybody cared if she researched the name. Who *was* Crator? She logged off and grabbed her jacket.

"I'm going for a walk," she whispered to Syra who was rocking Ana to sleep. Andru lay stretched out in his crib. Tara gently kissed his forehead then kissed her fingertip and placed it on Ana's head.

The night air was brisk. A chill ran through Tara's body, and she quickly zipped her leather jacket. Moving her laser to her front jacket pocket, she began walking behind the trailer. The open wilderness lying in front of her seemed dark and forbidding. Who was out there? What was out there?

Another chill caught her body. It was from fear. Tara was not accustomed to this emotion. She'd faced many enemies who had posed a more obvious danger than an old woman who babbled. What was there to fear?

The woman's words bothered her, she couldn't deny it. Although she'd written them off as the delusions of an old mind, Tara couldn't get them out of her mind.

You aren't through with your old life. You still have so much to do.

Tara shuddered as she saw the truth in those words. She was heir to the leader of all the Runner clans. The old woman couldn't have been more truthful when she told Tara that her old life wasn't done. Tara kicked the ground with the tip of her boot and scowled. That old woman couldn't have had a clue who Tara was or where she came from.

"What do you want to know about Crator?" The voice that came from behind her made Tara jump. She jerked around, and her laser pointed straight into Fleeders' chest.

He too jumped and his arms flew into the air. "It was just a question. You don't have to tell me if you don't want to."

"You startled me." Tara returned the deadly weapon to her pocket.

Fleeders' eyes followed it to its hiding place as he slowly lowered his arms.

"Who is Crator?"

"He is why we exist. Crator made all of this. Everything you see."

"Where is he? I want to meet him."

"You can't *meet* him." Fleeders laughed, then sobered immediately. "At least not until your life here is over. Crator created all life on Nuworld. He's a spirit. I'm sure Runners must have a name for Him. Who made you? Gave you life?"

"My parents gave me life. There's no spirit responsible for my life."

"We believe there is. Crator is responsible for all living things and for Nuworld itself. Are you saying Runners have no faith?"

"Faith?"

"What do you think happens when you die?"

"When you die, you're done. You exist no more."

"I don't think I could go through life if I believed that."

"Why couldn't I find information on Crator through the Network?"

"There's plenty of information on Crator. But, the council is watching you closely. I wouldn't be surprised if they know I'm here." Fleeders looked around him nervously. "Why this sudden interest in Crator?"

"I met someone today." Tara pointed to the dark, foreboding wilderness.

Fleeders' gaze followed her finger.

"Out there. She said something about Crator."

"Who did you meet out there?"

"I don't know her name." Tara shrugged. "Some old lady. Her words were mostly babble."

"You met an old woman out there?" Fleeders looked and sounded very worried. "What did she say to you?"

"I don't remember exactly." She wrinkled her brow and studied Fleeders' face.

He looked back at her anxiously, his eyebrows wrinkled.

"She didn't really make any sense. She said Crator knew things about me. Things I was supposed to do."

Fleeders stared out into the wilderness blanketed with darkness. It was as if he expected to see this old lady Tara had mentioned. There was a strange look on his face, one of fear and awe.

"Do you have any idea where she might live? I thought I would take her some food. She was an odd sort. I don't think she talks to anyone much."

"There's a legend about the Guardians, voices for Crator." Fleeders shuddered and turned away from the field. "There are animals that turn into people and tell us the wishes of Crator. It's just an old legend. No one's ever seen one. She didn't turn into an animal on you, did she?" Fleeders chuckled as he said this, but he sounded nervous.

He caught Tara's gaze and looked away quickly. She sensed how awkward the conversation made him. He really believed these legends of his, yet had no proof. She had the proof and didn't believe in them. A people with such faith could be very powerful, yet these people were scared and felt deserted.

"Why don't you go for a ride with me and let's see if we can find one of these Guardians?" Tara walked over to her bike.

"You're not going to go out there tonight, are you?" Fleeders stood firm, carefully focusing his attention away from the dark wilderness. "No one goes into the desert at night."

"There are good lights on my bike. We'll be able to see fine."

A sudden loud explosion from the town caused both of them to jump. They turned toward the sound; within seconds large flames began shooting into the sky.

"Something's on fire!" Tara straddled her bike.

"Oh no! It couldn't be!" Fleeders gave no explanation for his comment, but ran to Tara and squeezed onto the seat behind her. She took off slower than she would have liked out of deference to her passenger. Fleeders obviously wasn't familiar with a motorcycle; he kept fidgeting from right to left.

A large two-story building at the other end of the main street was engulfed in flames. As they drew near, Tara heard glass exploding from the heat. People ran from all directions toward the building. Trucks with long, thick hoses pulled up, and shouts came from many directions as the hoses were dragged from the truck and hooked up to small cylindrical objects attached to the ground beside the road.

The smoke attacked Tara and Fleeders, blurring their vision and making it difficult to breathe.

"Let me off." Fleeders squirmed behind her.

"What's that building?"

"It's a warehouse that's not being used right now. Our whole project was in there. Nothing in that building could have caused an explosion like that. Everything is ruined. Who would have known? Who could have done this?"

Tara pulled the bike to the side of the road, and the two jumped off. "What project was in there? Who would have known about what?"

"Nothing. It's nothing." Fleeders took off running toward the building.

A big, round-bellied man shouted orders as a large hose flooded the building with water. The fire withered from the attack.

Tara noticed another hose still coiled on the side of the truck. Why weren't they using it?

The smoke thickened.

People crowded into the street. It was easy for Tara to move closer and not be noticed.

Tara wanted to know what project had been going on in this building. Fleeders had looked as if he'd regretted saying what he had just before he ran off. Where had he gone?

The men putting out the fire seemed to move at a snail's pace. They acted content to let the building burn to the ground. A group of men stood across from the burning building. They watched intently and occasionally spoke with one of the security men who had come onto the scene. The crowd of onlookers was now being herded away from the building.

Tara stood down the street from the fire and avoided the security. She noticed handfuls of people trying to get into the side of the building that hadn't burned yet. The security guards were on them instantly, pulling them back.

Through the smoke, Tara noticed Fleeders, his tall skinny profile moving quickly through the thick haze to the group of men standing across the street. Tara watched as he spoke to one of them. He gestured wildly at a broad-shouldered man with long black hair. It was the man she'd seen the first day she arrived. She saw the broad-shouldered man gesture to several others, and the men took off running. It appeared he was giving orders to everyone.

Could that man be Gowsky? Fleeders said Gowsky had known she was there shortly after she'd arrived. Had Gowsky recognized her when he saw her pull in to town? The broad-shouldered man turned and looked directly at her.

A window exploded, this time from the second floor. Tara turned, as did others, and noticed a young woman waving her arms frantically.

"Help me!" she yelled to the men putting out the fire. "Please, you've got to help me!"

The potbellied man shouting orders looked up at her and then at the broad-shouldered man Tara guessed was Gowsky.

Fleeders lunged at the building, but several men grabbed him.

They weren't going to rescue the woman! Tara couldn't believe these people would let her burn. What was so awful about the project that they would let a woman burn for it? What could have been going on in this building that would provoke someone to set fire to it? She didn't know the answers to these questions, but she wouldn't watch someone die like this. Tara lunged toward the building.

"Hey! Get back!" The potbellied man gestured for Tara to move away. "What do you think you're doing?"

Jumping, she grabbed hold of the ledge above the window and swung her legs through the glass of the window. As her legs swung back, she turned and made eye contact with the broad-shouldered man.

As their eyes met, he froze, and his mouth fell open.

She turned to look inside the window, swung forward again, and dropped inside the burning building. The intensity of the smoke increased drastically as Tara landed in the room. It seeped through the broken windowpane, as she waved her hand in front of her face and began coughing. The room was dark, and Tara's eyes slowly adjusted.

She ran into a hallway. Smoke was billowing through the door at one end. Tara ran the other way. Several doors at the other end of the hallway were open. The farthest one opened into the large warehouse part of the building. Fire crawled along the floor at the far end of this cavernous room. Some of the rafters on the same side also burned. Tara guessed that within ten minutes the building would start to collapse. To make matters worse, fire swept the stairs, and the woman was trapped on the floor above!

Tara looked quickly around the warehouse. The large space was empty except for abandoned boxes tossed in a corner. She ran to the boxes and grabbed several, collapsing them as she ran back to the stairs.

"Hello? Can you here me?" Tara yelled through the smoke. She beat the fire with the flattened boxes until it had subsided somewhat. "I'm at the stairs. Are you hurt?"

She threw the cardboard down on the stairs and quickly bolted up to the second floor. Fire leapt at her from the walls and ceilings.

Tara entered a large, open room. The young lady was still standing by the open window. Tara ran to her and grabbed her shoulders. "Come on. The building is going to collapse."

"Who are you?" The woman looked horrified at Tara's foreign appearance. Tara had grown accustomed to the dark-skinned race reacting to her that way. She doubted many of them had ever seen someone with her pale skin color. The woman was young, of small build. Her black hair had once been pulled up, but long strands fell wildly across her face and down her back. "I don't know who you are."

"My name is Tara, and I'm going to get you out of here."

The lady, obviously in shock, looked around the room disoriented. She glanced at Tara and then down at the items she held in her arms. To Tara, they appeared to be loose papers and a small plastic container, similar to the kind Runners used to hold landlink discs.

"This won't stop anything, you know." The lady was obviously delirious. "Why would they want to stop us? They're not going to hurt us. They're stranded where they are."

"Come on." Tara guided her to the stairs.

"We've already communicated with them. I don't think they know that. This won't stop anything," the lady rambled.

When they reached the stairs, Tara saw that the fire had engulfed the collapsed boxes. The lady's body tensed, and she looked at Tara desperately. "We can't die. We've come too far. They can help us, you know. And we can help them. We call them Lunians, which was my idea. But I don't know if that's what they call themselves."

The lady continued to babble as Tara looked frantically around the room, saying to herself, "We need something to stamp down the fire before it takes out the stairs."

The crackling of the rafters and the heat from the floor let Tara know the structure was only a few minutes away from collapse. The fire was closing in. The heat was unbearable. They had to move, or neither one of them would make it.

She turned and looked out a window by the staircase. The men below still aimed the lone hose at the building. However, the broad-shouldered man who'd been talking to Fleeders was simply standing there watching it burn, calculating the minutes, probably, before they could go home. Through the darkness she could see him point to her, but none of the men moved.

It was too far down to jump.

"We've got to make a run for it," she said, turning back to the burning staircase.

"What?" The lady's eyes looked terrified. "We'll be killed."

"There's no time to discuss it." Tara grabbed the lady and threw her over her shoulder. The lady squirmed in protest, but Tara's grip was firm. She dashed down the stairs straight through the flames. She could feel the heat singe her hair and clothes. The stairs cracked and groaned under their weight. Large popping sounds indicated that one moment too long would send them falling through. Her foot did break through the last stair, and she pulled with a vengeance to release it from the torn board. Pain shot up her ankle, her knee, and then her thigh as her foot popped free from the burning wood. She grimaced as she put weight on it and limped through the large open room toward the window where she'd entered.

A large explosion told her the ceiling had caved in at the back of the building. Immediately, smoke from the collapsing wood filled the air, completely blinding Tara. The woman she carried screamed loudly, piercing Tara's eardrum. The woman's body went rigid with fear, and she made an attempt to jump out of Tara's arms. Tara held onto her tightly with one arm and used her other hand to feel her way down the hallway. She reentered the small room and ran to the window, her feet crunching over the broken glass.

"We can get out through this window." Tara released the woman. "Quickly, climb out. The ground is just a few feet below."

"You've saved my life." The lady climbed through the open window and then turned to smile at Tara. "I know who you are now. You are the Northerner I've heard about. Do you know about the Lunians?"

"No, who are they?"

"They are a colony living on the moon."

Tara froze in disbelief at these words as the lady stuck her legs out of the window and jumped. Another crash inspired movement and she, too, jumped out the window.

Her injured foot protested loudly as she hit the ground. Pain shot up Tara's leg. She fell sideways in response, and the rest of her body hit the hard ground. The crackling sounds nearby warned her that she still wasn't safe. Using her good foot and both hands, she moved crablike away from the building to a safe distance. As she stood, putting the weight of her body on her good leg, she looked up in time to see the building collapse to the ground.

The girl she'd rescued was gone. The crowd had dwindled, and the darkness, either from the night, the smoke, or both, made it hard to see. It was hard to identify which people were still hovering around the building. She didn't see the broad-shouldered man anywhere.

Tara turned and limped slowly toward her bike, thinking about what she had just heard. That lady had said something about a colony on the moon. She had called them Lunians. She said the Neurians had communicated with them. Tara squinted at the full moon. It looked the same as it always had.

She wondered what communication had transpired with this Lunian people. She'd never given much thought to the moon, although she relied on its light at night and had enjoyed its beauty. But now she studied it, looking for something she hadn't noticed before. The round object gave no indication that it housed life. But then, she felt sure with a good viewer she might notice something to indicate a city. Tara wondered what technology the Neurians possessed that allowed them to discover the people living there.

Without warning, a hand came from behind her, covering her mouth. Then, she experienced a sensation she'd felt too many times before—someone had stuck the end of a pistol into the back of her rib cage.

Tara turned instinctively and grabbed for the gun. Her aggressor was stronger than she was, but showed no knowledge of combat. She pulled the weapon from his grasp. Unfortunately, she turned and placed her weight on her bad foot. She grimaced in pain and let out a low shriek as she lunged helplessly to one side, unable to steady herself before falling to the ground.

The glow from the fire silhouetted the figure standing over her. The broad-shouldered man with long flowing hair stared down.

Still holding the gun in her hand, she aimed it up at him as she slowly forced herself into a standing position.

"I'm not foolish." The man's voice was calm, almost soothing. "It's not loaded."

She focused on his Neurian features. His brown skin was unblemished, and his dark eyes matched the color of his pupils. A small smile revealed white teeth almost glowing in the darkness. "I'm aware of your reputation as a warrior, and I had no doubts you'd be able to unarm me." His singsong accent was as distracting as his features. "You have not disappointed me."

Tara looked at the gun in her hand and then nonchalantly tossed it away. Relying on that distraction, she reached for her laser. The distraction didn't work.

The man's grin increased as he pulled another gun. "This one however *is* loaded."

"Fine, you win." Tara held up her hands. "Now what?"

"Can you walk?" The man continued to look straight into her eyes.

Knowing this to be the perfect way to intimidate an enemy, Tara returned the gaze. "It depends on how far. If I'm lucky, I can make it back to my bike."

"We'll get you home to your babies. First though, you and I are going to talk."

With no warning, the man pulled the trigger on his gun, and Tara's world went dark.

Chapter Seventeen

ೞ

The first thing Tara felt was pain. Her entire body reverberated with it as she slowly tried to focus on her surroundings. The throbbing in her foot matched the throbbing in her head. Tara realized she was lying down and lifted her upper body onto her elbows. Everything around her was spinning, and her muscles felt very stiff. For a second, Tara had no idea why she lay here. She searched her brain for an explanation for the pain and why she would be sleeping. It hurt to concentrate, but panic threatened, and Tara didn't like the sensation of fear beginning to consume her.

Then it came to her. The fire. She had jumped from the window and hurt her foot. Tara turned her head with effort, the blurred surroundings making her dizzy and looked at her foot. It also appeared a blur. She blinked and allowed her eyes to focus on nothing while she worked her thoughts into order. It made no sense why pain in her foot would make her brain so foggy. And where was she? She needed to find her bike and get to children. Tara made an effort to sit.

"You'll feel better in a few minutes," a male voice said.

She jerked her head toward the voice, and her vision returned.

The man who'd shot her sat several feet away in a metal chair. His features were perfect. Eyes like onyx stared at her with long lashes almost reaching thick black eyebrows. He had pronounced cheekbones and a long, straight nose. Tara noticed strands of his long hair were braided, but otherwise his mane fell free past his shoulders and behind his back.

His long legs disappeared into boots made of animal skin tied with leather straps just below his knees. He smiled, and his dark skin showed off his white teeth.

She noticed her laser sitting on his lap. "Where am I?" Tara continued her effort to reach a sitting position. Her head still pounded.

"You're in my barn."

Tara moved slowly to the edge of the makeshift bed, which felt like nothing more than a bench with several quilts thrown over it. As she shifted her legs over the side, one foot hit the floor, and she felt incredible pain shoot upward. When she leaned over to massage it, she noticed it was bandaged. She grimaced, swiping her hair over her shoulder. For some reason, her hair seemed longer than it should be.

"It was a pretty nasty scrape. Our doctor cleaned it up. He said it would hurt for awhile."

Tara glanced up at the man.

"Would you like something to eat?"

She shook her head, still dwelling on the pain in her foot.

He handed her a plate of sliced light-colored meat and a small vine of grapes.

Although she'd declined his offer, her stomach groaned loudly in protest, and she hated to admit she was famished. Reluctantly, Tara accepted the sustenance.

"I figured you'd be pretty hungry. You've been asleep for several days."

Tara was stuffing one of the slices of meat into her mouth and had begun to chew eagerly when she heard his last words. She almost choked when she heard how long she'd slept. Instantly, she thought of Syra and the babies. What would Syra have done when she didn't come home? Tara immediately feared the worse. There was no satisfactory outcome. Andru and Ana would have cried for her. Syra hadn't known the children that long. She wouldn't have been able to calm them.

"I've been asleep for several days?" Tara spat remnants of meat from her mouth and glared at the man. "How dare you keep me from my children for that long!"

"You were injured." The man shrugged.

"What about my children?" Tara raised her voice and felt the pain increase in her head. She felt too much outrage to care, but rubbed her hands over her face trying to understand what was happening. "Why are you holding me here?"

"Your niece and children have been notified. They are fine."

The man's calm made Tara want to smack him. "You haven't answered why you are holding me here," she said through clenched teeth. "And why did you keep me asleep for several days?"

"I don't run Semore by myself. The fate of all Neurians must be considered. It's obviously no secret how your war has affected us. Northerners are very different...your beliefs, your priorities —"

"And what do my beliefs and where I come from have to do with you holding me and keeping me from my family?"

"We have a duty to the Neurian people to ensure their safety." The man shrugged again.

Tara slowly stood, testing her foot. She started to put weight on it, then stopped. While she probably could walk, she decided it might be best not to let him know that fact. She was also very aware of her laser in this man's lap. "You seem to know more about me than I know about you. Who are you?"

* * * * *

The man's dark eyes watched her slim figure as she hobbled a few feet away from the bed. He knew very little about Runners, other than they were supposed to be incredible warriors, and they had defeated the Sea People. She was beautiful, even in her current state. Those blue eyes...like the color of the sky...and that pale skin...she was quite the distraction. He'd never seen a woman like her before, other than in pictures.

She limped slowly, but there was very little sign of discomfort on her face. He guessed even in her drugged state, she had enough training to prevent her expression from betraying emotion. His best approach would be to not second-guess anything about her, so he continued to watch her.

He'd heard that she'd united two nations and could claim leadership over both. What power, what beauty! He wanted to know the type of person who could master such a feat. She would have to be intelligent, with negotiating skills and the ability to influence positively. Otherwise, people wouldn't respond to her. And from the reading he had completed while she had been there, he realized not enough good things could be said about Tara.

He was definitely attracted to her. But if his plan was to work, he had to remain true to the role he'd agreed to play.

The council hadn't accepted his ideas on how to handle Tara, at first. In fact, he'd been forced to keep most of the arrangements from the council. They knew she'd been taken hostage. He'd brought her to them after he'd shot her. But they didn't know she was here, at his home. And they didn't know how long he'd kept her here. The council wouldn't have approved, but he knew he acted with the Neurians' best interests at heart. His conscience was clear.

He'd watched her as she lay under the covers, unconscious from the drugs. She became his sleeping beauty. There were nights when her presence haunted his dreams. He could have had sex with her, and she'd have never known. But that wasn't his style. He liked his women able to enjoy his ability to please them. No, it would have been rape, so he hadn't touched her — except in his dreams.

It had all started when the Runner, Kuro, approached him.

"You know there is a way to turn around the Neurian economy," Kuro had told him one night after they had enjoyed a fair bit of the Sea People's opiate wine. "And it would make you a hero."

"How's that?" Gowsky had asked, although he thought his friend a bit too intoxicated to be taken seriously.

"I grew up in a Runner clan known as the Blood Circle Clan," Kuro told him. "Their leader, Patha, has a daughter, Tara. She's a manipulative, hardhearted bitch, I'll tell you that. They say she is his bastard child, but she managed to lie and cheat her way into becoming Patha's heir. She'll lead all the clans after Patha dies."

"And what does she have to do with the Neurian economy?" Gowsky had no idea why his friend was talking to him about this.

"She charmed her way into the pants of the Lord of Gothman and gave him an heir." Kuro had poured more wine and then leaned back in his chair. "This is where it gets good, my friend. Tara and her children have entered Semore. They are right here in town."

"You are talking about the pale woman I saw yesterday?" Gowsky had been running errands when the young woman had driven her trailer into town. He had listened while she asked where she could keep her trailer, and then had offered gold as payment. The woman hadn't impressed him as coldhearted and manipulative, and Gowsky thought of himself as a good judge of character.

"She must be killed, Gowsky."

"Huh?" Gowsky choked on his wine. "Why does she have to be killed?"

"Gothman and Runners need oil. Your land is floating with the stuff. But Tara won't negotiate for it. Right now, she is probably devising a plan to take it without the Neurians knowing. That is how she is, my friend. But with her out of the way, the Neurians could sell the oil to a just Runner leader, themselves. And enjoy an economy better than they've ever known."

"And who would be the new leader?" Gowsky hadn't liked the idea of murder, but reestablishing the Neurian economy was imperative.

Kuro grinned. "Simple my friend. Me."

Gowsky pulled himself out of his reminiscing and focused on Tara. "I'm Dorn Gowsky," he said to her. "How's that foot?"

* * * * *

Tara glanced sideways at Gowsky. He watched her as if determining the answer for himself. That was something Darius often did. Guilt tugged at her. Noticing that this man was handsome was no crime, so why did she feel odd? She concentrated on his question in order to get her mind off him. "Your doctor's done a fine job. Please thank him for me. I would like to check on my children. Am I free to go?" She knew the answer to this question before she even asked it, but she decided to play his game and met his gaze with an innocent smile.

Gowsky smiled back. "Your children are fine. I would like to ask you some questions, if I may?"

"I'd like to see my children first. It's important they know I'm fine. I'll be more than willing to answer your questions after I see them. After all, I have nothing to hide from you or your people." She decided to take a chance and started hobbling to the door. There was no doubt in her mind that he wouldn't let her go, but she needed to make sure. If he had questions for her, he'd better start asking.

"Your children aren't in Semore anymore. Your trailer pulled out of here yesterday."

"You're a fool!" Tara turned and faced Gowsky. The rage burned in her eyes and her body tensed. She saw the amused look in his eyes and her anger intensified. "You better let me contact my family so I can tell them I'm all right."

"I might be able to arrange that." Gowsky stood and walked over to Tara, took her arm, and calmly but firmly escorted her back to the bench. "You handle pain well, but I wouldn't give that foot too much of a workout too soon."

She yanked away her arm and sat. Once again, her hair streamed over her shoulder. Lifting several strands in her hand, she realized her hair was definitely longer.

Gowsky dropped into the chair across from her, a serious expression on his face. He stared at her once again.

She glared back. "Go ahead with your questions."

"Why did you come to Semore?"

"I've never been south of the Trueland. I simply wanted to visit your town."

"You were looking for a job with our government."

"I liked it here. Your people have…" She hesitated.

"We have what?"

Tara reminded herself she had nothing to hide. "You have oil. We need oil. Getting a job with your government seemed like a good way to convince you to trust me so I could begin negotiations."

* * * * *

Gowsky was surprised by her answer. Could she be telling the truth? He suddenly worried he'd made a grave mistake. These people were so different. Could he trust her?

He told himself her beauty preoccupied him, and she could easily be lying to him. "Neurians have had their way of life stripped from them. Many of our people are without jobs. Regrettably, the dire situation has made us suspicious." Gowsky got up and stuck her laser into the top of his pants. He opened the door to leave. "I'll see if we can contact your trailer so you can talk to your family."

* * * * *

Tara stared at the door after Gowsky left, hearing the lock click into place. Cold air rushed her face, and Tara frowned. It felt like winter outside, but if Tara understood the climate pattern this far south, winter shouldn't be here for another five cycles.

She cuddled into the thick comforters spread over the bench and observed the dimly lit room. The floor was nothing more than smooth, packed dirt, and the ceiling was wooden. There were no windows, although sunshine peered through slabs of wood that constituted the walls.

She couldn't see anything indicating this room led to any other. It appeared to be a type of shed, yet Gowsky had said she was in his barn.

She noticed several different sets of footprints leading from the door to the bench and back again. Apparently many visitors had come and gone while she slept. She could only imagine who they might have been.

Tara rubbed her leg above the cloth wrapped around her foot. She could tell whatever pain reliever they'd given her was wearing off. She lifted her sore foot slowly onto her other leg, unpinned and unwrapped the bandage. There was a three-inch line of stitches along the side of her foot by her ankle

She studied the injury. There was no bruising and just a little swelling. As she ran her hand slowly over it, she noticed something that grabbed her attention. Next to the stitches was a faint scar, a scar she didn't remember having received, and it wasn't old. How strange, she thought as she rewrapped the injury and secured it with the pins.

Standing up was easy enough, but she worried about how soon she would be able to walk. She tried standing on one foot but was not successful. If she could master putting weight on her bad foot, she could kick through the wall with her good one. Her prison was not that sturdy, but her injuries made escape futile at the moment.

She hobbled over to one of the walls and looked through the slits in the wood. She could see a dirt yard and two trees. No other buildings and no roads were visible. She heard no sounds of animals, and no talking. Would Gowsky live outside town by himself? If that were the case, all she had to do was get out of this dilapidated structure and overpower one man. Child's play, if she weren't injured.

Had she really only been there several days? She thought about the faint scar on her foot. Could it possibly be from the injury she'd given herself climbing out of the burning building? So, why the new scar? Was somebody trying to make it seem like she'd been out of it for days when, in reality, it had been months?

Tara's heart began to pound, and she felt icy fingers creep slowly throughout her body. Something was very wrong. It was definitely wintertime. *How long had she been asleep?* She thought of her children, of Syra, and of Darius. What did they think? Had they tried to rescue her? She wondered why Gowsky wanted her to think she'd only been sleeping a short time.

Tara didn't see him for the next few days. She spent every waking minute exercising, trying desperately to rouse her atrophied muscles. The condition of her body proved to her beyond any doubt that she'd been asleep a long time. She was weak and out of shape. And she felt like a caged animal. Her body had always been in prime physical condition, and her lack of strength annoyed her.

Someone brought her a generous plate of food several times a day, usually dried meat and canned fruit. The same person never visited her twice, and no one talked to her. By the sound of their footsteps, she determined quite a few people worked for Gowsky.

She could sense the fear of each person who brought her food as they slid the plate through the gap between the door and the dirt floor, and then fled.

Her foot was mending quickly, but she decided it was best to give no indication of this. The room that was her prison was old and unstable. A week or two of recuperation and intense calisthenics, and her escape would be imminent.

In the meantime, icy breezes tormented her, mingling with dreams of her babies and loved ones. The blankets she kept wrapped around her provided little comfort. Tara's imagination made things even worse. She worried that her family was sick with worry, doing everything in their power to search for her, and growing frustrated when they couldn't find her. Yet while their images plagued her, they also added incentive to endure the cold and bring back her body to health.

Gowsky visited her nine days after she awakened. It was a bitter cold morning, and he pushed open the door with one hand and carried a pitcher with a steamy, hot fluid in the other. The morning glare was behind him.

Tara fought to keep her eyelids from shuttering against the light. He'd awakened her, and she forced her mind to clear before she moved a muscle.

He stood above her for a minute before sitting. Her body was stretched out under the comforters. She was on her side and the comforter curved over the outline of her hip. One of her arms draped across her body and her long fingers fell gracefully off the edge of the bench. Her sandy brown hair fell in strings.

"I do believe it's time to bathe you," Gowsky drawled in his singsong accent.

She focused one eye on him but didn't move. Every muscle in her body ached from the intense workout she'd put herself through the day before.

"I've been bathing myself successfully for many winters now," she answered.

Gowsky chuckled as he placed the pitcher on the ground next to him. "Does a hot bath sound good to you?" he asked and produced two mugs from his coat pocket. The steam floated up to the ceiling as he poured some of the dark liquid from the pitcher into each cup. It looked incredibly tantalizing, whatever it was. She licked her lips.

"It's good." He held out one of the mugs. "It also helps wake you up."

She opened the other eye and stared at him.

"Come on. You'll like it." He waved the cup under her nose. "Come on."

She felt its warmth brush her face. Sitting up slowly, she tried appearing to be in more pain than she actually was. The warmth of the mug in her hand felt so good that she wrapped both hands around it and sipped slowly. The liquid was thick and had a sweet honey and chocolate taste. She took another, longer drink and then looked up to Gowsky again. He had filled his mug and took a large gulp before setting the pitcher on the floor.

"How's your foot?"

She didn't respond, but instead situated herself on the bench carefully. She had taken the clothes she'd worn since she'd been there and laid them at the end of the bench while she slept. At the moment, she only wore a white pullover blouse.

Adjusting the comforter over her legs, she noticed he watched the action. His gaze locked on her bare legs, not looking away until she'd covered herself. Whether he noticed her muscles weren't as atrophied, or simply enjoyed seeing a partially naked woman, she had no clue. Something told her he enjoyed watching her. She knew interest in a man's eyes when she saw it. But how much had he watched her? For whatever amount of time he'd kept her here, he'd kept her unconscious. He could have enjoyed any part of her, and she wouldn't have been able to stop him.

When she met his gaze, he didn't look away but instead smiled.

She didn't smile back. "Why'd you tell me I'd only been asleep for several days?"

Gowsky's face looked completely innocent as he raised his eyebrows. "And what makes you think you weren't?"

"It's almost new winter. You've intentionally cut my foot and stitched it up so it would look like the injury from the building. How long have you had me here?"

"You've had plenty of time to think in here, haven't you?" Gowsky leaned back in his chair, crossed his arms, and stretched his long legs out in front of him. "Well, it's true. We made certain you'd remain unconscious longer than a few days. It was necessary at the time."

He said this so nonchalantly, the words stung. Anger brewed through her veins slowly, building to a boiling climax.

The Neurians had held her prisoner for cycles.

"I assume the Gothman and Runners believe me dead."

Gowsky looked at her with dark eyes and sipped from his mug. "Like I said, it was necessary at the time."

"So why did you bother to wake me now?" She matched his look of apathy. Her mind now, however, focused on a method of escape.

* * * * *

Gowsky shifted position, drawing his long legs underneath the chair and then stretching them out again. He thought of the best way to answer her question. It was one he had anticipated being asked and had thought of several convincing responses. He couldn't tell her it was the suggestion of another Runner. He wouldn't say, *sorry lady, it was politics, and Neurians need an income.*

He'd almost talked himself into doing away with her when Fleeders came forward and mentioned that Tara had talked to a guardian in the desert. Gowsky was a man of faith. He'd seen the dog-woman in his dreams a lot lately, and they'd made him uneasy. So he'd brought Tara out of her unconscious state. If anyone discovered her here, Gowsky knew he'd never be elected to another term

He desperately wanted to confide in Tara and tell her everything that had happened. The woman possessed a calmness, a sense of authoritative ease, that led him to believe she could talk through a dilemma and find a solution to please everyone. He wanted to share his dreams that he'd had during her time in captivity. He knew it meant Crator guided him when he dreamed of a Guardian, and he wanted to share this with her. She wouldn't understand though. She was a Runner, a member of a race without Crator. If she had seen a Guardian in the desert, it only validated his dreams; it didn't mean she understood Crator.

* * * * *

Tara realized from the way he hesitated that Gowsky wouldn't give her a straight answer. Her mind raced. Darius thought she was dead. Had he claimed another? Was someone else raising her children? What about Patha and Reena? Did her parents believe her dead, as well?

If so, Patha would name someone else to be his successor over the Runners. She would have to fight for her rightful title if someone else was named heir in her absence.

Her children were the heirs to two nations. When they grew up, Andru would lead Gothman, Ana would lead the Runners. She would not have that right taken from them. If Tara lost her title, she knew Darius would see that Andru became Lord of Gothman when he grew up, but Ana would be without a title.

Tara looked into Gowsky's dark eyes surrounded by that handsome face. Darius would never have to worry about her being unfaithful with this man. He was quite possibly as gorgeous as Darius was, but he had ruined her life.

"The Gothman were prepared to attack us when they thought you were a prisoner. We're not in a position for such an attack." Gowsky swallowed. "You died a warrior's death, saving one of our scientists from a horrible death. We escorted your family safely to a rendezvous point where they joined one of the Runner clans."

"How long ago was all this?"

He sucked in a breath and then exhaled loudly. "Six cycles ago."

Tara's muscles lurched. She wanted to leap from the bench and attack from midair. She wanted to pounce onto him, fists ready to injure with accurate stinging punches. She wanted to kill him.

Instead, Tara used every bit of power she possessed to remain calmly wrapped in the blanket, emotionless. "So now what?"

"We're not murderers. You were put to sleep to protect our nation. Time has passed and our nation is no longer threatened." His voice faded off as if to say, *The rest is history.*

"And so now you send me home." Tara seethed with the outrageous suggestion he implied. "Just like that?"

Gowsky reached for the pitcher and stood. "We'll discuss this further once you've calmed down." He walked to the door and opened it, letting cold air rush through the small shed. "Get dressed if you want a hot bath."

Tara sat in the same position for a long time after Gowsky left. Sunlight drifted through the cracks of the wood. She watched the dust rise through the rays of light as they shot through the room.

The Runners and the Gothman believed her dead. Darius had had six cycles now to mourn her and could quite possibly be ready to move on with his life. Andru and Ana would be over a winter old now. They would be walking and climbing and exploring their home.

Where *was* their home?

Were they living with the Runners? Or the Gothman?

She felt certain Darius would have them. They would grow up in his large house, exploring from attic to basement. The fields and hills surrounding it would be their backyard. And all of Gothman would be their playground. Tara groaned aloud. Oh, how she missed them. All of them. Somehow, she had to let them know she was alive.

Tara dressed quickly and threw the comforters to the side. The cotton pants she'd been wearing the night of the fire offered little to keep her warm in the shed. Her shirt sleeves were short, providing no protection for her long thin arms. Her flat leather boots, with their flimsy soles, would not do if she had to walk a long distance. Not only would her clothing not protect her from the elements, they would not protect her during battle, either. Somehow she needed to obtain different clothing.

She stood in the middle of the shed and jogged in place. Her foot had mended. It was sore, but she could live with that. After a bit, she dropped to the ground and began doing pushups. Her muscles were still far from the standard she normally expected from them.

Tara surveyed the walls of the shed. She could put her weight on her bad foot now. She glanced through the cracks in the wall and saw no one. Her time was limited. She took one of the blankets and carefully wrapped it around her leg. Using the laces of her shoes, she tied the blanket around her foot and leg. She stood up and tested the security of the blanket around her leg by jumping up and down. The blanket didn't move. It would serve well to protect her from the wood of the shed. She'd already tested the sturdiness of the four walls and knew which wall was the weakest.

Standing in front of the wall, she jumped into the air and kicked the wall hard with her foot. Several of the boards immediately cracked and a hole, several feet wide, appeared in the wall. The blanket caught in the wall, and Tara fell to the ground with her foot stuck up in the air. She pulled her foot loose and got up to survey the situation.

There was still no one in sight outside the shed.

Tara rolled up the blanket tightly. Quickly, she untied the shoestrings and re-laced her shoe. She draped another blanket over the hole in the shed so that it covered the splintered and broken wood and easily jumped out of her prison.

The bitter morning air slipped easily through her thin dress, and she shivered. Wrapping one comforter around her, and carrying the other under her arm, she glanced at the clear sky and got a sense of her direction.

Semore was north. All indications showed Gowsky's house to be on the southern edge of the town. If she moved south, she'd be out of town sooner. Then, she'd work her way west before heading north again.

Tara ran quietly through the yard. There was still no sight of anyone. She had no warm clothing, no food, no weapons, and no way to communicate with anyone. The odds for survival were not in her favor.

Within minutes, she stood surrounded by a clump of trees at the large yard. Tara turned back and looked at the house.

That was too easy.

Tara surveyed the abandoned shed back by the house. Did he want her to escape? Gowsky had said they weren't murderers. She guessed that they didn't know what to do with her. Were they just going to let her go?

"No," Tara said out loud to herself as she pulled the blankets tighter to fight the chill. "It would be foolish to let me go back to my people and tell them I've been put to sleep for six cycles by the Neurians."

She looked around at the trees and focused on the land south of her. Aware of how technologically advanced this society was, she searched the topography for potential restraining devices. An icy breeze rustled through the trees. Was it her imagination or did the trees half a dozen yards away not appear affected by the breeze? She reached down and picked up several rocks and threw one at the trees in question. The rock came back to her with such force she instinctively ducked.

So that was it…a force field of some kind. She walked in what she believed to be a parallel path to the invisible field, determining its location by tossing rocks until they bounced back at her. No wonder no one was pursuing her. She was fenced in.

Again, she studied the house. Were they watching her? Studying her? Figuring out what abilities she possessed?

Tara was perplexed. Without a landlink, she had few skills to handle her current situation. She couldn't just look at the field to see what it was made of, determine where it began and ended, or identify weak spots. She could throw rocks all day and quite possibly not learn a thing.

She climbed one of the nearby trees so she could perch high enough to see into the distance. Her blankets slipped and attempted to trip her several times, but she managed to settle on a branch, relatively hidden by dead leaves, and wrap the comforter around her. The force field contained her, but she would not surrender easily.

Sooner or later, someone would come out and check on her. Obviously, her whereabouts were important to these people.

Gowsky would probably be the one to find her. After all, he had risked much, holding her as he had for the past six cycles, working to keep her alive. He wouldn't revive her simply to let her sit out here, undisturbed, possibly freezing to death. His curiosity would get the best of him. His landlink would locate her.

Patience was a virtue, the Runners taught their young warriors. Tara had never done well with that lesson. She felt impatient. How long had she sat on this branch?

Tara thought she heard a noise so she listened for sounds other than leaves rustling. There it was again. Two Neurians were approaching her from either side. She immediately thought of the five Gothman she'd taken out in the forest the day she'd entered that nation. The memory brought a smile to her face. So, the Neurians wanted to see what she was made of, did they?

Two men, each carrying handguns, wandered through the trees toward her. They were looking in her direction, but she felt sure they couldn't see her. As they approached each other, they turned around slowly, focusing on the area beneath her. Their landlinks had led them to her.

She waited until they were within a hand's reach of each other. Slowly, the two men looked up into the branches of the tree above them.

Wait. Wait. Tara's muscles tightened, her adrenaline flew, and the breeze brushed her neck. Icy fingers crawled from her spine to the rest of her body. The excitement of the hunt sent chills through her. Her body and mind had been deprived of this for too long. She inhaled the cool air deeply. *Wait. Wait.* She watched the two heads tilt back, and then two sets of eyes looked up until they saw Tara.

Now!

She pounced onto them, the comforter acting like a cape as she took both to the ground instantly. One of the men pointed his gun at her. She grabbed the front of it with her hand. With the force of gravity to assist her, she fell to the ground, shoving the butt of the gun into his face.

"Do you plan to kill me?" she hissed.

The butt hit square on his nose, causing him to squint and howl simultaneously. His own blood blinded him. Grabbing the gun from his hand, she turned and shot the other square in the face. She landed on the ground, the two men underneath her.

"You broke my nose," the man howled, as he covered his face with his hands.

"I'm sorry, but I don't like it when people point guns at me." Tara tugged her blanket free from under the dead man and seized his gun.

Turning, she hardly had time to aim as a third Neurian, this time a large woman, lunged at her. The target was close, and Tara took her down easily. Two more Neurian women were right behind her. They, too, proved easy targets.

An incredible blow from behind sent Tara flying forward.

She hit the ground with excruciating force. Tara squirmed, absorbing the pain inflicted by rough ground tearing into her flesh. She scurried to her knees and crawled to grab the gun that had flown out of her grasp when she fell.

"Hold it right there." Tara aimed the gun straight into the mouth of a young Neurian man. His eyes doubled in size as her finger tightened on the trigger.

"That's enough!" A voice boomed through the air, jerking every muscle in Tara's body as she jumped in surprise.

She turned to look at the man who'd shouted the command. "You steal six cycles from my life, and then tell me this is enough?" Tara pulled the trigger and shot the Neurian in the mouth. At the same time, she grabbed the other gun from her pants' pocket and fired on the man who had issued the command.

The side of the man's face exploded. The sound of him falling to the ground echoed through the surrounding trees. Then, all was silent.

Tara turned quickly, arms outstretched, aiming the Neurian gun and her laser at anybody fool enough to step closer. Seven dead bodies lay on the ground around her. The smell of blood and gunpowder from the Neurian gun drifted as the breeze increased. She did not feel the coldness of it. Breathing hard, her body tensed. She listened to the silence and glanced quickly in all directions.

There were more. She could hear the occasional leaf crumple, the small twig snap. Gowsky walked slowly out from behind a nearby tree. His hands were outstretched, his movements slow and deliberate. She aimed one of the guns at him.

"Do all Runners fight like you?" He raised his hands higher, letting her know he was not armed.

"If they're good, they do." Tara raised the gun and aimed it at his face.

"We definitely have a problem on our hands." He smiled at her. "Do you shoot in cold blood?"

Gowsky must have believed she wouldn't shoot him, since he appeared before her with outstretched arms. But she knew he didn't trust her when four Neurians appeared from behind the trees. They aimed their guns at her.

Chapter Eighteen

ℬ

"I only shoot in cold blood if it's appropriate." Tara let the guns fall to the ground. The breeze whipped through the trees. This time, her sweat-soaked body felt the chill.

Gowsky noticed the seductiveness of her body through the clinging thin materials of her clothes. Tara had many sides to her personality, he noted. Those who didn't know her well would think she was simply a happy mama of two small children, looking for a new life. He'd seen what he wanted to see, however. She was the most incredible warrior he'd ever known. Briefly, Gowsky wondered why Kuro hadn't given him better warning of her unbelievable fighting skills.

Tara watched the four men closely, at the same time aware that Gowsky was summing up her abilities. Had he set her up simply to see what she could do? Her instinct told her this was probably the case. The man had sent seven of his warriors on a suicide mission to test her. For her part, Tara had no problem showing the Neurians her skills, or letting them know she would fight for her freedom. Now, she was curious what Gowsky planned to do with this knowledge.

Movement beyond the surrounding group of trees caught her attention. Automatically, she turned her head and looked through the trees. Something moved again. It was the old woman from the desert! She stood partially visible behind one of the farthest trees, returning Tara's stare. She gave the old woman her full attention.

Gowsky noticed Tara's attention was focused elsewhere so he followed her gaze. Concentrate as he might, he saw nothing, yet she was alerted by something. He stared harder. Still nothing. What was she doing?

Tara narrowed her eyes and scrutinized the old woman, who had finally stepped out from behind the tree and had begun walking toward her. Tara reasoned that the old woman had either been on this side of the force field or the shield had no effect on her.

To check her own wits, Tara shifted focus to the others. The four Neurians still held their weapons on her, and Gowsky was staring at her. None gave any indication they noticed the old woman approaching. Tara looked down at the ground and then slowly lifted her eyes in the direction of the old woman once again.

She walked into the open, allowing herself to be seen by the small group. Yet they didn't appear to notice her.

Were they testing her again? Tara tried to give no indication that she noticed the old woman approaching. The woman stopped next to Tara. She looked up and met Tara's eyes. It was the same woman she'd seen in the desert.

"Why are you here?" The old woman looked up at Tara. Her deeply creased dark brown face appeared healthy.

Tara didn't respond. Instead, she looked at Gowsky, who was giving her an odd look.

The old woman continued. "You have a lot of work to do. Tonight, you need to go home." She turned and walked back through the trees.

Tara glanced quickly at the old woman and then at the four men, still aiming their guns at her, before focusing on Gowsky.

"Take her inside," Gowsky instructed the four armed men.

Tara was escorted past the damaged shed to the house. For the first time, she noticed that her *prison* had been a shed with one wall attached to a large barn. She wondered what was kept in the barn, since she had never heard or smelled animals.

Her thoughts returned to the appearance of the old woman. Who was she? Tara remembered Fleeders' explanation about guardians roaming in the desert, but this woman had been flesh and blood, not the hallucination from some folk tale.

Gowsky led Tara inside his home, dismissing the guards before they entered. She found herself surrounded by warmth for the first time in days. As she entered a large room, Gowsky didn't seem to mind her self-guided tour, so she studied the room's contents.

Tara glanced behind her at Gowsky, who stood just inside the door pushing buttons on a wall-mounted pad. *Probably setting a security system.* Tara wished she had her landlink with her; she could then determine if force fields surrounded the house.

The room in which Tara stood was long and narrow. She noted a closed door at the other end of the room and a hallway to her left, which was shrouded in darkness. She guessed she stood in the living room, possibly used for conferences, judging by the number of chairs and sofas scattered about. The floors were carpeted, and the walls made of clay.

The door opened, and a woman appeared. She stared at Tara but made no move to enter the living area.

"You can show our guest to her room, Saysil," Gowsky said.

Tara focused on the woman as she passed through the room, heading for the dark hallway. Tara guessed she should follow and did so.

"These clothes should fit you." The woman, who was about the same age as Tara, opened the door at the end of the hallway and entered a room. Tara followed her, noticing Saysil had backed to the doorway as she pointed to clothes draped over a chair. She never took her eyes off Tara.

Tara was amused by the girl's fear. "Boo!" she said suddenly, and the girl jumped and ran from the room. Tara could hear her fumbling with the doorknob on the other side, desperately trying to lock it as quickly as she could. Tara laughed out loud and casually pulled the damp dress from her body.

She felt much more comfortable in the dark khaki pants and wool sweater she'd been given to wear. The small room where she'd changed had a large bureau and a small bed. She guessed it was a spare bedroom.

Absentmindedly, she noted it wasn't as nice as the room she'd been given in Gothman. The clay-plastered walls had no pictures hanging on them, and only one thin blanket spread over the bed — certainly not enough cover for this time of winter.

Left to her own devices, Tara decided to explore the room's contents. She found a pouch-like bag with straps that she tied around her stomach and hid under her sweater. She also discovered long underwear in the bureau and quickly pulled off the khaki pants to put them on before donning the pants again. She realized it would be wise to dress warmly should she decide to implement the old lady's idea and head home that night. Even though she had no idea how this plan was to be executed, she decided she would prepare for the occasion. It would only get colder the farther north she headed.

The sole window in the room looked out over the backyard. A large pane of glass was enclosed in a wooden frame that slid up and down on ropes. It easily unlocked, and she slid it up. The screen on the other side of the window would pop out easily, she determined after studying the manner in which it attached to the window frame.

She looked out the window at the side yard. Not too far away was a large barn. She could see the barn door flapping in the breeze and wondered if anyone was inside. Four guards had accompanied them to the house, but she didn't see any of them at the moment. She couldn't see the shed that had been her prison, but knew it was on the other side.

Carefully, she removed the screen and held on to it until the bottom touched the yard, then she let go and it landed silently on the ground. Gowsky obviously didn't use his house to hold prisoners. She wondered again if he had activated a security system when they first entered the house, and decided there was only one way to find out! For the second time that day, Tara planned her escape. She slid out the window, landing easily onto the ground.

She walked several feet away from the house and froze. At the corner of the building, Gowsky stood talking to another man! She hadn't noticed them from the window, since they wouldn't have been visible where they stood. The other man faced her way, but Gowsky had his back to her. If she made a move to the barn, she would be noticed.

The man talking to Gowsky pointed a finger in her direction, and Gowsky turned.

Tara saw him throw up his hands as if exasperated and quickly steer the man in the other direction. That's when Tara realized the other man was Fleeders!

Fleeders looked hard at her, saying something to Gowsky.

Tara seized the opportunity and bolted toward the barn. She heard Gowsky yell her name. He was running after her.

Tara got to the barn in plenty of time to shut the door and lower the wooden lock. She moved away from the door as Gowsky lunged against it.

"Open the door, Tara."

Tara ignored him and moved farther from the door, looking around her. Pieces of farming equipment, a tractor and seeder surrounded her. Irrigation supplies lined the wall. She saw several horse stalls and started examining each in turn. They appeared empty. She passed a pitchfork and picked it up as she continued investigating the stalls.

"Tara!" Gowsky yelled loudly this time, his frustration with his unwilling captive apparent.

"Where are all your animals?" Tara decided to feed his anger.

"Dead. Now open the door!"

"Dead? That's odd. How'd they die?"

"All the animals died, Tara." It was Fleeders' voice.

Tara reached the fourth and last stall. "Perfect."

She stared at her motorcycle parked in the space. It was covered with dust and straw. She brushed off the seat as she pulled it out. Her elation fell as she realized the landlink was missing from the dash. What else had they done to it? Would it run? Not far without fresh gas and oil.

Several gunshots came from the door, and Tara heard instructions shouted from the other side. "Aim at the lock."

A final shot broke the metal piece holding the wooden lock, and it slid across the hard dirt floor. Tara turned and watched the door swing open.

"Where do you expect to go on that?" Gowsky stood at the door, focusing on Tara who'd mounted the bike. "The force field surrounds the yard."

Tara smiled. She pushed the necessary buttons, and the bike started easily. "I guess I will have to have faith in your Crator."

She couldn't possibly realize how hard her words hit home with Gowsky. He looked at her with complete bafflement. He snapped his head to look at Fleeders, then turned back to Tara. "You don't believe in Crator."

"Well, it seems your Crator believes in me." Tara raced her engine, allowing the gas to flow through it.

"You have no right to speak about Crator. You know nothing about Him," Gowsky sneered. "And I doubt very much Crator would have anything to do with a Runner."

"If you say so." Tara shrugged indifferently. Her expression didn't change as she looked up and saw that he pointed his gun at her. "You know I saw her again today, don't you, Gowsky?" *Get him good and angry. He won't think as clearly.*

"You saw her?" Gowsky slowly moved closer, maintaining his aim on her right shoulder.

"I saw an old woman." Tara had no doubts that Gowsky would shoot her. But if he got just a bit closer, she'd disarm him. "She told me to go home."

"How convenient," Gowsky sneered.

Tara lunged the bike forward with no warning. Straight at Gowsky. He jumped to the side and pulled the trigger. Tara reached out and smacked Gowsky's wrist, causing the gun to shoot into the rafters. A blizzard of hay descended on them.

Tara maintained her grip as Gowsky yanked back.

Her hand moved with him as he yanked, offering no resistance.

He was prepared for her to pull back, assuming she'd try to take the gun from him. He used too much force to pull back the gun and lost his balance. Which is exactly what she hoped for.

As he hesitated, trying to regain balance, she stripped the gun from him, pulled the handlebar of her bike hard in the other direction and sped out of the barn.

Perfect! I'm properly clothed, armed, and I have my bike. This had worked better than she'd anticipated. She knew her skills exceeded those of the Neurians, but the accomplishments she'd just achieved almost appeared to be handed to her. But, how could that be?

Gowsky was right, she knew nothing about Crator. She'd never been asked to have faith in something she knew nothing about or had never met. She'd had faith in other Runners before, during battle. She knew they would do their part and if she did her part, they would be victorious. She'd had faith in Patha all her life. He provided for her and taught her everything he could. That was what she knew, and that was the faith she would use now.

Still if Gowsky and his people could believe in something they'd never seen, what could it hurt if she tried to do the same? Certainly, it seemed that *someone* or *something* had just helped her escape.

She skidded the bike around the barn and headed to the point in the force field where the old woman had entered. Tara would not slow down or hesitate in any way. This Crator-being, or the old woman…someone…had faith in her. She could reciprocate. She did not blink once as she drove at high speed.

* * * * *

Gowsky dove at Tara's bike but missed. He tore at the ground with his shoes as he broke into a full run toward his house.

"Turn off the force field!" he screamed, running through the house, knocking over an end table, heading for the small room off his living room. He screamed again, "Turn the force field off now!"

Fleeders was right behind him as the two stormed into the small room, startling the young woman sitting at a landlink.

"What?" She turned in her chair, looking surprised and bewildered at the unusual request.

"She'll electrocute herself." Gowsky almost knocked over the confused woman as he reached for the console in front of her. A beeping sound began, and a red light flashed next to one of several monitors. "She thinks she has some gift from Crator and can just drive straight through that thing."

The trio watched the monitor with the flashing red light. Tara could be seen driving at full speed through the backyard toward the trees. Another light began flashing, indicating the force field had been dismantled. Tara drove through the trees and disappeared from the screen's view. Gowsky hurried out of the small room, leaving the poor lady completely at a loss as to what to do next.

"You let her go!" Fleeders followed him.

"You heard her. She said she saw Crator. She was going to run right into that force field. Her bike is completely electronic — she'd have been fried to a crisp."

"She told me an old lady talked to her in the desert one night, and she just said she saw an old lady again. Maybe Crator *is* talking to her," Fleeders spoke quietly, as if afraid of being overheard. He looked around the empty living room. "She told me the woman disappeared into the darkness and then she saw a large dog. Gowsky, she knows nothing about the Guardians. She wanted to research Crator through our network but I told her..." Fleeders' voice faded quickly. He made eye contact with Gowsky and then shuffled from one foot to the other, suddenly very uncomfortable.

"You never told me that you discussed Crator with her. What did you tell her? And when did this conversation take place?"

"Well, uh, I told her it would raise suspicion if she started researching Crator."

"When did you talk to her?"

"Uh, the night that..." Fleeders hesitated, searching for words. He wanted to say the night that Gowsky burned down his life's work, the night their communication with the Lunians ended. "It was the night you brought her here."

Gowsky stared at Fleeders for a moment. So Fleeders had been communicating with Tara when he was supposed to be spying on her. The man possessed outstanding landlink skills, but his religious faith bordered on the superstitious. It amazed Gowsky that even the most intelligent of people could allow something as simple as faith in Crator to consume their life and affect rational decision-making.

Gowsky didn't have time for this. He gave Fleeders a look that said the conversation was not over. He straightened the small table he'd knocked over, opened the small drawer in it, and pulled out a gun. Shoving it into the side of his pants, he once again ran out of the house.

* * * * *

Tara didn't shut her eyes. She didn't blink. She didn't slow down. She felt the roots of the trees through the vibration of her bike and realized the tires probably needed air. She looked straight ahead as the trees cleared and could see the desert. And suddenly, she was in the desert.

She had done it. She had driven through the force field.

Was this the act of Crator? Who was this Crator? She looked ahead to the vast openness, glanced behind her to see the trees fading. Suddenly the frigid wind hit her skin, mocking the khaki shirt and the layers of material covering her legs, causing her to shiver uncontrollably.

Gowsky would follow her. Escape would not be this easy. She needed direction. West. She needed to go west.

Ignoring the waves of cold air streaming across her body, she veered the motorcycle. She was not accustomed to navigation without her landlink. But one of the tests she'd passed as a young warrior was finding her way back to the clan without the aid of her navigation program. She'd been one of the first Runners to make it back, and she remembered how proud Patha had been. He hadn't shown it in front of the rest of the clan, but that night, as she'd cleaned her bike, he'd told her. She'd never forget the look in his eyes — unconditional love.

Tara's eyes burned, and she began crying. The tears felt like fire, burning her face as they fell quickly down her cheeks. She tasted the salt in her mouth even though it was firmly shut to keep her teeth from chattering. She struggled with the tears as they persisted, fogging her vision.

Patha thought she was dead. Had he cried? She'd never seen him cry before. He was a true warrior and strong emotions would cloud judgment, she decided. Patha wouldn't cry. She decided it was more likely he'd been angry — angry that he'd let her go to Southland. Because she knew that Patha could have stopped her if he'd wanted to. Somehow she needed to let him know she was alive and coming home.

Tara looked up at the sky, noticing the sun was moving to the west. She knew the desert would drop below freezing once nightfall hit. However, the farther north she drove, the colder it would get. She was not properly dressed and would freeze to death if she didn't find heavier clothing.

Looking ahead once again, she quickly veered to avoid a large animal directly in front of her. Her bike slid in the sand, and for a moment she thought she would lose her balance. Once again, she cursed the clothes she was wearing. If she injured herself, she would only freeze faster. She slowed the bike and regained control.

As she turned, Tara's mouth fell open. The same old woman sat next to a fire, stirring something in a pot that hung over the flames.

Tara steered her bike up next to the woman and got off. "We meet again."

The woman didn't look up. "It's almost ready. Hurry and change clothes." The old woman pointed the wooden spoon to something behind Tara.

Tara turned to see a tan tent set up next to her bike. She looked at it in amazement, afraid to move. For the second time in days, she felt fear, and her shivering became uncontrollable. The tent had not been there a second ago. She was sure of it. Was she somehow still delirious from the drug she'd been given over the past six cycles? Maybe this whole thing was some drug-induced dream. For all she knew, she could still be unconscious, her inner thoughts creating this bizarre scenario.

She slowly turned to the woman who was still hunched over the fire.

"You'll freeze if you don't change. Your clothes are inside. I'll make you a plate."

Tara approached the tent, touching it gently, not completely convinced it was actually there. The roughness of the animal skin stretched over the wooden poles greeted her fingertips. Tara pulled the flap covering the entrance to one side and stepped inside. Immediately, warmth engulfed her. Her eyes adjusted quickly to the dimness, and she saw a small folding canvas chair set in the middle of the tent. Her Runner clothing was folded neatly on top.

She stared at the folded pile of black woven silk and smelled the crisp black leather before carefully touching them and picking up the top piece of clothing. It was her silk black undershirt! As she held the piece of material in front of her, she inhaled the familiar scent of her clothes—the sweet, fresh smell, as if it had just been washed.

As she finished dressing and put on her black leather jacket, Tara was instantly aware of the small laser in her right pocket where she always kept it. Tara left the tent and walked over to the old woman.

"Ah, that's better. Here, sit." The old woman gestured at her with a plate of steaming food in a crooked, wrinkled hand.

Tara took the plate and sat on the ground next to the old woman's feet. "How did you get my clothes?"

"Crator got them."

"Who is Crator?"

Their eyes met and the old woman smiled. "You'll know when your heart is ready, I guess." She nodded at the food. "Eat up. It's potato stew."

"Potato stew?" Tara looked down at the steaming plate of food. "This was my favorite meal when I was a child." She suddenly realized the old woman probably knew that.

Tara felt ashamed as she finished off the last bite of the wonderful stew. Her manners must have appeared insufferable. She hadn't stopped since taking the first bite. She stood up and took the plate over to the fire. Her insides were warm from the thick stew, and her body rejoiced at the comfort of her own clothing. She picked up her headscarf and wrapped it snugly around her head, securing it in the back. "You've been very kind to me. I wish I could repay you, but I have nothing."

The old woman ignored her and started to clean the dishes in a bucket of water on the ground.

"Let me clean up." Tara quickly squatted in front of the bucket and picked up her dirty dish.

"Don't worry, child." The woman took the plate from Tara. "You don't need to repay me. I'm simply a Guardian. You need to get that bike in order. You have a long trip ahead of you."

"What is a guardian?"

"I serve Crator and do as He says."

"Where is he?"

The old woman chuckled, apparently amused by the question. "Crator is everywhere, my dear." She looked up from her chore and again pointed the wooden spoon in her hand. "You'll find some tools behind the tent, I think." She sounded distracted, like an old person who wasn't sure where she'd left something.

"Do you live around here?"

"I go wherever I'm needed. Crator sends me."

Tara sighed. She wanted to know more, but wasn't sure which questions to ask. "So Crator takes care of you?"

"Child, he takes care of you, too." The old woman chuckled, placed the leftover stew in a bowl and put it into a travel bag. "Your faith shall grow, child, don't worry. You are young."

"My mission here wasn't too successful." She paused, studying the old lady's face, looking for the right words. "I'm glad I've learned of your Crator, though. I wish we had something like him in Northland."

The old lady slowly stood and moved next to Tara. "You've learned exactly what you were supposed to learn while you were here." She took Tara by the arm and, at a snail's pace, escorted her to the bike. "Child, Crator is everywhere, and He will take care of all who know Him." She let go of Tara's arm. "Take care of your bike, child."

Tara wasn't completely surprised to see exactly what she needed to tune up her motorcycle—spark plugs, a hand pump so she could inflate the tires and a large metal can, which, after smelling its contents, Tara realized was full of fuel.

Several hours later, the bike was in prime condition, ready for the long journey north. Tara cleaned the tools and returned them to the place she'd found them.

As she walked back around the tent, she noticed two things at once.

First, a large dog lay protectively next to the fire. Second, a vehicle approached the small campsite.

Tara pulled out her laser, prepared to fight for her life.

Chapter Nineteen

෪

The large beast curled up its lips and growled as the vehicle slowed just feet from the tent. The hairs on its back rose to full alert and its head lowered to the ground. Just as the animal prepared to jump at the intruder, an explosion rang through the air.

A horrific scream violated the campsite, curdling Tara's blood. The ground shook under her feet as the large dog fell to the ground.

"No!" Tara screamed and leapt out from behind the tent, firing her laser.

Gowsky stood next to his jeep, but his return shot missed her completely as the laser shot penetrated his right shoulder. This time the scream renting the night air belonged to Gowsky as he hit the side of his jeep and fell to the ground.

"Shoot again and you die." Tara's voice rang out. In her full Runner garb, she walked to Gowsky and ripped the gun from his hand before throwing it across the sandy terrain.

"Your clothes," Gowsky struggled to speak as pain racked his body, "they were sent back with your family."

Tara ignored him and instead moved to the side of the breathless animal. She stroked its bloody coat softly. "I'm sorry. I didn't hear him coming. I'm so sorry." She wept freely, and the tears mixed with the blood on the animal's coat.

Gowsky's groans didn't affect her as she cooed softly to the dead animal. "I'm so sorry. I'll give you a proper burial," she whispered into the ear of the dead canine and then turned to survey the contents of the campsite.

Gowsky crawled into his jeep, pulled out a small first aid kit and began to treat his wound. Tara ignored him as she looked for tools to dig a grave. All she could find were several large metal spoons and a large knife she used to break the dirt before scooping it away.

She was aware of Gowsky watching her as she dug a shallow hole in the sandy soil.

"Why do you care so much for this beast?"

"She took care of me, more than once."

"She was ready to attack me. I defended myself."

Tara turned and gave Gowsky a long hard look. She studied the handsome face and the onyx eyes. "Do you realize who you've killed?"

Gowsky looked at the dead animal and then back at Tara. His look was blank, but she thought she noticed trepidation lurking in his eyes. He held a cloth over his shoulder and got back out of the jeep, then walked over to look at the dog lying still on the ground. Standing over the dead animal, he said, "Obviously an animal you cared about."

"She was a Guardian. And you are a fool. She helped me more than once since I've been in your nation. She provided this camp, food, and the tools to tune up my bike. This entire setup was here when I arrived, with an old lady attending it. When you pulled up, she turned into a dog."

She watched him look around at the campsite in wonder. Tara turned and yanked the cloth away from the wound. "You'll live," she snarled and slapped the cloth back over his shoulder, glad she'd caused him to wince. "I came to Semore to see if you'd be willing to start trading with us." She felt frustrated she hadn't accomplished that task, but now all she wanted to do was go home. "We need a good source of fuel, and your land is full of oil. You shunned me and then you kidnapped me. Your people shall suffer for that."

Gowsky's body stiffened as she continued. "And there's nothing I can do about it. I could ask that you're given another chance to prove yourselves as allies, but I fear your crimes are too serious. Crator will decide what to do with you."

Gowsky secured the bandage to his shoulder. Then reaching down, he lifted the dead animal and placed it in the grave. He squatted next to the shallow hole and stared at Tara as she crouched on the opposite side. She scooped the dirt over the dog with the same pot she'd used to dig the grave.

Gowsky watched her graceful movements and thought how incredibly beautiful she was, and how deadly. With the power she now possessed, she could eliminate the Neurian race. Yet somehow, he felt she had no desire to do so.

He was worried. When Tara reappeared after six cycles, plenty of questions would be asked. And then what would he do?

Dimly, he heard her say, "I'm leaving, Gowsky. Go home to your people."

He paused next to his jeep as she continued to cover the animal with sandy soil. After a minute, he climbed into the vehicle, started it, and drove toward Semore. Suddenly, he turned the vehicle around and headed back to the gun lying on the ground. Skidding to a stop, he jumped out, grabbed the gun and squatted next to the jeep aiming the gun at Tara.

She didn't budge from her ritual.

He watched as she remained bent over the grave. After several minutes, Tara stood and moved to the tent. She began to disassemble it. The Runner had to be aware of his presence, yet she completely ignored him. Not once did Tara look up at him. How could he shoot a woman who simply ignored him?

Gowsky decided she must think he posed no threat. She must view Neurians as a soft race she could simply dismiss. Tara was challenging his warrior abilities, and he was furious.

After all, his pride was at stake. He couldn't turn and humbly leave as she suggested. Gowsky would show her that Neurians could fight! He jumped back into the jeep.

Tara folded the tent and pulled the twine attached to its outer side until it was a compact bundle. She secured it to the back of her bike. As she reached for the tent poles, she saw the jeep approaching at high speed—straight for her.

Jumping on her bike, Tara skidded out of the way just as he ran through the center of the small camp, sending pots rolling from either side of the jeep as he ran over them. Twenty yards or so past the camp he slammed on the brakes and turned the jeep around, preparing for a return drive-by.

She aimed her laser and shot out the back tire. She accelerated toward the jeep and then slammed on her brakes, skidding to a stop within a few feet of Gowsky.

Aiming her laser at his head, she said, "I told you to leave."

This time, Gowsky was prepared. He yanked the hand holding the laser. His strength overcame hers, and he pulled her forward off the front of her bike.

Tara came at him full force. The two flipped out of the other side of the jeep.

Gowsky twisted his body and landed on top of her. He slammed her hand against the ground and the laser fell free from her fingers. She completely relaxed her body underneath his, which caused him to relax his grip on her, although he watched her warily.

Instantly, Tara brought up her leg and kneed him hard in the crotch. He lunged forward, fell to the side, and she squirmed out from underneath him.

"You insult my fighting abilities and mock Crator," he snarled, doubled over on the ground from pain. "Do you really think our Crator would protect a Runner from a Neurian bullet? Crator protects Neurians — not Runners!"

"I'm not insulting Crator, Gowsky. But I am protected from your gun. A Runner's outfit is bulletproof." Her deep blue eyes shot daggers.

Gowsky raised his gun toward her.

She jumped into the air, kicking him straight in the chest,

He fell backward, and she pushed him to the ground.

This time, she was on top of him. She grabbed the laser with one hand, while her other hand leaned on his chest. Raising the laser to his face, she snarled, "I could kill you out of spite, and it would be completely justified."

"I can't just let you walk away."

She shoved the laser into his nose. "Then you'll die."

He looked at her eyes and could tell she meant it. "We're not prepared to be at war again."

She jumped off him. "Are you going to let me go?"

Gowsky scrambled to his feet, staring at the laser in his face. It was way too close for comfort. "I don't have much of a choice. You've disabled my jeep, and you have a gun pointed at me." He gave her one of his charming smiles which didn't faze her a bit. "Tara, I wish we could have known each other under different circumstances."

She backed off, but kept the laser pointed at him. She walked through the campsite backwards, looking at what was left, continuously glancing at Gowsky to make sure he didn't try to stop her again. The tent poles were bent and broken. Most of the food was smashed and scattered. She reached down, maintaining her watch on him, and picked up the grate that had been over the fire and one lone pot that had been on the grate.

Securing the grate and pot to her motorcycle, she straddled it and started the engine. Tara moved the bike slowly until she was next to Gowsky. "Good luck with your Southland."

Tara left him in a cloud of dust.

Gowsky brushed dirt out of his face and aimed his gun at her, firing several shots. To no avail. Her motorcycle soon disappeared from sight as he stood at the ruined campsite with a disabled jeep and an injured shoulder.

* * * * *

Tara continued to drive at high speed for several hours. She mentally tried to calculate the distance she would have to travel to reach Gothman. Yes, she would go directly to Gothman. Her children were there, she was sure of that. Patha would not oppose Darius in raising his own children, especially if Patha thought their mama was dead.

It had taken her a day and a half to drive to Semore in much slower transportation. However, she didn't know the best way to drive north. As she tried to determine her route, Tara's mind flickered to her children, Patha, Reena, Hilda, Torgo and Syra. And Darius.

She wondered if he'd claimed another woman. It was a recurring thought she'd had ever since Gowsky had told her how long she'd been unconscious. Night fell and Tara continued to drive, lost in her thoughts.

Tara imagined Andru and Ana walking. Her pudgy infants would now have legs strong enough to stand on. Which one had taken their first step? Tara imagined Ana would have taken the first step—she was the one who appeared more daring, putting everything in her mouth. But Andru would run first, she guessed, because he had to be fast to take everything from Ana and inspect it. Her heart constricted with pain at how much she had missed in her children's lives. For a moment, she couldn't breathe from the pain. With a deep inhalation, she told herself she would see them in the next day or two, and then work to make them know her again.

And what of Darius? If he had another woman in his life, perhaps she had attempted to make the children her own. Tara scowled at the thought. She would not allow someone else to raise her children. Not even Darius would be able to prevent her from being with her children, no matter the current circumstances.

She set up a makeshift camp when it grew too dark to drive safely, tore it down the next day, and drove through the wilderness without being disturbed by man or beast. Late that afternoon, she was riding along a high prairie trying to remember if she had been this way before. The hills and trees appeared in more abundance the farther north she drove, but after traveling for hours, all hills and trees appeared the same. She worried she had somehow altered course, although she still drove north.

Then she saw it. Ahead in the distance, several trails of smoke filtered slowly up to the sky.

Tara slowed her bike, her senses alert to the oncoming situation. Her body stiffened as instincts kicked in. The smells around her became more apparent. Any movement to the right or left caught her eye immediately. She heard every bird sing, every rock pop under the wheels of her tires.

She wasn't familiar with people living this far south of Gothman in Freelander territory. This land had always been uninhabited. There was no reason she would be considered an enemy unless these people knew of Runners and feared them. Still, caution was in order. Tara veered out of the prairie and decided to approach the camp through the trees bordering nearby hills.

She was ecstatic when she realized the camp was a Runner clan, though she didn't recognize the clan flag flying high from the center trailer. The black outfits of the men and women walking through camp were a welcome sight.

Several Runners noticed her approach and pulled their lasers. She knew they were skeptical because their equipment would not have acknowledged her as a Runner without her landlink.

"Hold it right there," the closest Runner approached her motorcycle as she slowed within yards of them.

Tara stopped her bike and held her hands out to show she came in peace but did not speak until questioned. She knew the routine.

"Runner, where is your landlink?"

"I've been to Southland. It was stolen. I'm lucky to be alive." She dismounted to show her non-warrior intentions as was customary. "I'm glad to see a Runner clan."

"You're welcome to hear the stories at the fire." This was the usual greeting offered to a visiting Runner, and Tara smiled her appreciation.

"I've got much to catch up on. I've been traveling for awhile."

"Come back for the test, have you?" They were walking now, and the two Runners led.

Tara pushed her bike. "The test?"

"Well, you have been out of circulation for awhile. No landlink, too. You navigate well."

"I wasn't sure I was, to be honest. What test?"

"The Test of Wills."

Tara stopped walking and stared at the Runner who had just spoken. The Test of Wills was given when the leader of a clan died or stepped down and had no heir.

"We will be continuing north in the morning. Most clans are headed that way, I'm sure. You're more than welcome to travel with us. We'll take you to Rolko, but I'm sure he'll give consent."

As Tara walked, her mind raced with questions. Why was the Test of Wills being offered? What happened to Patha? She decided to remain silent. If she made her presence known after the Test of Wills had been issued, it would stir up a commotion among the clans. Tara hoped she would learn more when she listened to the stories around the fire, later that evening.

She was accepted into the Four-Circle clan as a traveling warrior. This meant she could sleep by the main fire, use their water supplies, probably be fed, and if she still had her landlink, use their main board to transmit. To refuse their acceptance of her as a traveling warrior would dishonor the clan, especially since they were going in the same direction. So even though she would arrive at Gothman much sooner if she traveled alone, she graciously thanked Rolko for his hospitality.

Tara was left alone to move through the campsite after leaving Rolko's trailer. She decided to go immediately to the main fire, hoping for food and, if she was lucky, the offer by a compassionate soul to let her take a shower.

"Hey, wait up!" The voice came from behind Tara. "I'm Male, Rolko's daughter." A girl several winters younger than Tara hurried up. "Papa asked me to come get you and offer my hospitality. My trailer's over here if you'd like to clean up or anything."

Male's trailer was simple. The floors were bare; a wooden tile covered the kitchen and living area. The countertops were spotless, and two overstuffed matching chairs with a rectangular oak table between them, provided all the furniture for the small living area. A folding table extended from the wall of the kitchen and a shelf mounted on the free wall of the living area housed her landlink.

Male moved into her kitchen area and pulled a ceramic pitcher out of the small cooler in the wall. Handing a chilled lemon drink to Tara, she sat in the one chair at the kitchen table. She gestured with her cup to the matching chairs. "Sit. Be at home." She smiled and loosened her head cloth, revealing dark curls. "I hear you have no landlink. And that you've come all the way from Southland. Where are you going?"

"North, for the test," Tara lied.

"What were you doing in Southland? My papa will probably report you, you know."

"Report me, why?"

"Why? Because it's forbidden, that's why."

Tara wasn't sure what to say. What was forbidden? Male saw the confused look in her eyes and squinted at her. "How long have you been without a landlink? You do know Runners are forbidden to enter Southland, don't you? Patha of the Blood Circle Clan passed the law himself. That's why we're having the Test of Wills. His daughter died down there."

So Patha was alive. At least, it sounded like he was. If he had officially announced her death, she guessed her login number would be detached from the system. She would need a new number in order to access a landlink, any landlink. How would she explain no login number without revealing who she was?

"Would you like to contact your family?" Male asked.

"Would it be all right if I took a shower first?"

Male jumped up and walked down the six-foot hallway, opening the first door and turning on the light. She entered her room and returned immediately with a thick cotton towel.

The shower felt good. Afterward, Tara decided to walk around the camp. As she approached the main fire, she saw ten to fifteen Runners surrounding it, sipping ale and chatting among themselves. A large woman dipped wooden mugs into a barrel and handed them out. Tara slipped in inconspicuously and accepted the mug of ale offered to her.

She tried to remember the last time she'd enjoyed this Runner tradition. Gatherings around the evening fire at the end of a day, listening to the old Runners tell their tales of victories and places traveled — these were good memories. She recalled hearing the news from travelers of other clans, enjoying the screams and chatters of the younger children as they ran and played on the outer edge of the circle. These were the parts of her childhood of which she was most fond. This clan made her feel right at home.

The stories she heard that night shocked her. It was Rolko, himself, who explained the latest conflicts between the Gothman and Runners. Lord Darius wanted to be part of the judging for the Test of Wills. Rumors also circulated that several Gothman wanted to partake in the test. Many Runners had complained loudly to

Patha. The test was for Runners only. Rolko felt safe in assuming that Patha would not allow Gothman participation.

Tara wanted to say this was true. She knew her papa, and he would want a Runner to succeed him. They had an alliance with Gothman, but she knew he wasn't ready to integrate the two nations that quickly. Chaos would result if they did.

Tara was called upon to tell her stories of Southland. She found herself telling the Runners about Crator. She explained that the Southerners believed that Crator made the planet and all races on it. She told the myth of the Guardians, saying that they brought messages to the people from Crator and could take the form of animals. The Runners loved her stories and applauded as they refilled her mug.

She sat at the fire well into the evening, sipping the ale and catching up on the tales of the Runners. She felt relaxed, at peace and very much at home as she walked slowly back to the trailer later that evening. In a few days, she would have her children in her arms again. Then there was Darius. Would she make peace with him? She wondered once again if he'd found another woman. What would she do if he had? Probably kill her. Tara giggled to herself and realized the ale had hit her.

Tara knew no other woman would be able to prevent her from returning to her life. She hadn't asked to be gone for six cycles, and she never intended to be separated from Andru and Ana. It tore into her like a jagged warrior's knife that her children might not recognize her. Every time she thought of how the twins might react to her, she filled with trepidation.

Male was working at the landlink when Tara slowly pulled open the door to the trailer. "Did you catch up on all the latest gossip?" Male didn't turn around as Tara entered.

"It was great to sit at a fire once again and hear all the stories." Tara sat in one of the stuffed chairs and glanced at the monitor.

She leaned forward as she realized Male had logged onto the Blood Circle Clan site. Tara quickly scanned the screen, trying to see what the clan was broadcasting. She tried to sound nonchalant as she looked over Male's shoulder. "What are you looking for?"

"I'm going to submit the written part of the Test of Wills." Male glanced up at Tara and smiled meekly. "I don't expect to win or anything. Papa thinks it would be good experience. You'd have to understand what it's like to be the daughter of the clan leader, I guess."

Trust me, I do understand. "Why don't you print one off for me too?" she said instead. "There's no harm in trying, right?"

"Sure, as long as we don't get killed in the confrontation part." Male groaned. "I can handle the first part of the test, I think. But, I don't know about the second portion. Papa has never been too satisfied with my warrior skills."

"Maybe I could help you."

"If you want to take the time. It couldn't hurt."

Male printed two ten-page tests and handed one to Tara. She clicked through the information on the Blood Circle Clan and stopped on an article with a large color picture of Darius.

Tara's heart skipped a beat.

"Isn't he handsome?" Male leaned back and breathed deeply. "I hear he's an incredible warrior. He was able to defeat Patha's daughter, Tara."

"When did he do that?" Tara asked the question without thinking.

Male turned to stare. "I guess not everyone follows this news as closely as I do. That's how he claimed her as his wife. She couldn't tame him, though. So she left."

Tara couldn't help smiling and had to stifle an uncontrollable giggle that climbed within her. "Has he found another woman?"

"No. I hope to see him in person when we arrive at the Blood Circle Clan," Male said. "I wonder if he's as good-looking in person."

Tara wanted to say that he was much more handsome. She gazed at the picture of Darius on the monitor. Her body warmed as she studied the blond curls and deep gray eyes. She hadn't realized how much she missed him until that moment.

She wondered if she could trust him again. But then, only Darius could answer that. He would have to show her, through his actions, that he could be trusted. And that would take time. Tara's heart told her that now, she would offer him that time.

She smirked. Darius definitely had his work cut out for him, if in fact, he still wanted her to be his claim.

At least now she knew she wouldn't have to kill anyone.

Chapter Twenty

ഔ

The sunshine seemed a little too bright the next morning as Tara wiped down her bike and prepared for the day's journey. She had declined breakfast, but eagerly worked on her second cup of coffee. The camp was dismantled, and everyone appeared ready to leave.

"It's just occurred to me that I don't know your name."

Tara looked up to see Rolko speaking to her as he and two other Runners approached. "Good morning." She tried to sound polite as her mind raced for a response. "I'm Leetha," she decided quickly.

"Leetha, we've brought a landlink for your bike." He gestured to one of the men with him, and he produced a small flat black panel. "Which clan are you from?"

"The Blood Circle Clan."

"Well, we really are taking you home, aren't we?" He smiled, but the look in his eye let her know he had more to say.

She stood silently, showing her respect.

"You violated our law by entering Southland, Leetha. Male has told me you plan to enter the Test of Wills. I can't permit you to do that. I'll turn my report into Patha and make him aware of your violation. You'll have to approach him personally to argue your case once we arrive at our destination, before your entry can be accepted. I'm sure you're aware of the laws."

"Yes, sir. Thank you for the landlink, sir." Tara stood perfectly still until the men were finished with her bike and had left her. Her heart sank. The only way she could enter the Test of Wills now was by using her own login number. Furthermore, she knew the second Patha received a transmission saying a Runner named Leetha—from *his* clan—had just come over the border, her cover would be blown.

There was no Leetha in the Blood Circle Clan that she knew of. She could only hope Patha wouldn't review the reports from the clans right away. After all, there was a lot going on to distract him.

Somehow she needed to remain undetected until the Test began. She knew she could prove herself in battle. In fact, unlike Male, she looked forward to that part of the test.

Everything was ready to go. Tara tested her landlink, and the travel plan for the day appeared on the small screen. They were scheduled to arrive at the Blood Circle Clan that evening! This was perfect. Arriving in the dark could only be to her advantage.

She shut down the landlink and quietly entered Male's trailer. Tara already knew the young girl was not there. She'd taken off earlier to help some of the mamas organize their children for the day. It was a job that had often been assigned to Tara when she was that age. Male would be gone for a while.

She sat down at the landlink and took a deep breath. This would either work or it wouldn't. She held up her fingers, hesitated for a second, and then typed in her login number. The landlink buzzed quietly, and the proper lights lit up accordingly. She waited for what seemed like an eternity. *Come on...come on.* Male wouldn't be gone forever. Tara wanted to submit the answers to the written test before she was discovered. She couldn't remember the last time a landlink moved so slowly.

At last, the picture on the monitor flashed and the selection screen appeared. It worked! Her logon number hadn't been deleted. She realized that meant she'd not yet officially been determined dead. Why then, were they conducting the Test of Wills? She had no time to ponder this mystery but instead selected a blank page and began answering the questions that Male had printed.

She was familiar with the test but still read over each question carefully. Because the leader of the clans would have to know all the laws of the Runners very well, each test question asked about a particular one. Also required was the origination of laws, which one best suited a particular situation, and how she would interpret several selected laws. Tara typed quickly yet answered each question thoroughly.

After Patha reviewed the tests, he would name those who could compete in the Confrontation. This part of the Test was no longer a fight to the death. That law had been changed over one hundred winters ago because too many good warriors had been killed. The fight would last until the surrender of one of the competitors. Nevertheless, this still resulted in a fight to the death all too often, at least according to the stories. There'd never been a Test of Wills called as long as Tara had been alive.

Her fingers ached, and her back was sore. Over an hour passed. Tara clicked on submit and leaned back in the chair.

It was done.

Whether this would cut her throat or lead her to victory was undetermined. Tara knew if the test with her logon number was identified before she got to Gothman, Runners she didn't know would arrest her, and she would be delayed. But if she could get into Gothman before her test submission was discovered, she could speak to Patha, convince him of her need for the test to continue, even though, strictly speaking, it was unnecessary. Indeed, she could imagine Patha's outrage that she'd enter the Test of Wills instead of simply acknowledging she'd returned.

She stared at the blank monitor for a minute, wondering who would first notice a written test had been submitted on her logon number. Would they assume it was fraud, or would they suspect it was her?

Tara smiled to herself. Could she actually win the Test of Wills and be heir to Patha twice over? If so, she would rule the clans completely. Her authority would be unquestioned. And then there was Darius. She *wanted* him to see her earn her way to victory, conquering each hurdle every step of the way.

The winner of the Test of Wills wore the title of Head Warrior. It was the highest honor a Runner could receive and always fell upon the ruler of a clan. Not as many women won as men did, but Tara knew she hadn't lost a competition in — winters. She could not think of any warrior she couldn't defeat. And if Darius could witness her taking the title of Head Warrior, he, as well as all of Gothman, would see that a person's sex had nothing to do with what skills they possessed. Taking the title would be one more step toward earning the respect Tara needed from Darius, and from his people.

Her heart ached and her blood warmed as she thought of battle. Her pregnancy might have stopped her from participating in the last war, but nothing would stop her from using her warrior skills for the test. She was free to soar to her highest potential.

Who would the other contenders be? Would they be allowed to use weapons on a field, or would it be in an arena with hand-to-hand combat? How many finalists would there be? Tara had studied a few Tests of Wills during her childhood, and knew the leader of Runners had complete control over how the test would be conducted. Tara couldn't help but hope for an arena. More people could witness the victory.

Questions continued to swarm as Tara stared into the screen. The sounds of starting motors brought her back to the moment, and she jumped up. Turning off the landlink, she hurried outside to her bike.

By the middle of the afternoon, Tara began to recognize the countryside.

They were coming up on the southern tip of the Gothman nation. The ground was hard, and the dark gray clouds hung very low. Her eyelids burned from the cold wind that had slapped her face for the past few hours, and she guessed snow would fall before they arrived on the western side of Gothman where the clansite was located.

She suspected her logon number had been discovered by now. It wouldn't be difficult for the authorities to determine its source. It was quite possible Rolko would be notified that one of his landlinks had transmitted using her logon number. Then, they would search for the one who had used the number.

Tara wondered how much information Patha would give the clan leader. Would Patha tell Rolko that an illegal number had been used? Or would he specifically say that Tara's number had been used? She could only hope they arrived at their destination before Rolko was contacted.

Over the next hour, snow began to fall, drastically limiting visibility. Tara was forced to slow down, as was the rest of the clan.

She strained to see the passing countryside, trying to determine how far into Gothman territory they'd come.

The wind picked up. For a brief minute, she thought she saw something in the distance, but then it was gone. She focused on the ground immediately in front of her. Several riders ahead yelled, and she looked up. One of the Runners was pointing to something, and Rolko pulled up alongside him.

Tara looked in the direction the pointing finger indicated and could just make out several brown figures ahead. She squinted and refocused, watching through the snow as the figures drew nearer.

Four Gothman approached. Rolko, with the surrounding Runners, slowed to a stop. Her heart pounded through her leather coat as she watched the men talk to Rolko. She couldn't tell if she knew the Gothman or not.

The one speaking to Rolko was long-legged and broad-shouldered. Through the blowing snow, she couldn't determine his hair color. He turned his head to scan the Runners scattered across the meadow. Rolko gestured for the Gothman to follow him. They drove slowly through the hundreds of parked Runners.

Tara watched carefully as the four Gothman approached. *One of them was Darius!*

He passed within a few feet of her motorcycle, head held high in the blowing wind. Blond curls stuck out from underneath a black hat.

His hair is longer. Everything inside her reached to him like a magnet, yet he never glanced her way as he slowly drove by.

The Gothman and Rolko drove back to where the trailers were parked with the Runners congregating in their wake. Tara was near three Runners, and several others joined them to discuss the possible reasons for the Gothman's arrival.

"They said something about a wrong logon number being used."

"That doesn't seem like a reason to stop us in this bitter cold."

"The Gothman are looking for an excuse to search our clan."

"Why would Lord Darius come himself?"

And so the chatter continued.

Tara's mind was far from their conversation. Rolko would figure out what landlink transmitted the illegal number, and when the transmission had occurred. Once he had that information, he would know either his daughter, or she, had sent the transmission using the illegal number.

She couldn't conveniently disappear — she was surrounded by clan members. Even if she could slip away, the snow was blowing hard enough to become lost. Not to mention the fact that they could easily track her with the landlink they'd assembled on her bike.

Tara was trapped.

She waited for the inevitable to happen. Within a short amount of time, it did. A motorcycle approached their group, and one of the Runners who'd been with Rolko gestured to her.

"Come with me." He said nothing else.

She followed him through the snow silently. Some of the Runners watched her pass, but for the most part they huddled together in small groups, preoccupied in conversation. More than likely, they were discussing the anticipated test.

* * * * *

Torgo sat in the corner of the living room sorting through incoming tests. They'd been arriving by the thousands, and earlier in the week the program designed to receive and grade them had overloaded and crashed. Patha was impressed by Torgo's ability to save the information and rewrite the program. Now it moved twice as fast and sorted the tests, eliminating those with more than one mistake. This made the job of reviewing the tests much easier, and Patha praised Torgo's landlink abilities.

"He's a natural," he told Darius in Torgo's presence. "What he can't do on the battlefield, he makes up for on the landlink."

That comment stung at Torgo's pride, but he'd kept a straight face.

"I want an hourly report from you on all written tests," Patha ordered. "Assign any assistants you may need to help you."

Torgo had immediately called upon Syra. The perfect tests, and those with one mistake, automatically printed out with the logon number at the top. For the first few days, only one or two tests met this criterion. But as the day of the Test of Wills approached, several more tests printed out. Torgo had Syra manually check the answers before they were turned over to Patha.

"Here's Kuro's test," Syra said as she leaned back in her chair. Torgo came up from behind her and rubbed his hands down the front of her shirt as he leaned over.

"Not now, silly," she giggled and pushed him away.

"Perfectly answered, I assume." Torgo didn't like Kuro. He seemed fake and the way he'd buddied up to Darius annoyed Torgo for some reason.

"Of course," Syra shrugged. "Looks like he'll win the Test of Wills. I don't know about the rest of these people, but Kuro's quite the warrior."

"Well, I guess I'll take these reports to Patha for review. One of the clans reported a Runner who's admitted coming up from Southland. She's from the Blood Circle Clan. Her name's Leetha." Torgo grabbed the reports and stacked them. "I can take those tests to him while I'm at it."

"Uh-huh." Syra wasn't listening to Torgo. She was busy looking at a test that had just printed. "Torgo, look at this."

He studied it, then looked at her, confused.

She grabbed back the test. "Look! It's Tara's logon number. We forgot to delete it. Didn't Darius ask you to do that a while back?"

"Shit! Yeah, he did. But, the program crashed and I forgot all about it. I don't get it though. How come it's on this test?" Torgo reached around Syra and began pushing several buttons on her keypad. He pulled up the instructions for the program and then switched screens and typed frantically.

The screens on her monitor flashed. She tried to follow what he was doing, but his landlink skills outclassed hers. "It was submitted from a landlink in the Four Circle clan." He continued to type. "They're just south of us."

"What are you going to do?"

"Report it to Patha and Darius, I guess. Those are my orders." Torgo took the tests from Syra and walked to the door.

Syra jumped up and followed him.

Patha and Darius weren't in the house. After minutes of whispered discussion, the youths decided to drive to the clansite and look for the two leaders. They rode together on Torgo's bike, believing their information vital enough for it to be overlooked that they were together on the bike.

Balbo disapproved of the time Torgo and Syra spent together, considering his daughter too young for the physical relationship he felt sure the Gothman lad would instigate.

* * * * *

Torgo drove straight to Patha's trailer, which was parked next to Balbo's. Snow started to fall, and no one noticed the two disembark from the bike. Darius and Patha's bikes were parked outside the trailer. Torgo knocked on the door.

"Come," Patha's voice barked.

The two entered quickly, shutting the door behind them to prevent snow from blowing into the trailer.

Patha looked up at the young people questioningly.

Torgo handed him the two separate stacks of tests.

Darius sat at the landlink with his back to the two of them, not acknowledging their presence.

"You drove out here to give these to me?" Patha glanced at the papers. "I could have picked these up from you later today."

"There's something I wanted to bring to your attention," Torgo spoke calmly. He was working on mastering the coolness of voice his brother possessed.

Patha leaned back in his chair. "Go ahead."

"One of the written tests used Tara's logon number."

Lord Darius spun in his chair. "I told you to delete that number," he barked loudly.

Torgo cowered in his presence. "When the scoring program crashed, I spent so much time working on it; I forgot to delete the number."

"Let me see the test," Patha said.

"The answers are almost identical to the answers you gave us for the program," Syra pointed out.

"There's something else." Torgo wished Syra would let him do the talking. "It's probably just coincidence but I thought I'd —"

"What is it?" Darius snapped impatiently.

Torgo didn't like how mean his brother had become since Tara had left. "The Four Circle clan reports a Runner has joined them from Southland." Torgo held out the report to Patha. "Her name is Leetha, and she's a member of the Blood Circle Clan."

"There's no Leetha in my clan." Patha rubbed his head, then looked up at Syra. "Is there?"

"No, there isn't." Syra came out from behind Torgo. "I checked before we came."

Patha handed the papers to Darius so he could study them.

Darius looked up at the two young people and frowned. "So what are you saying?" He handed the papers back to Patha.

"We're saying it's a mighty strange coincidence," Syra spoke up quickly. Lord Darius annoyed her with his continual grouchiness. Once, she'd thought he was cute, but not anymore. He was the one that fucked up, and she wished he'd just get over his self-pity.

She continued, "A Runner joins the Four Circle clan from Southland. The report shows she didn't have a landlink on her bike so they weren't able to verify her identity, but she says she's Leetha with the Blood Circle Clan. The leader of the clan reports she's staying with his daughter. The next day, a written test is submitted from that clan on the daughter's landlink, using Tara's logon number. And the test answers match your answers almost perfectly. It just seems odd, and we thought you should know."

Syra glared at Lord Darius and then gave the same look to Patha. "Come on, Torgo, let's get back to work." She turned to leave.

"Wait a minute." Lord Darius growled.

Syra turned and crossed her arms, waiting for him to speak.

"Are you saying this is Tara?"

"If it's her, then why is she trying to sneak back up here?" Patha thought out loud and all three people turned their heads to look at him. Patha looked at the test answers more thoroughly and all three stood quietly, watching him.

The answers were almost verbatim to his. He could almost hear her vocal inflection in the writing style. It *was* a mighty odd coincidence. He looked up at Darius, nearly forgetting the others in the room. "It's always bothered me that the Neurians were never able to produce a body." He stood. "I want you to check this out."

Darius quickly grabbed his coat.

"Find out who used that number. If it's Tara—" but Darius was already out the door.

* * * * *

"Did you submit a written test for the Test of Wills after I forbid it?" Rolko barked at Tara as she got off her bike.

"Identify yourself, Runner," Darius spoke with authority and a coolness that had her heart pounding.

Her wide eyes stared, and she began breathing hard. Even though snow fell steadily, Tara no longer felt cold. In fact, she could feel her gloved palms grow damp from sweat. For a moment, she couldn't remember the name she had created to conceal her identity.

Darius stood in front of her, and in spite of his apparent intentions to look intimidating, all Tara could see was how incredibly sexy he looked. Six cycles had passed since Tara had been sexually active, and her body screamed for relief. But more than that, she wanted to cuddle into him. She wanted to hear how he had missed her. She wanted to hear how sorry he was that he made her leave. Tara wanted, more than anything, for everyone around them to disappear and leave her alone with the man she loved.

His presence almost overpowered her. Why did he make her feel like this? He had committed the ultimate of crimes and needed to beg for her forgiveness. She fought for words. "My name's Leetha."

* * * * *

Her voice hit him. There was no way he could react quickly enough to conceal his reaction to the sound of her. He stood staring, completely shocked.

His guards gave him a questioning look.

"I'll speak to her inside the trailer." His scratchy whisper sounded cruel, even to him. Darius made certain his expression appeared as harsh as he sounded. In no way could he betray his true feelings in front of his men and these Runners.

Darius wanted to grab Tara and run. His instincts had him ready to do anything to prevent her from moving an inch. Don't go away, he wanted to say. *Whatever you do, don't leave my sight again.* But he couldn't. The Lord of Gothman didn't behave like a babbling idiot. He did not take his eyes from hers for a second.

She returned the gaze.

Rolko grunted and gestured to the trailer. "Be quick about it, we have a clan to get settled."

Darius held out his hand for her to lead the way, and she obliged. He entered the trailer behind her and shut the door.

"There is no Leetha of the Blood Circle Clan. Who are you?" His growl was low as he watched the Runner walk slowly into the trailer.

She walked farther into the room and glanced up at him again once she'd reached the landlink.

He watched her every move, waiting for her to speak again.

Was *this* Tara? Damn! He wanted this to be *her* body, *her* voice. She was in full Runner uniform wearing the emblem for the Blood Circle Clan. What was she doing here, after all this time? And why was she entering the Test of Wills? "I asked you a question, Runner."

She put her gloved hands into the pockets of her leather jacket. "Do you have Andru and Ana?" She looked up.

This time it was Darius' turn not to answer. He moved quickly towards her and ripped off the headscarf. Her light brown hair fell past her shoulders and over her face.

She reached up and shoved the hair from her eyes.

His face softened the second he saw her. "Yes, I have them." His voice cracked with emotion, and he touched her face with his fingertips. He pulled his mouthpiece out of his pocket and wrapped it around his ear. Sliding his hand down it, he reached for the switch to activate it.

"No, don't." She grabbed his hand quickly. "You can't."

"What do you mean, I can't?" He took her hand in his before she could pull it away, put her fingers up to his mouth, and kissed them. "I have to tell Patha."

She pulled away her hand after a second. "You can't. It will ruin everything. If I announce I'm back, the Test of Wills will be cancelled. That would cause an uproar among the clans that can't be allowed to happen right now."

"Tara, there's no need for it. You're Patha's heir, you are. It's your nation, my Lady. You're not going to give that up."

"I have no intention of giving up my right to rule the clans." She looked at him defiantly. "I've entered the contest and shall win."

Darius laughed and reached out to her again.

He'd obviously put their past behind him, but she still felt they had unfinished business and stiffened. He ignored her hesitation and pulled her to him aggressively.

In spite of her intention to remain aloof, his presence in front of her was too overwhelming and arousing. She finally allowed him to literally pull her off her feet and into his arms. He held her with one powerful arm and lifted her face to his with his other hand. Without pause, he covered her mouth with his and kissed her passionately. The warmth of his body smashing hers softened all her defenses and she melted.

Finally, he moved his mouth away from hers and smiled at her again. Passions that had been asleep for many cycles soared to life. Tara felt intoxicated from all the emotions twirling inside her. She wanted to rip this man's clothes from his body and make love to him, forgetting the rest of the world existed. She wanted him to hold her, and talk to her for hours and hours, until they both knew each other's hearts again. But Tara also wanted to hear Darius swear unconditional loyalty — to her and their family. Tara wanted him to know that he would have to prove his love through his actions, and not his words. Although her heart needed to hear the words, too.

All of this, as important as it was, needed to remain on hold for the time being. A political agenda existed, and it must be handled first.

"So, my Lady, you plan on defeating all the other warriors, do you?"

She fought against his grasp now. He continued to hold her with one strong arm, and struggle as she would, she couldn't release herself until he let her go. She backed up and faced him as if he'd just challenged her.

"My Lady, do you know how strong some of the entries are?" Darius' gaze dropped as he looked her over.

"I will be triumphant. There's no doubt about that. Now, what you need to do is tell Rolko that I am Leetha, and you've agreed to let me take my argument to Patha when we reach the Blood Circle Clan."

"And why is it that I need to be telling Patha a lie?" Darius grabbed the side of her head, wrapping her hair around his fingers, and pulled her to him.

Tara pushed against Darius' chest so that her face was less than a foot from his. "You can't create more of a scene than you already have. These people are primed for the Test of Wills. I've heard the stories around the campfire of their predictions of victory. If I announce my presence, there will be much adrenaline, and nothing to do with it. It will cause a stir and create unrest among the Runners. A true warrior prepares for battle and then must fight. The

Test of Wills can't be reversed once the process has started. Do you understand what I'm saying?"

Something cold and brutal melted in those gray eyes. Darius' expression softened considerably. "So you'll put your life on the line to keep peace, will you?"

"I will live through this, Darius," she whispered, as she searched his face, and her hands went from his chest up to his shoulders.

"You'll be an outstanding leader, Tara. Your point is taken, and I'll inform Rolko, yes."

"You should do that now," Tara said, although she didn't want to leave his embrace.

"I'll not lose you again," he whispered, but there was a snarl in his voice, almost animalistic, definitely possessive.

"I assume you've learned some manners." Her whisper was just as harsh, and she hoped the fire in her eyes brought his blood to a boil.

"If anyone can teach me manners, it would be you." He kissed her again.

This time, she pulled back and tore away. "There are cold Runners out there." She ripped her scarf out of his hand and wrapped it around her head. Then she opened the door and walked out.

Chapter Twenty-One

ஐ

The Blood Circle Clan was alive with festivities. The snow had ceased, and its insulation on the ground made the night air crisp but tolerable.

Tara heard music and singing as she drove slowly through the camp. Nostalgia crept through her. Several huge bonfires sent streaks of fire shooting up into the cold gray sky. She could hear loud drunken stories and laughter coming from the fires as mugs were passed and ale poured. She smiled broadly to herself as she noticed so many familiar faces going about their business, unaware of her presence. So many newcomers arrived at the location that no one bothered to look up as she drove by.

She knew there was no way she could slip into one of the circles around the fires this evening. She'd be recognized the second she spoke. She had to maintain a low profile tonight, and she knew exactly how she would do it.

The land was so familiar to her it was as if she'd never left it. But she had, and there were two people she had to see immediately, her children. Darius said he had them, so she knew they would be in their bedroom, probably asleep. She wouldn't wake them but she had to see them, to touch their soft skin. Her heart ached as she slowly drove through the thick trees around the town and toward the large house on the hill.

* * * * *

It would take a skillful eye to track Tara as she moved through the woods. She knew how to stay invisible. It was just that skillful eye watching her now.

Darius sat motionless on the side of the road and observed her every move, following her as she passed among the trees and the large rocks jacked up out of the earth. He had known it was Tara as soon as the sound of her bike reached him. His landlink matched the code from the panel that had been installed onto her bike. Not that he needed confirmation.

Now she was moving at almost a dangerous speed, considering the limited visibility from the night and the snow. It suddenly occurred to him where she was going. He left the roadside and sped so quickly through the town to his house, more than one head turned and more than one body jumped out of the way.

Darius slid to a stop in front of the house and ordered the guard to put his bike in the shed as he ran inside.

Reena and Hilda looked up astonished as he bolted in the front door.

"Do not come upstairs." He barked the order and leapt up the staircase, taking three at a time.

* * * * *

The excitement in the community had proven to be an excellent distraction. Tara found herself behind the old familiar house before she knew it. She parked the bike in the seclusion of the trees and bushes and slowly moved toward the structure.

The best place to enter, she decided, was through her old upstairs bedroom. She easily climbed the trellis, free of ivy from the cold of winter. She lifted her body up onto the walls of the balcony and hopped nimbly onto the floor outside the closed door.

The room was vacant and dark, and the warmth from the house radiated toward her body. As she opened the door an inch to peek into the hallway, she heard voices coming from rooms below. The upstairs appeared to be quiet, and she moved slowly down the hallway to the nursery at the other end.

She was surprised to hear a low, quiet voice coming from behind the partially closed nursery door. It was Darius, and she was very much surprised to hear him softly singing a Gothman folk song. She couldn't see him through the half-closed door, but from where she stood, she could see Andru sitting in his crib watching his papa.

Tara froze at the sight of her son. He was so big! So grown up! Had she only been gone six cycles? He didn't look like a baby. His blond curls fell loosely around his head, and his eyes were big and a deep gray. She watched him move his small hands and wiggle the toes that were sticking out from under his blanket. He was pudgy but not fat, very cuddly looking.

She felt tears well in her eyes, and her vision blurred. It was a physical effort not to run into the room and scoop the small child up into her arms. She wanted to bury her face in him and whisper how sorry she was that he was taken from her. She wondered what kind of adjustment he and his sister must have gone through. How traumatized had it made them?

After several minutes of staring at her son in the dark hallway, laughter from downstairs brought her back to the reality of her situation. She stepped away and entered the bedroom she'd shared with Darius. The door adjoining the room to the nursery was closed, and all Tara could do was stand and listen to the song Darius was singing. He ended the song; several minutes of silence followed. She pressed her ear to the closed door and listened, trying to determine what Darius was doing. She heard nothing.

Suddenly, the door to the nursery flung open, causing her to jump backwards. She struggled to regain her balance in the dark room and not trip over furniture. Before she had her bearings, a large hand wrapped around her neck. Instantly she was lifted off the ground.

"What is it that you plan to do, m'lady?" Darius' whisper was more like a snarl.

She wrapped her fingers around his hand and struggled to no avail.

He threw her back.

She slid across the floor, skidding to a stop before she hit the wall. Tara flipped her legs around and looked like a cat ready to pounce as he came at her again.

"You are not taking these children anywhere!" This time the snarl was more apparent than the whisper. He lunged toward her.

She rolled out of his way and sprang to her feet. "Darius, all I wanted to do was see them." She stood there ready for him this time. "If I wanted my children to leave this house, I wouldn't have crept down the hallway while you sat in the nursery obviously waiting."

"Why should I believe you?" He reached out to grab her.

Tara dodged his hand and punched him squarely in the stomach.

He didn't flinch but instead, reached for her a second time.

She tried to turn away, but he locked her in his arms until her back smashed against his body.

"I guess you'll just have to trust me," she said, relaxing her body in his arms. With that comment, he released her. She looked toward the nursery door and then back at Darius. His expression remained wary, and the anger was still there. His gray eyes appeared almost black.

"Please, Darius, my children…our children…I need to see them." Her voice cracked and his gray eyes completely softened. Tara took off her headscarf and draped it over a chair. "Please, I need to hold them. I need to see if they remember me."

Darius walked over to her and wiped a tear from her eye. "Don't let them see you crying. I know they'll remember you." He took her by the hand and led her into the nursery.

The two children lay sleeping in their matching beds, and Tara cried all over again as she stroked their hair and squeezed their tiny hands. Ana pulled Tara's hand up to her face, and Tara felt the small child breathing gently against her skin. She knelt down and stared, stroking her beautiful baby girl's hair with her free hand.

Darius was behind her when she stood, and he wrapped his arms around her waist. "They're absolutely beautiful children, my lady," he whispered into her ear. Then he gently kissed her neck. "You'll be amazed at how smart they are and how they chatter all day long."

His grip around her waist tightened, and she placed her hand on his and squeezed back. "When I realized how long I'd been gone, all I could think about was getting back to my children." She turned around in Darius' arms and looked up. "I thought about you, too. I wondered if you believed I was dead. And I wondered how you felt after I left you."

With his hand on her back, he led her out of the nursery and back to the bedroom. "The Neurians that escorted Syra and the children back here were deeply sorry that you died in a fire, they were. They said you died a hero, that you saved one of their best scientists from burning to death." He put his hands on her shoulders and squeezed, then squeezed her arms and finally her waist. "You are so thin." His large hand held her face up to his. "And, my lady, you are out of shape. What did they do to you?"

Darius didn't share his feelings with her. She would allow him this much. If he wanted to discuss the facts first, that would be fine. But she would hear his formal apology and his desire to keep her in his life, without any other women.

Tara stood in Darius' arms and told him everything.

His arms tightened in anger as she spoke, and he pulled her very close to him when she'd finished. "I wouldn't accept the fact that you were dead. My mama kept saying I was denying your death and that I would be happier when I accepted it." He pulled her so close to him she could hardly breathe. "I had the strangest dreams, though. They kept repeating themselves. I was assured you were alive, and you would come home."

Tara whispered, "Was it an old lady who could turn into a dog?"

He stood there, shocked. His whole body went numb. "How'd you know?"

"I met her. She helped me escape. She told me my work wasn't done here. I know my muscles have atrophied, but I *will* be triumphant in the Test of Wills. Crator is behind me. I don't understand Him yet, but he wants me here."

"And this Crator is an old woman who can turn into a large dog?" Darius asked.

"No. The old woman isn't Crator. I don't know who Crator is. The old woman seems to know Him though. She has told me more than once what Crator wants me to do, or not to do. When I listened, things worked out the way they were supposed to."

"You will ask her to take us to see Crator, I'm thinking." Darius nodded. "Yes. That will work well. We will negotiate with him to help us further when we need it."

Tara laughed quietly and stroked Darius' cheek. "My Lord, I don't think it works that way. All you have to do is believe in Him."

"Believe in his what?" Darius frowned.

"Believe he exists," Tara said.

"Easy enough."

Darius picked her up and gently carried her across the room in his strong arms. He placed her softly on the bed and was on top of her instantly. "I'm afraid your work here will never be done." He kissed her.

She returned his kiss passionately. "What were your dreams about?" she whispered, once their lips had parted.

Darius propped up onto his elbows and looked down. "Ever since you left, I've had this one dream that comes again and again, it does. It's not like that usually, no. My dreams are of war, victory, making love to you." He kissed her again.

She felt him harden. His arousal started a fire smoldering deep inside her, an ache growing painfully. More than anything at this moment, she wanted to make love to him and hear him cry out his unending devotion.

"In this dream I was a child," he said as he kissed her on the neck. "I'm walking with a large dog—it's protecting me. Then I'm walking with an old woman, and she's teaching me. It's very important that I learn everything she says, I know." He slid down on the bed and unzipped her coat. "I've even written down some of the things she's said." His hands now worked on her black leather pants. "Remind me to show it to you some time."

"Why can't you show it to me now?" Tara ran her fingers through Darius' curls and held his head as he kissed from her belly button to her hip bone. He slid open her pants and tugged.

"I have something else to show you now." Darius' breath tickled her when he spoke. He continued to pull her pants.

She arched her hips, making it easier to remove them. "Do you?" Tara pushed herself to her elbows, kicking her pants to the floor when Darius had them to her ankles. She grabbed his shirt when he turned to crawl toward her and pulled it. "What do you have to show me?"

Darius crawled until his face was inches from her, and on hands and knees, he covered her body with his own. "It will take a lifetime, my lady."

Tara moved her mouth to say the word, "oh". But nothing came out other than a mere whisper of the word. The man had rendered her speechless, and although her thoughts jumped at what could take a lifetime to be shown, she wanted...no...needed to hear it.

Darius kissed her curved lips, sucking on her lower lip, then nibbled enough that she gasped at the tingles of electricity he sent through her with the action. She straightened her arms and collapsed onto her back, then reached for his shirt with her hands and tugged it up his torso. Darius pushed himself to his knees and pulled his shirt off.

Her fingers immediately tangled through his dark golden chest hair. "Tell me Darius," she whispered. His muscles jumped underneath her fingertips as she traced patterns down his chest to his pants. "Tell what will take a lifetime."

"My lady, it will take a lifetime to show you all the love I have for you." Darius flattened the lower half of his body against hers, preventing her from sliding her fingers into his pants, and then lowered his mouth over one of her nipples.

Tara gasped. The heat from his breath through the material of her shirt, and his words, brought her to her first quick orgasm, and she felt Darius smile over her breast.

Tara grabbed her shirt and pulled it over her head, and smiled up at him when his eyes feasted on her breasts.

"Do you love me, Tara?" Darius didn't make eye contact with his question, but instead lowered his body until he rested on his elbows and began sucking on her nipple.

"Oh." Tara arched into Darius and held his head in place as he adored her breasts. "I... You... Don't stop doing that."

Darius lashed her nipple with his tongue, rolled it gently with his teeth, and then sucked the hardened nub until Tara contorted her body, heat saturating her.

"Darius," she whispered. "Please."

Darius moved away from her breasts. Her nipples were still damp from his attention, and Tara suddenly felt chilled and exposed.

He began a trail of kisses down to her belly button. "I asked you a question, I did," he whispered into her belly button, sending shivers throughout her body.

"You did?" Tara lifted her rear end off the bed and pushed down on Darius' shoulders.

He chuckled as he scooted lower on the bed, then placed a hand under each of her legs, lifting and spreading them apart.

Tara kept her knees bent and reached between her legs with both hands to stroke herself while he watched. Tara spread herself open, running her fingers over her outer lips, and felt the moisture increase. She slid a finger inside herself, and then pulled it out, spreading the fresh wetness over her swollen nub, gasping as she did. She felt her muscles tighten and release, and she lifted her head to watch Darius, as his gaze fastened on the action of her fingers. She inserted a finger inside herself again, then pulled it out and extended it to his mouth.

Darius sucked her finger readily, and she smiled.

"Do you love me, Tara?" Darius asked when she pulled her finger free.

He moved her hands and held her outer lips apart with his own fingers, then gently kissed the swollen nub.

Tara felt another explosion surge through her body, gathering inside her, increasing the swollen sensation. "Oh please," was all she managed to gasp, as Darius teased her with his tongue. She heard his question, but her need to explode fogged her senses, and answering him didn't seem as important as having him inside her.

Darius made love to her with his tongue until she thrust her hips into his face and grabbed his hair. Rubbing against his face, her orgasm broke loose.

Darius freed himself and pulled away. Her vision blurred as she watched him strip. Finally, he stood at the end of the bed naked, his hardened erection dancing in anticipation.

She couldn't speak. Tara simply watched as he positioned himself over her.

"I need to know Tara, please." Darius made no attempt to touch her, but simply knelt between her spread legs.

She blinked several times and cleared her thoughts. "I never stopped loving you," she whispered.

"My lady, I will show you that I deserve that love. If it takes a lifetime, I will show you that you never have reason to leave my side again."

"There will be no other women." She knew his people didn't view his horrendous act as a crime, but she did, and he answered to her now.

"Tara, you are it for me, you are." His expression bordered on dangerous, his expression so intent. She prayed he meant what he said, but knew only time and his continual show of loyalty would convince her.

"Then prove that to me now." Tara reached for him, gripping his hardness in her hands, and stroked the velvety covering that moved over skin harder than stone.

Lifting her legs and spreading them at the same time, he knelt before her, pressing his hardness against her oversensitive entrance.

Tara watched those smoldering gray eyes. His expression didn't change when he shoved his steel hardness deep inside her.

Fire ignited inside her, spreading with a fury she couldn't control. Darius glided his massive shaft over her inner muscles, and she reached for him. "Darius. Please." The words were hard to form. More than anything, she needed him to soothe an itch that was about to make her crazy.

He spread her legs further, her inner thigh muscles stretching while he moved slowly out. When he plunged back inside, she screamed.

"Damn woman," Darius growled.

Tara managed to keep her eyes open so she could watch as he threw his head back and pounded into her. Tara climaxed again and again, arching her hips to allow him deeper.

When she thought he would explode, Darius stopped and pulled out. "Roll over." His voice sounded rough.

Tara pulled her legs from around him and struggled to flip over.

Darius helped her and then gave her rear end a sharp swat.

"Ouch," she cried, but she loved the sound of the spanking, and the brief warmth it brought to her rear end. Once she was on all fours, Tara arched her back.

Darius slid into her easily, and the new position had him pushing against a new area inside her that craved the attention. She kept her arms locked, pushing back against him. He felt so wonderful.

Hours passed as he moved her around and took her in every position they could master on the bed. She was numb and swollen when he finally allowed her to collapse into complete exhaustion. The smell of their sex and body sweat filled the air of the room. Even though it was very cold outside, neither of them felt a need to find a blanket. She fell asleep with his arms and legs wrapped around her.

"Darius?" a voice called.

Tara jumped with a start as she recognized Torgo's voice. She sat up quickly and reached for a blanket.

"Are you awake yet?"

"I'm awake, Torgo. I'll be down in a second." Darius rolled over and pulled Tara down on him.

"Hurry. The candidates are starting to assemble." Torgo's voice cracked as he spoke.

Tara could only imagine how much he'd grown. She pulled away from Darius and rose from the bed to walk across the room to the shower.

"How do you plan to get from here to the arena?" He admired her naked body as she picked up her clothes

"What did you say?" Torgo's voice came from the hallway.

"Go downstairs!" Darius' voice boomed, and feet were heard scurrying down the hallway.

"I'll make it." She smiled and shut herself into the bathroom.

It was Syra's voice Tara heard as she came back into the bedroom. She was on the other side of the closed door leading to the nursery.

Her heart leapt as she also heard two small babbling voices. They were content and happy. She heard an occasional squeal as one of them decided they deserved the toy the other possessed. Tara listened for a few minutes, anxious for the time when she would be sitting on the nursery floor, exploring the toys with her children.

Finally, she crept out into the hallway and back to her old bedroom. Darius was nowhere in sight, and she knew it would be just like him to leave her to her own wits in sneaking back out of the house. The house was completely silent, other than the noises from the nursery, and Tara assumed everyone had left to watch the test, leaving Syra to stay with the children.

Tara used the staircase by the kitchen and closed the back door silently behind her. She stood motionless in the yard for a moment, listening, as two guards stood on the far side of the house, laughing over something. Tara edged alongside the house in the opposite direction, and wondered if her new friend, Crator, had anything to do with her bike being parked where she had left it.

"I don't know who you are," Tara whispered to herself as she grabbed her handlebars and walked her bike away from the house. "But if you are taking care of me, Crator, I really appreciate it."

Tara started her bike once she had pushed it into the field, away from the house, and then drove over the rough countryside, around the town, and toward the clansite.

Hundreds of bikes were parked in a lower field. After she left her motorcycle with the rest, Tara began to hike the incline to the arena. The clansite buzzed with activity, considering the early morning hour, and she pushed her way through Runner and Gothman until she reached a roped-off area. Four large poles had been shoved into the ground to form a square, and several ropes were wrapped around the area providing a fence for the arena. Stakes stuck into the ground created an opening for contestants. Outside this area, competitors were checking in at several tables. Tara headed straight toward them.

"And to think, we'll be working together by tomorrow. You haven't noticed any competitor that you think could beat me, have you?" The voice caught Tara off-guard.

"I don't know all the Runners that are fighting, I don't. I've only seen the written tests. Can't really judge a person by what they write, you can't."

The second voice belonged to Darius, and Tara turned to see where he was. But that first voice, she knew that first voice. Who was it? She saw Darius a few yards away. His guards blocked her view of the man he was talking to. She continued to move through the crowd toward the tables.

"That's true. Drink with me to victory, my lord."

"It will definitely be a day to remember."

To whom did that first voice belong? Tara turned again, and this time she saw him. The man talking to Darius was Kuro.

She'd almost forgotten him. Her heart fluttered, and her breath left her momentarily. Her eyes immediately devoured every inch of his body, checking the familiar muscles, the remembered physique.

Kuro...her first love.

They had met as teenagers, and at eighteen winters he'd pressured her to marry him. They were madly in love, completely inseparable. But she thought she was too young to marry. She wanted the *Age of Searching*. He wanted to rule the Blood Circle Clan by her side. She'd refused his proposal, and in anger and humiliation, he'd left the clan.

That was five winters ago.

Now, here he stood, talking to the papa of her children, the man who had claimed her, and the man whom she loved as a woman.

It made sense that he'd return now. Here was his chance to do what he'd always wanted to do: rule the clan.

How had he met Darius? Had they become friends? And what was Kuro saying? He obviously assumed he would win the Test of Wills.

If he still possessed the warrior skills she remembered, it would be a challenge fighting him. Darius must have known she would fight him. Why hadn't he said something to her?

Suddenly she wondered what Kuro might have told Darius about her. Had he mentioned knowing her growing up? And if so, what else had he told Darius?

Suddenly, Kuro turned and caught sight of her. He gave her a distant look. Then, his eyes widened and he looked at her again.

Darius turned to see what he was looking at and both of them caught her eye.

She quickly turned and disappeared. Tara scanned the row of tables, and then approached a Runner she didn't recognize.

"You here to check in for the Test of Wills?" he asked, as he grabbed an armband.

"Yes. I'm Leetha with the Blood Circle Clan." Her heart pounded against her coat as she was given a white cloth to tie around her arm.

"Bordo, with the Kill Water clan." A booming voice next to her announced his arrival.

Tara glanced at the man and shuddered. His arms were thicker than her waist.

"And he's going to win!" A shrill female voice announced this information loudly, and several other Runners surrounding the large burly man began to cheer.

Tara was forgotten and shoved to the side, as Bordo's supporters pushed their way to the tables.

"Oh Crator, I'm doing the right thing, aren't I?" Tara mumbled, as she wrapped her coat around her tightly and began walking through the crowd.

Chapter Twenty-Two

℘

Tara knew that as long as she lingered in the crowd, it was only a matter of time before someone recognized her. The best thing to do was to remain in earshot of the arena, but find an isolated spot to wait — and hopefully remain unnoticed. Tara moved to the edge of the clansite, doing her best to avoid any Runners she recognized. Once in the trees, she climbed to a large branch and got comfortable on her perch. She would wait here for the competition to start.

Tara realized she'd been dozing when she heard Patha's voice boom through the loudspeaker. She'd dreamed about the old lady. Tara had sat next to her at the campfire in the desert. The old lady had kissed the white cloth tied around Tara's arm.

"Crator will guide you to victory. Have faith in Him."

Then she'd disappeared, and Tara found herself balancing on the large branch.

"Number eight and number three need to be at the side of the arena within ten minutes," Patha said. "The Test of Wills is about to begin."

The crowd screamed and cheered, and everyone began moving at once. All those who had been standing and visiting now hurried to obtain the best seat from which to watch the fights. Rows and rows of wooden benches were arranged stadium style, and the dull roar of people climbing to an available spot sounded like thunder.

Tara slid to the ground and headed to the arena. She was number three. She would be in the first fight. Was it good to be the first fighter? How had they determined who would fight first? "Quit worrying and have faith," she muttered quietly. *Crator will guide you to victory. You have faith that He'll do that, don't you?* After thinking about it for a second, she knew that she did. He'd proven his abilities. Whatever He was, He wanted this for her, and she would not let Him down.

Tara had to fight her way to the arena. The crowd was thick, and no one seemed interested in letting her pass. Her toes had been stepped on, and more than one elbow had jammed her by the time she removed her coat and entered the arena.

A referee confirmed her armband number, and then grabbed her hand and the hand of the other contestant. "Round one of the Test of Wills shall begin." The referee pulled her hand into the air.

Multitudes of bodies crammed the ropes at the outer edges of the arena and began screaming their encouragement at the referee's words.

"Let the fighting begin."

Tara looked at her opponent for the first time.

"I guess you'll do for warm-up," the tall, thin young man said. His pale green eyes appeared to mock her through his headscarf. The man lunged at Tara.

She responded with a hard blow to the side of his head, and he flew backwards, crashing to the ground.

His head fell back and hit a rock. He lay motionless.

Tara stood in the ring with her feet spread a foot or so apart and secured her gloved hands together behind her back. The crowd cheered, and she waited for the next contestant to enter the ring.

The next two fights were similar to the first. The fighters would aim one blow at Tara before she flattened them. A hard punch to the abdomen, a kick in the face, each caused the other fighter to fall, defeated. The third fight lasted for several punches.

A young, stocky woman came after her with full vengeance. She knocked Tara backward and punched her twice before Tara gained her balance.

Tara came back at her with several kidney punches, and the crowd groaned as they felt the woman's pain. As her opponent struggled to regain control, she once again stood still with her hands behind her back. The crowd screamed for her to attack again, and Tara glanced around the arena. It was not a fight to the death, and she refused to hurt the woman any more than necessary.

The woman finally pulled the white cloth off her arm and threw it to the ground, indicating her surrender. Part of the crowd moaned. Obviously, she'd been a favorite of one of the clans.

Between the next several fights, Tara scanned the crowd. The Gothman were sitting on one side of the arena, and she spotted Darius easily enough.

One of his guards was talking, and he listened intently.

She caught his eye as he looked at her, and he smiled. She glanced away quickly and looked at the crowd of Runners.

For the first time, she laid her eyes on Patha. He was staring at her.

She couldn't pull her gaze away.

Did he recognize her? How could he not, she decided. She shrugged. What could he do about it anyway? The competition was underway. As their eyes continued to meet through the crowd, she realized Reena was sitting next to him and also staring.

Suddenly Reena's hands went to her mouth. Patha steadied her, putting his hand on her arm.

Tara watched as Reena looked at Patha and said something. He nodded and they both turned and looked at her again. Reena started to get up, but Patha pulled her back. He then leaned back and crossed his arms across his chest. His face wore no expression.

She finally succeeded in pulling her gaze away from Patha as she took on the next contestant. After several more fights, Tara's adrenaline soared. She ignored the crowd now and focused on each contestant. By the tenth contestant, she began to feel more evenly matched. She and one fighter, a large burly man, fought for almost an hour.

There didn't seem to be anything she could do to make him fall. He was thick as a tree trunk. His punches served only to increase her drive to fight. At one point, he grabbed her from behind and slowly began to squeeze the life out of her. In a mad rage, she managed to reach behind and grab him by the neck. A hush fell over the crowd as she slowly turned until his neck cracked and he slumped, lifeless, to the ground.

The sense of battle took over all of Tara's thoughts. She no longer cared that Patha or Darius watched. She was a merciless machine, and each contestant who entered the arena felt her fury. At this point, she lost count of the contestants she'd eliminated. She was stunned back to reality when Patha's voice came over the loudspeaker.

"There will be a ten minute recess. Several of the contestants have withdrawn their application for the Test of Wills. We'll begin again shortly with the last ten contestants."

There were only ten more contestants? Two large Runners entered the arena and escorted Tara through the crowd.

"Make way for the next leader of the Runners," a young boy screamed not too far in front of Tara.

"You'll defeat the others, don't you worry," came another voice from beside her.

"Never seen anyone fight like you, lady," a man yelled.

Patha ordered her to be secluded in a white tent near the arena. She was given water as the two guards stood outside the tent preventing Runners and Gothman from entering to offer their allegiance.

Tara realized her hands shook as she sipped the water. The crowd outside pushed against the canvas, and guards yelled to step to the side. Tara exhaled and watched her breath appear as a puff of smoke in the chilly air. A Test of Wills hadn't been called for in over a hundred winters, and Tara couldn't recall from her history lessons if another warrior had successfully won every round. She felt exhilarated and nervous all at the same time.

"I'm meant to lead the Runners."

* * * * *

The crowd outside the tent and throughout all the benches buzzed with the excitement of the day. The same words were repeated everywhere: Who was she? Could anyone defeat her? Which clan was she from?

The Blood Circle Clan members knew exactly who she was. What they wanted to know was, how could she possibly be Tara?

Kuro pushed his way toward Patha and begged permission to speak with the leader of the clans.

Patha ordered his guard, who stood next to Kuro, to inform the young man it would be inappropriate to speak to a contestant during the test.

"You know who that is out there." Kuro looked past the guard and spoke to Patha anyway. "What are you going to do about it?"

Patha didn't answer and the guard stood between Patha and Kuro, telling Kuro to leave.

Disgusted, Kuro walked to the other side of the arena. He searched through the Gothman, looking for Darius. The Gothman were whooping and hollering and faking punches at each other as they downed the Runner ale.

Darius was still sitting on the bench with several men around him, including his little brother.

Kuro pushed aggressively through the men and confronted Darius. "That's Tara, isn't it?"

Kuro had bellowed the question, and Darius looked annoyed at the rudeness. The other Gothman pushed back Kuro and grumbled something about showing respect to the Lord of Gothman.

"She's supposed to be dead. What's going on here?" Kuro ignored the other Gothman and demanded an answer.

"You know as well as I do that Gothman aren't allowed to have anything to do with the Test of Wills, they aren't." Lord Darius showed no expression as he downed his cup of ale. "We're just here to observe."

"No one can fight like that," Kuro snarled, "except maybe Tara."

Darius stared blankly, and Kuro was furious. "I haven't seen her in five winters, and I can tell you without any doubt that is Tara. If you aren't so sure, than maybe your claim isn't as strong as you think. After all, you weren't able to keep her here the first time."

Darius leapt from where he was sitting and struck Kuro with his body while in midair. The two tumbled down the stadium benches to the floor. Gothman moved out of the way in all directions, clearing a path for the struggling men.

Kuro landed on his feet and stood inches from Darius' face. The rage on Darius' face was enough to make the largest of men back down. Kuro, however, stood tall and smiled. "I knew I could get a rise out of you, my friend," he whispered. "I won't hurt her, I promise."

Darius lifted Kuro by his coat and shoved him backward. Kuro stumbled a few feet before regaining his balance, and raised a fist at the lord. But Darius moved fast and grabbed Kuro's fist with his gloved hand.

Kuro stared hard at the handsome lord, whose face came within inches of his own. He hated the man for taking Tara, and despised him even more for somehow managing to bring her back. He wouldn't let the hatred show. First he had to win the Test of Wills, and so he relaxed his arm and forced a smile.

"Fight her like a man," Lord Darius snarled, undaunted by the chivalrous smile. "She'll take you down like one."

"Trust me, my friend, I know exactly what she's capable of doing." Kuro's eyes gleamed. He straightened his clothing and slowly walked away from the outraged lord.

Patha announced the fights would continue, and the crowd convened noisily. As Tara reentered the arena, the crowd volume increased by decibels. Gothman and Runners pounded their boots on the wooden seats and hollered and yelled.

She stood in the center of the ring, calm and unharmed from the previous fighting, letting the crowd show their respect. These people would follow her unconditionally, which was exactly what she wanted.

The next fighter entered the arena. He was a large man, standing head and shoulders over Tara, and she recognized him as the one who had checked in when she had. He turned and held his hands over his head as the crowd shrieked.

Tara realized he was drunk. With his back turned, she jumped in the air and kicked him hard in the small of his back.

The crowd roared as he stumbled but did not fall.

He turned and screamed. "Why you little bitch!"

Tara couldn't move fast enough when the man lunged forward, grabbed her, and then threw her as if she weighed nothing. The ropes stopped her from falling, but she found her torso twisted in them and took a second to gather her bearings and balance. Hands were all over her, and Tara felt as if some in the audience attempted to push her in, while others tried to pull her out.

Tara's clothes had twisted, and she felt groped as she finally faced her aggressor.

"You're going to lose this one, little bitch," Bordo sneered and made another attempt to grab her.

"And you're going to learn some manners," Tara hissed. She gathered her strength and jumped. Her legs went up, this time kicking him in the face. The heel of her boot hit him in the nose, and blood flew everywhere as he threw himself at her again. This time he picked her up and slammed her to the ground.

Tara lay without moving. The large man stood over her breathing loudly, but she didn't move. The crowd yelled for her to get up and finish him off, but still she just lay there.

Reena's hands went to her face, and she started to cry.

"Don't worry, woman, I taught her this," Patha whispered.

Reena slowly spread her fingers and peeked between them, unable to stop watching her daughter in action.

The large man approached Tara slowly, finally sticking a foot under her to turn her over.

Tara moved so quickly, most onlookers missed what happened. She grabbed his foot, jumped up with lightning speed, and raised it high into the air, causing the man to fall on his back. Before he could move, she was on him.

After several punches to his face, she wrapped her hands around his neck and twisted his head within fractions of the breaking point. Then she sat on him and waited. Each time he tried to move, she turned his head just a little farther.

At last, he realized his life was in her hands. He reached for the white cloth on his arm and threw it to the ground.

She jumped off, and the crowd seemed ready to riot.

The next several fighters were all huge men. They hovered over her, and she made it look like a struggle to defeat each one of them. Each time, they lost, bloody and mad as hell. Tara remained unharmed.

At last the moment she dreaded arrived. Kuro entered the ring.

A hush fell on the crowd as they saw the man predicted to win the Test of Wills stand before the undefeated woman.

Unlike the other warriors, Kuro stood facing Tara and bowed.

She stood undaunted and bowed in return. Then, to Tara's surprise, he assumed the position of the ancient warriors: bent knees, straight back, arms bent with hands opened. He held the position until Tara matched the pose.

The crowd grew silent. No one moved. Everyone sat on the edges of their seats.

The Gothman were not familiar with this method of fighting, and most Runners had not studied it. Patha had taught Tara and Kuro the ancient fight when they were teenagers.

* * * * *

Kuro knew this would be the last proof he needed to convince himself that this masked woman was indeed the first, and in fact, only love of his life. Love as he understood it, of course. Tara was worth wanting and loving, because with her came the rule of all Runner clans.

Kuro began moving slowly around the arena, stepping lightly, and keeping his knees bent. He watched as the woman in front of him matched him move for move and not a peep came from the hundreds of onlookers. With speed quicker than the eye, Kuro darted toward her and chopped with his hand.

She blocked the chop with her arm, spun and kicked him while jumping into the air.

He took the blow and returned one of his own. They continued to match each other, blow for blow. The crowd cheered, then quieted after each attack.

* * * * *

Thirty minutes passed, and Tara had had enough of Kuro's style. She felt he mocked her. Finally, she unleashed her power, raging at him with blow after blow, not allowing him the politeness of returning each blow.

* * * * *

Kuro went on the defensive, eager to find an opportunity to return to the offensive. The fear of defeat rose inside him, and not ready to accept it, he lunged and wrapped his arms around her.

She twisted, kicking and punching as he lifted her from the ground. She elbowed him hard in the ribs, causing instant pain to rack his body.

As he let her go, he reached out and ripped her headscarf from her face. Both Gothman and Runner alike howled as their suspicions were confirmed.

As suddenly as they had gasped their amazement, the masses quieted, wondering how a dead woman could be standing before them.

"What is this Test of Wills that you would have me fight a ghost?" Kuro turned and yelled to Patha. "No wonder she can defeat each warrior entering this arena. Will we let ourselves be ruled by a dead woman?"

The crowd stirred.

Patha looked across the arena to Darius who returned his gaze. Neither wanted a riot to break out.

Tara saw their gaze and knew it would take little to stir the crowd. She glared at Kuro who had turned away as he uttered his disrespectful outcries to Patha. She jumped up and kicked him hard in the square of the back.

"Does that feel like the blow of a dead woman?" she screamed. The crowd roared with laughter as Kuro stumbled forward.

Tara showed no mercy and kicked him again, and he fell. Once on the ground, she hit him so hard in the side, he was unable to rise. She jumped on him and pulled his head back by his hair.

"Which part of me do you think is dead?" she said as she punched him on the side of the head. She threw his head to the ground and leaped to stand on his back. She jumped, landing on him so hard not an inch of breath was left in his lungs.

"I'm not dead and have returned to the land and people I love." She shook her head enjoying the cold breeze on her sweat-soaked face.

The crowd cheered and slowly began to chant her name. "Tara! Tara!" The sound grew louder and louder. Gothman and Runner jumped to their feet and roared. "Tara! Tara!"

Kuro appeared lifeless at her feet, and for a moment she wondered if he were dead. The doctor soon entered the ring and called for a stretcher. With relief, Tara watched Kuro carried through the crowd.

She now stood alone in the arena as the crowd continued to chant. She turned to Patha, who looked at her with the serious face of a leader. She clasped her hands in front of her and bowed low in respect.

Patha stood and was assisted down the stairs by several attendants.

Tara noticed how slowly he moved and hurried toward him as he entered the arena. He waved away the attendants and eagerly took his daughter's hand as she helped him move to the center of the arena.

The crowd slowly sat and waited for the ruler of all clans to speak. He turned to his daughter and then slowly bent down and picked up her headscarf. As he reached to place it back on her head, she stopped his hand.

"No," she said loudly enough for all to hear. "I wear the clothes of the Runner to show the pride I have in my people. But, from this day forward, I will not cover my head in order to show pride in the people of my mama, the Gothman."

The crowd gasped as they heard about her mixed heritage for the first time. "I stand before you as rightful heir and future leader of all Runner clans. I also stand before you as the claimed one of Lord Darius, leader of Gothman."

Patha turned to Darius and raised his hand to salute and show respect to the Lord of Gothman.

Escorted by his guards, Darius led a small procession into the arena.

Patha took his hand and placed it in the hand of his daughter. He then turned and faced the crowd. "This day will be remembered for generations to come. All of you have witnessed one of the great moments of our history. We can tell our children and our grandchildren that we were present the day Runners and Gothman were truly united as a nation of two races that will never be defeated."

At this, the crowd stood and applauded loudly.

Darius turned to Tara and pulled her close. "You were incredible," he whispered.

"Crator told me I'd be victorious."

Chapter Twenty-Three

∽

The guards encountered a major challenge as they cleared a path through the crowds for Patha, Tara, and Darius. The leaders' motorcycles were brought to them, and once they were on them and surrounded by guards, they were able to move through the crowd with more ease. They rode slowly down the main street toward their home. Some of the crowd followed them, cheering their allegiance.

The party would continue through the rest of the day. Tara and Darius planned on joining them after a private family reunion.

Tara entered the house through the front door this time. She was nearly attacked by Reena and Hilda. Syra and Torgo were not too far behind. Hugs and kisses and tears followed.

Then, of course, there were the twins.

Tara collapsed to the floor and gathered her children into her arms. She felt immediate panic and dismay when the two did not respond as eagerly and, in fact, pulled away.

"Don't worry, child." Reena patted her shoulder. "You did the same thing to me when I had an opportunity to see you at times, you did. They'll learn who you are once again, I'm certain. It won't take you long to gain their trust, yes. Syra, be a good lass now, take them upstairs. Tara can come see them privately in a short while."

Syra reluctantly led the two toddlers by their hands and slowly climbed the stairs. "I miss out on everything," she mumbled.

"I can't believe you're alive!" Torgo cheered.

He had grown a good six inches in the past six cycles and stood taller than Tara. He was as skinny as he was tall, but his muscle structure indicated he would soon look just like his brother.

"I couldn't believe I was dead either." Tara laughed, feeling happier at that moment than she could ever remember.

The boy stood next to his brother. "You were incredible today. I've never seen anyone fight like that before."

"It *was* an incredible show," Darius added.

"More like unbelievable." Tara faced her family, beaming from ear to ear.

"Unbelievable is right." Patha entered the room. "Leave us everyone. I wish to talk with Darius and Tara alone." The tone in his voice quickly cleared the room.

Patha stood in front of his daughter with his hands on his hips. "Absolutely unbelievable!" Patha walked to the other end of the room and then turned, glaring at his daughter.

She looked at him blankly, her smile fading. She glanced at Darius and then at her papa. "I can't take all the credit, Papa."

Patha walked quickly to his daughter and slapped her across the face with his glove.

She stood frozen; not able to remember the last time Patha had struck her.

Darius' muscles tightened, but he didn't allow his facial expression to change. Gothman were taught as children to respect their parents and their rulers. He remained silent.

"That was an incredibly stupid stunt you pulled. You almost started a riot. And why? Your pride and that damn ego of yours. What were you trying to prove out there?" Patha snapped. Then he turned to Darius. "And you? You knew she was here. You probably thought this was all rather amusing. You two are pathetic!"

Patha turned and paced across the room again. He walked back and forth as the two stood there, motionless and expressionless, like two children waiting for punishment. Patha stared out the window, down at the town, which was lit up for the celebration. "How long have you been here?"

"I arrived yesterday, Papa. But I didn't do any of this out of pride or ego."

"Enough. You're my heir. The Test of Wills did not need to happen. Why didn't you contact me and let me know you were alive?"

"I didn't have a landlink. After crossing the border I came across a clan, and they took care of me. Papa, all their stories were about the Test of Wills—the glory it would bring them, the triumphs they would have. If I announced that I was alive, Runners would have been in an uproar. All those who entered the Test of Wills had attracted followers, individuals who believed, for whatever reason, that their applicant would be the best ruler for the Runners. I saw such turmoil in this one clan...I was sure all the other clans would be in a similar state."

"And you wanted all Runners and Gothman to follow you unconditionally. Well, Tara-girl, you have that. They will! But you could have sacrificed everything if you'd lost. Those were not good odds. It was foolish." Patha was still in a rage. He turned on Darius, "You went out to see if the written test came from Tara and came back and lied." His glare burned like hot coals. "If you were my son, I'd flog you for that. As my son-in-law, I believe I still have that right."

Patha stared at one and then the other. After a moment of silence he spoke, his voice slightly quieter. "I'm very happy that you're alive, my child. I simply will not tolerate being lied to. Is that understood?"

Both of them nodded silently.

"I fear your thinking is still too reckless to rule two nations," Patha continued and at this both Tara and Darius stirred.

"That's not true—" Darius began but didn't finish when Patha raised his hand.

"It is true. What would you have done if someone had started to win over her? Would you have shot them? That would have started a war. And a bloody one at that."

"Patha, I knew I wouldn't lose."

"And how did you know that? Are you returned from the dead? Can you no longer be killed?"

"No, that's not it. It's Crator. He told me I would win, if I had faith."

"*Crator?* Is that what you said? And what do you know about Crator?"

"Do you know about Him?"

Patha didn't answer. Instead, he moved over to the couch and slowly reclined. He looked up at his daughter with raised eyebrows, and Tara thought he seemed concerned. "So has the dog-woman come to you?"

Tara sat across from Patha. "Yes, she's come to me. I'd never have made it home without her."

"And now you believe, you have faith?"

"Yes, I do." She looked up and reached for Darius' hand, and he moved to her side. "Darius has seen her in his dreams, too."

Patha looked up at Darius. "I've also seen her in my dreams," he told both of them.

"So Crator has spoken to all of us," Darius said. "We now have an entity guiding us and protecting us. Tara, we can claim all of Nuworld!"

"I think Crator has always been guiding and protecting us. We're just now figuring out He exists." Tara looked first at Patha, then at Darius. "If we plan to claim every nation, I fear we'll work very hard to do so."

"But it will be possible." Darius grinned at the thought, completely putting the reprimand out of his head. "Look at what happened in that arena today."

"Are you saying I couldn't fight like that on my own?"

"According to you, you've never fought on your own. Crator has always helped you."

"It was an incredible fight, wasn't it?" Tara grinned.

"I don't think this Crator would have stopped you from making a fool of yourself, though." Patha still scolded. "You need to start acting like a ruler, child."

"I can rule." Tara felt challenged.

"Then no more running away from your problems!"

Tara was taken aback by this.

Darius suddenly looked awkward.

"You will prepare a report for me outlining everything you know about the Neurians." Patha slowly stood. "In six cycles, both of you will perform the Runner wedding ceremony. In front of all Runners and Gothman, you will take your vows to rule these two nations, remain with each other 'til death, and be loyal to each other from this day forward!" He looked at them fiercely, then walked to the kitchen door. "Now, prepare yourselves for the celebration."

Tara went to the nursery after she'd showered and changed. The twins delighted in the attention, although Tara was no more than a friendly face to them. She sat on the floor and let them show her their favorite toys and bring books to her. But if one of them got hurt or wanted a toy the other had, they ran to Syra, and then to Darius, when he entered the room. They did not honor Tara with this attention.

"They don't remember me at all." She was overwhelmed with sadness as she stroked the soft curls falling past Ana's shoulders.

"Give them time." Reena had stuck her head in behind Darius, and now entered. "They'll be demanding all your attention before you know it, my child, they will."

Tara affectionately hugged and kissed each child before she left the room. They were absolutely beautiful children, and she vowed that she would focus all her time on them starting tomorrow. They had a mama who loved them, and she wanted them to know it.

It was bitterly cold when Tara and Darius left the house. There were more people on the streets than had been there earlier that day. They cheered and waved as the two drove by. A few children who had been allowed to stay up late chased after them down the street.

The valley at the end of town was consumed by activity. Hundreds of Gothman and Runners flooded the area. Three bonfires were obvious from the distance. The closest one appeared to be a good fifteen feet up into the air and was eight to ten feet in diameter. A small crowd, all in black or dark brown leather, stood around the massive fire, laughing and talking loudly.

The crowd parted to allow Darius and Tara close to the fire. Tara accepted a mug of ale and soon lost sight of Darius as she mingled with the crowd, moving from conversation to conversation.

Several drunken Gothman standing nearby were loudly making jokes about the female Runner who defeated all rivals in battle that day. Their comments insulted her gender, but she knew she would have to let the two races work out their differences. If she'd ordered their silence at that moment, they wouldn't be any closer to accepting the equality of men and women.

She watched with interest as several Runner women approached the men and began challenging their accusations. The Gothman humbly begged forgiveness but continued to insult the women with their suggestive lewd comments.

"I must say I like the way these Runner women look in all their leather." A large, drunk Gothman grabbed one of the Runner women.

"I wish I could say the same about you." The Runner woman smiled as the Gothman grabbed her then sent a hard blow straight to his stomach.

The two other Gothman laughed loudly and slapped their legs as the first Gothman stumbled backwards and slid on the packed snow. "Looks like someone needs to teach you some manners," he said, working to gain his balance on the frozen ground.

The Runner knocked the man back to the ground before he could stand. She lunged at the other two Gothman but they, too, backed up. "We don't want to hurt you. We're just having a little fun."

"Oh, please, hurt me." The Runner woman mocked the men as she followed them, grabbing the back of their pants. "You're too cute to leave alone."

Disgusted, the men walked away.

The Runner laughed as she turned to face Tara. "Not bad, huh, sis?"

"Tasha, is that you?" Tara looked dumbfounded.

"Don't tell me you've forgotten your own sister? Although I guess I'm not as exciting as you are with all your adventures. Who'd of thought you'd show up for the Test of Wills?"

Tara noted disappointment in her sister's words. "I take it you were cheering for someone else?"

"Well, Kuro, of course. He's wanted to lead the clan for so many winters. If you hadn't broken his heart the way you did, he'd be leader, now."

"I think he wanted to lead the clan more than he wanted me, Tasha."

"It sounds like you just don't know how to keep your men happy."

Tara didn't like the tone in her sister's voice.

"It's a shame, that's all," Tasha continued. "Kuro had everything worked out so well. Considering how intelligent the Neurians are, who would have thought they'd turn out to be so superstitious."

"What did you say?"

Tasha hesitated for a second, then smiled again. "You should congratulate me, you know." She'd quickly changed the subject.

Tara was processing her sister's words about Kuro and didn't respond to her last statement.

"Fine, don't congratulate me. You're not the only one who can provide grandchildren, though. I'm pregnant!" she said triumphantly.

"Congratulations," Tara said simply. "Do you know who the papa is?"

"Of course I do. I won't upset you with such details though. I just hope it grows up to look and act just like its papa." Tasha smiled. "I'm sure we'll see each other again soon."

Tasha walked away, leaving Tara still sorting through what she'd heard. What did she mean by her comments on the Neurians? And when had her sister become so loyal to Kuro?

The snow was starting to fall again, and slowly the crowd thinned. Tara found herself near the makeshift hospital that had been set up for the wounded of the Test of Wills. She didn't feel obligated to see each and every contestant she'd injured. That would insult them. However, she wanted to see how Kuro was doing.

After politely listening to the opinions of several older Runners on how the navigational training should be taught to the next generation, Tara excused herself and entered the large tent.

"Now don't tell me you've discovered an injury." Dr. Digo smiled as she entered the sanitized environment.

"I'm sure I'll be sore in the morning." She smiled back and rubbed her arms.

"I'd be surprised if you're not. So, Tara, what can I do for you?"

"I thought I'd see how Kuro is doing."

"Oh?" The tone in the doctor's voice told Tara he remembered their steamy teenage romance.

"Yes, is that okay?"

"I don't see why not. He's behind the first curtain." The doctor hesitated. "Tara, you should know, he's badly hurt. If we get him through the night, he may survive."

Tara nodded but didn't respond.

The large tent had cubicles with walls made from animal hides. The thickness of the hides added to the warmth in each room. However, a generator had been set up to provide forced air heat into the pseudo-hospital.

Kuro lay on an elevated, thin metal bed. It was collapsible, and therefore could easily be set up, torn down and moved, as needed. He had a bandage wrapped around his head with visible red stains on it. His chest was bare, thickly wrapped with white bandages. Several tubes sent fluids into his body. Tara glanced at them, wondering how coherent he would be.

"Hey, beautiful." Kuro opened his eyes and smiled at Tara. "We put on quite a show out there, didn't we?"

"I got a serious reprimand for it." Tara smiled back at Kuro. "How're you feeling?"

"It's not as bad as it looks. How're you feeling?"

"My bruises are well covered," Tara lied.

"I'd love to rub salve on them." He smiled wickedly and then winced as he shifted position in the bed. "So, how did you like the Neurians?" Kuro struggled with a short chuckle.

"They weren't that friendly." Tara moved closer to the bed. "Have you been down that way?"

"Ah, now, aren't you the tricky one?" He waved a finger at her. "You already know everything, don't you? I never doubted you were the best leader, you know. I knew I would work at your side better than Lord Darius will. He's so jealous. You two would do nothing but try to control each other. It would be such a distraction for you. You and I would have ruled as a team, though, just the way we planned it when we were kids."

"But we're not kids anymore, Kuro. Why don't you tell me exactly what you were doing in Southland?"

"Exploring, just like you were." Kuro got a far away look in his eyes. "If they weren't so superstitious, everything would have worked out just fine."

"What would have worked out, Kuro?"

"You were supposed to return after I was ruler. Then we would fall back in love, and you would rule with me. It was planned so carefully." Kuro shrugged. "They needed to reestablish trade. No one wants that opium of theirs. Although I hear it makes sex fantastic."

"And you pointed out trade could be established with their oil."

"Yes, once I was leader."

Tara looked at Kuro in disbelief. "And so you devised the plan for me to be drugged?" Rage ran through her body. She looked at him coldly, her fists clenched. "How did you convince the Neurians to put me to sleep for six cycles?"

Kuro made another attempt at a chuckle, and his hand reached for his bandaged side. "Six cycles? Gowsky was supposed to keep you under a full winter. It just goes to show what kind of effect you have on men, sweetheart. I knew he wouldn't be able to do it. It made him crazy not to go help you in that burning building. I knew that."

He looked at her, smiling. "I told them if I ruled the clans we could negotiate a contract to buy their oil. I told them it would never work with the current leaders of the Runners and Gothman. They trusted me. But they trust that Crator-god of theirs more," he said these last words with disgust.

Tara pulled her laser and aimed it. "Your lack of faith in Crator has resulted in your own demise."

"You are so beautiful when you're angry."

Once she would have melted in his arms if he'd smiled as he was now.

"You won't shoot me. I know you still love me. I can see it in your eyes."

Tara aimed her weapon straight at his face.

The laser streamed through the air. Kuro died instantly.

Tara gasped in surprise. She hadn't shot him! Who had? She turned quickly and watched as Darius lowered his laser and returned it to his pocket.

Instead of looking at her, he turned and disappeared.

She looked back at Kuro, lowered her head and stood quietly for a long moment. Then, slowly, she walked out of the makeshift room and left the large tent.

The snow and wind had stopped. A heavy, gray sky showed patches of deep, rich black where the clouds had pulled away.

Most of the party had disappeared into the Runners' trailers when the snow had resumed falling. The lights from them lit her path as she followed Darius, who walked several yards before her, heading for their bikes.

"I would have killed him," she said as she straddled her bike.

"I felt I deserved the honor." He looked over at her.

Tara looked up at the sky. The moon appeared through a black tear in thick gray clouds, although the clouds threatened to obscure it at any moment. She studied it for a minute, remembering the lady in the burning building who had talked about the Lunians colonizing the moon.

"Do you think there are people living up there?" She turned and looked at the rugged features of Darius' strong face.

"I don't know."

"I was told there's a colony living up there."

Darius looked surprised. He stared at the moon for a moment. "I'm sure if there are people up there, you'd see to it that they follow you unconditionally, you would."

He started his bike and slowly took off on the packed snow toward the house.

Tara took one last look at the moon and followed him.

Why an electronic book?

We live in the Information Age—an exciting time in the history of human civilization in which technology rules supreme and continues to progress in leaps and bounds every minute of every hour of every day. For a multitude of reasons, more and more avid literary fans are opting to purchase e-books instead of paperbacks. The question to those not yet initiated to the world of electronic reading is simply: *why?*

1. *Price.* An electronic title at Ellora's Cave Publishing and Cerridwen Press runs anywhere from 40-75% less than the cover price of the <u>exact same title</u> in paperback format. Why? Cold mathematics. It is less expensive to publish an e-book than it is to publish a paperback, so the savings are passed along to the consumer.

2. *Space.* Running out of room to house your paperback books? That is one worry you will never have with electronic novels. For a low one-time cost, you can purchase a handheld computer designed specifically for e-reading purposes. Many e-readers are larger than the average handheld, giving you plenty of screen room. Better yet, hundreds of titles can be stored within your new library—a single microchip. (Please note that Ellora's Cave and Cerridwen Press does not endorse any specific brands. You can check our website at www.ellorascave.com or

www.cerridwenpress.com for customer recommendations we make available to new consumers.)

3. *Mobility.* Because your new library now consists of only a microchip, your entire cache of books can be taken with you wherever you go.

4. *Personal preferences are accounted for.* Are the words you are currently reading too small? Too large? Too...**ANNOYING**? Paperback books cannot be modified according to personal preferences, but e-books can.

5. *Instant gratification.* Is it the middle of the night and all the bookstores are closed? Are you tired of waiting days—sometimes weeks—for online and offline bookstores to ship the novels you bought? Ellora's Cave Publishing sells instantaneous downloads 24 hours a day, 7 days a week, 365 days a year. Our e-book delivery system is 100% automated, meaning your order is filled as soon as you pay for it.

Those are a few of the top reasons why electronic novels are displacing paperbacks for many an avid reader. As always, Ellora's Cave and Cerridwen Press welcomes your questions and comments. We invite you to email us at service@ellorascave.com, service@cerridwenpress.com or write to us directly at: 1056 Home Ave. Akron OH 44310-3502.

THE
☥ ELLORA'S CAVE ☥
LIBRARY

Stay up to date with Ellora's Cave Titles in
Print with our Quarterly Catalog.

TO RECIEVE A CATALOG,
SEND AN EMAIL WITH YOUR NAME
AND MAILING ADDRESS TO:

CATALOG@ELLORASCAVE.COM
OR SEND A LETTER OR POSTCARD
WITH YOUR MAILING ADDRESS TO:

CATALOG REQUEST
C/O ELLORA'S CAVE PUBLISHING, INC.
1056 HOME AVENUE
AKRON, OHIO 44310-3502

*Please be advised: Ellora's Cave is a publisher of erotic romance. Our
books as well as our website contain explicit sexual content.*

Cerridwen Press

Cerridwen, the Celtic goddess of wisdom, was the muse who brought inspiration to storytellers and those in the creative arts.
Cerridwen Press encompasses the best and most innovative stories in all genres of today's fiction.
Visit our website and discover the newest titles by talented authors who still get inspired — much like the ancient storytellers did...
once upon a time.

www.cerridwenpress.com